TALES OF THE
SHADOWMEN

Volume 3: Danse Macabre

TALES OF THE
SHADOWMEN
Volume 3: Danse Macabre

edited by
Jean-Marc & Randy Lofficier

stories by
**Matthew Baugh, Alfredo Castelli,
Bill Cunningham, François Darnaudet,
Paul DiFilippo, Win Scott Eckert, G.L. Gick,
Micah Harris, Travis Hiltz, Rick Lai,
Jean-Marc Lofficier, Xavier Mauméjean,
David A. McIntee, Brad Mengel,
Michael Moorcock, John Peel,
Joseph Altairac & Jean-Luc Rivera,
Chris Roberson, Robert L. Robinson, Jr.**
and **Brian Stableford**

cover by
Daylon
illustrations by
**Fernando Calvi, Cybele Collins, Daylon,
Gil Formosa, M. Gourdon, Jean-Michel Ponzio,
Rapeno, Albert Robida** and **Will**

A Black Coat Press Book

Acknowledgements: I am indebted to André-François Ruaud of *Les Moutons Electriques* (http://www.moutons-electriques.com/) for the use of the cover and back cover illustrations and to David McDonnell for proofreading the typescript.

Visit our website at www.blackcoatpress.com

Table of Contents

Arsène Lupin
by Daylon (2005)

My Life as a Shadowman

I became a Shadowman in 1963, when I was 9 years old.

The curriculum at the Catholic School of Grand-Lebrun in Bordeaux was strong on history (my favorite subject), geography, math, natural sciences, etc. but sorely lacked classes on such vital topics as sabotage, kidnapping and international trafficking. Or so I thought.

A few months earlier, a neighbor had thrown three bound collections of *Spirou* magazine into the trash. *Spirou* was one of the weekly comic books named after a popular character that I used to buy every week. Each issue contained about 20 stories, ranging from humor to serious adventure, serialized at the rate of two pages per week. Since no two stories ever began or ended the same week, there was ample motivation to buy the next issue when it came out, on Thursday. Later, the publisher would bind the issues returned by the news-agents and sell them as handsome collections.

The three collections the two neighborhood friends and I had been lucky to rescue from the trashman were old ones, dating back to 1955 and 1956. We each took home a book and devoured it

It is in that bound volume of old *Spirous* that I discovered the character of Monsieur Choc. Tall, lanky, dressed in a dinner jacket, he hid his features behind a medieval helmet. Monsieur Choc was the archenemy of two rotund detectives, Tif and Tondu, and the head of an international crime cartel called the White Hand. The page reproduced here, taken from the very same story I read in 1963, shows the nefarious villain preparing to commit an act of sabotage. The cartoony nature of the art barely made up for the rather serious and suspense-filled plot. [1]

Heavy stuff, especially when you're nine.

So, right then and there, despite my generally-accepted lack of tallness, lankiness, dinner jacket and medieval helmet, I decided to start a chapter of the White Hand at Grand-Lebrun, promoting myself to the title of Choc. I quickly enlisted two of my school friends, F*** and M***, and soon, we were on our way to becoming a world-spanning criminal organization.

---

[1] There is a chapter devoted to Monsieur Choc in our book *Shadowmen 2: Heroes and Villains of French Comics*, ISBN 0-9740711-8-8.

Le Retour de Choc
story by Maurice Rosy, art by Will (1956)

As far as I can recall today, our activities were mostly limited to exchanging secret notes in class to notify each other of secret meetings, during which we would devise more ingenious ways of exchanging secret notes. It might seem rather pointless and silly, but now that I'm a grown-up, I know that many Government organizations still work on the same principles, so it can't have been all that bad.

Alas, a few days later, an eternity in school time (which appears inordinately expanded to children), one of my notes was intercepted by the stalwart Mrs. B***, our lovely schoolmistress, and I was sent for a "talk" with the priest in charge of the "young children's" division, the tough-but-fair Father C***.

He tried to make me give up the identity of the mysterious "Hoc" who had signed the note, thereby crushing my hopes of a future career as a logo designer. I had thought it clever to turn the C of "Choc" into an open ellipse and write the "hoc" inside it. The good Father, probably because of his familiarity with Latin, had only read the *hoc* part.

The priests had ways of making us talk. Despite the threat of the dreaded detention, which meant coming into school on our day off, Thursday, to spend hours writing Latin conjugations, I remained obdurately silent and did not betray the secrets of the White Hand. That was probably as much due to the embarrassment of having to explain the name was *Choc*, not *Hoc*. But still.

The organization was in dire straits, with the personal blow to its leader, me, now under threat of having to write a hundred *amo, amas, amats* if I didn't start singing like the proverbial canary. The day was grim indeed. A Churchillian effort was called for.

The popular game in our age bracket that year was marbles. An entire secondary market had developed, with kids trading cloudy glass marbles, clear glass marbles, glass marbles with spaghetti-like motifs inside, larger glass marbles (*berlons*) and other exotic marble varieties. One school bully, the dreaded D***, assisted by two future little thugs-in-training, had taken to stealing marbles from smaller and weaker kids, which basically included everyone besides themselves. Fear of swift physical retribution had been enough to keep the matter hushed up. If you want to learn about *Omerta*, talk to a 9-year-old.

The next day, I returned to see Father C*** as I had been "invited" to do, presumably having had time to reflect upon my sins and now being prepared to make a full and uncoerced confession.

"It's D***, Father," I blurted out. "He steals our marbles."

"He steals your marbles?"

"Yes, Father. And then, he loses them by playing with the older kids." I had no particular evidence of this, but it sounded good. "That's why I sent the note to F***. To warn him," I added by way of explanation.

This blew the lid open on the Great Marbles Scandal of '63. Father C***'s robust investigation quickly exposed the dastardly D*** and his cohorts' villainy and they were properly punished, forced to apologize publicly and their loot confiscated. I was given to understand that D's father, in the military, had not been too pleased either.

I never had to write hundreds of Latin verbs on Thursday, but upon reflection, I did come to the conclusion than life as a mystery man was far too complicated. I had managed to extricate myself successfully this time, and expose a villain in the process, but could one count on such luck again?

So there ended my life as a Shadowman, while I turned my sights to the more realistic goal of becoming a soccer champion.

This third anthology again features the dreams and visions of writers from around the world–this time, Australia and Italy are added to our roster–who also once dreamed of being Shadowmen. Fantômas dances on Paris' rooftops, Doctor Omega defies the Lords of Vampire City, the Cat Women of the Moon threaten to plunge the world into chaos and King Kong falls in love for the first time; welcome once again to our annual merry-go-round of heroes and villains of popular literature, the *danse macabre* of of the Shadowmen.

Jean-Marc Lofficier

Although Paul Féval is not as well remembered today as Alexandre Dumas, he is one of the true giants of popular literature. His John Devil *and* The Black Coats *series are amongst the earliest examples of detective and crime stories; his* Wandering Jew's Daughter *is pure fantasy; and finally, his* Vampire Countess *and* Vampire City *are essential pre-*Dracula *texts for any serious scholar of vampire fiction. It is therefore fitting that Matthew Baugh opens this collection with a tale revisiting Féval's vampire metropolis, Selene, which has never before seen visitors like the fearless crew Matt has gathered in...*

Matthew Baugh: *The Heart of the Moon*

Selene, 1790

"Are you sure it will take all of us?" I asked. "It's just four men and a girl, and two of the men are old."

Prince Vseslav scowled at me. It was a terrifying expression he had practiced for the last 800 years.

"Don't tell me you're frightened, Yvgeny," he said. "Were you not a Cossack in life?"

This was true, though the implication that all Cossacks are fierce and bloodthirsty was simplistic and I found the comment vaguely offensive. I am bloodthirsty, but have never been exceptionally fierce, and the thirst has more to do with being a vampire than a Cossack.

"I'm not afraid, my Prince," I replied. "It's only that you require so many of us for this little job."

"You're still young in the ways of the undead," he said. "These men are vampire hunters. As such, they may be more than what they seem. Do I need to remind you of all of the mischief the Englishwoman wrought in our city with only a manservant, a physician and an Irish rogue to help her?"

I nodded, though without any real enthusiasm. Miss Ward's adventure was three years past, but it still rankled the elders. When they mentioned it, there was nothing we, the younger undead, could do but agree and settle in for the diatribe that was sure to follow.

Fortunately, there was no time for speeches now. I fell into rank with my ten companions and, at our lord's signal, we swept down on the campfire.

We moved as silently as shadows; only the green glow of our eyes could be seen. I do not know what it was that alerted them to our presence, but two of them sprang to their feet and drew weapons.

The younger of these two looked like a military officer, tall and broad-shouldered. He was no match for a vampire, of course, but I prefer not to exca-

11

vate pistol balls from my flesh if I can help it. I thought about going after the gaunt old man beside him. Slaying an armed fighter would garner some favor with my Prince. I decided against it when I saw the plain wooden cross around his neck.

I know that Ruthven and many others insist that the vampiric weakness to holy symbols is an outmoded superstition, but I have never chosen to test it myself. Vseslav says it is a chancy business, unless both you and your prey are atheists. Even then, he advises against it. In this instance, I thought the black-clad man's eyes burned with the same fire I remembered in old father Dimitri when I was a child. I decided to leave the religious zealot for someone else to fight.

The young girl's throat looked tender, but there would be too much competition for it. I decided to attack the other old man. He looked frail and had no weapons. As I neared him, he pulled a shiny metal device from his pocket and pressed a switch on it. It emitted a shrill sound that caused my head to erupt with blinding pain. I shot past the old man and into the woods on the other side of the camp.

I plugged my ears with my fingers and found that I could shut out enough sound to make the pain bearable. It seemed that I was the only one who had the sense to flee. My companions were doing their best to fight, despite the disabling noise. They were not doing at all well.

The girl and the fourth man, who had a twisted spine, were huddled close to my white-haired nemesis. The old fanatic was laying about him with a strange staff which had a cat's head fetish carved at one end. The cat's eyes seemed to blaze with eldritch fire and, with each blow, one of my brethren crumbled to dust and ash.

The young man had a curved sword which he used with two hands. He had already decapitated several of the vampires. This does not slay the children of Vseslav, but it does hinder us, and that gave him the chance to sprinkle a clear liquid from a silver flask on their bodies. Within moments, there was nothing left of my poor comrades.

"Such a bother!" the old man turned off his sound machine and put it back in his jacket. "Not one of them captured alive."

" 'Tis not possible to capture such as these alive, Doctor Omega," the other oldster said. "They all died long ago."

"Yes, yes," the Doctor answered with a show of impatience. "Technically you're right, Solomon, but you know very well what I mean."

"That was quite a demonstration of skill, Captain," the girl interjected. I had the sense she spoke largely to distract the two old men from a quarrel. "That is a *katana* such as the Japanese samurai use, is it not?"

The blonde man grinned and bowed gallantly.

"Indeed it is, Miss Amberson. I once visited Japan where I did a kindness for a man named Hanzo. He gave me this sword and taught me its use. It was forged by the great swordsmith, Muramasa."

"I notice you also carry a rapier."

"They're like lovely sisters," he replied. "Equally desirable, each in her own way. As I am unable to choose, I love them both."

"Promiscuity with women and swords will be your end," old Solomon growled. "You put too much trust in a heathen-forged blade."

"You're not in the position to call the kettle black," the Captain countered. "Your staff is a voodoo fetish."

The old man scowled darkly but said nothing.

"In any case, you both did magnificently!" the hunchback interjected, "And you too, Doctor! Your scientific device was amazing! I must learn the principles of its function."

"Just a trifle," the old man said dismissively. "We can save such chit-chat for tomorrow. I don't expect our friends will attack again tonight and I plan to get an early start. Maciste will be waiting for us in Stregoicavar."

I slipped back to report this matter to my Prince. Predictably, he was furious.

"The Captain, I know!" he said when his anger had abated. "He and his bent-backed companion are the most successful of all who hunt our kind. The old man with the staff reminds me of an English Puritan whom I had thought dead nearly 200 years. The others are not known to me, but they're clearly a danger. I must return to Selene at once and report this to the Elders. While I'm gone, it'll be up to you to stop these wretched humans."

"My Prince," I stammered. "I am your servant, of course, but how can one succeed where a dozen failed?"

"When one has been cunning enough to flee, one is clever enough to find a way," Vseslav answered. "I know that one is also wise enough to realize what will happen if one fails again."

I promised and then I stood back as my master took on the shape of a gigantic wolf. He howled once, and then bounded away at a speed that not even a falcon could match.

"Thank you, my Prince," I muttered bitterly. "I'm honored by the hopeless task you've set for me."

As I followed the little group, I learned of their habits. The hunchback was a scientist, though not nearly of the caliber of the mysterious Doctor Omega. He continually pestered the older man with questions. The girl, Telzey Amberdon, was the Doctor's companion and she, too, seemed to have a brain for science. The conversations between the three of them bored me to tears.

Old Solomon was the group's self-appointed scout and I was careful to steer as far from him as I could. By contrast, the Captain seemed lackadaisical.

13

He spent most of the time riding in the back of the wagon where he would nap, smoke odd smelling cigarettes, or flirt with the girl. The Doctor didn't seem to approve of this, nor did old Solomon. (In fairness, it was hard to tell if Solomon approved of much of anything.)

Three days later, the party came to the sleepy Hungarian town of Stregoi-cavar and rented several rooms at the local inn. By this time, I had come up with a plan that would afford me the best chance of success, not to mention survival.

The girl was the weak link. Though seemingly precocious, she was still in her teens and was left out of much of the socializing of the menfolk. That evening, the four of them left her in the inn and went to the tavern to try to learn any news of the man they were to meet.

The opportunity was ideal. I could not enter the inn–the rituals that humans use to bless their homes are more effective than they imagine–but I could call to her. I have learned the vampiric art of thought projection and was especially adept–if I'm permitted to brag–at using it to charm the fair sex.

I threw everything I had into entrancing her and to filling her head with dark urgings. After a moment, she looked up, then closed her book and set it aside. She rose and opened the door.

"Excuse me," she said. "Did you call me?"

"What?" I stammered, surprised that she could speak. Under my spell, she should have been like a sleepwalker.

"Did you ask me to come to the door?" She spoke slowly and clearly, as if she thought I was simple-minded.

"Yes," I answered. "Come to me, Telzey Amberdon, your will is no longer your own."

"You're using mental telepathy, aren't you?" she said. "I'm afraid you're not very good at it."

"I–I'm not?"

"I don't mean to be rude, but no."

I wasn't sure what to say to that. It occurred to me that it might be better to continue this conversation in a different place. I didn't want Solomon or the Captain turning up unexpectedly. I took a step in her direction, but she held out a cross.

"I thought so," she said. "You're one of the vampires."

"You could be too, my dear," I replied, throwing all of my charm and the full force of my will behind the words. "I can make you immortal, a creature of the night, eternal and powerful."

Telzey made a disgusted face.

"I'm afraid not," she said. "I can't really see spending all eternity living like a dog tick, thank you."

"It's not like that!" I protested. "My dark kiss will make you my bride. We will hunt the night together, remaining young, powerful and beautiful forever.

My kind are not like the cattle all around you. We're the only ones who are truly alive. Join me and no dark pleasure will be denied you."

"No, thank you!" she said. "Living off of other people's misery and death sounds beastly. Besides, you vampires have frightful breath."

I had to admit, given the choice, I would have made the same decision. Vampire life is not as glamorous as the Elders like to make it sound. Our society is a parade of self-absorbed tedium. broken occasionally by pretentious cruelty. All things considered, I had much more fun as a Cossack.

"Do you really believe in that symbol?" I asked indicating the cross. "I ask because you seem more the scientific sort of person than religious."

"The two aren't mutually exclusive," she replied. "I know plenty of scientific people who believe in some sort of higher power."

It seemed to me that she didn't seem to be including herself in that group, so I decided to take a chance. I lunged at her, intent on slapping the cross away and making her my prisoner.

Before I could grab her, Telzey touched a button on the side of the holy symbol. It began to glow with a deep blue light and I felt as if my skin was on fire. I fell backwards and tried to scramble away.

"It's ultra-violet," she explained. "That's the part of the Sun's spectrum that the Doctor told me affects the undead. I don't want to hurt you. If you'll promise to be my prisoner, I'll shut this off."

"I promise!" I croaked.

As soon as she turned the light off, I threw one of my shoes at her. It was the sort of tactic that Vseslav considered beneath a vampire's dignity, but I couldn't think of anything dignified that would work. I knocked the cross from her hand.

I was on my feet in an instant and caught the girl's shoulders.

"I'm not going to bite you," I said. "I just need to take you with me."

"I don't think so!"

The new voice came from a large, dark-complexioned peasant who had come up behind me while I was preoccupied. I let my eyes flash green and showed him my fangs. That is usually enough to send would-be rescuers running off into the night. Unfortunately, this man didn't look impressed.

"Maciste!" Telzey cried with obvious delight.

"I'll warn you once," the big man said. "Let the girl go and I'll let you leave."

He looked as strong as a bull, but the Elders are all in agreement, brute strength is useless against the undead. I shot out my right hand and caught his throat in a steely grip.

Maciste still didn't look impressed. With no apparent effort, he tore my hand free, breaking the bones of my forearm in the process. That was painful, but a vampire can repair damage like that in a few moments. Unfortunately, before I could heal myself, the big man reached out and broke my other arm in two places.

I bared my fangs defiantly. Maciste responded by shoving a ham-sized fist against my face. The impact tossed me backwards and damaged the stone wall. I tried to stand up, but found I didn't have the strength. I settled for spitting out a few teeth. They would grow back, but I would be a laughing stock without my left fang until then.

Fortunately, Maciste was ignoring me for the moment while he checked on the girl. I heard her thank him and say that she hadn't been in any real danger. That stung my pride but it also gave me the impetus to struggle to my feet. I loped away, my mouth bleeding and my arms dangling uselessly. It was humiliating, but at least I was free.

I rounded the corner of the inn and nearly collided with the Captain and old Solomon. The younger man drew his curved sword with a smooth motion. I felt a quick bite of pain in my neck as the blade passed through. The next thing I knew, my head was bouncing along the cobblestones.

I realized that the worst was yet to come.

I–which is to say my head–was tucked under Maciste's arm. This gave me a good view of the Captain and Solomon stuffing my body into a gilded coffin. I struggled as best I could but controlling one's arms and legs is considerably more difficult when one is not attached to them.

"Please tell me again, why are we doing this?" the Captain asked. "This is my coffin after all."

"When a vampire is gravely wounded, it is compelled to travel to Selene," the Doctor answered. "Our friend here will take us with him."

I tried to say something, but no words came out.

"What do we do with this?" the big man asked, holding my head out like a ball. "Shall I tuck it in the coffin?"

"Let me have it," said the hunchback. "I would like to perform some experiments to determine the most effective means of killing his kind."

"Doctor!" Telzey gasped. "That's inhuman."

"Don't worry, my dear," the old man said. "We aren't going to kill this vampire, or even experiment on him. We're best served keeping head and body separate for the moment, but we won't be cruel. I think I can even make something that will allow him to speak."

The Doctor's invention was a squat cylinder with a place to mount my head on top. When I spoke. it would release a stream of air across my vocal cords. I tested it by hurling all of the worst Cossack curses at my captors. When I calmed down, I told them my name and agreed to be their guide to Selene in return for the Doctor's promise that he would restore me to my body and set me free. I felt slightly embarrassed about my lack of loyalty to my own kind. I consoled myself with the thought that I would betray the Doctor and his group just as happily.

Doctor Grost, as the little man with the bent back was called, was unhappy with this arrangement.

"You can't let him go!" he shouted. "He is a vampire and will surely kill again."

"The Doctor is right my friend," the Captain said. "By releasing one, we gain the chance to kill many."

"Is that your purpose?" I asked. "To slay everyone in the Vampire City?"

"Would that it were," the Puritan replied.

"We're going to recover a piece of technology that belongs to me," the Doctor said. "That is, it comes from the same... the same group of which I am a member. It is a chronon nodal point generator."

"A what?"

"It is a component for a time-travel device," he explained. "Have you ever wondered how it is a normal clock will chime 13, 14, 15 times and all the way up to 24 when vampires are present?"

I shook my head.

"Logically," he continued, "vampires must either have some power that affects clocks–which would be absurd–or which affects the nature of time. Using the chronon nodal point generator, they can converge two parallel streams of time. When they do this, things seem to double. You hear twice as many chimes, not because the clock is defective, but because the chimes occur in two separate time streams. I believe this is also the technology that allows vampires to make doppelgangers of themselves and their victims."

I felt like shrugging but was deprived of shoulders.

"I just thought it was one of the odd things vampires do," I said. "Like the ability to float upriver, feet first."

"If all goes as planned, it is a trick they will not have much longer," he replied.

The trip was not terribly pleasant, though Telzey made me as comfortable as she could. The others mostly ignored me, except for Grost. When no one was looking, he would poke me with silver pins, or dab garlic juice on my skin, or some such thing.

One evening Solomon, Grost, the Captain and Telzey came to get my opinion on a matter they had been debating.

"What are the origins of your people?" the Captain asked. "Are you a lost race of man which traces its origins back to Lilith or to Cain?"

"I contend that you are human beings afflicted with disease microbes of some sort," the hunchback said. "The disease changes you into bloodthirsty fiends who cannot abide sunlight."

17

"I say you are humans who have been condemned by God for your sinful ways," Solomon added. "Though I have also heard you may be a servitor race created by the Old Ones who ruled the Earth in times primordial."

"I don't know," I admitted.

"Well, what do you think?" Grost demanded. "Vampires must have some idea of their own origins."

"I have heard the Elders say that the Moon is the fatherland of vampires."

"What does that mean?" the Captain asked.

"I don't know."

"It sounds like something the Doctor once told me," Telzey offered. "He said that the vampires come from a different planet. When they spread through the universe, they founded a scientifically-advanced colony on the Moon where they were ruled by three powerful and malicious space gods. After many millennia, one of the Moon-vampires used the chronon nodal point generator to revolt against the gods. The entities retaliated by stripping away the Moon's atmosphere. Most of the vampires were killed and the survivors were forced to flee to Earth. They built their city, and named it Selene in memory of their lost homeland."

"Really?" I asked.

"That was what he said," she replied, "but I don't remember if that applies to this time-stream or to another."

After a time, all of them drifted off to bed, except for the Captain who was on watch.

"I've told you what I know of my origins," I said. "It seems only fair that you tell me of yours?"

"Your kind murdered my family," he responded. "Now I live to kill them."

"What of the Doctor and Miss Amberdon?"

"Travelers in the Aether."

"And Solomon?"

"Cursed."

"That's rather vague."

"He believes that he's doomed to live until he can kill the Queen of all vampires."

"Ah! And what of Maciste?"

"He's the strongest man in the world."

"I wouldn't care to argue the point," I admitted, "but how did he come to be so strong?"

The Captain shrugged and took a puff of his cigar.

"He was born that way, I suppose," the Captain said. "All I know is that he's always used his strength to fight for the common folk. He is said to have turned back the Mongols..."

"The Mongols?" I interrupted. "But that was 700 years ago!"

He shrugged.

"I suppose you'll tell me that he also is cursed with immortality?"

The Captain smiled at my sarcasm and offered me a puff. I accepted but didn't particularly care for the cigar. Not having access to my lungs might have had something to do with that.

"Perhaps he simply rises from the Earth when his strength is needed," the Captain suggested.

"Captain," I said, "your stories remind me of a man I met once. His name was Munchausen."

"I'm not so great a liar as that," he said with a grin, "and you, Yvgeny–one who lives in a city of vampires–shouldn't be so skeptical."

We passed through Semlin and started up the Danube on the old road to Peter-wardein. During the day, my head was kept in a metal cylinder to protect it from the Sun so I couldn't see the lush vegetation give way to grey bleakness, nor the gradual darkening of the day.

On the other hand, I could feel the oppressive gloom that surrounds Selene, and the strange sense that each step towards our goal left us farther away. I felt, rather than saw, the total darkness that suddenly enfolded the group.

"Keep moving!" I cried, fearing what would become of me if they stopped. After several moments, I felt a change. We had arrived.

It took the group a little while to remember to take me out of my canister. This is understandable for the city is more fabulous than anything built by the hands of mortals and they were awestruck.

Selene is designed like a wheel, with six broad avenues radiating out from a central hub. The vast bulk of the city is composed of tombs to put King Mau-solus to shame, but the center is more spectacular still. A columned peristile which surrounds the great courtyard is filled with statues. These are made from the petrified bodies of beautiful maidens taken from the outer world. I heard young Telzey gasp with pity and Maciste growl angrily, and guessed that they had seen the look of helpless terror on the face of one of these. (In all honesty, I agree with them that the statues are in poor taste.)

In the center of the courtyard stands the vast tower which is the temple and ruling palace of the vampire race. It is taller than any human structure I've ever seen.

"How grand!" I heard the Captain breathe. "And the architecture is like that of Cathay and Japan."

"It seems to me more like the palaces of old Carthage," Maciste responded.

"No," came Solomon's voice. " 'Tis more like the cyclopean structures of the lost city of Negari in Africa, or perhaps the Tower of Babel."

"Doctor!" Telzey's voice was filled with wonder. "This looks like the ar-chitecture of Lessur..."

"All illusions!" the old man replied. "The distortions of time and space shape this place to our expectations. It's part of the effect of the chronon nodal point generator. That's why it's always night here, even when it's only a little before noon outside. That is also why the air is so still and the water of the fountains is frozen in place. We exist between seconds of time."

His voice was interrupted by the tolling of a bell which seemed to come from the very air.

"Hurry!" the Doctor snapped. "We must get inside the tower before the 24th stroke!"

I found myself jostled uncomfortably as Maciste threw the coffin with my body over one shoulder and tucked the can holding my head under the other arm. The bell tolled 13 more times before we came to a halt.

"Open the casket!" the Doctor commanded. A moment later, I found myself lifted from the container and set back on my own shoulders at long last. Though I was weakened from lack of blood, it was only a moment before I knit my parts back together.

I saw that we were inside the atrium of the tower on the ground floor. The building was made of porphyry, as translucent as amber and tinted a delicate green. In the center of the room was a dome of obsidian, as round as a colossal pearl and pulsing with a faint light.

"Open it, Yvgeny!" the Doctor commanded. "Hurry!"

"How?" I cried.

"If the blood of a vampire is spilled on the altar, it will open!"

By now the bells had tolled 19 times. At 24, the city would awaken. If I stalled, the vampires would overwhelm them and I would have saved my city. Of course, I would also be tortured for the next millennium or so as punishment for having led them here in the first place.

On the other hand, if I refused the Doctor's command, these vampire hunters would gladly find a different way to spill my blood.

I gashed my hand with my good fang and let the blood dribble onto the black surface. The fluid soaked into the stone like water into a sponge. A crack opened and the two halves of the dome rolled away to reveal a shining device floating over a deep shaft.

"Stop!"

All of us turned at the sound of the voice and saw the Lord and Lady of Selene as they entered. Baron Iscariot was regal in his robes of black. Baroness Phryne was bewitching in her daring cloak of scarlet.

I slid down behind one half of the dome and hoped that they hadn't noticed me.

Outside the tower, the undead had awakened and were rallying to the call of their rulers. The air was alive again, the water in the fountains was flowing, and I could sense the door of every tomb in the city opening. Outside the tower, we could see the shadowy army advancing.

"Dear guests," the Baroness' musical voice rang out. "Do not desecrate our holy altar. Throw down your weapons and let us welcome you."

Baron Iscariot
by Fernando Calvi (2006)

They say that, in life, Phryne was a courtesan whose loveliness no man could resist. That beauty, combined with the powers of a vampire queen, made her too much for even these vampire killers. They stared, their minds empty of all thoughts except her.

"Don't listen to her!" Telzey cried. Though not fully immune to the Baroness' beauty, women tend not to be as powerfully affected, and Telzey had mental defenses of her own. She ran from one to another of her companions, trying to shake them out of their trance.

"Doctor! Captain! Maciste! Please come to your senses."

It was old Solomon who responded. He shook his head as if to clear it.

"This place is Babylon indeed," he growled, "and you are its scarlet woman!"

He stamped his staff on the ground and a wave of green light swept through the room. When it struck the Baron and Baroness, their beauty melted away, leaving two mummified horrors. With the illusion gone, the Baroness' spell was broken and the men came to their senses.

"Hold them off!" the Doctor cried. "I only need a few moments to remove the device."

Baroness Phryne
by Fernando Calvi (2006)

Solomon raised his staff high and charged at Phryne. Powerful as she was, she did not want that weapon to strike her. With inhuman speed, she eluded him, laughing all the while.

The Baron took a more direct approach. He transformed himself into a wolf, as huge and terrible as my master Vseslav. He lunged at the Doctor, but the Captain stepped between them, firing silver bullets from both pistols. The Baron howled in pain but he still moved. The vampire killer drew rapier and katana and advanced on him.

Maciste hoisted a half-ton slab of the greenish stone and used it to push back the vampires in the entryway. Grost followed him with a brace of pistols and a flask of holy water to deal with any who slipped past.

"Only a moment more," the Doctor muttered as leaned out precariously over the shaft. The device was just beyond his reach and only young Telzey's grip on his other arm kept him from falling to his death.

It would have been so easy to reach out and shove him in, I thought. Then again, the girl had been kind to me. Besides, I wasn't about to expose myself.

These vampire hunters have a nasty habit of producing deadly weapons at the last moment.

Across the room, Phryne still led the Puritan in a dance of death. He would strike at her with the cat's head or stab with the sharp point at the other end of the staff, but always she slipped away with the grace of a luna moth. The old man was beginning to tire.

The Captain was doing better against his foe. His swords must have been inlaid with silver, or charmed in some other way. The cuts and thrusts left great rents in the wolf's hide which did not instantly heal as wounds inflicted on a powerful vampire usually do.

Maciste continued to hold back the horde with his impromptu barrier. This had been difficult enough when they were in human form, but now they were changing into dogs, bats, spiders, serpents, vultures and leeches. The smaller cratures were slipping past, which kept Grost busy stamping on leeches and spiders and dousing the smeared remains with holy water.

"I have it!" the Doctor crowed with triumph. Telzey pulled him back from the shaft, the alien device was in his hand.

"No!" Baroness Phryne shot towards him, with murder in her eyes.

Telzey stepped in front of the Doctor and raised the ultraviolet cross. Neither symbol nor imitation sunlight gave the Baroness pause. She slapped the thing from the girl's hand and it shattered against a wall.

"The Heart of the Moon!" the Baroness cried. "Give it to me!"

At that moment, Solomon finally caught up with Phryne. He drove his staff through her body like a spear.

"Babylon the great is fallen, is fallen..." he quoted with grim satisfaction.

Baroness Phryne's body was engulfed in eldritch flames. She threw her arms around the Puritan and together they fell into the open shaft. The Doctor stepped forward, a stricken look on his face, and there were tears in Telzey's eyes.

Gently but firmly, the old man moved his companion aside and began to tinker with the glowing device. Across the room, Baron Iscariot had fallen and reverted back to his human form. The Captain left him to join Maciste and Grost in their defense of the door.

"Hurry, Doctor!" the Captain cried. "We can't hold them much longer."

"That should do it!" the Doctor replied and raised the glowing device over his head.

At that moment, something happened that had never occurred since the city was built. With time unfrozen by the old man's tampering, the Sun rose over Selene.

There was a terrible cry from all around the city as the vampires felt the rays of light. The Sun is not fatal to all of my kind, but none of us welcome it. Those who didn't burst into flames or crumble into dust fled back to their tombs, screaming.

"Hurry!" the Doctor cried. "They may have a way to reverse the effect."

With that, the group ran from the tower and I was left alone. I examined the Baron who was badly injured, but would recover. I thought about finishing him off myself to avoid whatever punishment he might have in store for me.

"You are one of Vseslav's, aren't you?"

I spun to see the voice's owner. He was thin as death and hairless as a skeleton. In a city of the dead, his pointed ears, sunken eyes and tangle of sharp teeth still distinguished him. Orlok was the oldest of our kind, at least as far as I'm aware. He glided toward me with his long fingers twitching like epileptic spiders.

"I am Yvgeny, sir," I stammered.

"You may leave, Yvgeny. I will tend to the Baron."

I wanted nothing more, but I could see that the sunlight was only beginning to fade. I needed to stall for a few moments.

"Your Highness," I said. "The humans had an odd story to tell about our race coming from a lost civilization on the Moon. Can you tell me if it is true?"

"What else did they say about us?" he whispered.

"One said that vampirism is a disease," I replied. "Another that we're a different species of humanity. Yet another said that we are the servitors of dark and ancient gods, or that we are cursed by God for our sins. Can you tell me, sir, which is the true origin of our people?"

The ancient creature appeared lost in thought for several moments.

"People tell many stories about vampires," he finally answered. "They are all lies."

I left then, fearing what might happen if I didn't. The long years have driven Orlok mad, they say, and even other vampires are not safe around him.

I stuck to the shadows but I was still badly burned and blistered by the time I came to the city's exit. I looked back a final time on Selene, the city of wonders and mysteries. I would never see her again.

Just as well, I thought. I had never really liked the place.

Tales of the Shadowmen *prides itself on its unique international cast of contributors. So far, we have had writers from America, England, Belgium, France, Canada, and we now welcome our first contributor from Italy! Alfredo Castelli, the "father" of* Martin Mystère, *had his heart set on reconciling a bit of anachronistic information that appeared in Marcel Allain's 1919 non-Fantômas novel* Fantômas of Berlin *(a.k.a.* The Yellow Document*), in which in 1870, Kaiser Wilhelm refers to a Fantômas that obviously could not have been Gurn,* the *Fantômas of 1910. Castelli decided to "discover" what had happened to that forgotten Fantômas (and why he was forgotten in the first place)...*

Alfredo Castelli: *Long Live Fantômas*

Berlin, 1893

"Do you know what they call you, Krampft?"

"Will your Majesty deign to tell me?"

"My Court calls you the *Fantômas of Berlin*."

The Kaiser dropped onto a sofa and continued: "And that title is deserved. You have the audacity and the cunning of the man they nicknamed the Genius of Crime. The Master of Terror."

Conversation between Kaiser Wilhelm II of Germany and his private counselor, Doctor Krampft, as reported by Marcel Allain in his novel The Yellow Document or The Fantômas of Berlin, *New York, Brentano's, 1919.*

Naples, December 26, 1890

The Romans, whose eyes were trained to notice beauty, were the first to appreciate the spectacular scenery and temperate climate of Naples. The Grand Hotel was located on the very spot where, it was said, Emperor Augustus had a villa with magnificent views of Mount Vesuvius and the Bay of Naples.

The Hotel dated back to when Italy was not yet a unified country; from the day it opened, the establishment had been owned and run by the Vampa family. It was tastefully decorated and contained many pieces of antique furniture including some crafted locally, with stunning inlaid decoration.

A waiter knocked on the door of its celebrated Royal Suite, famous for its terrace and breathtaking view.

"Dottor Schliemann... Dottor Schliemann, are you in?"

But there was no reply.

After a while, the anxious waiter decided to open the door with a skeleton key.

He entered the tiled suite to search for the guest. At first glance, he wasn't in the reading room nor in the marble bathroom or on the veranda. The waiter, increasingly concerned, decided to look in the bedroom.

"Dottor Schliemann–" he began, before screaming in terror.

"You did a good job, Enrico, not that I would expect anything less from a Gioja," said the tall, dark-haired man. "According to the Police, Doctor Schliemann died from a severe ear infection. Nobody suspects anything else."

The man was dressed fashionably but not ostentatiously, in the manner of a British gentleman traveling abroad. Even though he had just entered his 50s, his face was surprisingly ageless, as young today as it had been 20 years before. He was registered at the Parker's under the identity of Marquis de Rosenthal, but of course, that was not his name. In point of fact, he had never had a name, only aliases.

"The poison is undetectable, Signor Saladin," said Enrico Gioja. "Besides, why would anyone suspect that the legendary discoverer of Troy was murdered? People consider him a hero. Why kill a hero?"

"A hero who has had dealings with some of the world's darkest powers. The treasures of Troy are priceless, and I'm not merely referring to the mundane value of the gold and jewels. Some of these stones have... power. Kings and anarchists, Masons and Illuminati alike, feared Schliemann. There are many things people didn't know about him, such as the fact that he's promised to sell the Stone of Priam to the Black Coats. I made him a good offer, but at the last minute, he chose someone else. A bad choice; for him... and for mankind."

"Is there any news of–our man?"

"No. Just as we were about to lure him into a trap in London two years ago, after those dreadful murders in Whitechapel, he suddenly vanished. We have no idea of his identity. But I'm pretty sure he'll show himself again soon. Those butcheries were only a rehearsal. I think he has greater ambitions. We must stay alert, Enrico, and when he makes a mistake, we must be ready to strike!"

Paris, 1894

Hyppolite Marinoni, director of *Le Petit Journal*, could have been a character in one of the *romans feuilletons* that the readers of his newspaper devoured daily. The son of a Corsican gendarme, he had kept pigs as a child and was inordinately proud of his humble beginnings.

When two agents of the Sûreté rather unceremoniously asked to speak with him that morning, his first reaction was one of surprise. *Le Petit Journal* made it a point to stay away from anything controversial or political so as not to incur the wrath, or the heavy fines, of the censors. The men asked to see a proof of the next issue of the popular *Supplément Illustré*, which was published on Sundays. That week, the eight-page color supplement featured a particularly funny comic strip by Draner, but otherwise contained only its usual medley of lurid news and risqué *feuilletons*, all garishly illustrated. These were redeemed by helpful, industrious advice for the hard-working families of France.

Marinoni pulled out the cover; it was a color engraving of a masked man holding a dagger as he towered over Paris. The caption read: *Fantômas: Il fait peur*.

In Marinoni's professional opinion, the accompanying article had everything needed to cause sales to jump by at least 10,000 extra copies:

"For the last four years, Paris has been devastated by a wave of cruel, unsolved murders. Some of these crimes were motivated by the clear and obvious purpose of stealing money or jewelry from the unfortunate victims. But many appear to have been committed for no other reasons than the pure, sadistic pleasure of the murderer, who has displayed a terrifying and twisted appetite for blood. Such horrors may have failed to attract the attention they ought to command, because in our decadent times, we take such aberrations for granted; they are all too often considered the natural product of the diseased minds which now plague our once-healthy cities. But *Le Petit Journal* has discovered that all these crimes are, in fact, the appalling work of a single man, a man whose name is whispered in fear by even the most dreadful figures of the underworld. Few have seen his face, and all those who did have died under the most horrible circumstances. Who is this grim wraith, this Fantômas? How did he come to be? The origin of the name 'Fantômas' remains mysterious; it is as if it merely bloomed, full-grown, from the Underworld like some dark, evil flower..."

The Sûreté agent stopped reading and slowly tore the journal from cover to cover.

"Fantômas doesn't exist, Monsieur. It is merely another of those idiotic urban legends which spring up from time to time and spread like wildfire, like Loup-Garou of Paris or the Phantom of the Opera."

"But, it was written by one of our most diligent reporters," Marinoni tried to interject, his mind already calculating what he could use as a replacement in the *Supplément*. "Claudius Bombarnac. He's accumulated notes, interviews..."

"After the Ravachol affair, the last thing we need is another criminal as hero, especially one who doesn't exist. Forget your Fantômas, Monsieur Marinoni, that is if you wish to continue publishing your lurid rag."

When the two agents left Marinoni's office, the editor looked at the shredded proof dejectedly. "At least they didn't destroy the cover illustration. I'll just have that artist... whatever-his-name-is... replace the dagger with a cornucopia full of cough drops so we can use it as an advertisement for that patent medicine."

Outside, the two agents had a brief conversation that would have much surprised the worthy Monsieur Marinoni had he been able to hear it.

"Who doesn't exist, hah! Do you think he believed me, Monsieur Clampin?" said one.

"I don't think so," said the man who had once gone by the name of "Pistolet" but was now an *éminence grise* of the Sûreté. "But you shouldn't give a damn either way, as long as he doesn't publish that article. Until now, we've managed to keep *his* existence hidden from the public. If people learned of *him*, he might become a much worse threat than Ravachol. *He* isn't a mindless anarchist with misguided bombs. *He* has the imagination and the power to really destabilize society."

"We're lucky *he* didn't respond to the Kaiser's overtures last year. To think of him working for the Boche–it's too awful to contemplate."

"I don't think *he* wants to work for anyone. *He* much prefers doing evil for the sheer pleasure of it. Maybe *he* derives some grim, perverse pleasure from flaunting the rules, customs and laws of society and knowing we're powerless to stop *him*. And if it appears we're ignoring *him*, *he* might do something foolish, you understand?"

Pistolet was right, as always.

While he was musing about the mysterious outcast's elusive motivations, at the Royal Palace Hotel, *he* brooded.

He realized that in London, *he* had been foolish to boast of his crimes. *He* had sent macabre messages to the press, defied Scotland Yard. Nevertheless, *he* knew that *he* had been lucky that day in 1889 to escape with *his* life. *He* had suddenly become aware that there were mysterious persons lurking in the shadows near *his* intended victim–a victim whom, upon reflection, he realized *he* had found much too easily. It had been too perfect. Too inviting.

It was a trap.

Luckily, swift as a phantom, he had escaped, giving his pursuers the slip in the fog-shrouded back alleys of Whitechapel, which he knew better than anyone.

Nobody knew *his* real identity: *he* had been extremely careful about that.

Yet, still there were men sniffing at *his* tracks: the Detectives, the Gentlemen of the Night, the forces of both light and darkness were arrayed against *him*.

He stopped killing, left London and came to Paris, deciding to be wiser–and more cautious. This time, *he* didn't choose a nickname as *he* had in London. But somebody had chosen one for *him*. The junior editor at *Le Petit Journal* thought he was only selling an advance copy of the paper to the competition. "Fantômas." A good name, much better than the one *he* had devised in London. Yes, *he* liked it.

But why had the paper not published the article? Was it possible that the Sûreté was so naive as to not realize that a single man was behind all those crimes? Unless it was, perhaps, another trap, one more subtle than the crude snares that had been laid for *him* in London...

He touched the jewel, which had been owned by King Priam and his son Paris. The stone gave him a new boost of energy. *He* must not succumb to his ego this time. Yes, they were deliberately teasing *him* in the hope *he* would make a mistake. Yes, it was another trap.

This time, *he* would disappear without giving them the satisfaction of ever catching him, ever learning who *he* really was. After all, the world was big enough.

Sartene, 1898

Saladin had celebrated his 60th birthday, but still looked ageless as ever. Enrico Gioja wondered if the old rogue hadn't somehow managed to find the Colonel's secret, the Colonel whom, they said, had never died.

"I think I have good news at last, Godfather."

"I need good news, Enrico," said the man known locally as Count Corona. "I do not like the ways of the world these days. I need something to warm my heart."

"We've followed *his* tracks all across Europe, Asia and Africa. As you know, when he was in Russia recently, *he* helped Pavel Krushevan write that pamphlet..."

"*The Protocols of the Elders of Zion.*"

"The same. *He* seems to think that ridiculous tract *he* stole from Father Rodin will somehow affect the destiny of..."

"Make it short, Enrico. Do you know who *he* is?"

"Yes. *He*'s a member of the English aristocracy, connected to the Royal Family, virtually untouchable. A man of great rank, great power."

"I see. Are you certain it's *him*?"

"We've checked the dates: London, Paris, New York, Cuba, Manila, Moscow, Cape Town. It all fits."

"Then you know my orders, Enrico. *Cut the branch.* How do you plan *to pay the law*?"

"*He* has an estate in England and a *garçonniere* in Paris, where *he* indulges in *his* vices. The estate is like a fortress; too well guarded. And since the Professor's death, our resources in England are not what they once were. We'd better act in Paris. But *he* is always very careful, as if *he* was afraid of something..."

"So? There must be a way. There always is."

"Yes. He can be gotten to, but only by someone he knows, someone he trusts. I think I have found that man."

"Enrico, you share the deplorable habit of never getting to the point with your late and regretted father, the Viscount Annibal. Who is he?"

"He is British, of course. He was trained by Paterson..."

"Per l'amor di Dio, Enrico! The name!"
"Gurn!"

Gurn had been lucky.

He and only three other British soldiers had managed to capture a Boer commando of a dozen men. Gurn had quickly recognized among them some of the men who had hunted him after he had defected and joined the British cause. Men who had dared threaten him.

"On your knees!" he shouted.

"Sir!" said one of the Boers. "We're soldiers. We've surrendered..."

Gurn shot the man who had spoken.

"On your knees," he said again, this time very calmly, before the body had even touched the sand.

They kneeled.

Gurn pulled out his army knife and handed it to the second man from the left amongst the line of kneeling prisoners.

"You will stab and kill the man on your left. Then the man on your right will take that knife and kill you. Then, the man on his right will do the same, and so forth."

"Sir! You're completely mad! I won't do it!"

Gurn shot him twice in the stomach. The man writhed on the ground in horrible pain. Gurn kicked the Boer and moved on to the next man.

"If you disobey, you each will die a long and painful death. But if you aim straight at the heart, you can at least dispatch yourselves painlessly. You may begin."

Sartene, Spring 1900

"Gurn is indeed a sadistic beast, Godfather," said Enrico Gioja. "He was going to be decorated for his courage by the British, but ended up almost court-martialed when his crimes were discovered. If it hadn't been for high-ranking protection..."

"From the very man we seek," said Saladin. "He was *his* aide-de-camp. They sympathized, if such men can ever do such a thing. They share the same... proclivities. Gurn has *his* trust, *his* confidence, and a powerful motive to help us."

"Can we be sure that he will give us the Stone of Priam?"

"We cannot. But have we got any other choice?"

Calais, Summer 1900

The Englishman: a tall, distinguished, white-haired Lord in his sixties, disembarked from the ferry that had carried him across the Channel. After the tiresome events of the *Man in Grey, he* was looking forward to a vacation in Paris.

A car with a chauffeur was already waiting for him. As always, Gurn had taken care of everything.

The ride to the Capital was smooth and without event. Inside the *berline, he* wondered what thrilling surprise his former aide-de-camp had in store for *him. His* hand already clawed and *his* mouth watered at the thought of their last escapade in the bowels of Montmartre. Gurn was without peer when it came to procuring the rare and exotic pleasures that his former Commander enjoyed. Pleasures such as these came with a cost, but thanks to Gurn's diligence, *he* had been able to disguise his secret life from his wife, the insufferably boring Lady Maud.

While the car drove on through the plains of Picardy, *he* felt the stirring in his loins subside. *He* knew that something in *him* was beginning to change, was no longer the same. Age, perhaps? An heir... Yes, maybe the time had come for *him* to look for a spiritual heir, a man worthy of someday following in *his* footsteps? Gurn? Perhaps. Should *he* speak to him?

He shrugged away the disturbing thought and returned to contemplate what Gurn had in store for *him. Mustn't damage the organs this time, he* thought.

Paris, Rue Lavert, Summer 1900

The car stopped near the *garçonnière*, No. 147 Rue Lavert, in the 20ème *arrondissement*. It was a small, insignificant street near Belleville, mostly deserted, which suited *him.*

He opened the outside door with his key, Madame Doulenques, the concierge, was absent, a further guarantee of discretion, and climbed the stairs, pleased to observe that *he* was barely out of breath when *he* reached the fifth floor.

He entered the small apartment and called out:

"Gurn? Gurn? Where are you?"

Suddenly, *he* heard the unmistakable sounds of passionate lovemaking coming from the small bedroom. *He* rushed in and discovered the sight of a beautiful blonde woman, her abundant hair surrounding her head like a halo, tied, spread-eagled, on the bed, in the throes of orgasm, while a man he knew all too well was plowing her helpless body.

"Maud?"

"Good morning, Lord Beltham," said Gurn, turning around. "Or should I say, *Fantômas?*"

A red veil seemed to cloud Lord Beltham's eyes. Gurn's taunts barely registered as his blood drummed in his ears. He pulled out a gun.

But Gurn was ready. He grabbed a hammer that he had carefully placed on the nightstand and, with a swift move of his hand, knocked Lord Beltham unconscious. He quickly jumped off the bed and, straddling the body of the Lord, grabbed his neck and squeezed.

Lady Beltham opened her mouth as she watched her naked lover strangle her husband, but before she could scream, Gurn's hand covered her mouth.

"Fantômas is dead. Long live Fantômas!" he whispered.

He returned to the body and slowly started to undress it. As he did so, he searched the clothes. Finally, he found a jewel hanging on a gold chain around Lord Beltham's neck. It looked ancient and eldritch. Gurn unclasped it and took it in his hand. He felt its power, its inebriating magic.

Lady Beltham looked at him in a daze, her eyes glazed.

Gurn began to dress himself with Lord Beltham's clothes. They were of the same stature and they fit him rather well. He then took a wig and perfected his disguise.

Under Lady Beltham's eyes, Gurn had become Lord Beltham.

Sartene, Fall 1900

"Here it is, Signore. Gurn kept his word."

Enrico Gioja presented Saladin with a small box.

"Thank you, Enrico. You have been a faithful member of our Brotherhood. I want you to take an oath…"

"An oath?"

"Yes. You will swear on the Santa Vergine that this jewel will be buried with me. This is the reason I wanted to buy it. To be sure that nobody would ever touch it again. Never, for any reason…"

"I swear on my honor, Signore. I know its power. It has fomented wars, death and many horrors. Schliemann was aware of this, but he didn't care."

"And he paid for that with his life. Now, leave me, Enrico, I want to be alone."

After Enrico Gioja had left, Saladin opened the small box. Inside was a small, seemingly harmless jewel, hanging from a gold chain. The stone, a yellow diamond, was shaped like an apple.

Saladin looked at the jewel that had started the Trojan War and which Homer called the *Golden Apple of Discord*. There was a small note with it:

"I don't need it. F."

"Fantômas."

"What did you say?"

"I said: Fantômas."

"And what does that mean?"

"Nothing... And everything!"

"But what is it?"

"Nobody... And yet, it is somebody!"

"And what does that somebody do?"

"He spreads terror!"

Dinner was just over and the company was moving into the drawing room.

It had been the immemorial custom of the Marquise de Langrune to have a few of her personal friends to dinner every Wednesday night...

THE BEGINNING

Barbarella
by Cybele Collins (2006)

When, in 1962, Georges Gallet, the editor of the French V Magazine, asked artist Jean-Claude Forest to create an adult comic strip featuring Tarzella, *the latter turned him down flatly as he wasn't interested in the concept of a jungle lady; but from that request sprang forth one of the most enduring icons of science fiction: Barbarella. Our regular contributor Bill Cunningham, who likes nothing more than to bring iconic characters together like flintstones to create a spark, postulates about the encounter between the Queen of the Spaceways and her opposite archetype...*

Bill Cunningham: *Next!*

The Future

"Quite frankly, I find this hard to believe."

The tall woman with the silky blonde mane stretched across her bed. He was going to make her explain it all over again despite the fact she was clearly ready for sex.

"Captain–James. May I call you James?" she asked, still seducing him with her eyes. She ran her fingernail slowly down his arm. "It's really quite simple. This is the 21st century..."

"But not my 21st century, an alternate one," he interrupted. This was going to be harder than she thought. Wasn't this man a "tomcat?"

"That's correct. In this universe, I have been tasked with creating a super-being. I am to be its mother, and you are to be its father. You have been selected and brought here across several realities and timeframes via the Chronosphere. Once we've accomplished *first contact*," she giggled, "then we can return you to almost the exact second you left. James, please we need you. I need you. "

"All this," he gestured to the luxurious envelope of space time they were lying in. For a mathematical construct, it was something else–cushions and food and atmospheres at the touch–all dedicated to sensual pleasures. He merely had to think it and anything he desired appeared. "It's a bit much. Why not simply take the DNA you need?"

Barbarella smiled mischievously. She got up to her knees and uncoupled the fastenings of her pleasure-skin revealing her tender flesh underneath.

"Where would the fun be in that? Besides, it's not like you haven't done this before."

And with that, the starship captain pulled her in for a kiss.

Barbarella jumped out of the sonic shower and grabbed an absorba-skin from the rack. She was refreshed after her energetic session with the captain. She would need all the sexual energy she could muster for her baby's next "father." Many more sessions were required before the right DNA mix presented itself–the right eye color, bone structure, skin tone, psycho-sexual proclivities–all matched and cross-indexed against the project template.

Barbarella tuned in her tele-viewer to see James back at his command and none the wiser. She actually hated doing that–wiping the event from his memory, but it was crucial to transdimensional integrity. A shame–for a man not familiar with the intricacies of 21st century technology, James sure could use a sense-all crystal to best effect.

She shivered at the thought, but turned her attention back to choosing the next candidate.

She commanded the tele-viewer to materialize multiple screens.

Barbarella jumped back into bed (the sheets had already changed themselves) and stared at the hovering images of her future suitors above her. It was very stressful saving a universe–there were so many choices:

She wondered why they called that one The Dark Knight, though she immediately got excited at the thought of counting his many scars with her lips.

The Man of Bronze was interesting too. Always in control. Always thinking, strategizing. Barbarella immediately wanted to see him lose control. Now that would be interesting!

The Lord of the Apes would be a challenge. She knew he would take what he wanted, but could the brutal savage give?

The Patchwork Man needed tenderness and understanding, and he gave great emotion.

The Thief was clever, inventive–qualities a superbeing would need.

Then there was the Diabolical One, The Alien, The Detective, and The Pilot–each of them with their own qualities and quirks. Then there were the dozens of others across multiple realities and...

Barbarella closed her eyes and pushed a button. Some days you just have to go with it. There was a brief flash and suddenly the time-space construct was filled with a chilling laughter.

"Hello, Ying Ko. Please sit down. We have much to discuss..."

One of the greatest satisfactions in launching our Rivière Blanche *science fiction, sister imprint in France in 2004 was the opportunity to track down some of my favorite genre writers from the 1960s. The legendary André Caroff, now in his mid-80s, was one of those prolific authors whose novels never failed to entertain, and whose characters, such as secret agent Bonder and starship trooper Rod, are still fondly remembered by myriad fans. In Caroff's polymorphic* oeuvre, *however, there is one creation that has since acquired the status of a genuine cult classic: Madame Atomos.*

Her real name is Kanoto Yoshimuta. She is a scientific genius whose family perished in the nuclear holocaust of Nagasaki. She has sworn undying revenge on the United States and has labored in secrecy for 20 years to hatch a series of diabolical plans, each one more fantastic than the last. She has only one purpose in mind: the infliction of as much pain and suffering as possible upon America. Invariably, she signs her actions: "Hiroshima. Nagasaki. With the compliments of Madame Atomos."

Rivière Blanche *has now begun to reprint all 18* Atomos *novels in a six-volume omnibus series, each featuring an all-new short story, taking place during the continuity of the series. If there is an event other than the bombing of Hiroshima that will forever be remembered in history, it is the Moon Landing of July 20, 1969. Clearly, such a cosmic enterprise, especially one launched by her hated enemy, could not leave Madame Atomos unaffected. The talented François Darnaudet, who appears in* Tales of the Shadowmen *for the first time, went looking behind the curtain (with a little help from the undersigned) and discovered the horrific truth...*

François Darnaudet & J.-M. Lofficier: Au Vent Mauvais...

Somewhere in the U.S.A.., July 1969

> *Et je m'en vais / Au vent mauvais*
> *Qui m'emporte / Deçà, delà,*
> *Pareil à la / Feuille morte.*
> Verlaine
> *Chanson d'Automne.*

The light of the television screen lit the entire room.

The location did not matter. It was an anonymous meeting room of a type found in millions of office buildings throughout the United States. There was a conference table, half-a-dozen leather chairs and four trite seascape paintings on the fake wood-paneled walls.

The television set had been tuned to CBS, where Walter Cronkite had been entertaining viewers with models of the LEM and conversations with Arthur C. Clarke and Robert Heinlein.

It had been a hot day, but now it was night; a rather hot night. The crescent Moon was tantalizingly high in the west. The Moon landing had successfully ocurred some six-and-a-half hours earlier. Now they were waiting for the first man to walk on another world.

On the table, quite appropriately, were a bucket of ice with a bottle of champagne and two glasses made of the purest cristal d'arques.

There were three people in the room, a man and a woman, sitting across the table, riveted by what was happening on the television screen, and a tall Japanese man in a chauffeur uniform who stood rigidly next to the door.

"Ozu, you may open the bottle of champagne now," said Madame Atomos. Few would have recognized the sworn enemy of America in this stunning young Oriental woman dressed in the latest Fifth Avenue fashion.

Her companion was a dark-haired man, handsome in a way that could only be described as "dangerous." His attire was European in style and he could easily have been taken for one of those European playboys who spent their lives jet setting from Saint-Tropez to Saint-Moritz.

"You will toast with me, n'est-ce-pas Monsieur Zemba?" asked Madame Atomos.

"Naturally, my dear," replied the man, with barely a hint of French accent.

"I believe that, this time, you have outdone your notorious grandfather."

The Frenchman could not keep himself from casting a covetous glance at Madame Atomos' long, shapely legs, alluringly covered by black silk tights, and which she crossed and uncrossed with consummate skill.

Zemba III, or Zemba The Third, as he liked to be called, smiled in self-satisfaction. Yet despite his outward calm, he was actually quite uncomfortable. He had heard of Madame Atomos; her sinister reputation, her obsessive ruthlessness and hatred for all things American had spread far and wide, even amongst the European Underworld.

She had been trying to hire a master-thief, and many in the game had turned her down, despite the truly staggering fortune she had offered.

More than the money, it was the nature of the assignment that had made Zemba III agree to take it. If he succeeded, his reputation would be made. He would no longer be a joke, a comical version of his prestigious grandfather, Gaspard Zemba, who had once been called the Master Criminal of Paris.

Ozu had opened the magnum of champagne in a manner that would not have shamed a sommelier at Maxim's; he was now carefully filling the two glasses.

On the television screen, Cronkite was becoming increasingly emotional. Understandably so, since he had been on the air 27 of the 30 hours it had taken the spacecraft to reach the Sea of Tranquility. The great moment had arrived. Soon, very soon, Neil Armstrong would step out of the LEM and would become the first human to walk on the Moon.

Madame Atomos and Zemba III grabbed their glasses.

"Look! It's happening!" he said.

"That's one small step for a man, one giant leap for mankind."

Armstrong had finally stepped off the lander's ladder. The reception was particularly good and the sound crackled, but it was spectacular nevertheless. Cronkite shed a tear.

"Americans are such children," said Madame Atomos contemptuously.

Zemba III said nothing. He didn't share Madame Atomos' obsession. On the contrary, he was somehow moved by the astounding venture.

"We still have a couple of hours to go, " he observed meekly. "Let us drink to the success of your enterprise."

"It has made you a very rich man," said Madame Atomos.

"For that, too, I am grateful, but now I can tell you: I would have done it for free."

Two hours went by. On the Moon, Buzz Aldrin and Armstrong were drilling core samples, photographing what they saw and collecting rocks. But finally, the moment they had been waiting for came: the planting of the American flag.

"Here it comes," said Zemba III.

Madame Atomos leaned forward to not miss a second of this historical event.

The House and Senate of the United States had stated, "This act was intended as a symbolic gesture of national pride in achievement and was not to be construed as a declaration of national appropriation by claim of sovereignty."

Armstrong grabbed the flag that had been mounted on the left-hand side of the LEM's ladder to make it more easily accessible. To protect it from the temperatures of up to 2,000 F during the 13 seconds of the touchdown, it had been wrapped in an insulating shroud consisting of three layers of stainless steel, Thermoflex and aluminum.

Armstrong began to unfurl the flag by extending the telescoping crossbar and raising it to a position just above 90 degrees. He then lowered it to a position perpendicular to the pole, where a catch prevented the hinge from moving. The upper portion then slipped into the base portion of the flagpole, which had been driven into the ground using a geological hammer.

It was an ordinary 3 x 5 foot nylon flag, which weighed only 9 pounds and 7 ounces.

"It's strange, it looks like it's flying in the breeze," said Zemba III, watching Armstrong salute the Stars and Stripes. "You don't think this is all a hoax staged somewhere in Nevada?"

"No," replied Madame Atomos. "They sew a hem along the top of the flag. A horizontal crossbar gives the illusion that it's flying."

A NASA secretary who had gone to the local Sears department store during her lunch hour purchased the flag for $5.50. Ironically, its insulating shroud cost several thousands of dollars.

"How did you ever manage to steal their flag and replace it with the one I provided?" asked Madame Atomos.

"Like you, I have my secrets," smiled Zemba III. "But if you must know, dear Madame, demonstration tests were performed to make sure that the flag would operate properly. Suffice it to say that the Jack Kinzler, the Chief of Technical Services Division who flew to Kennedy Space Center on June 25 to participate in a mock review of the lunar flag assembly may not have been who everyone else thought he was."

"I see. Very clever indeed."

"Thank you."

The bottle of champagne was now empty, as Zemba III found when he tried to refill his glass one last time.

"I drink to your victory, Madame Atomos. When will the flag now turn into your flag? The Stars & Stripes replaced by 'Hiroshima. Nagasaki. With the compliments of Madame Atomos.' I can't wait to see their faces!"

"It's not going to. Why would I want to do such a silly thing? I am above such petty vanities."

"But when you hired me, you said..."

"I lied. I told you what I thought a Frenchman like yourself would most likely believe."

"But then, why...?"

Zemba III never uttered another word. He collapsed on the table, dead.

"Make sure you remove the bottle and the glasses," instructed Madame Atomos. "The poison I use leaves no trace, but there is no reason to give the FBI any more clues than we have to."

The Frenchman had been right, thought Madame Atomos. It had been a most successful enterprise. She wasn't fooled by Congress' proclamation. Someday, America would colonize the Moon; the Imperialists wouldn't be able to help it. They would go there, build a domed city, a shrine for the site of their first landing, a memorial around their flag so conveniently abandoned on the surface.

And then that flag, in reality *her* flag, would spawn its deadly children and the first colonists would die in excruciating agony,

She had sown the first seeds of her hatred in the cosmos and an ill wind was now waiting amongst the stars.

If Tales of the Shadowmen *did not exist, it should have been invented just to make room for stories like Brian Stableford's unfolding Févalesque* feuilleton *and Paul DiFilippo's amazing contribution to this volume. Of all the French science fiction authors who followed in the footsteps of Jules Verne, perhaps the most important was Albert Robida, a writer-artist who also deserves a place in genre history as the founding father of science fiction illustration. Robida not only illustrated genre stories by Rabelais, Cyrano de Bergerac and Camille Flammarion, but he also wrote and illustrated his own scientific anticipation* feuilletons, *starting in 1879 with a deliberate homage to Verne entitled* Voyages Très Extraordinaires de Saturnin Farandoul, *in which the Tarzan-like Farandoul meets Captain Nemo. (This encounter will be included in the forthcoming Black Coat Press release of French proto-SF* News from the Moon*). However, Robida's masterpiece remains* Le Vingtième Siècle *(1882), devoted to the visual description of the mid-1950s. In addition to imagining futuristic devices, such as videophones, flying taxis, etc., Robida added the idea of the Moon being drawn closer to the Earth by a battery of giant magnets. So popular was* Le Vingtième Siècle *that he continued in this vein with* La Guerre au Vingtième Siècle *(War in the 20th Century) (1883), set in 1975, and* La Vie Electrique *(The Electric Life) (1890), set in 1955, which offered more of his satirical, pessimistic view of the future, and often contained frighteningly accurate predictions, such as the possibility of germ warfare. It is that fantastic, alternate universe, truly a future that never was, which is revisited by Paul DiFilippo in a brilliant "electricpunk" satire which unites Robida's amazing vision with another, entirely unexpected, fragment of popular fiction.*

Paul DiFilippo: *Return to the 20th Century*

The 20th Century

January 1, 1960, and the whole globe was atremble with anticipation. For today marked the start of ceremonies surrounding the official inauguration of the new man-made continent dubbed Helenia.

A truly unique milestone in human progress had been reached. The cunning assembly of millions of hectares of artificial land from great carved sheets of the Himalayas and Rocky Mountains, covered with rich topsoil dredged from the many productive ports and harbors of the whole world, and utilizing the scattered Polynesian isles as seeds around which to accrete, represented the supreme accomplishment of human craft and ingenuity to date. Although the startling and productive 20th century still had four decades to run, it certainly seemed to most of the citizenry that an apex of engineering, ingenuity and social coordination had been reached, one that would not soon be surpassed, if ever.

The 20th Century
by Albert Robida (1882)

But little did anyone suspect that a looming crisis would soon spur mankind on to an even greater feat of construction and ambition, all in the name of sheer self-preservation of their remarkable civilization in the face of a malign and unknown rival!

The capital city of Helenia, Pontoville, was abuzz this temperate day with the arrival of assorted dignitaries from across the harmonious globe. These eminences from all the spheres of culture, politics, industry and religion arrived by several means. By swift undersea rail tube, one such contrivance emanated from San Francisco (otherwise known as New Nanking), one from Lima, and one from Manila. By streamlined submersible and surface-plying oceanic vessels. And, of course, by innumerable aircraft, both immense ships of state, featuring lifting balloons large as castle and multifarious as a sculpture garden, and individual pinnaces and *veloces* from nearby territories such as the Sandwich Islands.

So heavily did the distinguished visitors plunge upon Pontoville, thronging the skies over the city of parks and towers and also its broad avenues and long piers, that they could not all be greeted individually by President Philippe Ponto and his first lady Hélène (nee Colobry). Later, of course, the President and his amiable consort would spend at least a brief interval of conversation with every superior guest, as they circulated at numerous state functions in celebration of the sixth continent's official birthday. But, for the moment, on this first day of the festivities, President Ponto had reserved his time for welcoming only the highest among the high. Su Chu Peng, leader of the Oriental Republic; Bismarck III, chancellor of Germany and its North American satellite, New Germania; Kulashekhara II, Emperor of India; and so forth down the list of exclusively great names–with two humble exceptions, the first being the President's immediate family.

Philippe and Hélène Ponto turned out in person at midday to greet Philippe's father (and Hélène's former guardian), Mr. Raphaël Ponto, the supreme industrialist, banker, speculator and visionary, whose titanic career had been an inspiration both to his son and the world at large. Accompanying the elder Ponto was his wife Josephine, herself well-noted for her role as an officeholder representing the Radical Feminist Party. And rounding out the party were Philippe's sisters, Barbe and Barnabette, along with their spouses and offsprings.

Philippe, a handsome mustachioed man barely past his first bloom of youth, clasped his stout father to his bosom, heedless of rumpling his official sash of office or of the impress of his many medals into his own and his father's chest. They stood upon the high, broad and busy aerial platform where the express from Paris had just docked.

"Father, I cannot believe you have finally made it to this new land whose creation owes everything to your own guidance and exemplary career."

43

Mr. Ponto, a stout and convivial iteration of his child, responded with bluff, hearty warmth and self-abnegation.

"Well, you know that a few small matters have kept me busy till now, during the year or two of Helenia's creation. The takeover of Portugal as a second pleasure park along the lines of Italy, for instance. But there was simply no way I would miss the official inauguration of such a monumental achievement. You have much to be proud of this day, my son!"

Philippe made some humble rejoinders of his own, before moving to greet his mother and siblings in similar open-hearted fashion. Meanwhile, Mr. Ponto's eye falling on Hélène, the elder man turned to his daughter-in-law, who so far had held back from the familial mingling.

"Why, Hélène, you look so distracted! Daydreaming perhaps? A privilege of youth. Still, it is most undiplomatic behavior on this splendid state occasion. I thought my days of lecturing you were over. But perhaps I shall have to take you once more in hand!"

Hélène, a slim, attractive, blonde woman of average build, did not respond immediately to her father-in-law's mix of chafing and jollying. Instead, she continued to stand at the ornate cast-iron railing of the platform, gazing up into the sky.

There, above the city of Pontoville, hung the daytime Moon.

The perpetual orb filled nearly the entire sky.

Some short time ago, Earth scientists had drawn the satellite much closer to its primary, by means of electrical attraction. Precisely speaking, the distance from one globe to another was now 675 kilometers, or roughly the gap between Paris and Lyon. Moreover, the rotation and gravitic interactions of the two planets had been locked and stabilized, so that the Moon neither rose nor set any longer, but remained perpetually in the sky over Pontoville, as a tribute to the importance of this new nation.

It was this very orb that seemed now to transfix Hélène. She murmured mysterious words at the blank visage of Selene, words which Mr. Ponto could interpret as he approached his daughter-in-law.

"*Alpha, we await your coming. Alpha, we are ready.*"

Mr. Ponto laid a hand on Hélène's shoulder, and the woman started, as if an electrical current had passed through her. She turned her face away from the lunar surface, its most minute details plain as the creases in one's palm, even by day, and addressed her father-in-law.

"Oh, sir, it is so good to see you! I am glad you have arrived!"

"Now, that is more like the reception I expected, dearest."

The reunited family consorted pleasantly for a few more minutes, amidst the hurly-burly of additional arrivals, with Hélène and her sisters-in-law exchanging news about the latest fashions of each continent. But their chatter was cut short by Philippe's exclamation.

"I see it! Jungle Alli's ship! The famed *Smoke Ghost*!"

All eyes turned to follow Philippe's pointing finger. The President of a continent was as excited as a schoolboy. Here came the second party for whom he had deigned a personal reception.

Moving swiftly through the sky like some celestial pirate ship, the *Smoke Ghost* radiated a *louche élan* not exhibited by any other craft. Suspended beneath a balloon shaped like a recumbent odalisque of Junoesque proportions, its baroque gondola was scarred by hard travel and not a few bullet impacts. As the craft approached the docking platform, the dashing figure behind the wheel inside the pilothouse could be more and more clearly discerned.

Jungle Alli, christened Alice Bradley at birth.

Alice Bradley had been born to Mary Hastings Bradley and Herbert Bradley in Chicago, the "second city" of the Mormon interior of North America. Directly from her first juvenile stirrings of reason and independence, she had resisted the conventional life outlined in advance for her, utterly rejecting a future that included the infamous Mormon polygamous marriage. Partly to tame her rebellious spirit, her parents had sent her to a private girls' school, *Les Fougères*, in Lausanne, Switzerland. But this rigid institution suited young Alice no better than her native patriarchy, and at age 16, in 1931, she had run away.

The next news of the renegade Alice Bradley came most unexpectedly from the heart of darkest Africa. At this time, the continent was not totally pacified and integrated into the 20th century as it is today, with its productive citizens indistinguishable–save for the hue of their skin–from their Paris or Berlin cousins. Pockets of sub-Saharan barbarism still existed, and one of the most brutish tribes were the Niam-Niams of Central Africa. Cannibals one and all, they derived their name from their blood-curdling war-cry of "Nyama! Nyama!" Otherwise, "Flesh! Flesh!" Feared by natives and Europeans alike, the Niam-Niams maintained an inviolate sphere of privacy and secrecy.

But even this hostile bubble had eventually to be pierced by the superior forces of technology, culture and capitalism, and in 1940, a trading expedition from Marseille entered the main Niam-Niam village under a flag of truce.

Imagine the consternation and discomfiture of the Europeans to discover, ruling over the cannibals, a young white woman!

Not precisely white any longer, after nearly a decade under the tropical sun. Nut-brown and nearly naked, save for a lion-skin skirt, with whip-cord muscles and long blonde tresses matted into elflocks hanging down to her shapely rump, Alice Bradley exhibited teeth stained brown and filed to points. She sat on a crude throne, clutching a feather-adorned spear. And she hailed the newcomers in the Niam-Niam tongue.

After overcoming their initial shock, the traders awoke Alice's long-disused French and were able to converse. She detailed a long history of conquest, first over the Niam-Niams themselves by one lone 16-year-old girl equipped with no more than a Krupp repeating rifle, 60 pounds of backpacked cartridges and an infinite supply of bravado and courage, and then, at the head of her adopted clan, of all the neighboring tribes.

When asked tentatively what her ultimate aims and goals were, Alice Bradley grinned in her ghastly fashion and replied simply, "Freedom." When asked if that goal were incompatible with her return to civilization, Alice said, "Not at all-so long as it's on my terms."

Thus began the public career of the astonishing woman soon dubbed by journalists everywhere "Jungle Alli."

For the next two decades, employing her obediently savage (and presumably dietarily reformed) cannibals as shock troops, Jungle Alli participated in the taming of the Dark Continent. Up and down the broad expanse of Africa, a mercenary in service of whichever government could afford her, Jungle Alli contributed to the establishment of law and order in pursuit of profit and fame. Her exploits became world-famous, from the overthrow of the dictator of Senegambia to the suppression of the Tuaregs of Biskra. Hundreds of pulpy novels, hardly exaggerated, had been written with her as the star.

However, of late, Jungle Alli had begun to seem like a bit of an anachronism. Now that her work was finally done amidst these former backwaters, Jungle Alli found herself on the verge of being outmoded. The modern pacified world seemed to have few assignments for a rogue of her nature, and she had spent the last few years in frivolous deeds of personal derring-do: mountain-climbing, big-game hunting, motorcar-racing and so forth.

Nonetheless, to those of young President Philippe Ponto's generation, she remained an alluring figure of romance and adventure. Even in this era of complete female suffrage and equality-female dominance, some would maintain-when many of the fairer sex had built exemplary careers, the ex-Chicago girl boasted a worldwide celebrity. Having grown up on tales of Jungle Alli's exploits, President Ponto had determined that she must grace the seminal celebrations of Helenia, conferring her iconic *mana* upon the new nation.

Thus her arrival today.

With Jungle Alli at the controls, the *Smoke Ghost* maneuvered delicately until achieving a mooring. Over the decks of the gondola swarmed dozens of Niam-Niams of both sexes, bare-chested and grass-skirted, fur cuffs at ankles and wrists. They dropped a plank to the platform, and carpeted it with zebra hides. Only then did Jungle Alli condescend to disembark.

Now 45 years of age, Jungle Alli remained an extremely attractive woman. Her lithe physique was modestly displayed by khaki pantaloons and blouse, complemented by high black boots. Twin pistols were slung at her hips, while bandoliers of cartridges crossed her chest. An unholstered machete slapped her thigh as she walked.

Jungle Alli's golden hair, admixed with threads of grey, had long ago been bobbed neat and short. Fighting aerial freebooters off the coast of Zanzibar ten years ago, she had lost an eye, and that sinister empty socket had henceforth been concealed by a patch. When she smiled, as she did now, the work of the best Parisian dentists was revealed, synthetic caps covering her cannibal heritage.

Accompanied by her honor guard of blackamoors, themselves a daunting entourage, Jungle Alli strode boldly across the gap separating her from President Ponto. She extended her right hand in the manner of her North American forebears, eschewing the more traditional European ceremonial double kisses. President Ponto took her hand and found himself wincing from the strength of her grip.

"Miss Bradley, allow me to extend the unlimited hospitality of our fledgling nation to one whose exploits have ever been–"

Jungle Alli interrupted the sincere but fulsome speech, employing her natal English. "No time for jawing now, chief. I've discovered that our planet is under attack!"

The state palace of Helenia consisted of a building inspired by Eiffel's Parisian Tower. But the Tower that reared over Pontoville was precisely five times as large, rearing a full 1600 meters into the empyrean and occupying a terrestrial footprint of many hectares. Nor did it feature mainly a lacy openwork construction, its lower reaches being walled off and devoted to governmental offices. And of course, the very tip of the enormous structure had been reserved for the sun-drenched Presidential chambers, serviced by a high-speed *ascenseur*.

Here, higher than clouds, sat now Jungle Alli, President Ponto and the President's father, Mr. Raphaël Ponto, the latter in his capacity as trusted advisor to his son and as representative of the international business community.

The legendary female African mercenary seemed utterly at ease, in comparison to the anxiety exhibited by the two men, and in fact had delayed imparting any more of her startling news long enough to enjoy a noxious cheroot, prefacing her indulgence by saying, "Damn nuisance not to be able to smoke in flight. But can't risk your whole ride going up in flames."

After a minute or so of contented puffing, Jungle Alli finally put aside her cigar, leaned forward in her chair, and pinned her fascinated auditors with her piercing one-eyed gaze, no less Gorgonish for its half power. When she spoke this time, it was in the French of her hosts.

"*Messieurs*, what is your opinion of the current relations between the sexes?"

The disarming question, whose relevance was not immediately apparent, took the men aback.

"Why," stammered President Ponto, "I hardly give the matter any daily thought. Absolute equality of the sexes has been the foundation of modern society for so long, that one might as well ponder the wisdom of raising capital through the means of a stock market, or of settling affairs of honor with duels, or of changing the government regularly by means of a decennial revolution."

The elder Mr. Ponto was not so hastily dismissive of Jungle Alli's question. He paused a moment before answering, then replied cautiously, "I must say that in the last election a year or so ago, when I ran for a seat against my wife, I was somewhat taken aback by the vituperative anti-male stridency of her campaign. At first, I chalked it up to some trivial personal arguments we had had between us, leaking into our professional lives. But as I heard other members of her party employ similar rhetoric against other men, I began to sense a certain shifting of the norms of discourse that had prevailed..."

Jungle Alli slapped her thigh with such a sharp report that both men jumped. "Exactly! The war between the sexes, long thought to be extinguished, is heating up! It has been obvious to anyone who has bothered to look during the past year. But the cause has been more obscure. It is not a natural affair! The animosity is being stoked by agents provocateurs–fifth columnists from beyond our planet! This is the nature of the assault on our world. And if we do not stop it, our civilization will go down in a cataclysm of gender warfare. Men and women need each other to continue supporting and advancing the elaborate mechanism that is 20th-century civilization. Neither sex can manage alone. But a wedge is being driven between the sons of Adam and the daughters of Eve."

Pontos Senior and Junior seemed nonplussed. The younger man, to stall a response, got up and walked to a wall tap where he was able to draw a steaming cup of rich *pousse-café* from the building's food and beverage network.

Sensing their hesitancy to embrace her admittedly grandiose revelations, Jungle Alli disclosed more.

"I have always been an admirer of the masculine sex. The drive, competence, certitude and ingenuity of males have been polestars by which I have guided my own career. Not to diminish either the charms or resources or native abilities of my own sex, which I have also honored and, ah, embraced. So you will understand that when, over the past few months, I began to experience unwarranted jealousy, anger and irritability toward the important males in my life, I began to suspect an outside influence on my own consciousness.

"By immersion in various shamanic meditative techniques of the Niam-Niams, I was able to establish the source of the psychic contamination in myself.

"It radiates from the Moon."

Instinctively the men looked out one of the office's huge floor-to-ceiling curving windows, where a segment of the pregnant lunar satellite was visible.

"On the Moon, amidst cyclopean ruins concealed in atmosphere-filled caverns, live the sparse remnants of an ancient race. A mere eight women, denominated Alpha, Beta and so on. They refer to themselves as the 'Cat Women,' a phrase emblematic of their egocentric mercilessness and predilection for playing with their prey. They possess the ability to tamper with human thoughts-but only those of their fellow females. To instill in unsuspecting female minds deadly seeds I term 'ideonemes,' which pass as native to the receptive brain.

"Once I discovered the existence of these Cat Women, I was able to establish two-way mental communication with Alpha, their leader. Boastfully, she revealed their full plans and intentions to me. I believe the loneliness of the Cat Women and their eagerness for contact inspired Alpha's loquacity.

"In any case, here is their intent. By fomenting an internecine war between Earth's men and women, they will weaken us to the point where the Cat Women can establish themselves as rulers of a wholly female globe, forsaking their sterile orb for our own fertile paradise."

President Ponto cleared his throat in polite dissent. "This presupposes, Miss Bradley, that your sex would prove victorious in such a combat."

Jungle Alli grinned fiercely, and although her teeth were no longer filed to points, both men experienced an impression of cannibalistic fervor. "Trust me, sir, we would. But please, I ask you, put aside all such chauvinistic quibbles and focus on the true import of my revelations. We are at war with a determined enemy, and we must take action!"

Mr. Ponto spoke. "Why is it only now that these hypothetical Cat Women have launched their attack?"

"It is our own hubris in moving the Moon so close to us!" responded Jungle Alli. "Previously, the vast distance between our spheres acted as a cosmic quarantine. Their mental powers were insufficient to bridge the gap."

President Ponto said, "All of this is so hard to credit. How can we possibly announce such an unlikely threat? Without proof, the practically minded populace would rightfully dismiss us out of hand. It would be akin to asking people to believe one of Mr. Verne or Mr. Wells' fantasies."

"Actually, we would not want to make a general announcement," Jungle Alli countered. "It would provoke a panic, and possibly force the hand of the Cat Women. They might forego subtlety and simply derange the minds of millions of women into a murderous rage. No, we must make an assault against the Cat Women under cover of a natural commercial impulse to integrate the Moon into Helenia's economy."

Now President Ponto finally balked, his immense respect for Jungle Alli counterbalanced by his stewardship of the infant nation and its resources.

"Miss Bradley, I am afraid I cannot commit my country's resources to such an unsupported crusade against imaginary enemies—"

Jungle Alli stood up. "Unsupported? Imaginary? Very well. You force my hand. I had not wanted to risk this. But it seems necessary now." Withdrawing one of her pistols from its holster-causing both men to blanch-Jungle Alli called out, "Alpha, appear! I summon you!"

Instantly, a fourth figure occupied the room.

The newcomer was a statuesque woman of immense beauty, clad in a black leotard that revealed every inch of her curvaceous figure. Her eyes were heavily kohl-lined, her painted lips cruel. Her dark hair was gathered up into an elaborate hive. Golden slave bracelets adorned her biceps.

"You dare!" said the Cat Woman known as Alpha.

"Let us end this here and now," replied Jungle Alli, and fired!

The bullet passed through empty space, smashing a narrow channel through a thick window. A thin stream of wind whistled from the pressurized interior of the building.

Alpha the Cat Woman had dematerialized in the instant Jungle Alli pulled her trigger, and reappeared on the far side of the chamber. The face of the Selene female was intensely wrathful.

"Your powers of mind are formidable, Alice Bradley! For an Earthwoman! You were able to take me unawares this time. But do not count on being able to do so again!"

And with that, Alpha the Cat Woman vanished entirely.

Jungle Alli reholstered her smoking pistol. "Gentlemen, do you grant credence to my story now?"

With shaking hands, President Ponto dabbed with a handkerchief at his wet trousers where he had spilled his *pousse-café*.

"Miss Bradley, the full energies of Helenia and its people are at your disposal."

The first of many official banquets meant to celebrate the birth of the new continent and scheduled for the upcoming week was held that very night in the Hall of Wonders. Larger than the largest aerostat hanger, the glass-and-cast-iron Hall of Wonders was filled with statues and paintings illustrating the tremendous progress made during the illustrious 20th century. Recorded in pictorial form were the invention of the conglomerate paper that substituted for wood; the parachute-belt; the chair-barricade; and so forth in a panoply of human ingenuity.

But even this extravagant exhibition did not preclude the temporary use of the Hall to hold hundreds of tables, topped with linens, crystal goblets, fine china and silver, all capturing glints from the many electric chandeliers.

At each place sat one of the many dignitaries who had voyaged hither for the ceremonies, patrician men and women from every nation of the globe, the "movers and shakers" of the new age.

At the head table, raised above the others on a dais, sat President Ponto and First Lady Hélène. Adjacent to the President sat his father and mother. At Hélène's elbow, Jungle Alli. The rest of the table was occupied by various officeholders of Helenia.

Focused on the table were a dozen telephonoscopic cameras, relaying the doings on the dais to a hundred screens set up throughout the Hall, thus providing a sense of intimacy for all attendees, however remote, with the doings at the Presidential table. Smaller screens at intervals conveyed the entertaining image and sound from a brilliant symphony orchestra.

The banquet commenced sharply at eight, after a rousing champagne toast. Thousands of servitors drew comestibles from the taps scattered throughout the Hall, ferrying steaming, deliciously prepared squab, pork medallions, sausages and other delights to the eager diners. Jollity and bonhomie, fueled by fine wines, reigned throughout the chamber. Although, truth be told, had anyone been in the frame of mind to scrutinize objectively the visages of President and Mr. Ponto, they might have detected a certain sham brittleness to their convivialness, as if the men were masking deeper concerns.

Likewise, the charming face of Hélène showed a certain distracted slackness and preoccupied inwardness.

This suspicious catatonia on the part of one so close to the powerful President of Helenia did not go unremarked by the perceptive Jungle Alli.

"Mrs. Ponto," said the adventurer gallantly and ingenuously, so low that only the two of them could hear, "your sweet face should be shining at this victorious hour with exuberance and animation. Instead, it is beclouded with melancholy."

With a visible effort, Hélène responded agreeably. "Please, call me Hélène. 'Mrs. Ponto' is my mother-in-law."

"And you may call me Alice. Well, Hélène, what troubles you? A burden shared is a burden lessened."

Hélène's brow furrowed. "It-it is hard to describe. Of late I have been pestered with odd notions. An angry unease with my husband-for no reason at all. And a sense that some imminent salvation is coming from-from the skies. I have no basis for either sensation-and yet they are intensely real to me. Is that not absurd?"

Jungle Alli laid a hand atop one of Hélène's and captured the younger woman's gaze with a fervent directness. "Do not ask me how, but I know these symptoms, and I believe I may be able to help you overcome them."

Hélène smiled broadly and genuinely for the first time that day. "Oh, Alice, if only you could! I would be forever in your debt..."

"We will discuss this more, later this evening. But for now, try to enjoy the occasion. I believe you will be surprised by the announcement that your husband has planned, and which I am privy to."

The dinner moved naturally through its many happy courses, until at last it reached the speechifying stages. After many lesser orations, the time came for President Ponto himself to speak.

"This hour should be dedicated, by common consent, to my new nation's recent accomplishment, shared by all mankind, in constructing a new continent wholly from scratch. These virgin lands-dubbed Helenia, after my charming wife"–here President Ponto pivoted to single out the lady so referenced, and Hélène's immense blushing face filled all the telephonoscope screens–"will serve as a necessary release valve for the population pressures of older lands, encouraging settlers to fresh heights of invention and enterprise. And I do so dedicate this shining hour to all the hard labor and visionary guidance that preceded it."

Here a rousing cheer from thousands of throats rattled the panes of the Hall.

"But," continued the President, "I would be disloyal to the spirit of Helenia if I focused solely on the past. For the future itself is that vast untouched territory that most concerns us, the frontier where we may unfurl untried and brighter banners of conquest and exploration.

"And so I choose this moment to announce a new project, one that will tax our every fiber, and yet reward us commensurately.

"Ladies and gentlemen, I hereby declare our nation's intentions to construct a bridge to the Moon!"

A stunned silence greeted this unexpected announcement. But as soon as the inevitable majesty of the notion penetrated the consciousnesses of the listeners, they let loose a lusty roar that outdid all earlier cheers.

When the din died away, President Ponto said, "This bridge–a transit tunnel of sorts, actually, such as those which link the continents of Earth under the seas–will open up vast resources and territory that our planet needs to move forward to her inevitable destiny. I know I can count on the support of every one of Helenia's citizens in this noble quest."

President Ponto resumed his seat to deafening applause, and the rest of the banquet passed in a furor of celebration, not unmixed with much wheeling and dealing, as various tycoons utilized telephonic service to reach their brokers.

Eventually, the occupants of the head table made their official exit, leaving the other revelers to continue the celebrations.

In the private backstage corridors of the Hall, President and Mr. Ponto conferred sotto voce with Jungle Alli.

"Your wild scheme is set in motion," said the younger man. "I only pray that the Cat Women regard the Earth-Moon Tunnel as harmless economic expansionism natural to our race, and not an assault on their citadel."

"Oh, I am sure they will welcome it, as diverting our resources. They of course, with their powers of teleportation, have no need of a material connection between our worlds. But we do. And once the bridge to the Moon is in place, we will be enabled to attack the nexus of their power. That ruined city beneath the lunar surface."

The elder Ponto now said, "There remains much to set in motion if this challenging feat of engineering is to be financed. I shall have to get busy right now. Son, I will need your assistance..."

President Ponto wearily signaled his assent to a long night of tedious governmental activity. "Miss Bradley, perhaps you would consent to escort my wife back to her rooms. She has been feeling unwell lately...."

"Of course."

Soon Jungle Alli was steering Hélène Ponto toward the younger woman's bedchambers. The wife of the President exhibited a slightly inebriated and confused manner.

Once the two women were inside the intimate Presidential quarters and all the maids were dismissed, Jungle Alli said, "You recall that I suggested I might be able to clear your mind of its recent confusions. Well, the process involves attaining a certain level of somatic and psychical integration between us, so that I might confer some of my innate immunity to such disturbances on you."

Hélène seemed on the point of swooning, and Jungle Alli had to catch her and lower her to a divan. With the back of one hand to her brow and eyes shuttered, Hélène said, "Anything... anything to restore my vigor and clarity..."

Jungle Alli quickly shucked her bandoliers and gun belt, then began unbuttoning her khaki shirt. "Just lie back, my darling, and the treatment will commence..."

At four that morning, when the Polynesian skies above the fresh-faced continent of Helenia were just beginning to display the first hints of dawn, President Ponto quietly opened the door of his wife's bedchambers. The dim electrical nightlights therein revealed the intertwined forms of not one but two women beneath the sheets of the large bed.

Her wilderness-honed senses snapping alert, Jungle Alli instantly sized up the intrusion and whispered, by way of explanation, "I believe my quasi-masculine touch has managed temporarily to break the spell of the Cat Women over your wife, Philippe. But additional male contact would certainly not be counterproductive... in neither of our cases."

Philippe smiled, shrugged with Gallic *savoir-faire*, and doffed his ceremonial sash. "Whatever is demanded of me to ensure the survival of our planet, Miss Bradley."

Grinning, Jungle Alli pulled back the bedcovers to disclose her scarred nakedness, and Hélène's alabaster skin. "Call me Alice, Phil."

The building of the Earth-Moon bridge instantly captivated the fancy of the entire planet, following as it did hard upon the excitement of Helenia's inauguration.

At least, the project attracted the eyes of that portion of the globe that was not concerned with the growing tensions between the sexes.

Not every woman on Earth was irritably chafing under the mental goads of the invisible and unsuspected Cat Women. But those lunar devils continued to prick the intelligences of many females in high places, who in turn inflamed their followers, thus fomenting dissent, altercations and contumely between the sexes.

For instance, the Women's Supremacy Brigade, normally inactive save during the decennial revolutions, had convened its members to patrol the streets of Paris by night, ostensibly to guarantee the safety of the city's *filles de joie*–a safety never actually in jeopardy. In reality, the Brigade functioned as a male-bashing squad, roughing up lotharios, boulevardiers and beau brummels.

But, as yet, this kind of intermittent breakdown in the social compact between the sexes formed a mere background rumble to the normal functioning of society and that society now strained at its brave limits to fulfill the incredibly ambitious program outlined by President Ponto.

Gathered in a meeting room with the chief engineers of the nation, President Ponto heard the first details of the plan to construct a bridge to the nearby satellite.

A bewhiskered savant named Professor Calculus explained, "The immense weight of the dangling bridge–in essence, a technological beanstalk or celestial *ascenseur*–must be counterbalanced by an equal weight outside the gravity shell of our planet, midway between Earth and Moon, at roughly the 337-kilometer mark. Practically speaking, the bridge will be suspended from this anchor outside our atmosphere, and simply tethered to the soil at either end."

"How do we create this anchor in the aether?" asked the President.

"We propose to launch by numerous rockets many millions of tons of magnetically charged material, all aimed at the desired nexus in the void. The multiple impacts will agglomerate naturally into the desired anchor. Then we will harpoon the anchor with a titanic cable fired from a super-cannon, the other end of which will remain fastened here, and use that cable as the armature to build upward. Once this leg of the bridge is constructed, building downward to the Moon will be trivial."

Mr. Ponto now intervened, exclaiming, "Superb! And I offer a sophistication. We shall construct upon this anchor planetoid an elegant space casino, just like the successful underwater one that punctuates the mid-Atlantic train tunnel. Baccarat and faro beneath the Milky Way! We'll make a fortune!"

And so, with the bridge and its refinements firmly conceptualized, construction began.

Never before in the history of the race had such titanic assemblages of men, material and energy been seen! The continent of Helenia was the focal point of tributaries of labor and materials from all quarters of the globe. Around the clock swarmed hordes of workers, stockpiling the steel plates and girders that would form the shell of the interplanetary tube, launching rocket upon rocket full of magnetite, coordinating the building processes.

Within several weeks, the anchor was complete, and the cable secured. Construction of the space-tube and its interior workings began immediately.

Throughout the gargantuan project, only four individuals knew the truth of the matter and appreciated the urgency behind the construction. President Ponto, Mr. Ponto, Jungle Alli and Hélène formed a secret cabal, a quartet of conspirators who alone amongst billions of souls realized that the whole planet was now in a race with the machinations of the Cat Women. Would humanity reach the Moon and stymie the Cat Women before terrestrial society tore itself apart?

For the tumult and tension between the sexes were increasing. Incidents proliferated and grew in brutality, as the perverted ideoneme of gender rancor disseminated itself through all levels of society, a virus cut loose from its original Cat Women source. Small riots and pogroms, both anti-male and anti-female, broke out daily, everywhere.

Luckily, Hélène and Jungle Alli maintained their sanity, thanks to their mutual inoculations of closeness, as well as frequent booster shots from President Ponto. Hélène's sharp wits and vast practical experience—she had dabbled in almost every profession under the Sun, before settling down as Philippe's wife—contributed much to the whole enterprise.

Six months into the project, the midway point in the bridge construction had been reached, and the moment of the casino's official opening loomed. But the ceremonies were actually a sham, to maintain the façade of innocent commercialism.

At the base of the space-*ascenseur*, President Ponto snipped a red ribbon, to much acclaim, his actions broadcast across the globe via the telephonoscope. He stepped aboard the car that occupied the interior of the space-tube. Hélène and Jungle Alli accompanied him. (Mr. Ponto was already at the casino, overseeing inaugural preparations and hundreds of workers who were preparing against the day when, God willing, the casino could function as intended in a world at peace.) The doors closed, and the car shot upwards inside the tube with remarkable speed.

Inside the private car, with its padded velvet couches, gilt trim, muraled walls and well-appointed wet bar, the trio fortified themselves against any further mental attacks by the Cat Women.

Within only half an hour, the capsule docked at the space casino. Its occupants barely had time to rearrange their clothing from the rigors of the passage before they were greeted by a boisterous string quartet in formal wear, and the smiling face of Mr. Ponto.

"Quite classy, Rafe," said Jungle Alli in her natal English. "Even if it is a little premature. Now where's the champagne?"

But this night of exclusive glittering gaiety was to be short-lived. Their welcome was a mere diverting moment of ceremony. Already the capacious capsule of the space-*ascenseur* was busy shuttling dozens of additional workers at a go to the anchor planetoid. For the past six months, rockets had been delivering tons of components for the next stage of the bridge. Protected from the cold and vacuum of interplanetary space by special suits of gutta-percha and *vitrine*, the workers were already forging the next leg of the link between the incompatible orbs.

For the next several months, the quartet of conspirators resided at the casino, its only patrons, supervising the construction. The task was wearisome, but the knowledge of how vital their mission was granted them endless strength.

Reports came hourly by telephonoscope of the accelerating turmoil back on the home world.

Due to the increased experience of the workers, and a skimping in certain ornamental details, the second half of the space bridge took only three months to complete.

Came the day when Jungle Alli and her three comrades, clad in their own anti-vacuum coveralls and bolstered by a squad of Niam-Niams, stepped out onto the lunar surface.

Now would the Cat Women find the battle brought to their very doorstep!

"All right, you may remove your helmets."

All the members of the Earth party, which consisted of Philippe, Rafael and Hélène, as well as the several savages, followed Jungle Alli's instructions, taking cautious breaths of the atmosphere found in the lunar caverns. As they doffed their suits, their movements were weirdly acrobatic and butterfly-like in the reduced lunar gravity.

Leaving a pair of Niam-Niams to guard the discarded suits, Jungle Alli said, "Follow me."

Leading the way through the luminescent lunar grottoes, the piratical mercenary soon brought her charges within sight of their goal.

The decayed city of the Cat Women, older than Nineveh and Tyre combined, a chunky set of fallen towers resembling a child's tumbled blocks.

Jungle Alli addressed her comrades. "Remember, the Cat Women can outmaneuver us by their powers of teleportation. But they are not supernatural. Our firearms even out the fight. And I believe if we can remove their leader, Alpha, from the equation, then the rest of them will collapse."

"Very well," said President Ponto. "Lead on, Alice."

Within minutes, the Earthlings found themselves crossing a broad plaza and entering a palatial building. They had not gone far before they found their way blocked by a living Cat Woman!

"I am Omega," said the alluring, dark-haired female, in every respect a sister to the aforeseen Alpha. "What do you humans want here?"

"Bring us to see Alpha. Our business is with her."

"She and the others are–are busy."

"Of course they are. Sending their evil thoughts into the innocent minds of our women!"

Quicker than a python, Jungle Alli had the blade of her machete against Omega's throat. "You might be able to vanish before my reflexes cause my muscles to slice, but I doubt it. You'll materialize in safety, perhaps–but with a severed artery! Now, lead us to Alpha!"

For whatever reason, Omega did not vanish, but complied. Perhaps she too chafed under the rule of the all-dominant Alpha...

The remaining seven Cat Women occupied couches in a large, column-dotted, temple-like room, looking like the Sleepers of Epheseus while they directed their malevolent thoughts Earthward. As the newcomers entered, Alpha instantly roused herself from slumber and stood.

"So," said the head Cat Woman, "you have decided to visit us at home, Alice Bradley! Forgive my ungraciousness as a hostess, but I cannot offer you any refreshments."

"We don't want any. We only demand justice. You will cease your assaults on Earth's females, or–"

"Or what? We will spontaneously relocate in the next second to a different part of the Moon, where you will never find us. And soon, your society will tear itself apart under our renewed attacks."

Jungle Alli pondered this boast, before saying, "This struggle is all about seeing which of our two races is superior, and deserves to inherit the Earth. Why not determine the same judgment between you and me alone?"

Alpha looked tantalized by the prospect. "You mean, individual combat?"

"I do."

"Very well, I accept. Rid yourself of weapons."

Jungle Alli swiftly complied. "And you will promise not to employ your powers of vanishment."

"Agreed."

Before commencing combat, Jungle Alli solicited a kiss from both Hélène and Philippe. Thus armed with their fond endorsement, she advanced on her foe.

The two women, each formidable in her own way, circled each other like wrestlers, looking for openings. Jungle Alli was sinuous as a snake, while Alpha, the larger of the two, resembled a panther.

At last they closed, with wordless grunts and exclamations. Grappling hand to hand, they struggled for mastery.

Jungle Alli was tossed to the lunar pavement first. Falling upon her stunned prey, Alpha was surprised to find Jungle Alli wriggling out of her grip and soon riding the Cat Woman's back! Alpha punched backwards, ramming knuckles into Jungle Alli's cheekbones, and causing her to loosen her hold. The women separated, regained their feet and faced off again.

For a seemingly interminable time, the two women fought, enacting a strange barbaric scene among the sleeping forms of the Cat Women–still pulsing out their deadly ideonemes–and the cheering figures of the wholesome Earth people. The battle inevitably took its toll: Alpha's long hair had come undone and disarrayed, while Jungle Alli's shorter pelt was plastered to her skull with sweat. The clothing of both women was ripped, revealing lush, bruised flesh. Their mutual panting sounded in the hall like the chuffing of some struggling engine.

The two resting apart for a moment, Alpha said, "You are a vigorous specimen, Alice Bradley. If all Earth women were like you, they might deserve to live!"

Falling into English, Jungle Alli replied, "We won't go on without our men-folks. You bitches have been deprived too long to know what you're missing!"

"Men!" spat Alpha. "Here's what all males deserve!"

With that, the leader of the Cat Women impulsively teleported over to Philippe and began to strangle him with her otherworldly strength! His face purpling, the President of Helenia seemed doomed!

But then Alpha shrieked, and blood began to flow from her mouth! She released Philippe and fell to the floor, dying as she hit the tiles.

Hélène stepped away from the body of the Cat Woman, Jungle Alli's red-dripping machete in her hand.

Jungle Alli surged to the side of Hélène, and began to comfort the stunned woman with petting and reassurances. But Hélène did not seem as distraught as one might have expected. She straightened her back, her eyes shining, and said, "So much for female supremacy!"

But whether Hélène was derogating Alpha or praising herself was unclear. Around the Earthlings, the six sleepers began to stir. Omega, who had stood on the sidelines till this moment, now mentally apprised her sisters of what had just transpired. The remaining Cat Women appeared directionless and disinclined to carry the battle further.

Massaging his throat, his voice something of a croak, President Ponto, supported by his father, said, "Our crisis seems at an end now, thanks to the efforts of my own wife and Miss Bradley. It remains only for us to carry the good news back to a waiting planet."

"You folks'll be heading back without me, I reckon," said Jungle Alli unexpectedly.

"But why?"

"I've plumb run out of lands to explore back home. Here I've got a whole new world to investigate. I need to see this place before there's a *Bon Marché* in every crater."

"But won't you be lonely?" asked Hélène.

Jungle Alli eyed the surviving Cat Women with a certain possessive passion.

"Oh," she said, grinning, "I figure I can do without the company of mankind for a little while."

The heroine of this story, Adelaïde Lupin, is the daughter of Arsène Lupin and American journalist Patricia Johnston, whom the notorious Gentleman-Burglar met in Maurice Leblanc's penultimate novel, Les Milliards d'Arsène Lupin. *Adelaïde was retroactively created and introduced by Win Eckert, one of our regular contributors, in "The Eye of Oran," published in* Tales of the Shadowmen 2, *to which this is a sequel. In his stories, Eckert is carefully assembling the pieces of a jigsaw puzzle that paints a fascinating picture of a post-World War II France that is further beset by the ever-encroaching powers of darkness...*

Win Scott Eckert: *Les Lèvres Rouges*

Paris, 1946

Ilona Harczy hung naked in the damp dungeon, her arms spread and chained at the wrist to the stone wall. She was unconscious. Her wrists and fingers were scabbed over with dozens of small cuts. A brown and withered vine snaked under her dangling feet.

When Ilona next awoke, the blonde woman was there.

Somehow, even in the darkness, the woman glowed, an icy bluish light emanating from a jewel hung at her throat. Her skin was pale, almost translucent, showing blue veins beneath. In a flowing white gown, she floated ethereally above the cobblestone floor. Her lips were painted bright red.

The woman gently took Ilona's wrist and made another small cut. Ilona moaned as blood welled. The pale woman kissed and licked Ilona's wrist. Only a few stray drops of blood escaped her lips, falling upon the floor and the almost-dead plant.

The blonde woman continued to kiss Ilona's wrist, and the bleeding stopped. Then she cupped Ilona's breast in her hand, and softly kissed Ilona's neck and short dark hair.

"Now my love, it is complete," she whispered. "You do love me, don't you? You must, you know."

The blonde woman moved away into a shadowy corner. Two humanoid forms were illuminated as the woman approached them, the light from the jewel glowing brighter and brighter. The woman embraced each in turn, pulling thick necks to her waiting mouth. She intoned nonsense words that Ilona didn't understand.

"*Iä-R'lyeh! Cthulhu fhtagn! Méne! Iä! Iä!*"

The jewel shone even brighter, its soft bluish light filling the room.

Then the three were gone, and Ilona lapsed once more into oblivion.

Nestor Burma looked up at the statuesque figure silhouetted in the doorway of the *Fiat Lux* Detective Agency's inner office. "How may I help you, Mademoiselle...?"

"D'Andresy. Monique d'Andresy." She stood in front of him, raven hair spilling over the shoulders of the London Fog raincoat belted at the waist with a loose knot. "You are working on a case with an American doctor? Francis Ardan?"

Burma leaned back in his creaky office chair and put his feet on the desk. The room's only light was a feeble cone emanating from a small desk lamp. He puffed at his bull's head pipe, red light from the coals illuminating his tired face.

"Mademoiselle d'Andresy, I may be an anarchist, but I wouldn't last long as a private detective if I made a habit of breaking my clients' confidentiality."

"But, Monsieur," she breathed, "my need is great."

She slowly walked around to the client chair beside Burma's desk. Instead of sitting, she stepped one leg up on the chair and propped an elbow on her upper thigh, leaning her chin on her hand. Long nails were done in a perfect French manicure. Facing him, took a drag of her cigarette.

"Perhaps we could come to an... understanding?"

Burma's eyes followed the curve of her leg from the four-inch pump to the lacy black top of a gartered silk stocking–and further. The folds of her raincoat fell away, the belt hanging loosely. Apart from the stockings and garters, she wore nothing else, intimate or otherwise.

"I am sorry, truly, but I don't think such an understanding will be possible."

Monique d'Andresy bent farther over him, providing a clear view of her rather ample charms. She was splendid, in every way.

"Mademoiselle, please..."

"What is it Burma, are you *une pédale*?"

"No, Mademoiselle, in fact you present quite a persuasive argument. But as tempted as I am, it is quite impossible." He puffed at his pipe again. "I believe incest is illegal in France. Now, perhaps I can help you with your coat? It appears you're catching a chill."

"What–?"

Two hands thrust out from darkness behind and gripped her upper arms. The hands were large and bronzed, tendons and muscles stretching across them like small cables. It was no use trying to struggle free.

She sighed.

"Doctor Ardan, I presume?"

"Adélaïde Lupin," Ardan replied.

She glared at Burma. "So Arsène Lupin is your father as well?"

"Not the man who raised me as his own son," Burma said. "But yes, I am Lupin's child from one of his many affairs."

"Clearly blood is not thicker than water." Adélaïde glanced meaningfully at the strong hands holding her solidly in place.

"Please, Mademoiselle d'Andresy–er–Lupin, I am not the one who slunk in here attempting a licentious seduction."

"Perhaps, but you obviously helped set me up. You knew we're siblings–"

"Half-siblings," Burma said.

"*Oui*. You could have said so earlier."

He shrugged. "We've never met before. I don't owe you anything. Besides, I wanted to see what angle you'd take. Quite inventive."

Another voice came from a dark corner as a third man stepped forward. "Your family reunion is very touching, but we have business."

"Yes, time is of the essence," a fourth added in a slight Germanic accent.

Adélaïde sighed. "Gentlemen, on the one hand, I'm not so immodest that I think you need reminding of my current state of *deshabillé*. On the other hand, as Burma said, it is somewhat chilly in here. Is this some bizarre burlesque, or might I be permitted to cover myself?"

Ardan freed one slender arm, and she awkwardly cinched up her coat. He applied gentle but firm pressure to her shoulders, forcing her to sit. She crossed her legs, one elegant and distracting thigh still exposed at the fold of her coat, and lit a fresh *Red Apple*.

"So, Francis, I said we'd see each other again, and here we are. I can think of better circumstances, though. Something along the lines of a snowbound cabin, roaring fire, a bearskin rug and a bottle of *Veuve Clicquot* '32 would do nicely," Adélaïde said playfully.

Ardan's bronzed skin, even under cover of the darkened office, turned ten shades of red.

"No reply, *mon chéri*? Pity. Well, what's it all about? I suppose the story of the Eye of Oran being a fake, and you working with Burma to track down the real Eye–that was all a charade to lure me here?"

Last month, Adélaïde Lupin had tricked Doctor Francis Ardan and the French Intelligence agency S.N.I.F., making off with a precious gem, the Eye of Oran–also known as the Silver Eye of Dagon–using Ardan's experimental Cirrus X-9 rocket pack.[2]

Doc Ardan nodded. "Yes, the story was a plant to draw you out. This man is a representative of the French government. If you turn over the Eye to me, they are prepared to drop all charges. You'll go free, no questions asked."

"All true, Mademoiselle Lupin." The third man said, stepping forward, limping slightly. He had grey haircut military style, and wore round-rimmed glasses. "Return the Eye and the matter will be dropped."

"I suppose you're S.N.I.F.'s Aristide? Sorry if I caused you some difficulties." A slight quirk at the corner of her mouth said she wasn't overly sorry.

---

[2] See "The Eye of Oran" in *Tales of the Shadowmen*, Volume 2.

"I'm not Aristide, and yes, your actions caused him no little trouble. You can call me Roger Noël. This is Jens Rolf, a mystic and expert on the Eye's occult nature."

The short German nodded curtly.

Noël continued, "Now, what do you say?"

"I say… I cannot."

"Mademoiselle," Noël replied, "if you don't return the Eye, you'll be locked up with the key thrown away."

"Don't you threaten me, you little bureaucrat. If you think any jail cell can hold Lupin's daughter for long, you'd better–"

"Enough," Ardan interrupted. "Gentlemen, would you excuse us please. I'd like a moment alone with Mademoiselle Lupin."

Burma looked at Noël and Rolf, shrugged, and got up. They all stepped into the outer office.

Adélaïde looked at Ardan, red lips parted expectantly. "Well, it's about time, *mon cher* Francis, I've practically been throwing myself at you."

"Drop the act, Adélaïde. I studied with your father when I was a boy. He was a thief and a scoundrel, but when push came to shove, he would do the right thing. I think you will too."

"Don't be so sure."

"I am. Do you have the faintest idea what Doctor Natas was planning to do with the Eye, before you conned us all and stole it? I've seen a lot and most can be explained without resorting to mysticism, but in this case, even I support the French in recruiting an occult expert to properly study and contain it."

"You, the medical man?" she scoffed. "The 'science detective'?"

"I grant you, almost all of the strange adventures my associates and I have had around the world have ended with rational explanations. But a few have not. When I was a young man, during the Great War, I saw a long whitish worm crawling over the skeleton of an infant, a victim of a satanic ritualistic sacrifice. Even today, I cannot classify that worm; it is unknown to science. In 1925, I encountered an entity which slaughtered many members of an Antarctic expedition. I have no explanation. Two years later, I observed our own Doctor Natas transmute lead into gold; I have not been able to reproduce this with any scientific means. In 1929, my colleague Doctor Littlejohn also traveled to the Antarctic, and had strange experiences which he, also a rational man of science, cannot explain. Three years ago, I was involved in a case in which an herbal concoction allowed its taker to see into the future. A specific prophecy came to pass. And now, the Eye."

" '*There are more things in Heaven and Earth, Horatio…*' "

"Precisely. Why won't you help?"

She shook her head. "Francis, first you must help me with a problem I've run into. If you can do that, I'll gladly abandon all claims to the gem."

The gold-flecks in Ardan's eyes seemed to swirl. "Adélaïde, I promise we'll help you with whatever trouble you're in," he said solemnly.

"All right, then."

"Good. Herr Rolf will secure the Eye while the rest of us tackle your problem. Once that's handled," he said, "I want you to return the rocket pack as well."

"Deal. But, Francis, you see, the quandary is... I no longer have the Eye."

FROM: Lieutenant Montferrand, Division Protection, Service National d'Information Fonctionnelle, Paris.
TO: SNIF.
DATE: August 21, 1946
SUBJECT: Silver Eye of Dagon

The Eye of Dagon is a large silver gem reputed to have occult properties. It is now in possession of a "Madame Elisabeth" who operates a series of brothels in Normandy and Brittany, with headquarters in Paris.

After absconding with the Eye outside Oran last month, Adélaïde Lupin (A.L.) was contacted by Madame Elisabeth. Elisabeth was holding a friend of A.L.'s, one Ilona Harczy, prisoner under the threat of forced labor in one of her bordellos. A.L. was instructed to turn the Eye over to Elisabeth as a ransom payment. To date, A.L.'s friend has not been released. Ardan and Burma's scheme to bait A.L. with a story that the stolen Eye was a fake unwittingly played into A.L.'s concerns about Madame Elisabeth's failure to release her friend. A.L. appeared in Burma's offices with startling alacrity.

It's unknown how Madame Elisabeth knew of the Eye in the first place. It's possible we have a leak, or perhaps she was in league with Doctor Natas, who also sought the Eye.

We have no prior intelligence on Madame Elisabeth, and are relying on A.L. for the following information. Elisabeth and a partner purchased the network of brothels known as the Cordon Jaune, *in January of this year. It is unclear where the money for this purchase originated, but the purchase was apparently intended as an investment. The venture went bad with the passage of the Marthe Richard Law last April, banning all such houses of ill-repute. We can guess that Elisabeth needs the Eye to mitigate her bad investment.*

Madame Elisabeth's partner in this venture is called "Le Chiffre," ostensibly a paymaster for the Syndicat des Ouvriers d'Alsace, *a Communist-controlled trade union. Le Chiffre is otherwise unidentifiable, having come out of the camp at Dachau last year with a case of incurable amnesia. He is always accompanied by two bodyguards highly skilled at personal defense and close range combat. He is described as small, with coarse reddish-brown hair and a voracious sexual appetite.*

Madame Elisabeth, too, is described as insatiable, but it is unlikely she satisfies her needs with Le Chiffre; during their one face-to-face meeting, she made a pass at A.L. which was "exceptionally forceful." Although A.L. portrays Madame Elisabeth as exceedingly charming and charismatic, she declined Elisabeth's offer. Doubtless Madame Elisabeth and Le Chiffre sample their wares on a regular basis. Madame Elisabeth's proclivities may also account for her failure to keep her bargain and release Mademoiselle Harczy, who is reported to be quite beautiful.

There should be no doubt: Madame Elisabeth and Le Chiffre are a deadly combination.

Under my "Roger Noël" cover, I have assembled a team dedicated to recovering the Eye of Dagon: Doctor Francis Ardan, Nestor Burma, the mystic Jens Rolf and Adélaïde Lupin. Unfortunately, we must again rely on A.L. At least, this time, we are dealing with a known quantity, but she is still a Lupin and I will proceed with care.

As an aside, A.L. learned–to her chagrin and my amusement–that Burma is also a Lupin, if only by an accident of birth. The so-called Gentleman Thief had nothing to do with Burma's upbringing, and despite Burma's leftist views I believe he will prove a reliable companion on this venture.

Recommendation: I suggest the establishment of a formal division dedicated to handling unknowable matters. The skills of those I have assembled are without peer, but they are not properly integrated as a team and have not trained together. We are far behind the British Diogenes Club and the American FBI's Unnameables Section in this regard.

"What are you doing here, Burma, slumming again?" Commissioner Faroux asked tiredly. "What brings you to the humble office of the *Police Judiciaire*?"

Burma pulled up a chair and made himself at home. "I want to know all you can tell me about a brothel run by a woman called Madame Elisabeth."

"Well, well, well. Don't your shady friends keep you updated on the latest houses of ill repute? What would Hélène say? She pines for you so–"

"Not for me, you dolt. I'm on a case, obviously."

"How are you involved? There have been three murders in the neighborhood of her establishment in the last two months! If you've been holding out on me..."

"Three murders? I came to you for information, remember? What's the scoop? And why is Madame Elisabeth still open for business?"

"Fine, fine. Her associate greases the right palms to keep it open. An unexpected expense since the Marthe Richard Law, eh?" Faroux chuckled. "Now there are three girls, all beautiful, all found dead in that neighborhood, their throats cut. We suspect they worked at Elisabeth's, no proof, no witnesses willing to say they saw any of the victims there."

"Of course not," Burma rolled his eyes. "None of this made the papers. You're holding out on me, Florimond. What else?"

"All right, all right. We've clamped down on the press, don't want to start a panic, you know. So here it is. All the girls? Not a drop of blood to be found, anywhere. Completely drained."

Burma whistled and exhaled. "Where's her place?"

"Not so fast, your turn now. If I can connect the murders to the *Cordon Jaune*, I can shut it down, bribes or no."

Burma puffed at his pipe. "Look, you're wasting my time and yours. Far be it from me to invoke government powers, but S.N.I.F. is involved. Cough it up, or don't. Either way's fine by me, I don't give a shit. Don't and the spooks'll be down here next. What'll it be?"

"S.N.I.F.? Jesus Christ, what're you into now? All right, she set up shop in the old Benet mansion. Place has been empty, gathering dust, since Doctor Benet kicked off back in '35. You know where it is?"

Burma nodded and got up to leave.

"Goddamn it, Burma!" Faroux shouted at his departing back. "You have 48 hours to fill me in, or I'll have you back in here for withholding evidence, S.N.I.F. or no goddamn S.N.I.F.!"

Burma gave a friendly wave.

In the parlor of the Benet mansion, the shades were tightly drawn against the afternoon Sun. Le Chiffre paced nervously back-and-forth in front of Elisabeth and took a loud snort from his Benzedrine inhaler.

"You can't continue disposing of the merchandise! This is the fourth one! We're practically insolvent as it is."

Elisabeth bestowed a serene smile upon him and stretched her feline body on the chaise. A clingy black gown set off blond curls. Wrists and plunging neckline were ringed in purple feathers, a silver-blue gem resting between her pale breasts. She looked like a Hollywood starlet.

A young, white-haired girl in a *negligé* lay curled on the floor, her head and one slender arm resting in Elisabeth's lap. The girl's eyes were open, but vacant. "Shhh. You'll wake her up." She caressed the girl's hair, but stared steadily at Le Chiffre. As always, her gaze had a tranquilizing effect.

"And why should I not use the 'merchandise,' as you so artfully call it, as I please?" She continued. "I own half of this venture."

Le Chiffre sat down and smoothed his dark suit. He put a *Caporal* in a cigarette holder and lit it.

Continuing more calmly, he said, "You cannot continue to kill these girls. Our financial situation is precarious and you're making it worse by killing off our only source of income. Not to mention the police are sure to become suspicious!"

"Ah, yes, isn't that always how it is," Elisabeth sighed, a faraway look in her eyes. "Always the peasants hound us, chase us on to the next village. Don't we have a right to peace and quiet, like everyone else?"

"Just promise me you'll stop. Eventually I may be able to sell off the *Cordon Jaune*'s assets, recoup our losses, but not if we're both in gaol, Elisabeth... Elisabeth!"

"Hmm? Oh yes, of course I promise, of course."

A discreet knock came to the parlor door, and one of Le Chiffre's bodyguards entered. The man was tall, with wide lips and slightly bulging, glassy eyes. He came over and whispered in Elisabeth's ear.

"Oh, by all means, do show her in, Denis, bring her to me!" Elisabeth clapped gleefully. At the noise, the white-haired girl awoke. "Plaster, we have a visitor. Go help Denis bring her to me."

The girl obeyed, and in a moment they escorted a tall, well-built redhead into the parlor.

Elisabeth looked at the newcomer and cocked her head in seeming puzzlement for a moment; then a smile spread across her face and she clapped her hands again in approval at Le Chiffre. "Beautiful! Splendid! What a find. All legs and curves and breasts. She'll do magnificently for us."

Speaking to the girl, Elisabeth said, "You understand our working arrangements, my dear?"

The redhead nodded.

Back at Le Chiffre: "Bravo, she's wonderful, quiet and shy as well. Herr Ziffre, you've outdone yourself. Denis, escort our newcomer–what is her name again?–yes, escort Jeannette to her room. No. 13 will do, I think. Yes, take her there straightaway, let's get her settled in, and rested. She starts tonight!" She blew a kiss at the retreating figures.

Le Chiffre looked at her warily. "You promised..."

"Oh, don't be tiresome, Ziffre. We've nothing more to discuss. You may leave me now."

Le Chiffre frowned once more, then shook his head and left.

A little while after he exited, Plaster returned the parlor and came to kneel before her mistress. Elisabeth took her hand. "Did you and Denis make our newcomer... comfortable?"

The girl nodded eagerly. "*Oui, Madame.*"

"Excellent."

Half a block down the street from the *Cordon Jaune*'s Parisian headquarters, a nondescript 1932 Citroën C6G pulled up at the corner. Roger Noël was at the wheel. Doctor Ardan sat next to him in the front, while Nestor Burma and Jens Rolf sat in the back.

Noël looked at his watch and ticked off the time. Adélaïde Lupin had gone in 20 minutes ago. Ardan didn't need the watch; his internal clock was as accurate as the atomic chronometer in his New York headquarters. His only response was a slight twitch of an index finger.

Burma noticed.

"Aren't you at all worried, Doctor?" Burma inquired. "Such a beautiful girl… Might she end up in a compromising position this evening?"

"Why should I worry, Monsieur Burma? She knows the risks. Besides, according to the plan, she'll be out of there long before evening falls."

"*Tu parles*. I've seen the way you look at her." He tapped the side of his head. "I'm a trained detective."

Doc turned away without responding. Was he flushed again?

"Do you mind?" the usually quiescent German asked Burma. "If I am allowed to concentrate, I may be able to sense the Eye from here and pinpoint its location."

Properly chastised, Burma settled deeper into the back seat and lit his pipe.

Adélaïde followed Denis and the white-haired girl through the corridors of the *Cordon Jaune*. She reflected smugly on her disguise's success. She had only met Elisabeth once, briefly, and had correctly predicted she would not be recognized. Ardan had objected, but Noël had wisely overruled him.

When these two left her alone in her quarters, she'd be free to explore and locate Ilona. Then back to the parlor to rip the Eye of Dagon from where it hung around Elisabeth's translucent neck.

The whole place had a freakish ambiance to it. Noël had briefed them all before sending her in. The mansion used to be the clinic of Doctor Felix Benet. Benet had used a new source of radiation–Radium-X–to cure blindness and other illnesses, and had been brutally murdered here. It still stank of death.

Add in the mansion's current occupants: Trollish Le Chiffre snorting his amphetamines. Languid Elisabeth… fascinating in a menacing sort of way, like a flame drawing in the moth that cannot resist. Did she have a slight Hungarian accent? And her two escorts, they were quite a pair. Denis with his bulging eyes and bluish-green, almost oily skin emanating a squalid fish smell; he was in serious need of a shower. And silent Plaster, a girl of no more than 20 with a shock of white hair. Was it the fear permeating this place that robbed her hair of color?

As they passed a large mirror hanging in the hallway, Adélaïde caught a quick glance in it and could have sworn… Had she really seen only her own and Plaster's reflections? No, she must have missed foul Denis' reflection because he was lumbering a few steps ahead of them.

No matter, she'd be in and out of here quickly. Free Ilona, snatch the jewel and disappear. It was a bit of a trek to Room 13, though, and they seemed to be headed toward the basement…

As they approached a heavy wooden door, Plaster's hand clamped over her mouth and nose with a chloroform-soaked rag. The last thing she saw was her friend, Ilona, shackled and hanging in the dank cellar.

When the Sun declined, the ladies of the *Cordon Jaune* were brought down for their evening lineup before Le Chiffre and Elisabeth. Counting the new girl–had anyone met her yet?–there were ten women currently working at this establishment. Last night, before Jeannette had come on board, so to speak, there had also been ten, but Claudette had left.

People came and went in this line of work, and the ladies weren't concerned. They might have been if Madame Elisabeth allowed them newspapers or radios–Claudette's body had been discovered nearby just that afternoon. Her corpse was completely depleted of blood, and the police, as usual, were baffled.

Le Chiffre, conversely, was concerned. Of the ten, only nine appeared at the lineup.

"Elisabeth!" he shouted, then turned back the women. "Back to your rooms, all of you! Now!"

Several of the girls, lead by the waif Cabiria, protested but complied on further threats from Le Chiffre.

After the ladies dispersed, he beckoned to his two looming bodyguards, and faced Elisabeth.

"Where is the new girl? Where is Jeannette!"

Elisabeth smiled at him lazily. "Ziffre, you really must learn to control your temper."

"Woman, you'll be the end of us all. Denis, Karl–" He snapped his fingers at the bodyguards "–take Madame Elisabeth to her room and lock her there."

Elisabeth began to giggle softly. She raised one elegant arm and pointed behind him, urging him to look.

Le Chiffre slowly turned and almost fainted. Denis and Karl's dark tailored suites were splitting at the seams. Eyes swelled in their sockets. Snouts elongated. Webs formed between fingers and toes of feet which no longer fit in discarded shoes. Oil seeped from bluish skin showing through the splits in once stylish clothing.

Thick red lips opened, showing row upon row of razor-sharp fangs. The incisors were particularly lengthy.

The jewel at Elisabeth's throat glowed momentarily with ice-blue intensity, and then softened.

"Gentlemen, Herr Ziffre is becoming a nuisance. Take him to the cellar. No, no! Don't hurt him–yet. He may still have his uses."

Karl punched Le Chiffre in the face, and the two fish-men started to drag him away, gibbering quietly to themselves.

"Oh, and gentlemen?"

The two creatures paused.

"Better stay out of sight. We wouldn't want to frighten the girls, would we, darlings? I'll call them down for this evening's lineup."

The two fish-men gesticulated in parody of a human nod, and continued to shamble away, dragging Le Chiffre and leaving a faint trail of fish-slime in their wake.

It had been too long. Adélaïde should have been out over an hour ago. Time for Plan B.

Doc Ardan and Jens Rolf had come into the *Cordon Jaune* with the evening's first round of customers. They had both noted the Eye of Dagon hanging from the Madame's neck, but the first order of business was to locate and liberate Adélaïde and Ilona. The Madame had made cooing noises over Doc, murmuring over the handsome bronze giant and making a point to caress his shoulders and biceps.

Elisabeth was undeniably mesmerizing, but Ardan could sense something vile and repellent at her core. He stoically bore the indignity of her touch, but when Elisabeth prattled on about what a lucky girl Plaster would be that night, Rolf kept things in motion, playing his part perfectly.

"Fraulein Elisabeth," the German snapped, consulting his watch, "if we could proceed, our time is limited."

"Of course, Mein Herr, forgive me. This girl's name is Manon. I presume she is acceptable?

"Quite, thank you."

Now both men were in separate rooms with the girls. Doc had broken a small glass tranquilizer under Plaster's nose and eased her into a comfortable position on the bed. As he exited, Jens Rolf silently came from the room across the hall. Through the open doorway, Doc could see the girl Manon sitting straight up in a chair, eyes open and yet vacant.

"A slight trance, she'll come out of it shortly," Rolf whispered.

Doc nodded, and scanned the corridor in both directions.

"That woman, Elisabeth," Rolf continued. "Something evil and depraved owns her soul."

Doc nodded again, and raised a hand for silence. After a moment, he pointed and the two men made their way toward a butler's staircase at the back of the house.

Nestor Burma was stationed out back of the Benet mansion at a basement window. His associate, a reformed burglar called Zavatter, worked at the lock.

"*Voila*," said the cracksman as the lock came loose. Burma paid him off, sent him on his way, and held his position.

After 30 minutes, Ardan and Rolf had still not appeared with the women and the Eye. Burma emptied out his pipe on the pavement. He sauntered casually from the back alley and down the block to the idling Citroën.

He said a few words to Noël, then retraced his steps, crouched, and went in the open window.

Adélaïde's wrists were shackled to chains hanging from the cellar ceiling. The room was featureless save for the tendrils of greenery which snaked the ground around her feet.

Adélaïde had been stripped down to undergarments and pumps. Her red wig was gone. She yelled at Ilona to wake up, but her friend was unresponsive. Adélaïde quieted when she heard the click of footsteps on the wooden stairs descending from the cellar door.

Elisabeth appeared, wearing black riding pants tucked neatly into black patent leather riding boots, and a white blouse cut low at the neckline. She held a riding crop behind her in both hands. Out for a day at the races.

"Welcome my dear, welcome!" She smiled broadly at Adélaïde, then whispered conspiratorially in her ear. "I knew it was you earlier today, as soon as you came into the parlor. I have an unusually strong sense of smell, and I could never forget your alluring scent."

"What do you want?"

"What? What do I want?" Elisabeth asked innocently. "Why my dear, shouldn't it be obvious? I want you."

Adélaïde shook her head in confusion.

"Oh, I admit, I probably should have left Paris long before now, but once I met you when you delivered the Eye–isn't it just exquisite, by the way?" She gestured at the luminescent jewel hanging between her pale breasts. "In any event, once I saw you, I knew it would be worth the risk of remaining a while longer. And I was right! Here you are, pretty as a package."

"I still don't understand. This was all a trap? For me?"

"But of course! When I met you, I could tell right away if I kept the Eye, you'd come here looking for Ilona. I'm a very good judge of character, you know."

"Why me?"

"Do I have to explain everything? Dear Adélaïde." Elisabeth pouted, puffing out her lower lip, then caressed Adélaïde's cheek with the end of the crop. Adélaïde stiffened.

"Oh, don't worry, this is just for show." She pointed at the cuts on Ilona's neck and wrists. "You see, no crop made those cuts."

Adélaïde shook her head.

"Oh, very well, I'll explain, though it doesn't matter in the end. Soon you'll be pleading to join me. So. Your friend, Doctor Natas. Remember him? Once you had escaped from Oran with the Silver Eye of Dagon, he was able to piece together what really happened. He discovered the true thief of his prize. And–surprise! He put a price out on your head and a reward for the Eye's return!" Elisabeth's smile illuminated the room.

"Word spread–I am somewhat well-connected in that area," she said modestly. "Natas' head of intelligence, Pao Tcheou, also sent out a personal dossier on you. Information on your parents, your friends, anything that might be of use. You can imagine my astonishment to find Ilona Harczy listed as one of your closest friends."

Adélaïde stared at her blankly.

"No? You are still confused?" Elisabeth sighed. "I once knew another Ilona Harczy. I was forced to kill her in Vienna, long ago. I counted it a stroke of good fortune to learn my late nemesis had a distant namesake! Out of curiosity, I sought her out, and discovered she was a chanteuse at the Calyx Bar–yes, the very place I took delivery of the Eye from you! I must say, the latter Ilona is much more beautiful than her predecessor, and once I saw her, I decided to keep her.

"Killing two birds, as the saying goes, I contacted you and arranged to exchange her for the Eye. After all, why not still collect on Natas' reward? When we met, I knew I'd have you as well. I was smitten, I confess. It's extended my Parisian stay a bit, and I probably should've moved on by now, but adding you and the lovely Mademoiselle Harczy to my stable will be well worth the risk and undue attention."

"Undue attention?" Adélaïde asked. "It's you. You've been killing those girls."

"Well, one needs to replenish, after all. I think I've been pacing myself quite nicely, but you're right, it is time we leave this place before the day breaks."

"I'm not going anywhere with you."

"Oh, you will," Elisabeth said softly, and kissed her cheek gently. "You'll beg to come with me."

In the upper cellar, Burma had discovered and released Le Chiffre from his cell. The small man was volubly cursing Elisabeth and Denis and Karl.

"Where is Madame Elisabeth, Monsieur? I must locate her."

"I have no idea," the other man growled, "and I don't aim to find out."

"Not so fast. You know your way around this chamber of horrors. You're going to help me find her, and the new girl–a redhead–who came here earlier today." Burma began to reach inside his trenchcoat, then stopped, slowly withdrawing his hand.

Le Chiffre had anticipated Burma, producing a gleaming Eversharp razor blade from the heel of his left shoe. "I'll flick this blade in your eyeball. Don't twitch, don't sneeze, you understand? Nod slowly if you agree."

Burma nodded, and Le Chiffre took off.

Ardan and Rolf approached the late Benet's laboratory. The scientist held up a hand, tapped his nose and raised two fingers. His sense of smell, akin to an ape's, far exceeded that of a normal human.

There were two... somethings... waiting in the laboratory.

71

Rolf understood Ardan's signal, and the two went in.

Nevertheless, neither was prepared for the ferocity of the attack. Sharp claws extending from rubbery webbed hands embedded in the wall inches from Ardan's head. Razor sharp teeth with exceedingly long canines snapped at his face. The scientist dove past the creature, and the creature's other set of claws raked across his chest, drawing blood. Doc jabbed a strong elbow into the creature's back.

The other fish-man backhanded Jens Rolf across the room, knocking him almost senseless. The second creature then leapt for Ardan, who rolled to the side and bounced up lightly on his feet.

The first creature freed its claws from the wall, and now both approached the scientist, backing him into a corner.

Four sets of claws came flying at Ardan.

"Never," said Adélaïde, "never will I willingly accompany you."

"You will, darling, but let us not argue. Soon you will love me."

"You're delusional. What you've said makes no sense. You decided to collect on Natas' reward, and yet you still have the gem and I'm hanging in your dungeon."

"As for you, I thought I had made myself clear. I have decided to keep you for myself. As for the Eye... I quickly discovered its special properties, and how to tap into them. One as well-traveled as I picks up quite a bit, you know. Human servitors are tedious; with the Eye I have created two completely loyal, relentless servants."

Her expression became wistful. "As the years have passed, it has become increasingly difficult to stay ahead of the forces of so-called 'justice,' moving from town to town, city to city, stopping only long enough to rejuvenate once or twice and then moving on. Now I can stop running, return home to Čachtice Castle. The Carpathians are particularly beautiful this time of year, as autumn approaches. As you'll see.

"These servants will go forth and gather the sustenance I require. All they'll need is the lake nearby the castle in which to replenish themselves. No more vagabond lifestyle. Home.

"So you see, I too have reason to keep the Eye for myself, and fully intend to do so. I am tired of running."

She went over to Ilona and began releasing her chains. "By tomorrow, we—the three of us—will be home."

Ilona slumped to the cold floor, senseless. Elisabeth left her there and returned to Adélaïde, made a swift cut above her left breast, and began to sup. As the blood flowed into Elisabeth's mouth, Adélaïde began to go into another world; it was pleasurable, but another part of her mind screamed silently in resistance.

Uncounted minutes passed, and Adélaïde came back into focus. She saw Ilona approaching Elisabeth from behind. Her approach seemed somewhat stealthy, and Adélaïde surged with hope. Elisabeth had made a tactical mistake in releasing the other girl. But she was weakened and pale... Would she be able to immobilize Elisabeth?

Ilona crept closer and closer, reaching in toward Elisabeth, who still was bent over Adélaïde, draining her life-blood. Adélaïde faded out and in once more again, and now Ilona was impossibly closer, about to grab the Madame and thrust her away from Adélaïde. Ilona took her shoulders, and Elisabeth reached back an arm, slipping it around her waist and pulling her in toward her victim.

Elisabeth kissed Ilona, covering her lips in Adélaïde's blood, then made another cut above the girl's right breast. The blood started to pour out, and she pushed Ilona's mouth down to the wound.

Ilona drank greedily of Adélaïde's blood.

The now-healthy and budding greenery which snaked around her feet seemed to be moving slightly, as if intercepting any stray falling droplets of blood.

Elisabeth returned to her victim's breast and joined Ilona in the feast.

Doc Ardan's superfirer pistols hummed busily, shooting hundreds of rounds of anesthetic "mercy bullets" at the two misshapen amphibians.

To no avail. The creatures advanced upon him. And advanced. Then stopped.

Rolf had regained his senses. He chanted words in an ancient and arcane language.

"*Ph'nglui mglw'nafh Cthulhu R'lyeh wgah-nagl fhtagn. Iä!*"

The two monsters who had been Karl and Denis strained. Their eyes swelled in their sockets but they were otherwise immobilized.

"Hurry!" the German mystic yelled at Doc. "This hex will not hold them long!"

Doc nodded once and went for the opposite corner of the laboratory, an area he had not been able to reach during the pitched battle.

Moving faster than most humans could conceive, the bronze man began to gather and piece together large pieces of old, dusty equipment.

"Faster!" Rolf yelled.

"I am," came Ardan's curt reply. Finishing the assembly, he hefted it under his massive, cabled arm. The object was black and conical, the tip coming to a rounded point of glass or some other transparent substance.

Doc reached inside his equipment vest and pulled out a small rectangular box. He wired the box to the cone, which came to life with a high pitched whine. The transparent emitter at the tip illuminated. He pulled out two pairs of goggles, put one on and tossed the other to the German.

Ardan nodded at Rolf, who released the spell and collapsed.

The two fish-men came toward them, moving faster than their deformed shapes gave them any right to.

Doc flipped a switch on the black cone, and the light of a thousand suns, powered by Radium-X, burst out from the emitter.

The beam hit Denis, then Karl, and both fish-men shrieked and burst into flames. Within moments, both had dissolved. All that remained was two piles of ashes on the floor, and a stench.

Burma came running into the room, pistol in hand, and stopped short at the sight and smell. "Mmm. Burnt rancid fish. My favorite."

Elisabeth and Ilona were still bent over Adélaïde. She became more and more pale, but paradoxically felt a strange warm sensation exploding out from the center of her body.

Mercifully, she had almost passed from consciousness when Ardan, Rolf and Burma burst into the dungeon.

"She's almost there! Don't stop!" Elisabeth ordered Ilona, and turned to face the men.

Ardan held the Radium-X projector under his left arm, a superfirer in his right hand. He sprayed Adélaïde's attackers with mercy bullets, but Elisabeth laughed it off, while Ilona continued to draw the remainder of Adélaïde's blood.

Ardan tossed the spent superfirer away and hefted the projector into position.

Simultaneously, Rolf uttered incantations–"Iä! Iä! Ph'nglui mglw'nafh Cthulhu fhtagn! Méne!"–and the Eye of Dagon exploded off of Elisabeth's graceful white neck in a detonation of blood and bluish light.

The gem bounced on the stone floor and rolled toward Ardan. Before he could seize it, the energy released from the Eye crackled and struck the Radium-X projector, frying and fusing circuits.

The projector began to heat up and blaze white hot in an uncontrolled reaction. Ardan dropped the projector before it could burn his hands. It bathed the room with sun-like light. Burma, *sans* goggles, was blinded.

Elisabeth and Ilona screamed and collapsed, writhing on the floor. "The light! The Sun!"

"The projector is going to blow. It'll take out the whole cellar, maybe more. I can't stop it!" Doc yelled at Rolf. He gestured to Burma. "Help him out of here. I'll follow you with Adélaïde and these two."

Ardan turned toward Adélaïde, but paused at Rolf's hand on his arm.

"These women," Rolf said. "I understand and respect your policy of humane rehabilitation. But these women are gone. You cannot help them."

Doc paused a moment further, then nodded and went toward Adélaïde.

Minutes later, he burst from the front of the Benet mansion. Adélaïde looked like a small child cradled in his massive arms, broken chains trailing from her wrists. He placed her gently in the back seat of the Citroën.

Roger Noël gunned the engine and floored it, Ardan mounted on the running board, as a violent explosion rocked the *Cordon Jaune* headquarters.

Just before sunrise, large boulders shifted and rolled down the piles of rubble in the debris of the Benet mansion. A large vine, now the circumference of a man's torso, pushed the rocks away. At one tip of the vine was a pod which vaguely resembled a Venus Fly Trap. The vine slithered free, and glided down the Paris streets.

Anyone who may have observed this singular phenomenon could also have heard, just at the edge of audible range, a tiny whispering voice, barely distinguishable from the slight breeze.

"Nourrissez-moi ! Nourrissez-moi!"

The murmurs gradually faded into the morning dawn.

FROM: Lieutenant Montferrand, Division Protection, Service National d'Information Fonctionnelle, Paris.
TO: SNIF.
DATE: August 26, 1946
SUBJECT: Silver Eye of Dagon

The Eye of Dagon has been secured and turned over to Doctor Ardan. Jens Rolf has provided Ardan with detailed and specific instructions for its safekeeping.

There was no sign of Le Chiffre anywhere in the Cordon Jaune *headquarters, nor of any of the other women employed in his house of ill-fame. It is presumed they all escaped in the confusion prior to the explosion.*

Burma's blindness was temporary, and Ardan has given him a clean bill of health. According to Ardan and Rolf, A.L. will suffer no lasting ill effects from her experience.

When the rubble was cleared from the lower cellar of the Benet mansion, Elisabeth and Ilona Harczy's bodies were recovered and taken to the morgue. However, the next day, the bodies were inexplicably gone.

Recommendation: The International Police Commission should be on the lookout for two women matching their descriptions.

Deep in the Arctic, in a solitary fortress, Doctor Francis Ardan checked on the Eye of Dagon. It was stored safely away from those who would use it for ill purposes. Likewise Doctor Benet's Radium-X projector.

He moved silently into the next chamber, a warm room decorated in the fashion of an Adirondack hunting lodge. Then, through the fortress' insulated walls, he heard the mechanical whine of rocket engines.

In a huge stone fireplace, embers from a once-crackling fire still glowed. A large bearskin rug in front of the fireplace was askew. A note was pinned on the mantle, near a half-empty bottle of *Veuve Clicquot* and one champagne flute (Ardan did not drink):

My Dearest Francis (the note began),

What a wonderful storehouse of treasures your little hideaway is! I left you the gem this time, although you know, of course, I easily could have taken it. Thank you for refueling the Cirrus X-9 for me. I know you'll be cross with me for making off with it again, but really, how else can I make certain we'll see each other once more?

Au revoir, mon sauvage.

Mon amour,

Adélaïde

He shook his head ruefully and smiled faintly. He just couldn't seem to hang on to those damn rocket packs.

But he didn't really care.

After his impressive and monumental two-parter, "The Werewolf of Rutherford Grange," which appeared in the first two volumes of Tales of the Shadowmen, *G.L. Gick chose here to pen a shorter story featuring the character of Doctor Omega, that mysterious traveler in space and time, last encountered in Matthew Baugh's opening tale. Gick uses Doctor Omega to revisit a genuine monument of French science fiction and does so with considerable skill and a wonderful economy of words. This tale is bound to bring a smile to our readers' faces when they realize on whose planet Doctor Omega has landed...*

G.L. Gick: *Beware the Beasts*

Planet Soror, the Future

It really was a lovely afternoon for tea. The brief summer shower had passed, filling the air with the pleasant tang of wet earth and grass. In the garden behind Jinn's villa, songbirds twittered from tree to tree, while a red squirrel, looking for nuts, paused inquisitively upon a branch to gaze down at the strange party, then dash back into the leaves, tail twitching furiously.

"Another cup, perhaps?" Jinn asked his honored guest.

Doctor Omega leaned back in his chair and abstained, contentment practically pouring out of him.

"Oh, heavens, certainly not. I couldn't eat another bite."

"More jam, Tiziraou?"

Phyllis, Jinn's lovely wife, proffered a dish to the little creature sitting next to her.

"Thank you, please," the tiny, macroencephalic Martian chirped in its high-pitched voice, pushing its plate forward, perhaps more eagerly than necessary. Unable to chew most solid foods, the small alien was often forced to make do with more liquified sustenance. As a result, he had become practically addicted to the melange of sweet jams and jellies his planet had never produced, but that were so easily obtainable in far-off Normandy.

The Doctor tut-tutted, but otherwise said nothing. After nearly dying in his heroic attempt to help save this world, he figured that Tiziraou was entitled to a bit of gluttony.

At the edge of the pond, a swan-like creature dipped its long, elegant neck deep into the water, looking for food. Along all sides of the villa, Phyllis' beloved flowers were in full bloom, attracting the pleasant buzzing of honeybees.

"I still don't know how to thank you, Doctor," Jinn stated. "If not for you and Tiziraou, Soror would have ceased to exist, in the blink of an eye. How could we possibly repay you? We owe you everything."

Doctor Omega
by Rapeno (1949)

"Oh, I wouldn't say 'everything,' my boy." The Doctor casually waved off the compliment, but his face was a blazing display of self-satisfaction. "I'm hardly responsible. Indeed, we wouldn't even have known of the whole affair if we hadn't encountered that lost spaceman during our travels, would we, Tiziraou? Too bad he refuses to leave my *Cosmos* to join us, but I'm not going to force him."

Steepling his fingers together, he gazed into the sky and harrumphed. "The mere effrontery of it all. This Q creature... Deciding he doesn't like the way a planet is shaping up, so he takes it upon himself to create a variant, to change things to see if he likes it better another way... Still, we certainly placed a spanner into his works, didn't we, hmm? Perhaps he'll think twice next time before playing with the timelines again."

"I certainly hope so, Doctor," said Jinn.

"You know what you have to do now, hmm?" said Doctor Omega, looking at them sternly.

Phyllis put in quietly. "I still cannot get over the notion..."

"I know what you're going to say, my dear. But you have no choice."

"Do we?" Jinn's voice was raised in protest, but he refused to raise his eyes to meet the Doctor's. "What can we do? We're merely two people. Yet you ask us to alter hundreds of years of hatred and..."

"Entire worlds have turned on the actions of just one person, Jinn. Believe me. I know. And it has to begin somewhere."

"But–but you don't understand!" Phyllis cried. "From our very childhood, we are taught to hate and fear the beasts. Of all creatures, only they hunt and kill for the sheer pleasure of it; only they slaughter for the sake of slaughter. Even their own kind, they kill. The beasts are *monsters*, Doctor. How can you ask us to put all that aside?"

"Because you must, child. Because for all the just, equitable society you have tried to create here on Soror, it still amounts to nothing if even one sentient creature cannot participate in it. You say the beasts are monsters? You're right; they are. I know that better than anyone. They're killers. Murderers. But they are also so much more." Once again, he glanced to the sky, as if gathering his thoughts. "I have seen the destinies of countless races throughout this universe, my friends. I have seen entire civilizations born, grow and die, either slowly or quickly, all too often by their own hands. But rarely have I seen one with so much potential, so much ability to turn their ways to either good or evil. It would be a crime against the universe if you did not allow them that chance." Pushing his cup aside, he leaned forward expectantly. "And remember, to them, *you* are the beasts. You are the ones who hunt them without cause; who seem to hate them for the mere sake of hating them."

Doctor Omega pointed a finger up to the alien sun above. "Finally, also remember that your planet originally had no existence. You're a slice of time brought into existence by Q. Your civilization, for all its greatness and wonder, exists only because of a whim. Once his experiment was done, he would have destroyed you, if we hadn't happened along... You say you owe me? Then repay me by letting the beasts into your society. It can be done. If you want to."

Slowly, Jinn and Phyllis looked at each other. Then, slowly, they bowed their heads in acceptance.

"Good," said the Doctor, smiling. "I knew you'd agree. As I said, you are a just society. You, too, deserve to be part of the universe. And I'm certain you'll make it."

Reaching into his frock coat, he pulled a large gold watch. "Time we got back to the *Cosmos*, eh, Tiziraou? We've still got to get that astronaut back to his own time and space. Come along!"

He stood, then wagged one finger warningly. "If you ever doubt the rightness of letting the beasts into your society," he said, "think on how they treat your own people on their world."

Gravely, he shook hands with his hosts. Tiziraou bowed comically. Then, with a promise to return one day, the two travelers sauntered off deeper into the garden, where they had left their ship.

Phyllis settled in next to her beloved Jinn.

"Could it be true, darling?" she asked. "Could we really civilize those creatures and let them into our society as equals?"

Frowning, the chimpanzee shook his head. "I don't know, my love. Man is such a peculiar beast..."

There is something about prehistoric fiction that truly thrills our senses. Almost the only thing people remember from Jules Verne's seminal Journey to the Center of the Earth *is the all-too brief description of a humanoid creature–"his height was above twelve feet. His head, as big as the head of a buffalo, was lost in a mane of matted hair. It was indeed a huge mane, like those which belonged to the elephants of the earlier ages of the world"–watching over a herd of mastodons. Micah Harris, a new contributor to* Tales of the Shadowmen, *revisits Verne's vision, adding to it an extended cast of equally famous protagonists...*

Micah Harris: *The* Ape Gigans

London, Skull Island, 1843

Benjamin Disraeli looked up from the file that lay open on his desk and peered intently over his reading spectacles at the beautiful woman who sat before him. Her white frock with the quaint Empire waist suggested an innocence belied by the fox-face and reddish-blond hair visible beneath her bonnet.

"Well, Miss Sharp," he said dryly as he shuffled the papers to their proper order and returned them to their folder, "for an insurgent who has survived a failed *coup d'état* and, consequently, spent the better part of 1842 fleeing for your life across the African wilds"–here he caught his breath–"I must say, you look most... refreshed."

Becky Sharp sat rigidly upright, hands on her lap, and successfully resisted the urge to squirm under the unyielding gaze of her austere superior. She had, after all, mastered long ago the ability of not shrinking under a withering glare, when, as a waif of 16, she seemed to regularly displease the head mistress of the finishing school where she had taught French in return for board and picked-over meals.

Maintaining her own cool gaze, she said, "Sir, do you mean to hold me responsible for the failure of the Kor Affair? Do I have to remind you that I was but a pawn? That I was to be your puppet queen? And as for my being 'refreshed'... well, that is your doing as well."

"Is that accusation in your tone, Miss Sharp?" Disraeli asked stringently.

"Indeed it is, sir! Do you deny your men were under orders to toss me into that column of fire? Was it not your plan that that flame endow me with the same preternatural qualities it had given the queen I was to supplant? And the entire scheme was hatched and enacted without my knowledge or consent! I only knew we were looking for a rare, natural resource in the environs of lost Kor." Here, Becky affected a shiver, tucked her head and brought a clinched handkerchief to her mouth. "I thought I would burn horribly."

"Frailty thy name is woman," Disraeli said caustically, leaning back and steepling his fingers before him.

Becky's hand with the handkerchief dropped into her lap, and she raised her cool gaze to meet Disraeli's again. "You owe me an apology, sir!"

Disraeli laughed. "Your country owes you no more than a hangman's noose, Miss Sharp!"

Becky scowled in silence, for she could not deny it: she had first come to his attention–and that of this secret organization he served, the Meonia–when she attempted to sell to insurgents in India certain military secrets which she had acquired from her last victim, one Colonel Joseph Sedley.

Disraeli was in charge of the British Special Branch which had arrested her. Recognizing in her the amoral nature which made for an apt special agent, the Meonia had given her a choice: come into the fold or hang.

"So, what happens now?" Becky asked Disraeli.

He picked up the closed file and slapped it back down to the desk. "If we can trust your report, that this 'She–Who–Must–Be–Obeyed' possesses a mystical means of surveillance–well, she'll be more vigilant than ever now, shall she not? Thus, there seems to be nothing we can do on that front. Our mission is hopelessly botched; we both stand in the displeasure of my superiors. But fear not, Miss Sharp. There is a way we may both disentangle ourselves from this untoward affair."

"Go on," Becky said.

Disraeli patted the folder containing her report. "You mention in your notes that the flame in the caves of Kor issued up from somewhere far deeper in the subterranean realms. The source of the flame, then, lies elsewhere, and if we could find that source, then we need no longer be concerned about our failure to take the throne of this 'She–Who–Must–Be–Obeyed.' "

"That all hangs on a rather enormous 'if,' sir. First, one would have to find appropriate ingress into the Inner Earth..."

"Yes, well, it appears 'one' has. The Meonia is secretly backing an expedition to Antarctica to locate a polar entrance into our allegedly hollow world. It is to be led by a prodigious German youth named Lidenbrock and his assistant Miss Fatima Talisa."

"He has a female colleague?"

"Yes. A most taciturn young lady in public, but Lidenbrock's looks toward her during our preparatory meetings indicate she has much to say to him in private. Frankly, Miss Sharp, there is something unsavory about the whole business. We of the Meonia sense it, yet none of us attempts to stop it. But we have determined to manipulate the manipulator.

"Your mission, then, is to enter the underworld through the South Pole with the Lidenbrock expedition. Secretly, you will search for the wellspring of the flame of Kor. You will have one other associate in the expedition who shares this intelligence, Mr. Lemuel Beesley.

"You should, of course, seduce Lidenbrock so that you may replace Miss Talisa in his regard. Your agenda may, at times, be at odds with hers. In which case, your interests–by which I mean 'ours'–must prevail.

"I suspect you will have a worthy rival in Miss Talisa, Miss Sharp, one whom you must supplant, perhaps even crush." Here he smiled, leaned back, and templed his fingers again. "How I wish I could be there to watch you at work. Keep an account of it all, will you?"

From the Journal of Becky Sharp
February 16, 1843

I have met the sphinx Talisa.

And Disraeli was correct: she does have some hold over young Lidenbrock. The looks they exchange are the same that have passed between myself and Joseph Sedley before he met his untimely demise. Lidenbrock fears her.

All the others on the expedition, all men, sense he is cowed by that female and regard Lidenbrock with contempt. They do not know what such a woman is capable of. I do. I am such a woman.

Talisa senses this. Indeed, she tries, as much as is possible on a ship in middle of the ocean, to avoid me. Unfortunately, the same limited confines make it difficult to get Lidenbrock alone.

February 17

Something will have to be done about Lemuel Beesley. Tall, muscular, balding, with a pocked complexion and waxed mustachios, the man is as determined to adhere to me as Talisa does to Lidenbrock. I could not have been out of his sight for five minutes when he found me taking refuge on the quarterdeck.

"Sir, I realize you have been charged by our superior to keep an eye on me. But we are miles out to sea. The scenery here is monotonous enough; must it include your face everywhere I look?"

"But the sight of you is all that makes these endless miles of sea bearable, Miss Sharp," he rejoined with a smile, twisting by turn each tip of his mustache as though snuffing a wick between thumb and forefinger.

"I assure you, you will be as sick of me as I am you once we are shut inside by the frozen climes and no longer have the use of the deck."

"You haven't realized, then."

"Realized what?"

"We're no longer sailing for the South Pole. We haven't been for days."

I was taken aback by this revelation. "Well, where then?"

"I am not a prophet, Miss Sharp. As of the moment, we are veering in a Southeastern direction, but as for tomorrow? I suspect we will not know our destination until young Lidenbrock tells us we have arrived. Though, perhaps a face prettier than mine might persuade him otherwise. Until then, I shall trace our course so that you and I might find our way back, should we part ways with the good Professor."

"I suggest, then, that you spend less time following me, and more tossing bread crumbs on the water in our ship's wake. Good day, sir."

Remarkably, he did not follow, nor have I seen him since. He is giving me space so that I might have latitude to approach Lidenbrock and gain with feminine wiles that knowledge which cannot be discerned from the stars.

I must thus circumnavigate Talisa.

February 18

At last I have had the long desired interview with the good Professor Lidenbrock.

Wagering that Talisa would surely not accompany him to the ship's water closet, I caught him as he exited, pretending I was about to enter.

"Oh, Professor, I am mortified that you have found me dealing with nature's... necessary business," I said demurely.

Although visibly chagrined, he strove to be chivalrous. "Miss Sharp, do not be embarrassed. Our quarters are close after all."

As he started to pass, I took his elbow and gently drew him back. "Pardon me, Professor, but I need to speak to you alone. And you and Miss Talisa are usually all but joined at the hip."

"I... I...," he stuttered.

"I do not mean to exacerbate your humiliation, Professor. But it is clear to me that she is a harsh mistress. Let us cast aside all social niceties, and tell me frankly all your woes."

He immediately drew away. "I must say that if you believe Miss Talisa to be a source of woe to me, you are quite mistaken. I owe all to her."

"Certainly not 'all.' "

"She did not grant me my genius, no, but she gave me focus. 'twas she who introduced me to the notion of a Hollow Earth, the theories of Symme. More than once, when I have been wearied by this endeavor, she has taken my head in her lap and sung of the heart of the Earth as though she has been there already, assuring me that where one would expect, at best, to find all opaque, one discovers a most brilliant, most pellucid world."

Initially, I was taken back at the revelation of this touch of tenderness. But, of course, I understood very well the technique of "punish then stroke." And so I responded thus to his rhapsodizing:

"And you believe her fancies?"

Lidenbrock blinked rapidly, as though incredulous that I could not. "You would have to hear her, I suppose..."

"And is it to Miss Talisa's singing that we owe our change of course?"

"What do you mean?"

"You know well what I mean: we are no longer headed for the South Pole. And if we are following only your siren's voice, then I feel I justly fear this vessel's fate!"

"But how did you know? The captain and crew have been paid well for their silence..."

"Come, Professor Lidenbrock! To achieve your goal, you have sought sponsorship from certain powerful personages. Did you really think they would be so trusting that they would have let you out to sea without a system of checks in place? Now, explain yourself, or I assure you, this vessel will be turned back to England so quickly your head will reel!"

"Miss Sharp, please. It is not mere fancy that guides us. Miss Talisa and I discovered a journal with a map in the Royal Society's secret archives. That map charts our destination."

"Produce it, then. I want to see it. Now."

"First, I must confer with Miss Talisa—"

"And then you will confer with myself and Mr. Beesley *tout d'suite*! We will meet in the mess hall in one hour. You have this one opportunity to make your case, so bring more than Talisa and her repertoire of sea shanties!"

Our interview had taken a turn I did not foresee: I ended up being most stringent with him, but if it means having all his cards face up on the table, then so be it.

February 18, later

I have spent the balance of the day with Beesley, Lidenbrock, Talisa and Captain Marsh in closed quarters. Talisa stood against the far wall, apart from the rest of us. Several times I found her eyes riveted upon me. Clearly, she knew I had forced Lidenbrock's hand.

Her expression made it clear that when she retaliated, I could expect no pity. The sphinx Talisa had spoken.

"We were never journeying to the South Pole," Lidenbrock said. "Forgive my deception, but I could not risk another learning of our true destination before we were well underway. I assure you that we have secretly stored attire appropriate to warmer climes. You see, we sail to an island described only in the journal of one Bishop Brom Cromwell, a 16th century missionary to Malaysia.

"When he heard of a forgotten civilization far west of Sumatra, he set out to preach to these souls as well. He named their island 'Golgotha,' because of the skull-like appearance of its most prominent mountain.

"Upon landing, he observed 'ancient serpents that did walk upright as did Satan before the Fall, dragons filling the land, sea, and sky.' Further, among abandoned ruins he discovered a temple built round a bottomless pit from which, he learned from the island's human inhabitants, the isle's creatures had issued."

"There are people there, then?"

"It is unlikely they've survived. In Brom Cromwell's day, they were already dwindling in the shadow of a great wall their ancestors built against the rising tide of claw and fang. And they were already in the decadent state of a pagan civilization, as described by the Apostle Paul, which 'worshipped the creature more than the creator.' "

"But why should you regard so seriously this religious fanatic's account of 'dragons'?" I asked.

"Because, Miss Sharp," he answered, "skeletal remains of 'ancient serpents that did walk upright' have been excavated since ancient Greece. Fatima–Miss Talisa–suggested to me that, should one dig even deeper, one might discover living specimens. And, indeed, it is from the depths of the Earth that Brom Cromwell says these beasts emerged."

Lidenbrock paused, surveyed our small group, and then announced: "Gentlemen and Miss Sharp, I mean to find this island with its bottomless pit, and from there journey to the center of the Earth!"

(*The above entries are all that remain of Becky Sharp's account of the failed Lidenbrock expedition of 1843.*)

Seething in tropical steam, rivulets running from its twin, upper apertures, like tears streaming from empty sockets, the mountain's death's head veiled then unveiled, veiled then unveiled its skeletal visage from within the shifting folds of an ephemeral shroud.

Is the giant skull breathing out the vapor through which we sail? Becky Sharp mused as heavy droplets materialized on the railing under her hands.

"Miss Sharp!"

Becky looked about for the source of the disembodied summoning. Its note was urgent. Who sought her out under cover of the fog?

"Professor Lidenbrock?" she asked, proceeding cautiously.

Then a horrific shape divided the mist and lunged toward her. Becky screamed, narrowly avoiding the slicing of the creature's claw. It caught instead in her sleeve, rending it.

Becky turned and fled, vainly hoping the fog would be enough to shield her from her attacker. But even were she hidden to its yellow, reptilian eyes, the nostrils on either side of its saw-like beak had already taken in her scent. Now the creature spread scaly, leathery wings, lifted, and flew after her.

Becky stumbled and fell. As she attempted to rise, the gargoyle descended upon her, flattening her to the deck. Becky screamed again, covering her head with her arms as the creature's beak just missed clipping off an ear.

And then the voice again: "Miss Sharp, I am much disappointed. I thought you to possess more grit than you are displaying."

"Whoever you are," Becky cried, "please! Drive this creature away!"

"But I am the creature. I, Talisa."

Becky started, incredulous: this revelation alone was stunning, but she realized now that the voice was inside her head!

"It's too fantastic," she gasped out. Now she could hear the rapid patter of feet, men calling, but the fog! They were drifting into a thick patch, and it would hinder the speed with which they could come to her aid. She must purchase the necessary time.

"Talisa?! How can that be?"

"The woman you have all seen among you these past weeks was only an illusion. The Mahars–all of my kind, in the world from which I came, possess supreme powers of mesmerism."

"Your world? You mean the world below? Then, your plan all along has been to return there. You've mesmerized Lidenbrock–you've mesmerized the entire Meonia to serve your ends!"

"Astute girl. Have you also grasped my plan for you?"

The cries and footfalls of the others seemed yet, in the fog, impossibly far away. In a small, childlike voice she asked, "Why kill me?"

"True, the pressure you exerted on Lidenbrock to tip his hand did not abort my scheme. But your will is formidable, Miss Sharp. I cannot risk your further interference."

"I shan't interfere! I understand now: you only wish to return home."

The creature's screeching laughter drilled through Becky's head so that she winced. "No, no, Miss Sharp. It is not as simple as that. There is to be more, much more, which you would most strenuously oppose should I allow you to live!"

A talon lashed out, ripping away Becky's frock from collar to shoulder. Becky screamed, wild and shrill, as the serrated beak began to cut painfully into her exposed flesh.

A flash suddenly lit the fog and a musket ball struck the Mahar's arm. It shrieked, and Becky looked up to see a startled crewman, still holding his musket out and staring wildly.

Now the other men's footsteps were closer, coming from both sides. The monster that was Talisa hissed in rage–

–then, shrieking again from the pain the effort cost her, she grabbed up Becky and leapt over the ship's railing, vanishing immediately into the mist.

Lost in the cloud, borne along on the wings of the Mahar, Becky had no sense of up or down, a sickeningly disorienting experience. The screeching of the creature was terrible to hear, for each labored beat of her right wing exacerbated her pain.

Finally, she was forced to release her hold, and Becky was suddenly plummeting. She twisted and turned her body in the air as she slipped through a parting of the mist into the lunging, tumbling breakers beneath her. A wave immediately lifted her again, as though to toss her back into the sky –

–then thrust her ashore instead. She clawed into the sand, dragging her body forward over rough, scraping shells.

No sooner had she gained dry earth than she saw, just a pace apart, the fallen form of her captor. Becky rose cagily, looking about for a stone she could use to smash the gargoyle's skull...

Finding none, she still crept cautiously forward until she stood over the Mahar. Suddenly, its yellow, reptilian eyes flew open and quickly filled Becky's mind...

She fought losing control and felt Talisa's surprise at her strength. In her head, she saw Talisa in her reptilian form, expelled to the surface world by others of her kind through a dormant volcano. Becky gleaned from her mind the surprising fact that Talisa had been a political revolutionary...

The creature tightened her psychic grasp, but not before Becky saw Talisa's attempted return through the same opening after much time in exile, only to find the volcano alive again, rivers of incinerating lava blocking her passage...

...and then Becky's will was gone. There followed only impressions of being shepherded by Talisa, pushing through jungle foliage filled with fluttering, feathered lizards that cawed; of large, rough fronds, licking out, catching; bramble sticking her as she tore through scrim after endless scrim of vines and branches; sweat stinging eyes that always seemed to blink too late to flick the drops from her lashes...

Becky came to on her stomach, her face pressed down into soft, rotting vegetation. Her muscles ached and her skin was scratched. She slowly peeled her face from the jungle floor, and rolled onto her back. Just inches from her, the Mahar hunched.

She felt again the hateful voice in her mind: "Up, stupid cow! How can I herd you if you do not walk?"

Becky rose to her knees, a queasy sense of violation passing over her. "You took my mind," she said accusingly. "How dare you...?"

"Your will is not so strong, it seems, when I have no need to appear human, and can focus my mesmerism entirely upon you."

"Why did you drop your illusion when you attacked me on the ship?" Becky asked.

"So that your death, should it be seen, would be blamed on one of the aerial beasts of the island. Then that fool shot me. The pain was so intense, I knew I could no longer manage the illusion of humanity among so many. I took you then to discourage their firing after me; I take you with me now because..."

Here, the creature's beak parted slightly, a serrated smile, "...because I must eat, Miss Sharp."

Becky rose shakily, knees atremble. Her eyes darted wildly about: the jungle hemmed her in from every side. She had no idea of how many days they had been traveling, whether Lidenbrock and the others were searching for her or not.

And that thing... she couldn't outrun its influence, not once it brought all its attention to bear on her again.

She faced her captor, her eyes narrowing. "I am only one," she said coolly. "And, as you said, your wound keeps you from reassuming human form. If you abandon your designs on me, I will help you procure the others for your... appetite."

The Mahar laughed. "My wound is almost healed. And they are to feed my sisters and myself when I return with them–those we do not need to take us back to Europe."

Becky's jaw went slack. "Europe? What do you want with Europe?"

"My dynasty no longer rules the world beneath, so this world shall be our domain and our feeding ground!"

Becky's lip curled with revulsion, and, drawing back her fist, she lunged forward to strike the monster–

–and then, once again, her will was gone.

She came to, standing upright, before an enormous amphitheater in the ruins of an abandoned city. The jungle had long ago, in a fecund green tide, swept up along the buildings of hewn stone. Branches erupted from their sides; plants burst through the fissures of the flagstones upon which she stood.

A horrible screech was emanating from within the amphitheater, and with that screech Becky's full consciousness had returned. She realized it was Talisa, and, whatever that scream meant, it had caused Talisa to lose her hold on her.

She turned and ran.

For half-a-day, she put distance between herself and Talisa without incident. Then the jungle trees parted to create a glade. Becky was halfway across when an upright lizard, eight feet from snout to tail, propelled itself over the glade in a series of hops that ended with its hind talons atop Becky's shoulders, bearing her to the ground.

Becky screamed as its opening jaws rained saliva upon her. Then the air cracked and cracked again. A small hail of musket balls slammed into the lizard, one plowing a trench in the earth by Becky's head. The monster sprang back, releasing her.

"Lidenbrock! Beesley!" she cried out. "I'm here!"

"Stay down, Miss Sharp," Beesley shouted out as flashes of smoke heralded another round of fire. Staying where she was seemed to be a good way to be shot, so bending low, she scampered toward her rescuers. While the Englishman and some sailors moved in on their saurian quarry, Lidenbrock ran to meet her.

"Are you all right, Miss Sharp?" Lidenbrock asked.

Becky grabbed at him desperately. "How long?" she sobbed. "How long since that creature flew away with me?"

"Almost a fortnight. We had given you up as lost. Thank Providence your path crossed ours."

More musket shots. Becky looked back: the twitching giant reptile lay supine on the ground.

"This is such a miracle–to lose you both in one day and then, find you both alive and well!" Lidenbrock was beaming.

"Wait–both of us?" Becky asked, placing her hand to his upper arm.

"Miss Talisa, Miss Sharp! She vanished from the ship, carried away, she tells us, same as you. We found her about a mile or two on the other side of this glade."

Lidenbrock winced, and looking down, saw that Becky's nails were biting into his bicep. "Miss Sharp... my arm..."

Becky released him, turned and began striding purposely across the glade. Yes, there she was, just emerging from the trees. The infernal harpy! Whatever made her scream in that temple, it hadn't meant the end of her. And after two weeks, she was healed enough to cast her spell on them all again.

She walked up to Beesley. "Hallo, Miss Sharp! Very glad to see you are unspoiled," he said by way of salutation and then tweaked the tip of each waxed mustachio.

"Is your musket loaded, Mr. Beesley?" she asked.

"Ho! You wish to take a shot at this miserable beast! Just on principle, eh? Well, here you go, lass," he said, cocking the long gun and handing it to her. Becky put it to her shoulder and turned it on Talisa, who now stood less than 25 feet away from her.

Talisa's eyes widened. Becky fired–

–just as Beesley knocked her to the ground, insuring the musket ball went off mark.

"That bitch is a monster!" she shouted up into his face. "Do you hear? That thing will be the death of us all!"

"Have you gone daft?!" Beesley asked, wrenching the gun away. "That's Miss Talisa!"

By now, Lidenbrock had reached them, having begun to run when he saw Becky aim the long gun at Talisa.

"Do not do it, Lidenbrock!" she shouted at him. "Don't take her to the pit! Do you hear? You don't know what you'll be setting in motion! Lidenbrock– 'twas she who flew away with me!"

Lidenbrock shook his head in pity. "Poor creature," he said. "This infernal Sun has been too much for her. I'll fetch some rope–"

"*No!*" Becky cried desperately. "Beesley! Get off! You can't tie me–you have to listen–*No! No!*" she cried as he turned her over on her stomach, and soon her arms were bound behind her.

Her legs were left free to allow her to walk. During the journey under Talisa's guidance to the abandoned city, Becky continued to vilify her adversary, salting her adjurations with such profanity that even the sailors began to complain. Finally, the grieved company as one consented to her gagging. Becky thus seethed in silence.

Lidenbrock all but swooned at the sight of the ancient amphitheater, Brom Cromwell's temple of the pit. Soon, he was urging them through a large open archway through which a solitary stone pillar was visible. The theater's floor consisted of flagstones. In its center, a 15-foot tall stone idol of an ape perched vigilantly on a large, round pedestal.

"Why, it is the *Ape Gigans*?" Lidenbrock said and peered at the figure's base. "There is writing here, in the esoteric characters of the West African G'harne fragments. It says that, long ago, this city's inhabitants, the Blessed People, enjoyed a benign existence, 'not as much as a snake,' to threaten them. Game was plentiful. But the god of the dead, Malgoghphoni, 'miserable in his underworld,' envied their bliss.

" 'Malgoghphoni opened the Earth, and sent from his domain his prodigy: great serpents who walked. They came forth continually. All stood in jeopardy.

" 'Then from the same depths rose our salvation. Before man, when the gods fought, Malgoghphoni made eternal prisoners of those...' "

Here Lidenbrock frowned. "Apparently, they identified the ape on this dais as belonging to some demigod class out of their mythology. They appear to have regarded his sudden appearance as the fulfillment of a prophecy. Let me start again:

" 'Malgoghphoni made eternal prisoners of those demigods who opposed him. But one, Kong the cunning, torn free of his fetters, came now to the Blessed People's aid.

" 'Kong did what men could not do: by his strength, he beat back the serpents and took a great stone, sealing the pit against Malgoghphoni's prodigy...' "

Now Becky understood Talisa had screamed in frustration at encountering this unexpected obstruction.

" 'In the doing, Kong severed himself forever from his brothers, captives in darkness below. Never could he return to free them, lest he unleash again Malgoghphoni's brood upon us.

" 'To console his loneliness, the Blessed People to this day offer him brides of our own virgins, and here we also set up his image over the pit.

" 'Thus were our days extended, but because of the increase of Malgoghphoni's prodigy, the time will come when we must leave forever the works of our fathers' hands. Great is Kong, the bane of Malgogphoni's brood. Blessed is he.' "

Lidenbrock looked at the idol. "We will have to blow that thing up, then," he said, and Talisa smiled. "It's the only way in. You men–bring the powder kegs."

"I'll take Miss Sharp back a pace–to that pillar in front of the archway," Beesley said. "That should shield her. You should come along, too, Miss Talisa..."

While the other men prepared the powder, Beesley took Becky to the ancient column and began untying her arms preparatory to resecuring her. The moment her hands were free, Becky reached up and snatched her gag away.

"Beesley, listen to me!" she implored. "You mustn't allow them to open that pit! It will be the beginning of the end!"

"Bosh! We can handle these thunder lizards all right," he said, retying her wrists before her. Just above Becky's head, he had noticed an iron ring in the pillar, and so had left a length of rope to tie her to it. "Sorry, lass, but I don't trust another to hold your leash, as I'm the one who has to answer for you to our Meonia masters."

He secured the rope through the iron ring, pulling her hands over her head. Becky groaned, turned her face from Talisa's victorious sneer and began pulling against the ring. It held secure. Perhaps, she mused, Kong's brides tended to be unwilling.

There were shouts now from the area of the idol. Becky looked from around the pillar to see Lidenbrock, Marsh and the sailors sprinting for cover. Toward the dais and its statuary, a flame was slithering and sputtering along a trail of jet...

With a *boom* that left all their ears ringing, as though the idol itself roared with defiance and indignation at its dethronement, the pit erupted in a shower of stone and earth. Pieces of statuary sprayed as far as Becky, flung over and beyond the sheltering pillar.

She was just beginning to peer around it at the resulting rubble when there was another terrible roar, this from far behind her, beyond the abandoned city itself.

"Somewhat of a delayed echo, that," Beesley commented.

"This island possesses unusual acoustics along with everything else," Lidenbrock responded. Talisa stared intently into the smoke still boiling over the pit.

Amazingly, more than half of the pedestal, *sans* ape, still obstinately plugged the hole. But there was enough to pass through. Talisa's eyes flashed with triumph, and she bolted for the ingress.

"Wait!" Lidenbrock called after her. "We must yet be cautious! Talisa, stop! The ground about may give way..." Orpheus reversed, he followed his Eurydice toward the underworld.

She reached the edge, almost toppling over it, but Lidenbrock caught up to her just in time, pulling her back over the lip of the half crater. "Wait, Talisa! We need ropes to begin our descent."

As the others thus prepared, Becky found herself momentarily alone and forgotten. So when she heard trees crashing in the jungle beyond the city ruins and cried out to them, she was ignored.

The men had secured a rope ladder and lowered it into the pit when a roar sounded that was clearly neither echo nor distant.

Bending to squeeze his black, hairy bulk through the large archway, Kong re-entered his temple.

"It is the *Ape Gigans* himself!" Lidenbrock gasped out.

Rising now to his full height, which fell just short of the amphitheater's great walls, Kong stretched out his long arms, and then brought his fists back against his enormous chest, drilling them in a rapid-fire staccato. He roared again, eyes riveted on those who stood guiltily among the rubble of his image.

The pillar to which Becky was tied placed her right before the towering hulk, but he had yet to notice her. She yanked furiously at the rope that held her, but to no avail. And so, she at last gave in to her fear and screamed.

Kong looked down and immediately reached for her.

"*No, No, No!*" Becky pleaded as she was enveloped in the sweaty, fleshy folds of the great palm, fetid with musk. With his other hand, Kong snapped the rope free of the pillar.

Becky's wrists, still bound, now dropped before her. She used her bunched fists to strike back and forth at the monstrous hand grasping her, as the leathery skin of the ape's face molded into what Becky recognized as a grotesque parody of a human smile.

This offering was unlike any he had seen before: her clothing enveloped her body, but the skin which was exposed was white, and her long hair shone like flame. He twisted her waist-length locks around a fingertip, tugging Becky's head back so that she thought he would tear it from her shoulders. She screamed again, and Kong ceased his pulling.

"Lidenbrock!" she cried out. "Beesley! *Help me!*"

The sailors were already rushing to her aid. Lidenbrock stood at the edge of the pit, suspended on the cusp of two worlds. Talisa, seeing that the giant ape's attention was turned, began to scramble down the rope ladder.

Lidenbrock moved to join her, and immediately felt Beesley's musket barrel in his ribs. "Not so fast, Professor. Miss Sharp first!"

Meanwhile, the sailors were already loosing their long guns upon Kong. One ricocheting ball grazed Becky's head. She heard her captor roar in anger, and the last she saw was his long arm lashing out, sending the sailors scattering like tenpins...

Pain returned with Becky's consciousness. Her bound hands touched gingerly at her blood-scabbed scalp. She opened her eyes and found herself upon a large leafy mat in an enormous cave. It was well lit, and she quickly saw why: two large, paired apertures in one of the cave walls above her were flooding the cavern with light.

A deep, rapid stream flowed through the cave. Still a bit dazed, she crawled to it, and, lowering her mouth, drank. The icy cold bit when she splashed it over her face and into her hair with her bound hands.

She suddenly realized that the twin openings above her must be those of the island's mountain topography. But how had she come here? The answer hovered as a shadow at the furthest periphery of her consciousness: she flinched against it. And then it seemed the shadow would not be denied, that it had slipped from her mind and now blocked the Sun from the openings above...

Becky looked over her shoulder as though against her will and screamed at the large dark form hovering behind her. Kong's hand reached for her, but instead of snatching her up, he first gently brushed with his fingertips her injured head.

She now rose shakily to her feet. The giant anthropoid shifted, and the sunlight struck Becky full on, making each tiny hair along her arms an incandescent wick, her reddish-blond head a conflagration. A look of wonder spread over Kong's face.

Becky backed away, but he imposed his hand behind her, grabbing her up again. On some level, he had understood her need for healing rest and thus had spared her his more robust attentions. But now that she was awake, he meant to renew the investigation of his catch in earnest.

He reached for where the dress was already torn over her shoulder, revealing the intriguing pale skin. He caught the loose fabric, pulling down and popping free the buttons that held the back of her frock together. Part of the chemise beneath ripped away as well, revealing the shapely protuberances of her shoulder blades. Becky flinched as Kong stroked her, tactilely savoring both her softness and the distinct, unfamiliar textures of the shredded outer and under garments.

The loosened dress slid off Becky's shoulders and to her bosom, where her bound hands desperately caught it. She was soon compelled to let drop the clutched frock to box the returning, worrying thumb and fingers.

Now only in a torn chemise and boots, Becky fought more frantically against the ape's plucking, which nevertheless soon reduced her undergarment to hanging tatters. The abundance of unfamiliar white skin in the ape's palm dazzled in the bright sun, a wonder from outside Kong's existence, as though he suddenly held a handful of snow.

Becky continued to fight him off with her bound fists. Then the ape caught the dangling length of rope from between her wrists and ripped her bonds loose. Becky yelped at the rope burn. Still, caressing her stinging wrists, she muttered, "That much was useful, at least."

Now Kong focused on the flaming hair, curling the reddish-blond strands about his fingers. This time, however, he took care not to tug as hard as he had before.

"He remembers," a breathy Becky spoke to herself as he let her long hair gently unwind.

She realized her fascinated captor would never willingly free her. And she suspected his former brides had angered him by attempting to escape–hence this prehistoric Bluebeard's perennial need for a new one. One bid for freedom was all she would have.

Kong plucked and gathered fruits which, for Becky, were the size of melons. She ate, which necessitated visits to a tall, thick bush by the cavern stream. When he followed her warily, she would squat behind the bush, shooing him while rattling its branches. Once he connected that rustle with certain odors, the ape seemed to grasp her desire for privacy. He would turn away until the rustling stopped. Having established this pattern, Becky slowly began increasing the time she rattled the bush and was thus out of his sight.

When Kong ventured out, he was always careful to place her on a high outcropping for safekeeping. From this vantage spot, through one of the high, twin apertures, Becky could look out over the island.

And it was from here that she saw the distant wisp of smoke like that from a camp fire. Her heart leapt. Did this represent a party searching for her? She must risk all and hatch her scheme as soon as Kong returned.

After much pacing about, she heard her captor lumbering home. She quickly composed herself lest he smell her desperation. He entered, carrying more melons which he let roll to the cavern floor. Then he collected Becky. As usual, he poked, stroked and pulled at her person. She now wore a tiny loin cloth and another rag that barely contained her ample breasts, both fashioned from her chemise's remains. For days, she had been unraveling into string the discarded outer frock and the rope that had bound her.

Upon her release, Becky went through the motions of eating as Kong peeled and ate the melons as though they were oranges. While he concentrated on slaking his thirst and hunger, Becky produced her latest little bundle of string from where she had hidden it in the grass mat.

Tucking the thread into her bosom, she moved toward the bush. The ape sucked the sticky juice from his fingers and watched her. Once concealed behind the bush, she quickly added the most recent bit of thread to a long single strand, already tied there, whose length she had been increasing every trip to the privy.

Kong sensed something more was going on than simply answering nature's call. He moved toward the bush. Becky quickly pulled the string, rattling the branches. The ape hesitated, then, by force of habit, looked away.

Using the thread to continue tugging on the bush, Becky kicked off her boots and slowly waded into the stream. She didn't even feel the sting of the cold as the water rose over her thighs, her fast-beating heart had so suffused her body with warmth. Now she let the quick current carry her along, unfurling the string behind her, all the time still tugging it.

The speed of the stream increased, and shot her out of the cave and into the sunlight–just as an angered roar sounded behind her. Suddenly, she was yanked back like a fish on a line. She released the string and swam hard, fearful to look back, trying not to think of what would happen should Kong recapture her–

But the stream was carrying her along now even faster, and Becky realized she had entered a rapids. She went limp, bumping off of large stones, shielding her head for fear of being knocked unconscious. The ground beside her shook with the ponderous *thud, thud, thud* of Kong's bulk going up and down as he ran on his behemoth's hands and feet, now coming alongside her. Becky frantically ducked underwater, but upon resurfacing, saw he still kept pace with her.

She ducked beneath again, and when she burst to the surface saw a new reason for fright: a waterfall. The inexorable rush of the stream left her no choice. She looked desperately now to the ape along the bank–just as the rapids took her over. Simultaneously plunged underwater and falling, she could still hear her captor's roar of frustration and failure. She struck the river below, plummeting to the bed, then writhing back to the surface in a rhythmic, sinuous flow of her supple body.

Becky broke the surface, gasping in sharp, painful draws of breath as she splashed frantically and peeled away the hair plastered over her face. Her starting eyes looked about for the giant ape. No sign yet. And the swift flow of the river was taking her further away every second. She was bruised, but no bones were broken or out of joint. Her trip over the rapids and waterfall, however, had cost her her last, scant rags.

She had no idea where she was now in relation to whoever had started that campfire. But if she set one of her own–might they come to her? Would she also draw Kong's' attention–or any of the other island creatures? As she came ashore far down river, she decided that risk was better than blundering blindly through the danger-laden jungle.

Becky had learned how to start a fire in the wilderness during her time in Africa. As always, the process of striking stone to twigs was frustrating and she nicked and scraped her fingers more than once, provoking bursts of swearing. But she finally succeeded, sending and maintaining a plume of white smoke above the tree tops. She tried to stay awake, but her ordeal had exhausted her, and she fell asleep by the fire.

A crash of the jungle foliage moving in her direction roused her, along with shouting: "Miss Sharp! Miss Sharp! Are you there?"

It was Beesley's voice. With the men approaching, she suddenly felt keenly her nakedness and scampered for shelter behind some large fronds.

"I'm here!" she shouted and a few moments later, Lidenbrock, Beesley, Captain Marsh and the sailors who had survived the jungle were grouping around her fire. "Gentlemen," she said from the fronds, "I fear my ordeal has left me *au naturel*. Will one of you be so kind as to toss me your shirt?"

Lidenbrock immediately removed his, and, averting his gaze, handed it to Becky behind the fronds.

"Thank you, Professor," she said. "You are most solicitous."

Here, Lidenbrock's face burned, and he was glad to be turned away. "Alas, Miss Sharp, to my shame, I must admit Mr. Beesley had to persuade me to pursue you and not follow Fatima–Miss Talisa–into the pit."

"I do not think poorly of you, Professor," Becky said. "I'm certain you were not completely yourself." Becky now emerged wearing the shirt, which reached only as far as her knees. Still, she could hardly begrudge her gallants a display of leg after their efforts on her behalf–especially if it added to her powers of persuasion.

Marsh and Beesley looked on appreciatively while Lidenbrock blushed, and said, "Once you are safe, I intend to descend after her."

"Listen to me, Professor," Becky said, placing her hand on his arm. "You must not! We must reseal that opening in the Earth, else that pit shall be the threshold of doom for many."

"And desert my Fatima? Miss Sharp, how can you suggest such a thing?"

Here Beesley drew her aside. "Are you forgetting your mission in all this?" he asked, voice low. "You have certain obligations it is my duty to see you fulfill –"

"Disraeli sensed there was something insidious about this expedition," she whispered. "I have confirmed that."

"And what proofs do you have to offer? Because he will require them, as do I."

Becky started to speak, but caught her tongue. She dare not bring more insubstantial, fantastical railings against Talisa, lest she be bound and gagged again.

"If you do not seal the pit upon our return," she said instead, "I promise you, you will soon have all the proof you need. But it will come too late."

"Then, Cassandra, I will acknowledge you a prophetess. But now let us get moving."

The group began its march through the heated stillness and into the lengthening jungle shadows.

They walked through the night non-stop, arriving back at the ruined amphitheater with the dawn. There, they paused for food and rest, though it wasn't long before Lidenbrock was urging them to begin their descent. Beesley, however, argued they return to the ship first and see that Miss Sharp be outfitted properly for the journey below.

"Surely Miss Sharp, after her recent ordeal, has no desire to risk more peril," Lidenbrock snapped. "Now, I have seen to her safe return, Beesley! Just as you required. But I will put off seeking Fatima no longer, even if I must do it alone!"

Beesley started to retort, but the angry twist of his mouth froze on his face. His eyes widened at something happening behind Lidenbrock. Marsh and his men immediately began cocking their long guns, and Lidenbrock turned to see what was the source of their agitation.

Slipping through the pit's opening, like a grub from under a moved stone, came a winged, human-sized reptile, one of the Mahars, Talisa's true people. The narrow egress slowed its progress, and before it could clear itself, it was so shot through that instead of taking flight, it fell dead to the ground.

"Miss Sharp was right," Beesley announced. "Fetch powder–we'll seal this hell-hole immediately!"

Lidenbrock opened his mouth to protest when Casptain Marsh pointed at the hole and shouted: "Look!"

Guns were immediately trained upon the pit.

"No!" Beesley shouted. "That's a woman's hand!"

Lidenbrock sprinted for the pit. "Do not shoot, you fools!" he cried. Reaching the hand, he took it, pulling its owner up and free of the crevice.

"You are not my Fatima," Lidenbrock began, his tone one of surprise, but not complete disappointment.

For the possessor of this hand was a beautiful, winsome blonde, completely nude, the abundance of her peach-flushed flesh the effulgence of the morning Sun.

Smitten, the men lowered their guns and stared instead in a stupor of delight. Even Lidenbrock did not shift his gaze but willingly drank in the feminine radiance.

"Bloody hell!" Becky swore. "Another one!"

A second naked beauty, whose hanging reddish locks barely concealed her voluptuousness, rose from the hole.

"And another!" Becky remarked. "And another..."

Soon, a display that would rival the *crème* of the finest seraglios now lolled and beckoned about the pit's opening. Beesley and the others dropped their long guns to the ground and moved to join Lidenbrock, who remained planted to the spot.

Becky snatched up a rifle and fired a musket ball in the direction of the "women," furrowing instead the pate of one of the sailors.

"Damnation! I missed!" Becky exclaimed as the man fell. She didn't know how to reload, but several pairs of long guns were at her feet. All of the men–including Lidenbrock–were already running back for her, and before she could fire again, they had tackled her, then pulled her roughly to her feet. Becky looked back at the women. To her horror, she saw Talisa–the only one who appeared clothed–had come up from the pit to join them. Lidenbrock, his clothed–had come up from the pit to join them. Lidenbrock, his expression bliss, took a step toward her, but she nodded him back. All the women nodded, a silent communication to the men...

One sailor drew Becky taut. Beesley brought his open palm hard against her face, then the back of his hand across her mouth. She saw with satisfaction that the skin of his knuckles was blood-scraped from her teeth.

He looked back, as did all the men, at Talisa and her sister-things, who tittered and nodded again.

Now Becky was pummeled by all: to her stomach, to her ribs, blows placed to her kidneys. Sagging ground-ward, she was hefted up for more punishment, the unnatural tittering urging it on–

–With a roar, a rapacious storm of black fur, claws and fang descended upon Becky's molesters, tossing them carelessly. Kong plucked up Lidenbrock and flung him far afield. He careened over the flagstones on his stomach, his head striking the sacrificial pillar so that he blacked out. The man holding Becky to be beaten dropped her to the ground to flee, but was halted when the titan's paw snatched him up by the neck and quickly wrung it so that the body tore free of the head. Becky saw Beesley sliding down the amphitheater's wall, his skull opened, his exposed brain leaving a trail like a giant slug.

The mangled corpses of the sailors who had not successfully fled now littered the amphitheater floor. The same deadly paws that had put them there gently picked Becky from the ground and brought her close to Kong's burning, amber eyes. On her back in his palm, Becky weakly turned her head and nodded toward the women. Then she wondered–would he be susceptible to their charms as well?

Kong's upper lip curled, exposing fangs, his eyes narrowing. Gently, he placed Becky down and then, with another roar, he propelled himself on his knuckles and hind paws upon the harpies.

It seemed Kong was vulnerable only to true beauty.

In panic, the Mahars dropped their useless guises, launching themselves to meet the charging ape. They dropped on him from above, from behind, and head on, flailing at his eyes. They hooked him with their beaks and talons, biting deep into the flesh of his head and body. The Ape peeled them from himself, tossing them as he had the men. But those whose necks he had not rung, or whose vitals he had not torn free with his fangs, returned to bite and snatch and tear again.

Only Talisa had not joined in the attack–or changed her appearance. Skirting the edge of the battle, she was able to get behind Kong and at what he guarded so valiantly: Becky Sharp.

Bruised and sore as she was, Becky managed to rise to her knees at the approach of her enemy and raised her fist to strike her. Talisa rushed forward, grabbing the wrist, and, putting her other hand over Becky's mouth, pushed her back to the ground, pinning her there.

"These ape creatures long plagued my kind–" Becky again heard the words in her head "–we had thought them long eliminated. Their resistance was always robust. My sisters will require more than this dead human carrion the ape has let fall. You will provide fresh flesh and blood when they are done."

Kong suddenly dropped flat on his back to the ground, flattening the three winged reptilian creatures who had returned to attach themselves there. But there seemed no end of assailants left to bite and rake him

Now he eyed the partially opened pit which he had sealed long ago. He regarded the temple wall rising behind it, just as his adversaries hooked fast into his neck, into his abdomen, into the flesh above his right kidney. Roaring in anguish, he ran for the wall, springing upward, grabbing the top and propelling himself and the Mahars which clung to him over the side.

Talisa smiled. "The brute in his torment has forgotten you, Miss Sharp, and seeks to escape his adversaries. t'would seem you drew the weak-minded of his lot."

Then the section of the wall behind the pit buckled, dust of ages first unsettling, stirring in clouds; then cracks shown in the masonry, and the first stones began to topple over into the pit...

From over the wall flew the screeching Mahars who, unable to thwart the ape's purpose, quickly descended into the pit as the wall continued to crumble and spill into it behind them.

Talisa's eyes widened with realization. Releasing Becky, she scampered for the pit as fast as she could–

Too late! The section of the wall completely tumbled over the opening, leaving Talisa to throw her arms over her face against the rising plumes of dust–

–and then find herself suddenly before the great ape who stood hunched, bleeding and torn, swaying on his great knees. His amber eyes lit with anger at the last of his enemies, ready to deliver upon her full recompense for the grievances he had suffered lately from her kind.

Talisa shrieked the sound of nails scraping slate. Kong lunged for her–

–and a long gun fired!

By chance, the ball grazed his great head at the proper spot with only the necessary impact to steal his consciousness. His great form fell forward on top of the screaming Talisa.

Becky looked back to see an aghast Lidenbrock lowering his long gun. "*No!*" he screamed. Then he was running with the long gun to the prostrate behemoth.

"Lidenbrock!" she cried out, trying to gain her feet against the pain. "She's dead! Crushed! It's too late!"

"Not to avenge her!" he shouted back. He aimed for Kong's temple–only to have the hammer click with no sequel. "No powder!" he shouted in rage, then raised the gun's butt, ready to beat it to splinters against the colossal head before him.

"Stop, Professor!" Becky shouted, now to her knees. "You'll only rouse him! We dare not tarry—we must flee to the ship! I am weakened by the beating you participated in! I need your help! Now!"

The gun's butt hovered for long seconds, ready still to strike, then Lidenbrock lowered the musket, teeth pinching blood from his lower lip, eyelids beating back tears...

Groaning, he turned and sprinted for Becky, gathered her up and began carrying her back to the ship, leaving behind the strewn corpses of fallen comrade and foe alike.

From over his shoulder, Becky watched Kong, still except for the rise and fall of his great breast. Amidst her fear that he might yet rise and carry her away, never to escape again, she found herself strangely touched and wondering:

Why had he sealed the pit—two times now—and denied himself return to the world from which he came? Did he realize, as Talisa said, that the rest of his kind were long dead? That in this world or the one beneath, he was still ultimately alone?

Safely aboard Captain Marsh's ship now, her bruises bandaged, Becky rested against the railing and regarded the island's skull-like topography that she had lately inhabited. There had been no sign of Kong during their flight, though once out to sea, she had heard an inhuman yet despairing wail from the now distant isle.

Professor Lidenbrock joined her. He, too, stared silently toward the island they left behind. Becky was surprised to discover that he, like she, had left it forever, abandoning that ingress to the Inner Earth.

"That way holds too much grief for me," he said. "Part of me died back there with her."

"Yes," Becky thought, "that part of you which she held captive."

"So let us not speak her name ever again," he said. "I never shall. But that does not mean I will forget her, nor ever cease looking for another opening into the Earth's center. Though it become the work of my life, I am comforted that she, after a fashion, will carry on with me."

Becky looked again toward the island's colossal skull formation, particularly the great stone dome that made the cranium. Did Kong wander about the cavern inside, an atavism beyond recall, a hermit memory taken residence in a long dead giant's discarded skull?

She wondered, did she in turn still stir inside the head of the *Ape Gigans*? It was unlikely he would ever see white skin again or other hair as radiant as her own. Perhaps, over time, she would seem to him some phantasm, something from a half-remembered dream. If such as he *could* dream...

Fantômas
by Gil Formosa (2005)

Travis Hiltz is also a newcomer to Tales of the Shadowmen. *For his first story, he has chosen to pay homage to the visually striking imagery of the Louis Feuillade serials which are the very essence of French popular fiction:* Fantômas, Les Vampires, Judex, *etc., with their wonderful procession of black-clad assassins crawling through the sewers of Paris or dancing on its rooftops .In this tale, as befits a collection subtitled* Danse Macabre, *it is no ordinary adventure...*

Travis Hiltz: *A Dance of Night and Death*

Paris, 1909

Night fell over the city. The sounds of Paris drifted away from the boulevards and the streets and into the homes, the theaters and the cafés. During the day, it was a city of strollers, automobiles and tree-lined avenues, but when night fell, one sought out the public places, crowded, well-lit–and safe. For the monsters came out at night. Thieves, scoundrels, killers and phantoms.

In one particular neighborhood, the houses huddled close together. They were not houses lived in by the rich, but rather the moderately well-off. At a modest two-story dwelling, the lights on the second floor went out. A window opened. A woman stepped out and slid gracefully onto the slate shingled roof. Lithe and shapely, she moved with a dancer's grace. She wore a black, skin-tight body suit. The hood fit tight around her head, with a round opening for her face. Her features were well-formed, the kind of full lips, pale skin and deep, sensuous eyes that, at a party, would have drawn numerous suitors to her side, asking for a dance or the permission to fetch her a cocktail.

Now, on the rooftop, in the moonlight, her eyes were alert and searching; her face had the grim look of a predator on the hunt. This black clad huntress was Irma Vep and she was the newest member of a feared gang of thieves known as the Vampires.

Her steps were light and sure as she made her way across the rooftops. She leapt nimbly across the narrow gap between the houses, making her way down the boulevard. She had a destination in mind, a house at the end of the street. The Belthams owned the house. The current Lady Beltham had become a bit of a recluse after the murder of her husband. The house had been ripe for the picking for many months. It was a perfect opportunity to fill the coffers of the Vampires. A worthy test of their newest recruit.

Irma Vep reached the end of the street and estimated the distance between her current perch and the roof of Beltham House. She held out her arms, took a few steps backwards, and launched herself into the air with a grace and power that many a ballerina would have envied. With nothing stronger than a mild breeze blowing, the jump was no challenge to her. Her only worries were if she had misjudged the distance, or the fear that the neighborhood might contain an amateur astronomer or a late night stroller.

Irma Vep landed, catlike, on the roof of Beltham House, digging her heels in between the slate shingles to steady herself. She stood up, took a breath and nodded, please with herself.

Suddenly, a quiet sound drifted on the night air and caught her attention. The sound of light applause. Irma Vep peered about, anxiously. Someone had spotted her!

"Very good, little Vampire," a voice said, from higher up. "Most impressive."

Beltham House was a three-story manor house, each story featuring an ornate bit of baroque overhang. Irma had landed on the second peak. Her taunter stood upon the third. She caught sight of the glowing tip of a cigarette, as he stepped out of the shadows. He was a tall man, dressed in elegant black evening wear, including an opera cloak, white gloves, top hat and a slender black cane tucked under one arm. He also wore a distinctive black domino mask.

Irma Vep took a step back, despite the distance between herself and the new arrival. His clothes, and especially the mask, told her who he was.

"Fantômas!" she breathed, feeling a chill creep along her spine. He merely tipped his hat in acknowledgment. The Vampires were feared and hunted across Paris. They were considered the most devious thieves this side of Arsène Lupin. Wealthy men felt for their wallets and double-checked their safes at mere mention of their name. But, Fantômas–his very name struck terror all across Europe! He had been known to kill in the most horrific manner, merely to distract the police from discovering a minor scheme. Fantômas would burn a hospital to the ground, just to eliminate a single man that had earned his wrath. Even hardened criminals would weep in terror if they thought Fantômas has reason to be displeased with them. The Vampires worked hard to not attract the police's attention–and even harder to not attract Fantômas'.

Fantômas stubbed out his cigarette against the balcony and strolled casually towards Irma Vep, a slight smile at the corner of his mouth.

"I have read of your exploits and found them mildly entertaining," he said, in that same low, emotionless tone. "You and your playmates are quite clever. Which is why I have allowed you to operate unhindered in my city, thus far..."

"Your city?" Irma snapped. Despite her fear, her pride could not stand his patronizing tone.

"My city," Fantômas repeated. "Paris and all who dwell in it, or merely pass through it, are mine. If there is thievery to done, murder to be committed, or terror to be spread, it shall be done either by my hand. or with my approval." He tapped his cane against the roof. "This house and all its contents are not for you to plunder, my little Vampire. Go home. Find another target."

"Why?"

He halted for a moment, raised an eyebrow, as if having someone questioning him was so rare that he was unsure how to respond. "Because, I have said so," he replied simply. "I have allowed the Vampires free reign over Paris, mostly because it suited me, but also because you chose your targets wisely and avoided crossing my path." He twisted the handle of his cane and slowly drew out a razor-thin sword. The blade glinted like silver in the moonlight. "You have a choice to make, my little Vampire."

There was a smile on his lips, but when Irma Vep locked gazes with Fantômas, she saw that it did not reach his eyes. There was a longing there, a foul hope that she would be foolhardy enough to challenge him, and a promise. A promise of death. Ugly, painful death.

Irma Vep drew in a deep breath and straightened her shoulders. She brought up her hands. Her already long fingernails were augmented by a set of metal claws built into the fingertips of her gloves. "I suppose it would have come to this eventually," she said, taking up a defensive stance.

Fantômas nodded to himself, mildly impressed. "Clever girl," he murmured, dropping nimbly down from the third floor to the second. He casually reached inside his coat, as if to draw out a cigarette case, but pulled out an ornate dagger with a heavy blade. He raised both weapons in a mock salute. "Let the dance begin then," he said, lunging forward.

Irma Vep tensed, waiting for Fantômas to make the first move. Yet, when it came, it caught her off guard. His movement had been almost accidental, the light cane twirl of a Parisian dandy. Next thing she knew, there was a gash across her ribs. The flimsy sword cane, while looking like a mere toy, was sharp enough to part the fabric of her body suit and the flesh beneath. It just broke the skin, causing a light trickle of blood. Irma clasped a gloved hand to the wound, sucking in her breath. Distracted as she was, she barely registered that the dagger was on a downwards arc, rushing for her heart. She twirled, like a ballerina, feeling the wind of the weapon's passage as it missed her by less than an inch.

Claws barred, Irma Vep slashed at Fantômas. He brought up his weapons. Blades and claws clashed, raising sparks. Both combatants struggled to push the other back. Fantômas had the advantage of strength, as well as the high ground, but the pads in the soles of Irma's feet were made specifically for keeping secure footing on uneven rooftops. She also had a strong dose of fear to bolster her determination to succeed. Death at Fantômas' hand would not be quick, or painless. Satanas would look upon her surviving this encounter, while failing at her original mission, with strong disapproval. Neither option appealed much to Irma Vep. But, to survive an encounter with Fantômas, and to return to the Great Vampire with riches from Beltham House, would place her at the pinnacle of the Paris underworld.

"Stop daydreaming, little Vampire," Fantômas growled, flinging his arms upwards. He then brought both blades swinging viciously downwards. Irma spun to the left, pirouetting past Fantômas until she was behind him. He spun quickly, to slice her down. Irma fell to the roof in a split, then leapt to her feet, the claws of her right hand raking up Fantômas' sleeve as she went. Her claws weren't sharp enough to do more than tear the cloth, but instinctively, the master villain flinched back. Irma then brought her left fist down hard on the hand holding the dagger. It fell from Fantômas' grip and skidded down the sloped roof.

Fantômas swung his sword and Irma clamped her claws around it, blocking the attack. The two combatants froze for a moment, locked together, their heavy breathing causing faint clouds of mist in the cold night air. Their gazes met and Irma Vep could not stop from gasping. The cruelty she had seen in Fantômas' eyes earlier had now spread, turning his handsome features into a brutal mask. His teeth ground together and a low animal snarl escaped his mouth. The disguise of the suave gentleman was gone. Irma was glimpsing his true face.

Shocked, she stumbled backwards, barely able to fend off her opponent's frenzied attacks. Irma came to a halt, as her back struck the edge of the tiered roof. She could feel the sharp edge of the slate shingles biting into her back. Fantômas made a savage slash that passed within an inch of her wide, frightened eyes.

His top hat tumbled off his head and the arch-villain casually rested the point of his sword against Irma's breast as he bent down to retrieve it. Irma Vep felt as trapped and helpless as a butterfly pinned to a collector's exhibiting board.

His sword arm steady as an iron rod, Fantômas smoothed down his hair and then replaced his *chapeau*. "So, my little Vampire," he growled. "Regretting your choice?"

Irma was, in fact, regretting it. She was by no means squeamish about pain and death, so long as it happened to other people. Two things kept her defiantly silent. The first was that she was damned if she would admit defeat to any man, whether the police, the Great Vampire or even Fantômas himself. The second was the fact that it was only by biting her lip that she kept from crying out in pain as the sword pierced her body suit and then slowly bit into her skin just below her collar bone.

Irma Vep held Fantômas' gaze for several seconds, while her mind frantically rushed through her scant options for escape or survival. Unfortunately, most of them required a miracle.

Apparently, though, fortune does indeed favor the wicked, as just at that moment, Fantômas' right heel slipped on the shingles .It took him only seconds to recover his balance, but that was all the time Irma needed. She twisted away from the sword, and trapped it between her arm and her body. A second twist and she was able to wrench it out of her enemy's grasp.

Fully recovered, Fantômas straightened his hat and peered darkly at Irma Vep. "Most impressive, little Vampire," he murmured, his usual predator's growl tinged with a slight tone of surprise. "Given time, you could truly become a challenge..."

Irma gave a slight, mock curtsey and then tossed away the sword. It clattered down the slates to the pavement below.

Fantômas flexed his arms, so that twin blades dropped from concealed holsters in his sleeves into his gloved hands. "So, we'll just have to ensure that you aren't given that time," he snarled. The knives sang as they flew through the air. One grazed Irma's hip. The other buried itself in her shoulder. Irma clasped her hands to her injuries. She stumbled backwards, lost her footing and fell. Pain raced up her side, as she dug in her heels to keep from sliding closer to Fantômas. The master villain strolled over to where his dagger lay.

Irma clutched at her aching hip and struggled to sit up. It proved to be more than she could manage. She then reached for the knife embedded in her shoulder. The slightest pressure on it sent a white-hot pain through her body and she bit her lip till blood flowed to hold back a shriek of pain. Her vision blurred and she let go of the knife. Desperate as she was for a weapon, removing that knife would only leave her too weak and helpless to use it once Fantômas returned.

Irma dug her claws into the tiles, hoping to pull herself along. She had seconds left before Fantômas would retrieve his weapon and she had no doubt he would kill her, quickly and brutally. Then her fingers brushed against metal. Fantômas' other knife! Breathing a silent prayer, she grabbed the knife while struggling to turn as she heard footsteps clicking along the shingles.

"Little Vampire," Fantômas said, drawing closer. "It is time to end our dance." He raised the dagger high, preparing to strike. Irma flung up one of her arms to distract him, then hurled her body up into a sitting position and drove the small silver knife into her enemy's thigh, burying it up to the hilt.

Fantômas' roar of anger and pain echoed across the neighborhood, as he staggered backwards, clutching at his leg. He lost his footing on the shingles, and soon lay sprawled on the rooftop, glaring across the distance at Irma Vep.

Eyes locked with his female foe, Fantômas clenched his jaw and ripped the dagger free from his leg. Irma slumped, her muscles trembling with the effort. She forced her much abused body up into a sitting position. Every inch of her ached and part of her wanted to just give up. If Fantômas didn't kill her tonight, she knew he would hunt her down. He was not one to forget a grudge. She would spend the rest of her life looking fearfully over her shoulder.

Somehow that fear opened a floodgate inside her. Letting loose all the fear, anger, pain and frustration that came with growing up in poverty, being looked down upon by her so-called betters, clawing her way through life and finally into the membership of the Vampires, where her being a "mere" woman meant having to prove herself twice as much, work twice as hard, and be twice as cruel and cunning as any of the male members. She let all these emotions well up and surge through her until, wincing with pain, she stood up. If Fantômas was going to kill her this night, Irma would not face him on her knees. Her legs trembled with the effort, but held.

Fantômas watched her while wiping his blood off the knife with a silk handkerchief. If the pain of his wound or the trickling of blood down his leg bothered him, he showed no sign of it.

"Come, Fantômas," Irma snarled, yanking the knife free from her shoulder. "Let's finish this!"

The arch-villain limped forward, then paused, as if studying his opponent. His face, a mask of cruel fury, shifted as the corner of his mouth was drawn up in a smile. Then, he lunged, quickly slapping the knife out of Irma's hand and caught both of her delicate wrists in the iron grip of his left hand.

With a gloved finger under Irma Vep's chin, Fantômas raised her eyes to his. "No, my little Vampire," he murmured. "Our dance is far from over. You have a spark. It would be a shame to stamp it out so quickly. Let see if instead we can fan it into a flame."

Irma faltered. Fantômas' finger moved to her lips.

"No idle threats or clever words," he said. "It would ruin the moment and then I would change my mind. Tend to your wounds, little Vampire, and stay out of my way. I will see that I stay out of yours until the time is right." Fantômas ran his finger down Irma Vep's cheek as he stepped back and released her hands. An almost tender look played across his wolfish features.

As Irma nodded in agreement to his terms, Fantômas slashed out viciously at her with his knife. It cut through the fabric of her body suit and left a raw gash upon the top of her right breast, in the shape of a jagged "F."

Irma glared up at him, clutching at her new wound, her eyes wide and full of hate for the well-dressed villain, as he strolled away across the roof.

"Don't go mistaking a moment of compassion for soft sentiment." He bowed and then disappeared down a trap door set into the roof.

Irma glared at the spot where Fantômas had been. Blood seeped from between her fingers and she trembled with both fierce emotion and the growing chill of the night.

Irma Vep lay back on the settee, dressed in a silk robe, bandages wrapped around her wounds. She took a sip of brandy and closed her eyes.

"You are looking better than I expected," said Satanas.

"That's because you expected to see me stretched out on a morgue slab," Irma murmured drowsily in reply. She opened her eyes and gave the Great Vampire a weak, loveless smile.

He patted Irma's non-bandaged shoulder lightly and sat down across from her. "If any of us could survive the wrath of Fantômas, I knew it would be you."

Irma took another sip of her drink, finding little comfort in his words. The flame of hate that Fantômas had lit inside her still burned bright and the sight of that smug man only added fuel to it.

"With Fantômas busy at Beltham House, our men should have met no difficulties breaking into the Crédit Foncier," the Great Vampire added. There was the sound of a doorbell. "In fact, it sounds like they're back already."

A thickset man in workman's clothes entered the room, supported by a butler, and clutching at a bandage around his head.

"The police... They were waiting for us..." the Vampire muttered, groggily, as he was lowered to a chair. "The others... captured... or dead."

"But how?" Satanas snapped.

"Fantômas," replied Irma Vep, smiling as she swirled the brandy around in the snifter.

Like Win Scott Eckert, our regular contributor Rick Lai has been slowly assembling his own storyline through his contributions to Tales of the Shadowmen. *In Rick's case, the saga focuses on two dynamic female protagonists: one, Josephine Balsamo, Arsène Lupin's arch-enemy, and the other, her rival, Irène Chupin (or Tupin), whom Rick "rescued" from the Spanish cult horror film* La Residencia *(a.k.a.* The House That Screamed*). While the following tale can be read independently, readers wishing to refamiliarize themselves with Irene and her ghastly trials at Madame Fourneau's College for Young Women may find it useful to reread "Dr. Cerral's Patient" in our second volume before reacquainting themselves with...*

Rick Lai: *The Lady in the Black Gloves*

Provence, 1885

In November 1885, a lecture on French literature was being delivered by Madame Fourneau, the headmistress of the College for Young Women, an exclusive boarding school in Provence. She was a middle-aged widow with brown hair, dressed in a stern black skirt and a white blouse, with a dark brown tie. She always repeated her comments twice while her students, approximately 30 girls, recorded her words in their notebooks.

"Alexandre Dumas was... Alexandre Dumas was... an extremely meticulous writer... an extremely meticulous writer... His historically accurate novel... His historically accurate novel... *Joseph Balsamo*... *Joseph Balsamo*... revealed the true role of the title character... revealed the true role of the title character... in fomenting our great revolution of 1789... in fomenting our great revolution of 1789."

A 15-year-old girl raised her hand. She was slender, with dark hair, and wore a dark orange dress. The headmistress acknowledged her.

"You have something that you wish to say, Mademoiselle Tupin?"

"I disagree, Madame. Monsieur Dumas severely distorted Joseph Balsamo's activities. He was merely a charlatan known as Count Cagliostro. Dumas later compounded his fabrications by exaggerating Balsamo's role in the Affair of the Queen's Necklace. Dumas' assertions about Balsamo's secret passages in the Rue St. Claude are wild speculations, typical of an author who claimed that Louis XIV was replaced with his twin brother."

"So you disagree with my assessment of Dumas, Mademoiselle Tupin?"

"I do, Madame."

"Are you calling me a liar?"

"No, Madame, I am not."

"Then, why are you arguing with me?"

"At my previous school, we were allowed to question our teachers."

"We follow other methods here. But I feel there is an ulterior motive behind your statements."

"I do not understand what you mean, Madame."

"By denying Cagliostro's achievements, you are, in effect, criticizing a fellow student, one whom I have entrusted with a large amount of responsibility."

"No, Madame, I am not saying that at all."

"Yes, you are, Mademoiselle Tupin. I must insist that you apologize for your behavior."

"I will not. I have done nothing wrong."

"Then, you must be punished."

Madame Fourneau approached the desk occupied by a 17-year-old student. She had blonde hair, a delicate chin, deep-set eyes and high cheek-bones. She wore a black skirt and a brown blouse, with a black tie.

"Mademoiselle Balsamo, take Mademoiselle Tupin to the isolation room."

The blonde girl rose. The headmistress gave her a key. Pulling Tupin by the arm, Balsamo dragged her out of the classroom. The brunette was taken up a flight of stairs to a Spartan room with a bed and two chairs.

As the blonde was leaving the room, she addressed the younger girl:

"My dear Irene, you brought this upon yourself."

"What do you mean, Josephine?"

"You should have agreed to my offer. As I told you before, I really run this school. "

Two hours later, Josephine returned with Madame Fourneau and two other girls. The headmistress harangued the detainee.

"Mademoiselle Tupin, are you now willing to apologize for the slanderous remarks that you made earlier?"

"No, Madame."

"If you do not recant, you will have to be punished appropriately."

"If that is your wish, so be it, Madame."

"It is not my wish, it is *your* wish, Mademoiselle." Madame Fourneau handed a whip to Josephine. "Mademoiselle Balsamo will administer the punishment."

A week later, Irene stood before Josephine and two other girls who helped her in her prefect duties at the school. The trio was sipping tea.

"Irene," intoned Josephine, "the last time you were here, I asked you to join our sisterhood. You foolishly refused. I extend that offer again. Do you accept?"

"Yes, Josephine."

"Very wise. But we need to clarify certain matters. You did not wish to discuss them before. Are you willing to do so now?"

"Yes, Josephine."

"Your mother's maiden name is Victoire Chupin, but there is no mention of your father's name. Who was he?"

"I don't know."

"Your parents were unmarried. Doesn't that make your mother little more than a common harlot?"

Irene nodded.

"You really have to speak up, Irene. What did you just acknowledge that your mother is?"

"A harlot."

"And you are little more than a common thief. Are you not?"

"That is a lie. I have never stolen anything."

"The interview that Madame had with the lady who brought you here would suggest otherwise. That lady has a son, four years younger than you. Your mother was his nurse, wasn't she?

"Yes, his name is Arsène, although his mother calls him Raoul."

"Arsène's mother claims that a valuable brooch was stolen from one of her friends, the Duchess of Dreux-Soubise. This brooch was later discovered in your room. Do you admit your crime?"

"No. Arsène stole the brooch. He hid it in my room."

"Irene, don't make an 11-year-old boy a scapegoat for your own inept actions. If you tell any more lies, I will see to it that you are punished again."

"..."

"To protect your mother's reputation, you were even registered at the school under the alias of Tupin. Admit it. You stole that brooch."

"I stole the brooch."

"You are lucky that thieves are no longer branded with a *fleur-de-lys* on the shoulders as they were in the old days. In Arabia, they remove the hands of the offenders. Fortunately for you, punishments of such a cruel nature are no longer used in this enlightened age. The College received a letter asking about your well-being. It came from a gymnastics professor named Théophraste Lupin. Who is he?"

"He is Arsène's father."

"Is he *just* Arsène's father? The surname Tupin is very similar to that of Lupin..."

"That's just a coincidence."

"Is it? It seems strange that Arsène's mother left her husband and abandoned his surname. She now uses her maiden name of d'Andresy. I can only conclude that Théophraste and his wife argued over some important matter. Perhaps it was your very existence?"

"I don't know. I told you earlier that I don't know who my father is."

"My dear Irene, isn't it logical to assume that Théophraste Lupin is also your father?"

"Perhaps."

"Good. Now that we have come to an understanding, I have an assignment for you. I have seen your work in art class. You really are quite talented with those firm hands. I want you to draw my portrait."

Provence, 1889

Now approaching her 21st birthday, Josephine Balsamo was scheduled to graduate in the spring. But a new development caused her to leave the College for Young Women sooner than anticipated. Madame Fourneau had received a letter from the wife of Noel Moriarty, the British railway expert, currently residing in Naples. Because she had a three-year-old boy, she wished to engage a governess fluent in both Italian and English. Josephine spoke both languages.

"You will be pleasantly surprised," said Madame Fourneau, "to learn that Mrs. Moriarty is the former Mademoiselle Catarina Koluchy, your predecessor as my prefect. I have reviewed the terms of her offer and they are very generous. There is only one issue that remains to be settled."

"What issue would that be, Madame?"

"That of your successor."

"There is no question, Madame. Only one candidate exists. She has proven her reliability, although her first few months were difficult."

"As yours were too," chuckled Madame Fourneau.

"I have not forgotten." Josephine remembered all too vividly her own flogging. "Do you concur with my recommendation, Madame?"

"I do. In fact, she is already waiting outside." Opening the door, Madame Fourneau said: "Irene, will you please join us?"

After the meeting, Josephine made her farewells to Irene.

"You have been a loyal friend, dear Irene," she professed. "I have a little gift for you."

Josephine handed the girl a small box. When she opened it, she saw a silver brooch in the shape of a five-pointed star.

"A pentagram," indicated Josephine, "a sort of good luck charm. You may need it in your new role."

Naples, 1889

At the Villa Corbucci in Naples, Josephine Balsamo met with Mrs. Moriarty. She was a regal woman with dusky hair, rosy lips and extremely dark blue eyes.

"Josephine," she began, "I've been guilty of a slight deception. Although I was truthful about my marriage and my child, I do not really need your services as a governess. I have a different position in mind for you. I have been managing a philanthropic organization, a Brotherhood, since I left the College. It is a branch of the Black Coats. I would like you to become one of my assistants."

"I know the Black Coats, Catarina. My late mother was one of their members."

"Indeed. I have to say, however, that some of my associates fear that you may bear a grudge because of the disciplinary actions I took against you at the College."

"Not in the least. Any unpleasantness between us was entirely Madame Fourneau's fault. You only followed her directives. If I recall, by the time you left the College, we had become friends."

"And I proved it when I recommended you for the position of prefect. I was surprised that Madame so readily agreed. You were only 16 at the time; others were older, had more experience."

"I had ways of endearing myself to Madame Fourneau, Catarina."

"She did enjoy your sketches of her."

"A family trait, perhaps, this obssession with artwork. Did you know that she is the sister of Gaston Morrell?"

"The deranged artist who strangled all those women in Paris during 1878?"

"The same. Naturally, her three children are unaware of this. Her daughter is studying in Paris. Philippe pursues his education in Geneva, but the other son, Louis, is still at the school, due to ill health."

"So the young whelp hasn't gotten over his asthma. He must be about 16 now. Madame Fourneau still keeps him tied to her apron's strings?"

"Very much so. In fact, I have devised a scheme to manipulate him in order to repay Madame Fourneau for her mistreatments."

"I am happy to hear it. Like you, I had some distasteful experiences at the hands of Madame Fourneau during my tutelage. What is your scheme?"

"I plan to seduce Louis and turn him against his mother. I have gained his affection; he is not yet ready, but he soon will be. Because Madame Fourneau forced me to draw her portrait, I intend to induce Louis to present her with an artistic effigy assembled from... very unusual materials. Her son will soon be following in his Uncle Gaston's footsteps."

"A wonderful strategy, Josephine. You enlist the children of your enemies to act as your underlings. Was it difficult to arrange secret meetings with Louis?"

"I had an accomplice. The new prefect. She made excuses for my dalliances with Louis."

"Is this girl smart, Josephine? Should I recruit her for my Brotherhood?"

"Certainly not. She is merely a petty thief with delusions of intellect. She has no idea about the overall scope of my plan."

"Like Jeanne de La Motte, whom your ancestor manipulated into stealing the Queen's Necklace."

"Her fate will be similar to Madame de La Motte's, Catarina. She, too, will be branded as a thief!"

Paris, 1896

In the autumn of 1896, Paris was plagued by a series of unexplained murders. Five women had been found, strangled, their bodies floating on the Seine. The crimes bore a strong resemblance to those of Gaston Morrell, the notorious strangler who had terrorized Paris 18 years before under the sobriquet of Bluebeard. Gaston had drowned fleeing the authorities, but now he seemed to have awakened from his grave. *L'Echo de France* dubbed this imitator the "second" Bluebeard.

(Pedants observed that he should really be the "third" Bluebeard since the original Bluebeard was unarguably Gilles de Laval, Baron de Rais, the slaughterer of children from the 15th century.)

The hysteria gripping Paris was compounded by the reception of letters sent to the newspapers and accurately predicting each murder. All contained the same identical phrases: "*History will repeat itself tonight. Bluebeard will strike again.*" They bore the signature of a woman: *Clio Gosart.*

La Maison de Repos de Ville-d'Avray was an insane asylum situated in that small community just outside Paris. It consisted of several buildings spread over a large area, enclosed by an extremely steep wall. One large edifice housed the administrative staff.

Its director, Doctor Maubeuge, was a man of indeterminable age with piercing eyes and a walrus mustache. Seated at his desk, he had been reviewing the file of a 23-year-old patient who had committed suicide that evening. His perusal, however, was interrupted by a visitor.

Doctor Maubeuge critically eyed the young woman seated opposite him. He judged her age to be in the mid-twenties. Tall and slender with black hair, she wore an orange dress with a brooch in the shape of a pentagram on the right side. A short black scarf was tied around her collar. Black silk gloves adorned her hands. Silver bracelets were on her wrists. She had presented a business card that identified her as Irina Putine of the Chupin Detective Agency.

"Are you Russian, Mademoiselle?"

"Yes. I immigrated to this country three years ago."

"I must commend you on your French. You speak it like a Parisian."

"Thank you, Doctor. You have an unusual name. Are you from Flanders?"

"I'm not from the city of Maubeuge, if that's what you mean. I'm from Switzerland. Five years ago, I came to France to become director of this sanatorium. Sometimes, names can be misleading. This recently deceased young man was such an example. Despite being christened Louis Fourneau, he was generally known in Provence by the Spanish variant of his first name, Luis."

"I'm well aware of the College Girl Murderer's background, Doctor."

"The College Girl Murders was a foolish name given to my patient's crimes by sensationalistic newspapers six years ago. I'm rather surprised you heard of his suicide. We only sent a message to the police within the last two hours."

"I didn't know of Fourneau's death until my arrival. How did he die?"

"He cut his throat with a razor. We have concluded that an orderly dropped it in his cell after shaving him. Needless to say, his employment has been terminated. If you didn't come because of Fourneau's death, then why are you here?"

"A simple request from a client who wished to rule out the possibility that Fourneau may have escaped to become the new Bluebeard."

"A ridiculous assertion," stated Doctor Maubeuge. "Like Gaston Morrell, the new Bluebeard strangles his victims. Fourneau, on the other hand, slew them with a knife and mutilated their bodies. I see no parallels. Why would your client espouse such an absurd theory?"

"My client learned of a family connection between the two killers. My client was Fourneau's sixth victim."

"Your client must be lying about her identity then, Mademoiselle. The account of Fourneau's crimes contradicts that claim. The murders were committed in a boarding school for young women between September 1889 and January 1890. Louis Fourneau was the headmistress' son. Detaching the flesh of his victims, he took grisly trophies to a locked storeroom in the school's attic. He was trying to construct a woman in his mother's image. He was confronted in the attic by a student who indeed became his sixth victim. Immediately after this murder, Madame Fourneau found the girl's mutilated corpse in the attic. Louis then locked his mother in the storeroom with the grotesque caricature fashioned in her likeness. Her screams were heard by a janitor. He ran into the attic, overpowered Louis and ultimately discovered that the headmistress had died from heart failure."

"Certain facts are missing from your file, Doctor. First, my client was merely knocked unconscious by Louis Fourneau, rather than slain."

"That makes no sense. Why didn't he kill her outright? It goes against the pattern of his other crimes."

"Perhaps he was acting on special instructions from his Muse?"

"His *Muse*?

"Louis told the police that he had performed his atrocities at the bequest of a woman whom he described only as his Muse."

"Perhaps it was Mary Shelley? Louis' crimes were obviously inspired by her famous novel, *Frankenstein*... But before we continue any further, I'd like to know your client's name."

"Is it not in your file already?"

"My file does not mention the names of Fourneau's victims."

"Yes, the victimizers are often remembered better than the victims... In any event, my client wishes to remain anonymous, Doctor. But I can tell you that her first name was Irene."

"Very well then. I can't imagine how this Irene survived. Even if she'd been merely unconscious, she'd have died from loss of blood. Fourneau had severed both her hands."

"As I said earlier, certain facts are missing from your file. A doctor treated the girl's wounds and rushed her to a hospital. Some months later, her health improved, but she had been mentally traumatized by her ordeal. Her guardian dispatched her to a private nursing home in England. She spent three years there before returning to France." [3]

"I see. That must have been awful for the poor girl. Do you have any further questions, Mademoiselle?"

"Did Louis Fourneau write anything during his confinement?"

"Only meaningless scribbles," said the voice of a man who just entered the office. "My name is Doctor Biron." As Irina Putine introduced herself, he kissed her gloved hand.

"The good doctor is a fellow colleague from Passy," explained Maubeuge. "He was visiting here when this unfortunate suicide transpired. Doctor Biron asked to examine the writings of the deceased."

Biron handed Irina a sheet of paper. It had the heading: "*Je m'abuse*" (French for "I abuse myself"). Under it were the words "*Louis – Louis*," repeated for seven rows.

"I would also like to see the body, Doctor Maubeuge," asked Irina.

"I see no harm in granting your request."

Maubeuge escorted Irina to a morgue. He lifted the sheet that covered the cadaver. The body was that of a thin, handsome man with brown hair.

As Irina left, she was met by Biron. He was accompanied by a lean man with grey hair and a beard. The man wore tinted spectacles. He was dressed in a black Inverness cape and a top hat.

"Mademoiselle Putine, a police inspector has arrived to inquire into this suicide," announced Biron. "Permit me to introduce Inspector d'Andresy."

"D'Andresy?"

"My name seems familiar to you," remarked the Inspector. "Have we met before?"

"No, but I have heard of a Raoul d'Andresy."

"A distant cousin. My name is Maurice."

Van Klopen, Tailleur pour Dames was a prestigious dressmaking shop in the Rue de Grammont. Its original owner, Van Klopen, had sold his establishment

---

[3] See "Dr. Cerral's Patient" in *Tales of the Shadowmen 2*.

in 1892 to a London clothing firm, the House of Crafts. The new owner, Mrs. Moriarty, was commonly addressed by her employees as Madame Koluchy.

She was presently having tea in her office with three of her subordinates. Koluchy was dressed in an elegant black gown. Seated at her right was Josephine Balsamo in a bright green dress. The other two attendees were attired less flamboyantly. They both wore black skirts and brown blouses with black ties. They were Mary Holder, a pale looking woman with dark hair and eyes, and Helen Lipsius, a damsel with a piquant smiling face and charming hazel eyes.

"Josephine, my husband is impressed by your usage of the Morrell motif in this current operation," said Madame Koluchy. "He is quite an admirer of Gaston Morrell's artistry, and has his painting of his fourth victim."

"I knew that your husband owned works by Jan Gosart and Jacques Saillard, Madame, but I was unaware that he also possessed a Morrell."

"He purchased it from the Duke of Carineaux's collection."

"Please tell Mr. Moriarty that I am very pleased with the work of his protégé, Mabuse. How did they meet, if I may ask?"

"Mabuse was recruited by my late brother-in-law before his tragic death in 1891. Poor James met him in Switzerland."

Mary Holder refilled her own cup of tea. She noticed that Josephine's cup was nearly empty.

"More tea, Mademoiselle Balsamo?"

"The correct title is Countess," said Josephine coldly. "You are guilty of a breach of etiquette, Mademoiselle Holder. I could have you sent to the Alteration Room."

"I apologize, Countess," beseeched Mary. "I meant no disrespect."

Being the daughter of a genuine Italian Count, Koluchy knew that Josephine's claims were a sham. Nevertheless, she permitted her affectations since the blonde was her most valuable assistant.

"Do not fret, Mademoiselle Holder," interjected Koluchy. "Mistakes are allowed, provided they are not repeated. Countess Cagliostro committed a much more serious mistake two years ago, and suffered no other punishment than being temporarily banished to New Orleans. She tried to recruit Arsène Lupin as her pupil, but he outsmarted her and is now a major threat to us."

"Lupin will soon be eliminated, Madame," said Josephine.

"Josephine, I have a fondness for you that dates from our days together as students, but I warn you. Our society will not tolerate a second failure in this matter." Then, indicating that the matter was now closed, Madame Koluchy added: "The dresses worn by our two colleagues may have a certain nostalgic flair. They are from the new clothing line inspired by those uniforms that the late Madame Fourneau gave us as gifts."

"Madame intends to propose a new name for our organization to the High Council," said Helen Lipsius.

"What name?" asked Josephine.

"The Black Skirts."

Chief Inspector Lefevre of the Surete had investigated the original Bluebeard killings of 1878. He was now in his late fifties and was entrusted largely with supervisory duties. He had delegated the new Bluebeard case to Inspector d'Andresy.

Born in Martinique in 1850, Maurice d'Andresy had become an official in the constabulary on the island. During 1895, he had achieved considerable fame for breaking up a smuggling ring active in the Caribbean and the Gulf of Mexico. Working closely with American authorities, d'Andresy had tracked the leader of the crime network to New Orleans. Regretfully, the detective was afflicted with pneumonia while fruitlessly pursuing the master criminal in the Louisiana bayous. After his recovery, d'Andresy was transferred to Paris in the same year.

The Inspector coughed slightly. Lefevre attributed that cough to a consequence of the investigator's earlier pneumonia. D'Andresy was summarizing the case to his superior.

"Since Morrell strangled the women whose portraits he painted, our supposition has naturally been that the new Bluebeard must also be an artist. All of his victims posed for either painters or sculptors. Our suspicions focused on the sculptor Boris Yvain, because three of the victims were amongst his models, but he has no connection to the other two. He also has an unbreakable alibi for the night of one of the murders. I now have a new suspect, Jacques Saillard."

"The painter whose work is said to be even more erotic than that of Monet and Renoir?"

"Yes, the same. All the victims had posed for him at some point. There's also an intriguing point about Saillard. He has never appeared in public. His physical appearance remains a mystery. I have a suspicion that he may be related to Morrell."

"Why do you believe that?"

"Madness runs in that family. Morrell's nephew was the recently deceased College Girl Murderer. His brother, Philippe Fourneau, vanished from a Swiss boarding school in 1891. I viewed the corpse of Louis Fourneau in order to get some idea of Philippe's probable appearance. My theory is that Philippe is both Bluebeard and Saillard."

"Have you been able to trace any of Saillard's other models?"

"He's done a rather conservative portrait of the celebrated Isadora Klein."

"But she's in Germany. Do we have any other leads on him here?"

"So far, no. I hope to locate him by interrogating Maurice Joyant, the art dealer who exhibits his paintings."

"I've never met Saillard," answered Joyant. "The delivery of the paintings, as well as any financial dealings, have all been handled through an intermediary."

"Who is he?" asked d'Andresy.

"Saillard's proxy is a *she*, Inspector. In fact, she posed for his painting, *The Lady in the Black Gloves*."

"Is that painting here?" asked Lefevre.

"No, it's in London," replied Joyant. "It was sold last year to a wealthy British collector, Noel Moriarty."

"What's the model's name?"

"Irina Putine."

The Chupin Detective Agency was a large three-storied building. The firm had been founded in 1868 by Victor Chupin. When Inspector d'Andresy arrived, he immediately asked to see Chupin, but was informed by a secretary that her employer was working on a case in Spain. She directed him to Chupin's chief assistant, Irina Putine.

As the policeman entered Irina's office, she rose from her desk to greet him.

"Inspector, this is a surprise, please have a chair. When I met you the other day, I didn't compliment you on the extraordinary job that you did in the Caribbean."

"Thank you, Mademoiselle. My only regret is that I didn't apprehend the ringleader of the smuggling syndicate in Louisiana. I hope that you'll assist me in finding an equally elusive quarry."

"Whom do you seek?"

"A painter named Jacques Saillard. He's sought for questioning in the Bluebeard murders."

"I'm not surprised. My own investigation has concluded that Bluebeard is killing Saillard's models. You must have uncovered my role in the exhibition of his work. I'd like to help you, but I'm bound by the rules of confidentiality to protect Saillard's identity. You've placed me in an awkward position."

"No, Mademoiselle, you've placed yourself in this awkward position. Do you claim that your so-called client is someone other than yourself?"

"I'm not sure I understand the meaning of your question, Inspector."

"I had initially assumed that Saillard was a man. But now, the thought occurs to me that a clever woman with artistic ability could easily produce such paintings under a male pseudonym. This would be particularly desirable if the artist in question is pursuing a bohemian lifestyle. I assume from the title of your self-portrait that you only wore two small articles of clothing?"

"You have clearly not viewed *The Lady in the Black Gloves*, Inspector. I posed in attire similar to what I'm now wearing. My portrait is no more controversial than the painting of Isadora Klein."

"Doctor Maubeuge told me the details of his earlier conversation with you. You are aware of the connection between Gaston Morrell and the College Girl Murderer?"

"Yes. We appear to have both researched Morrell's family thoroughly."

"Let us talk about the woman whom you identified as Irene to Doctor Maubeuge. Have you heard of the *Werewolves*?"

"Yes. They were a criminal gang that emerged during the late 1860s. In 1893, their leader, Lothaire Stepphun, was arrested in New York for murder. Soon after his incarceration, he was fatally shot while trying to escape. What relevance does this have to Irene?"

"A minor member of the Werewolves gang was a prostitute who acted as a courier between Stepphun and his fence. She was little better than a 'prostitute.' Her name was Victoire Chupin. She came from the same criminal family that spawned the founder of your agency; in fact, she's his sister."

"It is true that my employer had a checkered past, but he's made amends for it decades ago. Mind you, the same was true of the founder of the Sûreté."

"Victoire was arrested in 1868 for transporting stolen goods and sentenced to a year in prison. After her release, she gave birth to a daughter named Irene. I put it to you that this is Louis Fourneau's sixth victim."

"I do not dispute the fact, Inspector."

"In 1872, Victoire became the personal maid to Henriette d'Andresy, a banker's daughter. The following year, Mademoiselle d'Andresy was disowned by her father because she chose to marry Théophraste Lupin, whom he believed to be unscrupulous gold digger. Whether or not Théophraste truly loved Henriette, I don't know. But what I do know is that, prior to his marriage, he had long been Victoire's lover. In fact, Irene was their daughter. Théophraste and Henriette moved into a new residence. Despite the awkwardness, Victoire and her daughter were allowed to live with the Lupins. In 1874, Henriette gave birth to Théophraste's legitimate child, Arsène. Victoire then became the young boy's nurse. Arsène Lupin, who now calls himself Raoul d'Andresy."

"Are you related to him, Inspector? You implied as much when we met at the asylum."

"The Lupin marriage soon dissolved after Henriette realized that Irene was Théophraste's bastard child. She fled, reassumed her maiden name, changed her son's first name and even forgave Victoire for her betrayal. Henriette perceived her as a stupid woman who had been entirely fooled by Théophraste. Henriette supported herself by being a servant in the household of old friends, the Dreux-Soubise. A few years later, however, Irene followed in her mother's criminal footsteps. She foolishly stole a brooch. When the theft was discovered, Irene was exiled under the alias of Tupin to Madame Fourneau's boarding school."

"Maybe Irene wasn't guilty of the theft of the brooch, Inspector."

"Please enlighten me, Mademoiselle."

"A couple of years prior, the Dreux-Soubise had been robbed of a diamond necklace. Was Irene in the household at that time? No, she wasn't. What a pity! We can't blame her for that earlier theft. On the other hand, Raoul was. But please, continue with your narrative. I'm curious to see where it'll lead us."

"When Henriette died in 1886, Victoire could have retrieved Irene from the boarding school but instead she busied herself with raising Raoul. Besides, Irene's letters indicated that she was very happy at Madame Fourneau's College."

"The mail was rigidly censored there, Inspector, by the headmistress' prefect. Do you know who she was at the time?"

"No, I do not, Mademoiselle, but I fail to see the relevance..."

"Her name was Josephine Balsamo. Have you ever heard of a historical figure called Joseph Balsamo, Count Cagliostro?"

"Yes, I've read of him in novels by Dumas."

"Have you any clues as to the identity of Clio Gosart, the author of the letters predicting the new Bluebeard's murders?"

"If I did, I would not share them with you, Mademoiselle. I will merely remark that Clio is the Muse of History and Jan Gosart was a Renaissance painter."

"That artist was also known as Jan Mabuse because of his Flemish origins. And Clio Gosart is an anagram of Cagliostro, Inspector. The role of Clio in mythology also suggests that Josephine Balsamo was the Muse, whom Louis Fourneau cited as the inspiration behind his crimes."

"That anagram proves nothing, Mademoiselle."

"Have you ever heard of an alleged descendant called Countess Cagliostro?"

"Yes, I remember such a name figuring in a few unrelated cases, but I can't see its connection with these recent deaths."

"There was a confidence trickster calling herself Countess Cagliostro active in Paris during 1870. Twenty year later, a woman appeared in Panama under that name. While too young to be the earlier Countess, she was the right age to be the Josephine Balsamo from the College. This 1890 Countess romanced Caratal, an important witness in the Canal scandal. Following his disappearance under highly unusual circumstances, there was speculation that the Countess betrayed his movements to the conspirators behind the swindle. Previously, in April 1889, a woman only identified as 'the Countess' allegedly ruined General Boulanger's political career by convincing him to flee France after his indictment for treason."

"These are cases of high finance and politics, Mademoiselle. We are dealing now with a murderous lunatic."

"Josephine Balsamo could be playing a complicated game for higher stakes. Months after Boulanger's disgrace, she visited her former school. The College Girl Murders commenced following her departure."

"Mademoiselle, you are the one playing games. You have been seeking to divert me from my primary inquiry. I have made two accusations, and you have yet to answer them. Are you Jacques Saillard? Are you Irene, Louis Fourneau's sixth victim?"

"Regarding the first charge, no. I met the real Jacques Saillard two years ago in Berlin. Otto Klein, the sugar magnate, engaged the Chupin Detective Agency to prevent his wedding reception from being disrupted by burglars. The bride introduced me to Jacques Saillard, and I posed for him. Isadora Klein later hired the Agency to assist in the selling of his work. As I said, I'm not at liberty to reveal Saillard's identity, but Madame Klein is. She arrived in Paris yesterday and is a guest of the Royal Palace Hotel. If I explain the circumstances in a letter that you can present to her, she will likely disclose his whereabouts."

"There still remains the matter of Irene. Irina is the Russian form of Irene... You talked about anagrams earlier. Your current surname is a virtual anagram of Tupin. In other languages, your surname would be spelt without an 'e.' The extra letter is essential in French to mimic the Russian pronunciation."

"Are you not forgetting a blatant fact, Inspector? Irene's hands were horribly severed. I have a pair of hands, as you can plainly see."

"Yet, you always wear gloves, Mademoiselle. I have heard rumors of great advances in the creation of artificial limbs. Someone may even be able to paint with such appendages. I would like you to remove your gloves."

"You're dangerously close to becoming offensive, Inspector, but I will comply."

Irina doffed her gloves. She displayed a set of perfectly formed human hands.

"You may wish to touch them to make sure that they are real. You have my permission."

She rose from behind her desk and then presented her hands to the Inspector. He felt them and concluded that they were surely not synthetic.

"Now that I have acceded to your ridiculous demand, Inspector, please let me write the letter."

At the Royal Palace Hotel, d'Andresy requested an interview with Madame Klein. It was granted by the raven-haired socialite.

"I hope that you were not too upset by Irina's refusal to disclose Jacques Saillard's identity, Inspector," said Madame Klein after having read the letter. "She was bound by promises of secrecy."

"I overstepped, Madame. I falsely accused Mademoiselle Putine of being Saillard."

"That is ironic. Irina told me that she had been an artist in her youth. But she's abandoned such pursuits to join the Chupin Detective Agency." Then, she added: "I understand the gravity of the situation, Inspector. I will answer all your questions, but you must promise not to make my answers public if they clear Saillard of all suspicion."

"Your terms are acceptable. Who is Jacques Saillard?"

"I am. I use a pseudonym to overcome the prejudices of male art critics. My first painting was a self-portrait."

As Isadora Klein was in Berlin during all of the killings except the last, d'Andresy returned to police headquarters. He reviewed the files on the College Girl Murders. They contained information on Anatole Cerral, a surgeon who advocated outlandish medical procedures. He had treated the injured Irene.

The Inspector retired to his home in the Rue St. Claude. There, he removed the fake wig and beard as well as the glasses that hid his true appearance, that of a much younger man. He then perused a series of papers in which the name of Raoul d'Andresy appeared very frequently.

Among these papers was the birth certificate of Arsène Lupin.

The same night, Irina Putine was conferring with a middle-aged woman inside her office at the Chupin Detective Agency. The lady was her mother, Victoire. There existed a strong degree of resentment in Irina towards her mother, due to events in the past. As a result, they rarely saw each other. But now, the circumstances demanded it.

"I have asked you here because I need information about Papa,"said Irene. "He was more than just a professor of gymnastics."

Victoire did not respond.

"He was Lothaire Stepphun," asserted Irina.

"How did you discover that?"

"Your earlier association with the Werewolves. Lothaire Stepphun is an anagram of Théophraste Lupin. I believe the daughter of one of Papa's enemies has been using anagrams, too, for her own purposes."

"Who are you talking about?"

"Before I disclose her identity, we need to have an open discussion of a certain event in 1880. The theft of the reconstituted Queen's Necklace from the Dreux-Soubise. Uncle Victor briefed me about that affair, I know Raoul stole the necklace and gave it to Papa..."

"I don't want to talk about this."

"Neither do I, but it's relevant to my current line of investigation. I do have but one question, anyway. Did anyone try to steal the necklace from Papa?"

"Yes, there was this woman who posed as a purchaser for the gems. I never knew her name, but she belonged to the Black Coats. They attacked your father. One of his paramours stabbed her. I later heard that she died of her wounds."

Victoire's revelation enabled Irene to grasp Josephine's scheme. The dead woman must have been her mother, the 1870 Countess Cagliostro, who likely had coveted the Queen's Necklace because of its connection to her ancestor, Count Cagliostro. The current Josephine had been orchestrating a complex scheme of vengeance against the Lupin family in order to avenge her mother's death. Irene's own debasement at the School was merely part of this vendetta.

"Mama, did Papa commit that murder in 1893 that led to his death in New York?"

"No, your father was a thief and a swindler, but he wasn't a murderer. Evidence was fabricated against him by one of his enemies."

"Probably by the Black Coats. The daughter of the woman who was stabbed in 1880 is behind it all, Mama. Her name is Josephine Balsamo."

"Josephine Balsamo! Arsène never mentioned any connection between her and the Queen's Necklace."

"Arsène! What does he have to do with her?"

"Oh! I shouldn't have said anything. I'm sorry, but I can't tell you. Arsène swore me to secrecy."

"Oh really, Mama, we shouldn't keep secrets from each other. We're one happy family," said Irene sarcastically. "I keep my distance from Arsène, but I have followed the news about him. He lives in Normandy with his wife, Clarisse. What's the problem? Were he and Josephine lovers?"

"Stop it! I agreed to conceal from him that you're back in France. He still thinks you're in England. In exchange, you're not to bother me about him. Why can't you make peace with him? Do you realize that you haven't seen him for 11 years?"

"But we must discuss it, Mama. I will not have you place his interests over mine, your own blood. Now, tell me. I want to know what happened between Arsène and Josephine."

But Victoire remained silent.

The next day, a letter bearing the Clio Gosart signature was received at *L'Echo de France*. The police were immediately notified that Bluebeard was about to strike again.

Maurice d'Andresy informed Chief Inspector Lefevre that there were only two of Jacques Saillard's models left in Paris: Isadora Klein and Irina Putine. Although the real Saillard had been cleared, the two policemen still agreed that the killer was targeting his models.

The pair formulated a strategy to protect the two ladies. Lefevre would take a squad of policemen to shield Madame Klein. Meanwhile, d'Andresy would bring Irina to that same location.

When d'Andresy arrived at the Chupin Detective Agency, Irina was attired in a comparable fashion as the day before, except that her dress was dark red. He requested that she accompany him to a safehouse guarded by the Sûreté. His request was quickly rebuffed.

"I'll be safer here surrounded by my own operatives," argued Irina. "I'm convinced that you and your colleagues have been grossly incompetent so far."

"You're acting like a fool, Mademoiselle. Is there anything that I could do to persuade you to change your mind?"

"Being a member of the d'Andresy, you must know about their affairs. There's a connection between Raoul d'Andresy and Josephine Balsamo. If you can tell me what it is, I'll accompany you."

"Agreed, but I will only divulge it en route to the safehouse."

"I will accept that condition, but I'll add one of my own. We'll use the cab maintained by the Chupin Detective Agency. If I find that you're supplying me with either false or incomplete information, I'll order the cab to return us here."

The Inspector assented to Irina's request. Irina carried a large handbag with her into the carriage. Entering the cab, the Inspector gave the driver an address in the Rue St. Claude.

"I await your information," stated Irina.

"Raoul d'Andresy first met Josephine Balsamo two years ago..."

"Please call your cousin by his real name: Arsène Lupin."

"If we're dropping aliases, then we should do the same with yours. I've read about Dr. Cerral's controversial experimentation with hand transplants. [4] Your bracelets cover surgical scars."

"Then there is no need to engage in further subterfuge. I am indeed Irene."

"Josephine seduced your half-brother in order to turn him into her lieutenant in crime."

Irina silently concluded that Josephine had devised an elaborate strategy of revenge against the children of Théophraste Lupin. Josephine had recruited Théophraste's offspring as an expendable pawn to be liquidated at her leisure.

"Are they still partners, Inspector?"

"No, Arsène turned against her."

"Tell me the truth now. If you don't, I'll turn this cab around. How do you know all this?

"I am Arsène Lupin, sister," he admitted with a sigh. "I went to Louisiana to help my cousin, the real Maurice d'Andresy, pursue the leader of the smugglers. Maurice caught pneumonia and died. I assumed his identity."

"Intriguing. Have you been misbehaving?"

"I have formed an organization somewhat similar to the old Werewolves."

"Let us return to Josephine. Did your affair with her occur after your marriage to Clarisse?"

"It happened before. That was a very impertinent question, sister!"

"Consider it just retribution, brother. You asked me several rude queries yesterday."

"My truculence was motivated by a sense of shame. My own inquiries unearthed all the nasty details of your conduct at Madame Fourneau's boarding school."

"Do you realize, brother, that I am being judged morally unfit by a man who just confessed to be the leader of a criminal fraternity? The question is not

---

[4] See "Dr. Cerral's Patient", q.v.

whether we are brother and sister of the flesh, but rather brother and sister of the spirit. Both our souls have been tainted by Josephine Balsamo."

The cab arrived at its destination, Rue St. Claude. Irina ordered it to return to the Detective Agency. As they entered the house, the cabdriver noticed that Irina waved goodbye to him with three fingers.

Across the street, there was another cab. A man and a woman sat inside.

"The mousetrap has been sprung, Herr Mabuse," commented the female.

"One Lupin sibling will destroy the other, Fraulein Lipsius," predicted her male companion.

Inside the house, Maurice and Irina entered a large living room. Irina's back was briefly turned to her companion.

"I have a difficult decision to make, brother." She quickly turned around after taking something out of her purse. She was holding a pistol and pointing it at Maurice.

"Sister, what are you doing?"

"I am debating whether I should kill you now or turn you over to the authorities, brother. You told me a pack of lies and half-truths in the cab."

"I told you the truth!"

"Josephine Balsamo is still your lover! You're still in partnership with her!"

"That's not true! I love Clarisse!"

"You weren't in Louisiana assisting the real Inspector d'Andresy to chase the chief smuggler, brother! You were the ringleader! Your only truthful assertion was about the assumption of the genuine Inspector's identity when he perished from pneumonia."

"Sister, you're letting your resentment against me warp your judgment! Can't you see Josephine's scheme? She started the Bluebeard murders to reawaken your rancor towards me! Her aim is for you to murder me!"

"Brother, have you ever read *Le Vicomte de Bragelonne?*"

"Have you lost your mind, sister? Do you want to turn our conversation into a literary discussion?"

"Answer the question!" demanded Irina.

"Of course, I have. It's a famous book by Alexandre Dumas."

"Doesn't it concern Louis XIV and his twin brother, the Man in the Iron Mask?"

"Yes, but I don't understand why you're bringing that up now!"

"The man incarcerated in the Ville-d'Avray asylum wrote *Louis* twice for seven rows. In other words, he wrote *Louis* 14 times! The same inmate also wrote the words *Je m'abuse.*, which evoke the alias of Jan Gosart known as Jan Mabuse because he came from Maubeuge, a city in Flanders. Maubeuge is the name of the asylum director..."

"Surely Maubeuge would have deduced the contents of this alleged message. Why show it to you?"

"Maubeuge didn't show it to me, brother; a visiting physician Doctor Biron, did. In Dumas' novel, conspirators replace Louis XIV with his twin. Maubeuge works for Josephine Balsamo, alias Clio Gosart. So he replaced Louis Fourneau with a look-alike–his own brother, Philippe Maubeuge must have abducted him in Switzerland and transported him to the asylum, keeping away the outside world, except that the prisoner wrote that cryptic message, hoping that it would be deciphered by someone. Philippe didn't commit suicide, Maubeuge murdered him because an accomplice in the French police was about to reveal the family connection between the College Girl Murderer and Gaston Morrell!"

"Maubeuge may be a killer, Irina, but I had nothing to do with the death of that inmate!"

"Au contraire, you had everything to do with it, brother. I have been calling you 'brother' not because we're brother and sister in the flesh, but because we're brother and sister in the spirit. Both our souls were corrupted at the same boarding school. For you're not Arsène Lupin! You're Louis Fourneau! Bluebeard"

The man posing as Maurice d'Andresy took off his wig, false beard and tinted spectacles. The face of a handsome man with brown hair was revealed. He looked exactly like the cadaver at the Ville-d'Avray asylum.

"It's been a long time, Louis," announced Irina. "You went to New Orleans after your liberation from the asylum. You used the Inspector's pneumonia to mask your own asthma. You must have diverted the police into guarding Isadora."

"Lefevre is at her hotel."

"Very clever. But your ploy to pose as Arsène was inconsistent with your behavior yesterday. The true Arsène would never refer to his beloved Victoire as a 'prostitute,' or a 'stupid woman,' even in the middle of a masquerade."

Louis Fourneau let the pieces of his disguise drop to the floor.

"The usurpation of my brother's identity was intended to lure me into this house, but it hints at a more complex motivation for your crimes," continued Irina. "The name Arsène Lupin has yet to be attached to any significant crimes. I believe Josephine's plot is to blame him for the Bluebeard murders. If I'm killed, the police would follow the trail here. There must be evidence in these premises that Inspector d'Andresy is Arsène Lupin in disguise. The traditional method of the Black Coats to *pay the law* by framing an innocent would spring shut, and my brother would be latched on by the authorities as a convenient scapegoat. Do you take pride, Louis, in butchering five innocent women as part of such an elaborate charade?"

"It's your own fault, Irene, that those ladies were strangled. Josephine only traced your present identity a few months ago when she saw Saillard's portrait of you at the home of its owner, Noel Moriarty. Besides the resemblance, she recognized the pentagram brooch. After some inquiries in the art galleries of Paris, she uncovered your alias at the Chupin Detective Agency. She was under the misapprehension that you were Saillard, but the real facts still fit her false scenario: Arsène was driven to murder by his sister's connection to scandalous paintings. You have only yourself to blame for those deaths."

"You argue like your mother, Louis. You always blame the victims for the abuse that you unleash upon them, and some are all too ready to take it. Josephine gave me this brooch to ensure my blind subservience. I wear it to remind myself never to behave like such a fool again."

"In that case, my dear Irene, you have failed in your purpose," shouted a new voice. "I also gave that brooch to mock your early ignorance of your father's secret life. My gift is the sign of the werewolf, but you have transformed it into a badge of imbecility."

Josephine Balsamo, wearing her customary green dress and holding a gun in her right hand, stood behind Irina, the barrel of her weapon pressed against the back of the detective's head.

Taking Irina's gun and handbag from her hands, Fourneau deposited the articles on a nearby table.

"I've been an idiot!" confessed Irina. "This house is in the Rue St. Claude, where the original Cagliostro lived. It must have been part of a string of buildings that he secretly owned and equipped with secret passages."

"I still remember when you refused to accept their existence."

"This is a rare occurrence for you, Josephine. You usually don't take a direct role in your murders. The Black Coats have trained you well, as you tried to train Arsène, but I understand he's started his own competing gang. Your colleagues must not be too happy with that fact."

"You should be more concerned with your brother's carelessness," retorted Josephine. "A spy inside Arsène's gang has assured us that he has no alibi for the murders. The intense scrutiny following the discovery of your corpse will cripple his syndicate and send him to the guillotine."

"Enough of this talk!" yelled Fourneau. "I have been waiting a long time to become reacquainted with Irene."

"Louis has always been frustrated by the fact," said Josephine, "that when I designated you as the final victim in the College Girl Murders, I had specifically instructed him to avoid killing you during the mutilation."

"Why did you order that?" asked Irina. "Did you want me to bleed to death?"

"If you really must know, Irene, dear, I was hoping that the loss of your precious artistic hands would drive you insane."

"My sanity remains intact!"

"Are you sure? There are times when you act most irrationally."

"Josephine, stop bickering!" exclaimed Fourneau. "Let me get on with my work!"

"If you must, Louis, do what you do best!" said Josephine as she backed away from Irina.

Fourneau removed his tie. "I really want to slit your throat, Irene, but such a procedure would upset the standards established by my uncle..."

Fourneau threw the tie around Irina's neck and started to pull. As the girl gasped for breath, Josephine lowered her gun.

Irina grabbed her pentagram brooch and pulled it from her dress. She stuck the uppermost point of the star into the middle of Fourneau's throat and pulled the brooch across his neck. The murderer released his hold on the tie and fell to the ground with a severed jugular.

Josephine raised her gun. Irina swung forward. She slashed her enemy's hand with the point of her brooch. Shouting in pain, Josephine dropped the gun. Irina grabbed her by the throat and pushed her against the wall. Irina now held the uppermost point of the pentagram against Josephine's neck.

"You seem to be at a loss for words, Josephine, dear. Do you admire how the points of your gift have been sharpened like razors? I could cut your throat, but I wish to work within the law. I will be happy to see you dispatched by the guillotine, but first there's something I must do. Because of you, I was branded as a thief. The least I can do now is to return the favor."

Irina pulled Josephine by the nape of her neck and slammed her against the wall. The blonde slumped to the floor, a stream of blood running from a gash in her forehead. Removing her scarf, Irina bound Josephine's feet. She used Fourneau's neck-tie to secure her hands. She then retrieved her handbag, took out its contents and performed a certain act upon her unconscious foe.

Irina then searched the house. Locating the birth certificate and other papers that implicated her brother in the murders, she burned them in a fireplace. Irina had no love for Arsène. Her destruction of evidence was motivated by self-interest. An investigation of Arsène would reveal too many secrets from her own past.

Leaving the house, she walked three blocks before finding the cab from the Chupin Detective Agency. She had silently signaled the driver with her hand to wait that distance from the building. She told the man to take a message to Lefevre at the Royal Palace Hotel, to inform him that Bluebeard now lay dead at Inspector d'Andresy's residence.

After dispatching the driver, Irina returned to the house. To her consternation, she discovered that Josephine was missing. Only the corpse of Louis Fourneau remained.

Irina greeted Lefevre when the police arrived at the Rue St. Claude. The Bertillon measurements confirmed the identity of the false Inspector d'Andresy. Irina never mentioned the name of Arsène Lupin. At her suggestion, Lefevre had the handwriting of the Clio Gosart letters compared with certain archives that the Avignon authorities had salvaged from the aftermath of the College Girl

Murders. A warrant was issued for Josephine Balsamo's arrest, but she was never apprehended for her role in the Bluebeard crimes.

Dr. Maubeuge never reappeared at the Ville-d'Avray asylum. He left France to seek refuge in another country.

In *Van Klopen, Tailleur pour Dames*, there was an area called the Alteration Room. There, tailoring mistakes were corrected and clothes were altered to fit patrons. The room contained various knitting devices, ironing implements and branding tools.

There, Josephine Balsamo now stood before Madame Koluchy, Helen Lipsius and Mary Holder. Her forehead and right hand were bandaged. At Madame Koluchy's insistence, she wore the same dress from the Rue St. Claude.

"This is a formal hearing," said Madame Koluchy. "There will be no Christian names or self-bestowed titles of nobility employed here, is that understood, Mademoiselle Balsamo?"

"Yes, Madame," answered Josephine.

"Mabuse's cab was assigned to transport Putine's corpse to the Seine. Instead, he found you tied up like a calf. Do you acknowledge this?"

"Yes, Madame."

"You also appear to have been branded. There are marks on the shoulders of your favorite dress, drawn with ink. What are those marks, Mademoiselle?"

"They are both the letter 'V,' Madame."

"What, in your opinion, is the significance of that letter?"

"It stands for *voleuse*, Madame," Josephine replied, using the French word for *thief*.

"Your two friends here lack the benefit of a strong education in French history. You have expertise in this area. Explain to them the historical significance of those marks."

"Jeanne de La Motte was punished by being branded with these marks."

"They are the marks of a thief, are they not?"

"Yes, Madame."

"Do you confess that you have stolen from the Brotherhood, Mademoiselle?"

"I have stolen nothing, Madame."

"You have stolen the Brotherhood's dominant position in France by accidentally creating a major competitor in Arsène Lupin. You have stolen the opportunity to rectify that mistake by allowing yourself to be outwitted by Irina Putine. You are a thief, Mademoiselle Balsamo."

"I am a thief, Madame."

"Those marks are an appropriate punishment."

"These marks are an appropriate punishment, Madame."

"Remove your dress, Mademoiselle Balsamo, and give it to Mademoiselle Lipsius. An alteration clearly needs to be performed."

Josephine complied with Madame Koluchy's commands and handed her dress to Helen.

"Mademoiselle Lipsius, please examine the dress in order to duplicate those marks on a softer and more delicate surface," commanded Madame Koluchy. "Mademoiselle Holder, please assist me in ensuring that the surface in question remains stationary during the duplication."

Josephine saw the three other women rise from their seats and advance towards her.

"This can't be your wish, Madame!" pleaded Josephine.

"No, it is *your* wish, Mademoiselle Balsamo."

Some minutes later, the Alteration Room was filled with the screams of Josephine Balsamo.

In addition to being the talented author of The League of Heroes *and other novels and a contributor to* Tales of the Shadowmen, *Xavier Mauméjean (whose story comes after this one, in alphabetical order) also co-edits the* Bibliothèque Rouge, *a series of French anthologies mixing articles, timelines and original stories devoted to fictional characters such as Arsène Lupin, Sherlock Holmes, Fantômas, etc. The following tale was written for his forthcoming volume devoted to Hercule Poirot and finds the Belgian detective with his first Mystery From Outer Space...*

Jean-Marc Lofficier: *The Murder of Randolph Carter*

Ghent, 1928

My friend Hercule Poirot had come to spend a few days in Ghent to relax and reacquaint himself with the warm atmosphere of a town he had often visited during his youth.

Acting upon my recommendation, he had booked a room at the Pension Doucedame, Rue du Vieux Chantier, an old but respectable lodging house.

Alas, as increasingly happened to him these days, the horrible specter of crime haunted his every step, even in our beautiful city.

An American tourist named Randolph Carter was found murdered in the library one grey morning. And what a murder it was! The victim's body appeared to have been torn apart by some unfathomable monster who had vented its anger on him; his face reflected only unspeakable terror.

My friend's reputation preceded him; his crime-solving exploits during the Great War were still fresh in the minds of the Belgian Police; the investigation was entrusted to him in the hope he would quickly find the murderer and thus help calm the protests of the American Consulate.

After a week of arduous investigation, often thwarted by the lies and contradictory statements of the suspects–three other Americans who had arrived at the Pension soon after Mr. Carter–Poirot gathered us all in the library in the presence of Inspector Owen to inform us of his conclusions.

Everyone's attention was focused upon the detective as we all waited for his definitive solution to the murder of Randolph Carter.

"*Ph'nglui mglw'nafh Cthulhu R'lyeh, n'est-ce-pas, wagn'nagl fhtegn! Aaaaiiiiii!*" said Poirot, holding in his hand a copy of Quentin Moretus Cassave's renowned Flemish translation of the *Necronomicon*.

"*Fhtagn*," corrected Charles Dexter Ward.

"*Pardon?*" said Poirot.

Hercule Poirot
by Daylon (2006)

"*Fhtagn*," said Dexter Ward. "It's pronounced *Fhtagn*. I can't understand you with your damned French accent."

Poirot shook his head in irritation.

"*Fhtegn*. That is just what I said, Monsieur Ward. Please, pay attention. This book, a 17th century edition, once part of the Comte d'Erlette's collection, a fine example of Belgian engraving, it is one of your obsessions, *non*? You can recite entire passages from memory. You and Monsieur Carter had both come to Ghent to negotiate the purchase of this rare book. But Monsieur Carter, he arrives a few days early and he buys the book before you. You are upset, *naturellement*, but you repress your anger and you go and talk to Monsieur Carter in this very room where we stand. You offer to buy the book from him for twice the amount he paid. He refuses. The anger, it becomes very strong. Then, you suggest that you should combine your expertise and exploit the book together. He turns you down again. And then, you learn that Monsieur Carter, he has bought the book with only one purpose: to burn it!"

The audience shivered with palpable surprise.

"I found a *briquet à amadou* in Monsieur Carter's pocket, a lighter powerful enough to produce a strong flame. Look at the corner of the book, here. The binding is charred. So Monsieur Carter, he was trying to burn the book, but he did not succeed. Why? I blame the damp that pervades this house," he said, throwing an unkind glance at Monsieur Doucedame, our hotelier. "Still, one fact leads to another. When you find out his purpose, you become furious. I made inquiries about you, Monsieur Ward. It seems you are afflicted with a serious personality disorder. You are subject to violent episodes during which even your friends, they say they do not recognize you..."

"I suffer from some gastric problems, yes," said Ward dismissively. "I have a sensitive stomach. What has that to do with this case?"

"*Eh bien*, when Monsieur Carter, he reveals his intentions to you, you become overpowered by your insane passion and you grab the first thing at hand, this Arumbaya fetish, and then, you strike!"

"You have no proof of that!"

"*Au contraire*! In your rage, you break a piece of the ear of the fetish, a piece that I found in your coat pocket later."

"You dirty, lying, Belgian weasel," screamed Ward, while being dragged away by Inspector Owen's men.

I thought that, because of his political connections, he would be quickly extradited and would not have to suffer Belgian jails for long.

"This nightmare is finally over," said Lavinia Whateley. "Thank you, Monsieur Poirot."

"I fear, Madame, that it has only begun."

The young woman blanched, if that was at all possible considering her extremely pale complexion. She was seven months pregnant and had told the Police she had come to Ghent for the waters. When apprised of the fact that there was no thermal source in our beautiful town, she had merely replied she had been misinformed.

I was no MD but her belly seemed abnormally large. I also could have sworn–but no doubt it was a trick of the light caused by the dimness of the *lampes à quinquet* that lit the Pension–that I'd seen it tremble and quiver, as if under a pressure exerted by some inhuman thing incubating inside.

"The nightmare of a young mother alone, pregnant with a child whose father is unknown," continued Poirot. "Please note, Madame, that I do not judge the scandalous behavior of a certain depraved American youth. Undoubtedly, you were the victim of some fiendish Oriental drug. A man, most evil, took advantage of your passivity... Your body barely conscious, pliant, supple, ready to yield to his bestial transports..."

Poirot's eyes glazed over, becoming lost in the distance. No doubt, his little grey cells were actively gathering clues, working to solve this baffling mystery.

"Poirot!" said Inspector Owen.

"*Ah oui, je m'excuse*," he said, batting his eyes. "The nightmare, as I was saying, of a young mother alone, pregnant, who fears to lose the inheritance she is counting on to provide for herself and her child!"

"Heavens! How did you know this?"

"*Très simple, Chère Madame*. Your cousin, Wilbur Whateley, he dies recently in a hunting accident. Normally, you would inherit his vast fortune. But then, you receive a letter from Monsieur Carter informing you that he, too, is a cousin of Wilbur. And according to the antiquated laws of the State of Massachusetts, it is the male cousin who inherits! So you take the first ship for Belgium where you know Monsieur Carter is going–I checked the passengers manifest of the *John Flanders*–because you want to plead your cause in person. At first, Monsieur Carter, he seems reasonable. He is ready to abandon the inheritance. *Mais voila*: he puts a condition to his offer. A horrible condition. I do not dare to repeat it here, but you know what I am talking about, do you not, Madame Whateley?"

The gesture of the young woman, clutching her hands over her stomach to protect her unborn child, answered more clearly than any of Poirot's remarks might have. I even thought I heard a hiss of rage that sent Murr, the Pension cat, slithering out of the room, but it was more likely the wind gusting through the fireplace.

"That night, your decision is taken," continued my friend. "You know that Monsieur Carter, he likes to nap alone in the library after dinner. You walk down very softly, armed with this three-pronged garden weeder that I later found hidden in the tropical fish aquarium. There, you find Monsieur Carter, battered by Monsieur Ward, but still breathing. And you strike, with all the ferocity of a mother seeking to protect her child!"

Inspector Owen's men took Lavinia Whateley down to the station. The woman was in tears and I knew that no jury, be it Flemish or Walloon, would have the heart to condemn the poor child after such an ordeal. No doubt her child would grow up to become an outstanding citizen that would help Belgium project its pacifying influence abroad; a fearless reporter with a tuft of hair, for example...

"Congratulations for a fine piece of crime-solving, Monsieur Poiret."

"*Mais non*, I am not yet finished, Monsieur Marsh. And my name is Poirot, not Poiret or Popeau."

That David Marsh was a strange and repulsive man. A native of the small town of Innsmouth, he had a narrow head, bulging, watery-blue eyes that seemed never to wink, a flat nose, a receding forehead and chin, and singularly undeveloped ears. His skin was rough and scabby, indications that he either suffered from a rare firm of Ichtyosis, or that he was allergic to the *carbonade* drink served by Monsieur Doucedame.

"I had you investigated, Monsieur Marsh," said Poirot gravely. "You and your family are smugglers, pirates, the leaders of a town of pirates and smugglers. Your ships, they bring back drugs, slaves, pagan idols and God knows what else from the Southern Seas. But one man knew of your nefarious traffics: Monsieur Carter, who had gathered in the taverns of Antwerp enough evidence to have you all put under lock and key. Evidence which he was preparing to give to the Federal investigators. You were sent by your accomplices to insure his silence, in the most definitive fashion."

"I protest!"

"Do not interrupt me, Monsieur Marsh. You arrive in the library after Madame Whateley has left. The twin shadow of the Manneken Pis which so puzzled me, it was you! That detail, it confuses me, until I remember how much water you drink with each meal. You come into the library and there, you find Monsieur Carter, writhing in agony but not quite yet dead. Madame Whateley, she is a weak woman. So you see an opportunity to have someone else accused of your crime. You put your hands, your vile, slimy, viscous, strangling hands, around the neck of Monsieur Carter and you squeeze, squeeze, squeeze..."

"Poirot?"

"*Ah oui*, excuse me again, Inspector. Once your sinister task, it is concluded, you go back to the dining room and order your favorite dish, a plate of mussels. But instead of asking for them *à la crème*, as you usually do, you ask for *moules provençales*, a recipe that contains much garlic. Why? Because Monsieur Ward, he has told you of his stomach problems and you are trying to divert the attention, but Poirot, he isn't so easily fooled, *oh non, mon ami*."

"Please, listen to me," said Marsh. "It's true, I did come here to kill Carter, but when I saw the job the other two had done on him, I decided to leave things alone. I didn't lay a finger on him. He was still alive when I left the room."

"You lie, Monsieur Marsh. Only your face–you will excuse me for speaking frankly, your repulsively, obscenely hideous face–can explain the expression of unspeakable horror on the dying Monsieur Carter."

"I'm not hideous! Ask Pht-thyar-l'yi!"

"He is delirious. A typical sign of dissociative personality common amongst murderers. Take him away, Inspector."

"Do you really think he killed Carter?" I asked Poirot after the Police had removed the suspects and we prepared to leave the Pension Doucedame. "He seemed sincere."

"The little grey cells, they do not lie," said Poirot, lightly tapping his forehead. "Once we have eliminated the impossible, then whatever remains is bound to be the truth, even if, as was the case here, it is very strange. Because, if Monsieur Marsh is not the murderer, then the only hypothesis left is that the house itself killed Monsieur Carter; but houses, they do not kill people, *n'est-ce-pas*, Monsieur de Kremer?"

Poirot shut the front door of Malpertuis behind him and together we stepped into the darkened street.

Xavier Mauméjean's contribution to our Madame Atomos *series is a delightful romp that takes place between the last of the original* "Angoisse" *novel and the final book, published much later in the* "Anticipation" *imprint of Fleuve Noir. The '70s were about hair, glitter, drugs, rock 'n' roll, women's rights, flared suits and bell bottoms, and nowhere were they more alive than in London. It is, therefore, in the very heart of the British Empire that Madame Atomos experiences all the excesses of that decade crammed in a single day, a very* bad *single day...*

Xavier Mauméjean: *A Day in the Life of Madame Atomos*

London, 1972

Mayfair, 10:30 a.m.

Madame Atomos woke up.

Ever since her body had been rejuvenated by the effect of her multiple teleportations, she enjoyed life as she had never before done.

She now looked forward to her occasional days off in her posh Mayfair flat. Somehow, the delicacies of life tasted much more succulent since she was once again young.

She felt the silk sheets against her flawless, naked skin as she stretched, and purred like a kitten.

Under the almost scalding water of the shower, she thought about the day ahead.

Check in with the Gardener in Berwick Street. Tea at Biba's. Meeting with Sinclair at the Depository Bank of Zurich in the City. And, of course, the night was full of promise.

Madame Atomos wrapped herself in a yukata kimono and went into the kitchen to make a cup of tea. Lapsang Souchong, naturally.

In moments like these, she valued her privacy, tolerated no interruptions, wanted no servants to interfere with her. Even her loyal, hulking Isadori had been instructed not to disturb her. Madame Atomos wanted to be alone to reflect on her life, and the mayhem and destruction she would soon inflict upon America.

The living room was white. White walls, white carpets, white bamboo screens, white enameled furniture and an original 1918 Malevich White-on-White. Even the London sky was milky white this mid-morning, the sun barely breaking through the cloud cover.

Madame Atomos sipped her tea sitting on a silk cushion while contemplating a *shogi* problem on the low coffee table. She was aiming to disable her opponent's *yagura* defense–perhaps reach a *jishogi*–when, suddenly, a single sound, a *taiko* note, rang clearly and loudly in the room.

Madame Atomos delicately put her cup of tea back on the saucer.

The note rang again

She sighed, then pressed a square on the *shogi* board. A heavily accented Japanese voice that seemed to emanate from nowhere broke into the silence of the room.

"Hai, Mistress! This is Shoichi Yokoi. Hydra Bruderschaft has taken over our secret base in Guam."

Madame Atomos sighed again. Since Baron Strucker's disappearance after Hydra Island sunk, Madame Hydra had done everything she could in the Pacific to rebuild her empire.

"Madame Hydra will want to avoid scrutiny; they will remain discreet. Do you have a cover story?"

"Yes, Mistress," said the voice. "I will say that I spent 28 years in the jungle because I didn't know Japan had lost the war. The foolish *gaijin* will swallow anything."

"Very well. It is but a minor setback. Hiroshima and Nagasaki will be avenged."

"Hiroshima, Nagasaki! *Hai!*"

The silence returned.

Now, her morning had been spoiled, thought Madame Atomos. Should she do some *Sahaja Yoga* before going out? No, it was getting late already.

As she got up, a *shuriken* star whizzed by her face. Madame Atomos plucked it from the air, while diving to avoid two more deadly stars. In a graceful *zhong chui* gesture, she then threw it back at the Si-Fan ninja who had crawled down from the roof onto her balcony. The black-clad warrior collapsed, dead.

Madame Atomos glanced distractedly at the corpse, whom Isadori would get rid of later. Fah Lo Suee did not share in her father's misplaced idealism, but unlike him, she decidedly had no sense of humor, she thought.

She grabbed one of the *shuriken* planted in the wall and walked into a small, adjacent office. Isadori had left some mail for her on her desk. She used the star to slice open the envelopes.

The first was an invitation to a party from Derek Flint. A highly talented man who seemed to know virtually everything, including how to talk to dolphins. He wished to present his latest piano sonata.

Madame Atomos decided to go. Flint was, like herself, a pragmatist–and therefore, not to be trusted–but his sense of style was impeccable. Besides, it would be an opportunity to try that new Paco Rabanne original made up of tiny metal pieces.

Then, there was a letter bearing a familiar design. Madame Atomos sniffed it before opening it. She detected the faint odor of spikenard. It was poisoned of course. She nevertheless opened it. Anyone but she would have been dead within seconds.

Sumuru wished to discuss their respective interests over tea at the Reform Club. I think not, thought Madame Atomos. She needed Sumuru's help like she needed more mutated Teraphosa spider eggs. She would not go. She carefully incinerated the letter. It would not do for Isadori to find it. Good servants were hard to clone.

Having disposed of the day's mail, Madame Atomos dressed and went out.

As she stepped into her Rolls Sedanca de Ville, she noticed the odd couple outside: the dandy with the bowler hat and the umbrella she knew to be deadly, and the seemingly daft-looking girl with the Mary Quant mini-skirt and leather boots dressed straight out of a Carnaby Street shop window.

Mother is sniffing around, she thought. She might have to sell her flat and move. Again.

Soho, 1 p.m.

The Gardener–no one knew his real name–had a small, unremarkable shop off Berwick Street.

The market was still going strong. Madame Atomos stopped at a stall selling fresh eggs. She had more botulism germs in inventory than she knew what to do with. Perhaps... But no, another time.

She walked into the store. It was full of glass jars, amphoras and barrels filled to the brim with roots, exotic seeds and other mixed herbs. The ambient smell was that of compost. The stuff on display was quite harmless, of course, but the Gardener liked to discourage visits. The real goods were not even in the back shop, but in the secret cellars beneath.

The Gardener had promised Madame Atomos a brand new type of Black Lotus, cross-bred with a particularly elusive kind of Blood Orchid found only in Pnom Dhek.

The Gardener, unfortunately, would no longer delight anyone with the fruits of his inventive genius. He was dead, his body wrinkled like an old prune.

Madame Atomos bent over and examined the cadaver. Not that she needed to. She recognized the mark of Alouh T'ho. Madame Atomos was a scientist who had long since stopped believing in the fairy tales of her childhood, but at that instant, she wished all the dire fates the *Oni* could be visited upon the ex-Chinese Empress.

There was nothing more to do here. Either Alouh T'ho had stolen the new Black Lotus for her collection, or she had destroyed it, making sure no one would produce a new one. It was hard to tell which.

In any event, thought Madame Atomos, her plans to plunge Hawaii into madness were now moot.

She sighed. This day was not turning out to be that good after all. But she had had worse.

She derived a modicum of consolation from cleverly avoiding being recognized by Clarissa de Courtney-Scott as the red-haired, murderous nymphomaniac walked into the alley.

Kensington High Street, 4 p.m.

The rejuvenated Madame Atomos loved wandering around Biba's. She loved getting ideas from the great ambiance, buying fab clothes and makeup, and always grabbed something to eat upstairs; it made her feel like she was part of the "in" London scene—even though she wasn't really part of any scene.

The bullet that had earlier crashed onto the special glass that made up the tinted windows of her Rolls had had her name on it. She knew who had fired it of course. Well, she would deal with Greta Morgan later. What she really needed now was that elusive moment of peace and fun that had eluded her all day.

Unfortunately, a tall, beautiful Eurasian woman came from behind and grabbed her arm.

"What amazing luck," said Tania Orloff. "We must have tea! Come on! I shan't take no for an answer!"

A long, two hours later, Madame Atomos managed to escape from Tania. She had seriously considered poisoning her, but she was working with her uncle on a new breed of deadly butterflies, soon to be tested in Africa; the murder of his favorite niece would cast a pall on the enterprise.

She had also fleetingly considered poisoning herself, rather than continue listening to Tania's long rambling stories about her unrequited love for that French prig; a man who had been responsible for the death of Madame Atomos' protégé, the "Samurai of a Thousand Suns."

Tea with Tania Orloff was enough to drive anyone to suicide.

The City, 8 p.m.

Night had fallen and some remnants of the once-mighty London fog were slowly creeping into the narrow streets of its financial district.

Isadori had returned to tell Madame Atomos that her plan to appropriate the Pink Panther diamond had failed. The Black Lizard had gotten to it before her own force could move in to execute her carefully planned scheme.

Madame Atomos consoled herself with the notion that the stone was cursed. It would serve her rival right.

She was lost in dark thoughts of revenge and failed to see Sinclair emerging from the darkness. The little banker handled all of Madame Atomos' financial assets in Europe. They never met in his office, of course, but in this quiet back alley, after everyone had gone home.

She also failed to see the tall figure, dressed in a ragged coat and a floppy hat, shamble out of the fog.

Two crimson eyes blazed death and struck Sinclair.

Madame Atomos
by Jean-Michel Ponzio (2005)

At once, the small man, the only one who knew the numbers to all of her secret bank accounts, collapsed in a pile of unattractive charred remains.

Madame Atomos sighed, for the umpteenth time that day.

Two metal plates she had carefully reengineered on her original Paco Rabanne dress produced a deadly burst of disintegrating rays. She only felt a pleasant tingle on her nipples, but the small dacoit who carried the death-ray apparatus harnessed on his shoulders half-vanished, leaving behind a foul-smelling carcass of entrails and blood.

Madame Atomos cursed Miss Ylang-Ylang. The leader of the international cartel known as SMOG had obviously not forgiven her for pilfering some of their secrets after SMOG's failed "Operation Dark Knight" orbital misadventure.

She would deal with SMOG later.

It had been a miserable experience, but she would rebuild, as always.

Now, she had a party to attend.

Ladbroke Grove, 11 p.m.

Madame Atomos arrived suitably late at Flint's party. It was well underway. The band was playing Alkan's *Symphony for Solo Piano Number Four* to waltz-time.

She waved at Catherine Cornelius, avoided Mephista, made small talk with Mrs. Butterworth and danced with Vic St. Val.

All in all, her definition of fun.

Then, it happened.

The outrage. The embarrassment. The crushing blow. The final humiliation in an otherwise abominable and dismal day.

Modesty Blaise entered, Willie Garvin on her arm

She was wearing the very same Paco Rabanne dress as she!

The bitch, thought Madame Atomos.

She stamped her feet and walked out.

The world will pay, she cursed. *Oh, how they will!*

Paul d'Ivoi (1856-1915) was the first to be the second (or third or fourth...) on the block after Jules Verne. As a result, he is somewhat neglected today, even though valiant publishers periodically try to reissue some of his novels; his best-remembered being Les Cinq Sous de Lavarère, *a rip-off of Verne's* Around the World in 80 Days. *Doctor Mystère is d'Ivoi's own version of Captain Nemo, and would be mostly forgotten today were it not Alfredo Castelli's (yes, the same Castelli from earlier in this volume) brilliant idea of making his world-famous comic-book hero Martin Mystère a descendent of Cigale, Docteur Mystère's teenage sidelick. David McIntee, a name well-known to* Doctor Who *fans, decided to tell a story featuring Docteur Mystère in Bollywood...*

David A. McIntee: *Bullets Over Bombay*

India, 1896

I had read, in many spiffing adventure stories, of characters experiencing "thunderous silences" and the like, and had never believed that such a thing was even remotely possible. Until that day, when two Colt single-action Navy pistols fell silent, with a shock that startled me, and made me whirl round to see what was happening.

I am afraid I am somewhat getting ahead of myself, and for that I must beg your forgiveness, for the telling of tales–no, let me rephrase that, lest it imply tall tales and lies–storytelling, is not as natural a profession to me as is the hunting of great cats. Oh, tiger-hunting is not a profession I had sought out–far from it–but when the Service wanted someone to help out with a man-eater some years ago, they knew I was something of a sharpshooter back in the 95th, and requested my skills. We had staked out a goat near a watering hole–this was down by Panaji, by the way–and shot the beast quite easily when it came to feed. There was no question that it was the man-eater, as several local men had previously wounded it in self-defense, and this animal bore the identical scars. At any rate, from that moment, my rather dubious destiny was assured: whenever there was cat trouble, which happens a couple of times a year, I would be given a brief leave of absence and seconded to help out with the hunt.

But, I'm sorry, now I fear I have gone too far back rather than too far ahead; I can see it on your face. Please forgive me. I'll send the Boy for another round; that should help loosen the tongue.

Where was I? Ah, of course, the "thunderous silence" matter. Dashed queer business, all told. It started the night the Lumière brothers brought that–what do you call it? their magic lantern show–along to Bombay.

I had heard about it, of course; the stories say that people in Europe and American ran screaming from displays of their work, when they thought that steam engines were charging through the portable theaters. Nothing like that happened here, I must say. Indeed, the exhibitions of this almost magical new medium were met with wonder and amazement to be sure, but also with a certain amount of calculation. The Indians as a people are quite diligent and ambitious, and I shouldn't wonder if before too long they have outstripped the *Frères* Lumière and their ilk in this new art form.

The *Frères* Lumière were not alone in their expedition, however, and, quite aside from representatives of the Raj and the British East India Company, they had somehow added to their company an apparently exiled Hindu Prince. Thought he was a Sikh at first, actually; he had that kind of turban and that trim of beard. You know the look I mean. Turns out that's geographical rather than religious; it's the tradition in the area he comes from. Well-dressed chap too; proper morning suit, waistcoat and so on. Wouldn't look out of place at Buckingham Palace, apart from the turban and beard. When I asked the Lumière *sahibs* what his role was, none of them were quite sure.

As for me, well, it seems the Lumières had also brought along all the apparatus and impedimenta used in the creation of these wondrous moving picture displays, and they had developed something of a desire to make a show about a tiger hunt. So, of course, your and my mutual friend, Freddy Rowbotham, recommended me, and before you knew it, the Lumières had sent me a telegram.

I have to admit that I maintained a certain curiosity about their extravaganzas, so I packed up a couple of Henry rifles and the usual gear for a tiger-shoot, and went to meet them.

I caught up with the group while they were filming a local wedding. A high-caste were celebrating a marriage, and the Lumières wasted no time in capturing the event for eternity by means of their technologically marvelous contraptions. I'm afraid I can't even begin to explain how it works, but in essence it's a camera of sorts, and they were using it to take these moving pictures of the wedding.

An Indian wedding is a dashed colorful affair, and always has been. Everything was decked out in red and yellow blooms, as were most of the members of both families. When I arrived, the bride and groom—A Mr. Khan and a Miss Chopra—appeared to be singing to each other, while both families cavorted and danced in a very respectable and pleasant fashion throughout the courtyard. I must say it was a damned shame the *Frères* Lumiere had no means to record the songs as well, without which their moving images will probably lack considerably in the atmosphere that suffused and seduced us all. Perhaps someone should introduce them to that American chap who has invented a wire sound recorder? There may be some business worth doing with that.

At any rate, the celebrations were most pleasant, and it was there, by a buffet table, that I first spoke to this Hindu Prince. When I asked him his name, he

146

was most well-spoken and replied that the members of the French expedition referred to him as *Docteur Mystère*, and that he consulted both on medical matters, as his title implied, and on the technical matters of how the moving pictures were created. He was, by all accounts, quite a technical wizard, and traveled in his own carriage, which the people in the group called an "Electric Hotel." Rather rum name, but I'll tell you more about it in a moment.

I attempted to make small talk and explain the purpose of my visiting the group, but he seemed mostly concerned with discussing some technical matters with his apprentice, a lad called Cigale. Cigale was a pleasant lad, and had the vigorous practicality that can be so strangely lacking in today's youth. I found Dr. Mystère and Cigale much more our kind of people than the Lumières, and was a little disappointed that they were so preoccupied. I could not really complain, of course, for what is so terrible about efficiency and professionalism in playing one's part?

I circulated for a while then, ignoring the sobbing mother of the bride, who seemed to be having some kind of argument behind the scenes. Eventually, I noticed a rather shifty fellow, whose name I never did discover, who was only watching the festivities. He was the very image of a villain from a penny-dreadful: unkempt, scar-faced and wearing an eye patch. He openly leered at the dancing bride, much to the annoyance of many other celebrants, before getting leaving most rudely.

I followed him a short distance, but lost him in the dark. When I turned to return to the group, I was startled to find Dr. Mystère almost right at my shoulder. "Mr. Williams," he asked, "Did you know that man?"

"No, I just thought he seemed a little out of place. I know it probably isn't my place either, but- Do you know him?"

Dr. Mystère put his hands behind his back and said the oddest thing: "I hope not, for all our sakes."

Yes, it put a dampener on the evening for me, this hint of danger and threat. I asked what he meant by it, but Dr. Mystère shrugged the questions off, saying that I was missing some good food and drink. That is something that is hard to argue with.

I had shared a dormitory room for the night with Cigale and two cousins of the groom, off the courtyard where the celebrations had taken place. The bride and groom had left for their new abode a few streets away, where they undoubtedly had been enjoying the *prima noctis* more than I had been enjoying Cigale's snoring. So the last thing I expected the next morning was for the bride's distraught father to rouse the company with shouts and wails of the deepest and darkest despair. I had thought I had known darkness in my drinking days, but this man, Bachchan, was in a torment that no drug, no form of alcoholic depravity, could have sent a man to.

Dr. Mystère, in britches, shirtsleeves and braces, answered him, and quickly ascertained that some tragedy had occurred. He motioned to Cigale, telling him to be sure the Lumières stayed with their equipment and did not accompany he and the suffering father. He then said to me, "Mr. Williams, would you be so good as to come with me?" I had no idea what had happened, or what possible aid I could give, but his tone was so grave that I felt I had no choice but to acquiesce.

The old man took us to the home of the newlyweds and some other members of their family, and a more horrific charnel house I have never seen. I will spare you the details; I know such things aren't to your taste, but I must impress upon you that a truly terrible death had visited the young man and everyone in the neighboring domiciles. I saw at once why Dr. Mystère had asked me to come: the marks on the bodies were not made by knives or bullets, but unquestionably by the claws and fangs of big cats. The way the throats were bitten is quite distinctive. "You understand?" Dr Mystere asked. I dared not speak lest my voice betray my nausea, so I could but nod.

We went next to a missionary hospital. It appeared that the bride had survived, and truth to tell, I believe that this fact was to her misfortune. The injuries that she must have sustained were hidden beneath the most modest bedclothes, but her face was pale and sweating, and her eyes pits of despair. I could hear a clock ticking, though I could not see one in the room. I could see only a bed and two dozen members of her family who had somehow entered the room.

Dr. Mystère was allowed to her bedside. I doubted that I would be so allowed, and I had no desire to trouble her or her family, so I remained by the door. When Dr. Mystère returned, his eyes burned with anger. "Will she live?" I asked him.

He balled his fists. "No. But her last breath has avenged her." Outside in the empty corridor, he extracted a notebook from his pocket, and neatly wrote down some instructions to an outermost part of the city. "Take this to the *Frères* Lumière, and tell them they may have their cat hunt. Tell them they will have the most exciting moving picture they can imagine. Cigale and I will go on ahead and prepare the groundwork." He hesitated a moment, then said. "Your Foreign Service and Freddy Rowbotham say you are the best tiger-man in Bombay. Is that true?"

I did not wish to seem a braggart, but could not deny that many held the opinion that I was the best tiger-man in Bombay.

"Then we shall have sport tomorrow," he said, "for I was once counted the best tiger-man in Bengal."

We–I mean the Lumière's group and I–followed Dr. Mystère's instructions precisely. I had thought that we would be traveling out some distance from Bombay, to one of the villages or even some jungle, but to my astonishment we simply circumnavigated the city, and were still within its environs when Dr. Mystère's strange Electric Hotel came into view once more.

When I call this superlative and quite mystifying vehicle "Electric," I am not merely using the name by which its owner refers to it. It is, indeed... Electric! Not only is it illuminated with a incredible arrangement of electrical apparatus–I've heard that Mr. Tesla is jealous to a fault over the vehicle, and young Cigale warned us more than once to keep our eyes peeled for spies from Tesla's company–but it was surrounded by an atmosphere of tension and suppressed excitement that is quite draining. Electric, as I said; being around the Electric Hotel was like awaiting the discharge of a massive thunderstorm. Like the building storm, it quite gave me a headache, and I needed something of a pick-me-up while in its vicinity.

While the Lumières and their attendants and lackeys began unpacking their most singular equipment, Dr. Mystère approached with Cigale. To my surprise, the good Doctor carried a Henry rifle and wore two Colt Navy revolvers belted around his morning coat. "A cat hunt, then," he said with grim cheer.

The officials who had been playing host to Dr. Mystère and the brothers Lumiere had gone to great lengths–too great, I began to think; *the lady doth protest too much* and all that–to assure us that big cats were unknown in the city. His attempts to mollycoddle us came to naught, when we were approached by a man–with the odd name of Lever–in charge of what used to be a village, before it was subsumed into the city, who begged that I would shoot the leopards which had killed several of his family.

Dr. Mystère and I exchanged knowing glances. Leopards could easily have committed the atrocity after the wedding, and I at once knew that Dr. Mystère had already heard of this case, and linked it to the wedding killings with remarkable speed. I was very much astonished by this, for I had never before known either tigers or leopards to wander so close to human civilization.

Nevertheless, the wounds I had seen the previous day were certainly caused by a leopard rather than a tiger, which is larger and heavier.

Lever informed us that these beasts had been sighted coming from a slum on the city's southern reaches, as if they were human residents. He accompanied us to this fetid hive of poverty. I had considered myself quite used to the poverty that the lower-caste Indians existed in, but the conditions in this deplorable suburb were more horrifying than any I had ever seen before. Finally, Dr. Mystère described to the old man the unkempt man whom I had seen at the wedding. Lever recognized the description, and seemed to think that this person was bad luck. Lever gave the mysterious ruffian a name, Dutt.

Upon our hosts', shall we say, vociferous doubting of this man's statement, he drew our attention to numerous pawprints, which had somehow survived being obliterated by those of the multitude which had passed over them. These prints were going in all directions, back and forth through the very streets and between the houses, and none of us could deny that the cats seemed to have been walking about the district all night.

I recognized the tracks immediately, of course, as did Dr. Mystère. Examples of the spoor were both new and old, and tended to cluster along the wheel-ruts formed by carts and wagons bringing grain from the fields. Dr. Mystère knelt beside one such track, heedless of the mud that was soaking into the tail of his coat.

"What do you make of this?" he asked.

"Leopards right enough," I said. The pawprints were nowhere near large enough to have been produced by tigers, and tigers were far more solitary creatures. Groups of leopards were not unheard-of the way a group of tigers would have been.

"Leopards indeed, Mr. Williams. But it is their singular interest in these cart-tracks that I would like to hear your thoughts upon."

"I have no thoughts on the matter, Sir. Unless it is to say that the creatures may be following wagons which are carrying something with an attractive scent."

"Meat."

"They are carnivores."

Dr. Mystère nodded slowly. "And even a cargo of fruit is pulled and driven by beings of meat." I could not help but shiver. "Let us get ready," he said.

The slums petered out to small fields, and there were trees dotted both among the fields and even between the smaller shacks and shanty buildings. As the Moon was near the full, Dr. Mystère and I determined to sit up in trees at night, and sent Cigale on to our lodgings to make the necessary preparations.

Cigale quickly and efficiently engaged some local men to erect two platforms in trees about half a mile apart. Round these nests we had hides formed of boughs with soft leaves, this to prevent any rustling or noise. Cigale brought two goats, which were tied with strong ropes some 15 yards from our hiding-places, in such positions that, as the full Moon reached its high point, they would remain clear of the shade. My tree was on the cart-road, that of Dr. Mystère was nearer the slum, both in open cultivated ground, but clear of crops.

The Lumières set up their cameras on the roof of a nearby temple building. I had no idea whether their cameras would even work in this kind of moonlight, but they themselves were too excited to be troubled by the issue.

It was about ten o'clock when I saw the first leopard come out from a tumbledown shack and stand in the clear moonlight not more than 100 yards from my tree. I was certain that he would come along the road and I should get a good shot right down his throat, when suddenly, another leopard came skylarking at him, and, with a playful growl, they both ran across and disappeared behind a rising ground. Dr. Mystère fired at once, and one of the leopards came bolting back towards my hide. I shot it between the eyes.

Nothing more happened for an hour, but neither of us descended from our positions, as I had discerned the tracks of many leopards in the area, not just a pair.

We had almost decided the night's work was over, when suddenly, a black swarm poured out of the shanty huts and the ditches in the field. They were leopards, dozens of them!

I began to fire immediately. They were so densely packed that it was almost unnecessary to aim; any shot was bound to hit one. I fired and reloaded as quickly as I could, the barrel of the rifle becoming red hot in my hands. I could hear and see the shots from Dr. Mystère's hide, matching mine in speed and accuracy.

Suddenly, something slammed into my back, throwing me to the floor of the hide. Damn me, it was another leopard. It had climbed up behind me and leapt into the hide! The strangest thing of all was that it seemed to be standing on its hind legs, upright like a half-cat half-man thing. Then its jaws were at my throat. I jammed the rifle into its mouth and fired.

I was now out of ammunition, but there were still two or three leopards trying to ascend to me. I hard more shots, and saw Cigale, with a rifle, potting leopards. Behind him, Dr. Mystère's hide burst into bright flame, lighting up the ground below. Cigale turned to look at it, and a leopard leaped at him. I could only vault over the edge of my hide, and crashed into the beast's powerful shoulders. I had no bullets left, but used my rifle as a club to crush its skull while it was stunned.

The sounds around us were terrifying–growls and roars, like those of a feral cat magnified to cyclopean proportions. Leopards were everywhere, and I was sure we were finished.

Then Dr. Mystère's Colt Navys boomed rapidly. He too had run out of rifle ammunition, but the Colt Navy's bullets were heavy enough to kill a leopard. He ran to cover us, spinning this way and that, shooting the ravenous creatures left and right until there was only one left.

And that was when that terrible silence impacted upon us.

The Leopard circled warily, its tail straight out behind it. Dr. Mystère carefully replaced his Colt Navys in their holsters, while Cigale reversed his rifle, ready to use it as a club as I had. Even with three of us, I had no desire to face such a creature as this leopard. Eventually, it reared, standing on two legs.

Dr. Mystère kicked it in the belly at once, and it curled up. We beat it to death. It is a terrible thing to do to such a magnificent animal, but it was our only true chance of survival. We all caught our breath, and Dr. Mystère eventually managed a savage grin. "Only one beast left, Williams. The worst of them."

He led us through the shanty town, following the densest sets of leopard packs back to their source, which proved to be a boarded-up Christian church. We stepped into the shadows. "Cigale, if you please?" Cigale nodded, and produced, of all things, a stick of dynamite from his pocket. He affixed it to the door and lit it.

The door was blown in with a loud bang, and we piled through. I had no idea what I expected to find, and could only hope that Dr. Mystère did. I most certainly did not expect to find a blood-slicked statue of Kali, festooned with the leopards' table-leavings, and the rough-looking man from the wedding holding a sword. Dutt attacked at once, and Cigale and I tried to fend him off with our rifle-butts. Dr. Mystère had no such weapon, and, I suspect, had no real need of one. Using some form of Eastern Boxing, he neatly disarmed the man, and ran him through with his own sword. Only then did he relax, and let the mix of elation and despair that comes with the end of battle wash over him.

"I suspected as much when I saw this man Dutt at the wedding," he said. "He had trained the beasts to attack people, and starved them to make them more vicious."

"But why the wedding party?" I asked. Wagons I could understand; there have been robbers as long as there have been people.

"Politics. The groom and his family are friendly to France and hostile to Russia. Foreigners hire these old survivors of the Thuggee cult to do their dirty work in India. Believe me," he said. "I know."

And that's about the size of it, old chap. The Lumières and Dr. Mystère have continued on their world tour, and I wish them all well. I can't help wondering whether the brothers indeed managed to make a moving picture of our adventure. If so, the people who fled the moving image of a train will probably want to lynch them. I cannot for the life of me imagine that people would want to see such things for mere entertainment, especially here in India. Never in a million years.

Like Win Scott Eckert, Brad Mengel (our first Australian author!) chose 1946 Paris as his stage; a post-war Paris transformed by the Cold War into a shadowy world of espionage, a city of Folies Bergères *and murderous back alleys where East meets West, a theater of* femmes fatales, *secret agents and desperate interlopers. Smell the* Gauloises *and hear the sound of the blues as we enter the smoke-filled rooms of one of the City of Light's best-known cabarets...*

Brad Mengel: *All's Fair...*

Paris, 1946

Pigalle sang like an angel and had a body to match. Admirers flocked to the backstage of the *Picratt's* in Montmartre where she sang to mostly male audiences. No one in Paris could compare to her beauty. Some admirers were there to just be a little closer to the raven-haired siren. Others, if they were lucky enough to catch the eye of this goddess, were granted an audience.

James was lucky enough to catch her eye this night. Pigalle didn't know what it was that caught her eye; the Naval Commander was certainly handsome but so were many other of her admirers. Perhaps it was the cruelty she saw in his eyes, or the scar on his cheek which lent him the air of a pirate. Whatever it was, many had fallen for it before and most likely many more would fall for it in the future.

Pigalle dispatched her current "husband," Maurice Champot, a.k.a. *La Grammaire*, to invite the dashing Commander to dinner with her. *La Grammaire* was currently trafficking in information, often blurted out on his wife's satin sheets, and looked upon Commander Bond merely as a juicy morsel. He returned with the news that the dashing Englishman would be delighted to join his wife for supper–and a reminder that she had already made other plans...

Frédéric-Jean Orth was waiting in the bar where he had arranged to meet Pigalle the night before. As *L'Ombre*, he had recently been all too busy avoiding the attentions of Commissaire Voisin and a night on the town with a pretty companion was a welcome diversion.

Whilst waiting for his date, he had struck up a conversation with a wealthy Louisiana planter, Hubert Bonisseur de la Bath. Orth liked Americans; they were always full of energy and filled with hope. Young Hubert was no different. They spent a pleasant hour discussing President de Gaulle's resignation and the first meeting of the U.N. Then, Hubert explained he had a previous engagement and insisted on paying for the drinks.

Orth smiled as he watched the young American leave. It was then that Maurice arrived and advised him that Pigalle sent her regrets.

Hubert Bonisseur de la Bath was under no illusions about Maurice *La Grammaire*. He knew the man pimped out his wife to compromise wealthy Americans who, later, could be blackmailed by his Soviet paymasters. His own boss at the OSS had briefed him adequately, before sending him into Pigalle's arms. After all, two could play the game...

OSS 117 knocked eight times, then once, then three times at the discreet metal door in the alley behind the cabaret. Maurice opened the door.

"I'm here to see P'Gell," the young American said.

"Of course you are," said Maurice. "This way, please."

Hubert's sense of alarm alerted him a bit too late; he had already stepped halfway into the broom closet when he was shoved inside and he heard the door locked behind him.

L'Ombre laughed as he pulled off the wig, tore off the latex and wiped off the makeup that had enabled him to impersonate Maurice so convincingly. "Now *à nous deux*, my dear Pigalle," he thought.

Orth crossed a small courtyard and stepped through the *sortie des artistes* door and into the bustling backstage area of the *Picratt's*. But suddenly, he stopped. At the other end of the cabaret, he had just spotted his nemesis, Commissaire Voisin, accompanied by two Inspectors and the Manager.

"Our anonymous tipster said *L'Ombre* is here," said the Policeman. "I want the place searched from top to bottom."

Orth decided to forego the pleasures of a night with Pigalle and, almost blending in with the darkness, disappeared in the darkened alley.

James Bond smiled as he saw the adventurer beat a hasty retreat. *L'Ombre* was well-known to MI6, of course, and as soon as he had spotted him, he had taken steps to eliminate the competition. A quick phone call to the Police Judiciaire had produced the anticipated visit by the uniformed men which had sent the mysterious Mr. Orth (not even M knew his real name) packing.

The Commander proceeded towards Pigalle's dressing room, a bottle of Veuve Clicquot Ponsardin under his arm, when he saw *La Grammaire*, rubbing a pronounced bump on the back of his head, amble towards him.

"Is Mademoiselle Pigalle in, Monsieur Champot?" asked Bond.

"*Mais non*, Commander Bond," replied the Frenchman with a forlorn air. "She just left with the other gentleman, the one with the Jewel of Gizeh."

Swearing under his breath, Bond burst through the door.

He was greeted by a note written in lipstick on the mirror of Pigalle's dresser.

"All's fair in love and war," and it was signed with a haloed stick figure.

Writing something pithy about Michael Moorcock is like facing the Everest: a daunting challenge, to say the least. Philip José Farmer coined the Wold Newton concept, but Moorcock gave us the Multiverse. His signature character, Elric, has met his eternal counterparts, Erekose and Corum, at the Vanishing Tower, Conan the Barbarian in the pages of Marvel Comics, and even Roland, the hero of the Chanson de Geste, *in* Stormbringer. *Jerry Cornelius and the fantastic Una Persson have crossed literary boundaries, meeting other characters from comics and pulp fiction. It was the gifted Chris Roberson who happily suggested that Moorcock grace* Tales of the Shadowmen *with a story, and he has done so in a yarn in which a well-known albino crosses the path of several notorious French villains...*

Michael Moorcock: *The Affair of the Bassin Les Hivers*

Paris, 2006

I. Le Bassin Les Hivers

Until the late part of the last century, the area known as Les Hivers, was notorious for its poverty, its narrow, filthy streets and the extraordinary number of crimes of passion recorded there. This district lay directly behind the famous Cirque d'Hiver, the winter circus, home to performing troupes who generally toured through the spring and summer months. Residents complained of the roaring of lions and tigers or the trumpeting of elephants at night, but the authorities were slow to act, given the nature of this part of the 11th arrondissement, whose inhabitants were not exactly influential.

The great canal, which brought produce to most of Paris, branched off from the Canal Saint Martin just below the Circus itself, to begin its journey underground. For many bargees, what they termed Le Bassin Les Hivers was the end of their voyage and here they would rest before returning to their home ports with whatever goods they had purchased or traded. Surrounding the great basin leaned a number of wooden quays and jetties, together with warehouses and high-ceilinged halls where business had aways been done in gaslight or the semi-darkness created by huge arches and locks dividing the upper and the lower canal systems. The banks rose 30 meters or more, made of ancient stone, much of it re-used from Roman times, backing onto tall, windowless depositories built of tottering brick and timber. The Sun could gain no access here and, at night, the quays and markets were lit by gas or naphtha and only occasionally by electricity. Beside the cobbled canal paths flourished the cafés, brothels and cheap rooming houses, as well as the famous Bargees' Mission and Church of Our Lady of the Waterways, operated since the 9th century by the pious and incorruptible White Friars. Like Alsatia, that area of London also administered by the Carmelites, it formed a secure sanctuary for all but habitual murderers.

The bargees not continuing under the city to the coast, and even to Britain, concluded their voyages here, having brought their cargoes from Nantes, Lyon or Marseille. Others came from the Low Countries, Scandinavia and Prussia, while those barge-folk regarded as the cream of their race had sailed waterways connecting the French capital with Moscow, Istanbul or the Italian Republics. The English bargees, with their heavy, red-sailed, ocean-going boats, came to sell their own goods, mostly Sheffield steel and pottery, and buy French wine and cheese for which there was always a healthy market in their chilly nation, chronically starved of food and drink fit for human consumption. It was common for altercations and fights to break out between the various nationalities and more than one would end with a mortal knife wound.

And so, for centuries, few respectable Parisians ever ventured into Les Hivers and those who did so rarely returned in their original condition. Even the Police patrolled the serpentine streets by wagon or, armed with carbines, in threes and fours. They dared not venture far into the system of underground waterways known collectively as the Styx. Taxi drivers, unless offered a substantial commission, would not go into Les Hivers at all, but would drop passengers off in the Boulevard du Temple, close to the permanent hippodrome, always covered in vivid posters, in summer or winter. The drivers claimed that their automobile's batteries could not be recharged in that primitive place.

Only as the barge trade slowly gave way to more rapid commercial traffic, such as the electric railways and mighty aerial freighters, which began to cross the whole of Europe and even as far as America, Africa and the Orient, did the area become settled by the sons and daughters of the middle classes, by writers and artists, by well-to-do North Africans, Vietnamese, homosexuals and others who found the rest of Paris either too expensive or too unwelcoming. And, as these things will go, the friends of the pioneering bohemians came quickly to realize that the district was no longer as dangerous as its reputation suggested. They could sell their apartments in more expensive districts and buy something much cheaper in Les Hivers. Warehouses were converted into homes and shops and the quays and jetties began to house quaint restaurants and coffee houses. Some of the least stable buildings were torn down to admit a certain amount of sunlight.

By the 1990s, the transformation was complete and few of the original inhabitants could afford to live there any longer. The district became positively fashionable until it is the place we know today, full of bookshops, little cinemas, art-suppliers, expensive bistros, cafes and exclusive hotels. The animals are now housed where they will not disturb the residents and customers.

By the time Michel Houlebecq moved there in 1996, the transformation was complete. He declared the area "a meeting place of deep realities and metaphysical resonances." Though a few barge people still brought their goods to

Les Hivers, these were unloaded onto trucks or supplied a *marché biologique* to rival that of Boulevard Raspail and only the very desperate still plied the dark, subterranean waterways for which no adequate maps had ever existed. The barge folk continued to be as clannish as always. Their secrets were passed down from one family member to another.

When he had been a lowly detective sergeant, Commissaire Lapointe had lived on the Avenue Parmentier and had come to know the alleys and twitterns of the neighborhood well. He had developed relationships with many of the settled bargees and their kin and had done more than one favor to a waterman accused unjustly of a crime. They had respected Lapointe, even if they had not loved him.

A heavy-set man in a dark Raglan overcoat and an English cap, Lapointe was at once saturnine and avuncular. Lighting a Cuban cheroot, he descended from the footplate of his heavy police car, its motors humming at rest. Turning up his collar against the morning chill, he looked with some melancholy at the boutiques and restaurants now crowding the old wharfs. "Paris changes too rapidly," he announced to his long-suffering young assistant, the aquiline LeBec, who had only recently joined special department. "She has all the grace and stateliness of an aristocratic whore, yet these stones, as our friend de Certau has pointed out, are full of dark stories, an unsavory past."

Lapointe had become fascinated by psychogeography, the brainchild of Guy DeBord, who had developed the philosophy of "flaneurism" or the art of *dérive*. DeBord and his followers had it that all great cities were the sum of their past and that the past was never far away, no matter what clever cosmetics were used to hide it. They had nothing but contempt for the electric trams, trains and cars which bore the busy Parisians about the city. Only by walking, by "drifting," could one appreciate and absorb the history which one inhaled with every breath, mixing living flesh with the dust of one's ancestors. Commissaire Lapointe, of course, had a tendency to support these ideas, as did many of the older members of the *Sûreté du Temps Perdu* and their colleagues abroad. This was especially true in London, where Lapointe's famous opposite number, Sir Seaton Begg, chief metatemporal investigator for the Home Office, headed the legendary Whitehall Time Center, whose very existence was denied by Parliament, just as the Republic refused to admit any knowledge of the Quai d'Orsay's STP.

LeBec accepted these musings as he always did, keeping his own counsel. He had too much respect to dismiss his chief's words, but was also too much of a modern to make such opinions his own.

Reluctantly, Lapointe began to move along the freshly-paved quay until he had reached the entrance to a narrow canyon between two of the former warehouses. Rue Mendoza was no different from scores of similar alleys, save that a pale blue STP van stood outside one of its entrances, the red light on its roof turning with slow, almost voluptuous arcs while uniformed officers questioned the inhabitants of the great warren which had once housed grain and now was the residence of publicity directors, television producers and miscellanous media people, all of whom were demanding to know why they could not go about their business.

Behind him on the canal, Lapointe could see a faint mist rising from the water and he heard a dozen radios and TVs, all tuned to the morning news programmes. So far, at least, the press had not yet got hold of this story. He stubbed out his cigar against a masonry-clad wall and put it back in his case, following the uniformed man into the house. He told Le Bec to remain outside and question the angry residents as to their whereabouts and so on. There were no elevators in this particular building and Lapointe was forced to climb several storys until at last he came to a landing where a pale-faced young man, still in his pajamas covered by a blue check dressing gown, stood with his back to the green and cream wall smoking a long, thin Nat Sherman cigarette, one of the white Virginia variety. He transferred the cigarette from right to left and shook hands with Lapointe as he introduced himself.

"Bonjour, M'sieu. I am Sébastien Gris."

"Commissaire Lapointe of the Sûreté. What's all this about a fancy dress party and a dead girl?"

Gris opened his mouth, but there was no air in his lungs. His thin features trembled helplessly and his pale blue eyes filled with helpless fury. He could not speak. He drew a deep breath. "Monsieur, I telephoned the moment I found her. I have touched nothing, I promise."

Lapointe grunted. He looked down at a pretty blonde girl, her fair skin faintly pockmarked, who lay sprawled in the man's hallway, a meter or so from the entrance to his tiny kitchen filling with steam from a forgotten kettle. Lapointe stepped over the body and went to turn off the gas. Slowly, the steam dissipated. He took a large paisley handkerchief from his pocket and mopped at his head and neck. He sighed. "No name? No identity? No papers of any kind?"

The uniformed man confirmed this. "Just what you see, Monsieur le Commissaire."

Lapointe leaned and touched her face. He took something on his finger and inspected it carefully. "Arsenic powder," he said. "And almost certainly cochineal for rouge." He was growing depressed. "I've only seen this once before." He recognized the work on her dress. It was authentic. Though unusually beautiful for the period and with an unblemished skin, she was as certainly an inhabitant of the early 19th century as he was of the 21st and, as sure as he was alive, she was dead, murdered by a neat cut across her throat. "A true beauty and no doubt famous in her age. Murdered and disposed of by an expert."

"You have my absolute assurances, Monsieur, that her body was here when I got up this morning. Someone has done this, surely, to implicate me. It cannot be a joke."

Lapointe nodded gravely. "I fear, Monsieur Gris, that your presence in this building had little or nothing to do with the appearance of a corpse outside your kitchen." The young man became instantly relieved and began to babble a sequence of theories, forcing Lapointe to raise his hand as he dropped to one knee to inspect something clutched in the corpse's right fist. He frowned and checked the fingernails of the left fingers in which some coarse brown fibers had caught. The young man continued to talk and Lapointe became thoughtful and impatient at the same time, rising to his feet. "If you please, Monsieur. It is our job to determine how she came to die here and, if possible, identify her murderer. You, I regret, will have to remain nearby while I question the others. Have you the means to telephone your place of work?"

The young man nodded and crossed over to a wall bearing a fashionably modeled telephone. He gave the operator a number. As he was speaking, LeBec came in to join his chief. He shuddered when he saw the corpse. He knew at once why their department had been called in. "1820 or perhaps '25," he murmured. "What's that in her hand? A rosary? An expensive gold crucifix, too? Poor child. Was she killed here or there?"

"By the look of the blood it was there," responded his chief. "But whoever brought her body here is still amongst us, I am almost certain." He turned the crucifix over to look at the back. All he read there were the initials "J.C." "Perhaps also her murderer." With an inclination of his massive head, he indicated where the bloodstains told a story of the girl being dragged and searched. "Did they assume her to be a witch of some sort? A familiar story. Her clothes suggest wealth. Yet she wears too much makeup for a girl of her age from a good family. Was she some sort of adept or the daughter of an adept, maybe? What if she made her murderers a gateway into wherever they thought they were going and they killed her, either to be certain she told no others or as some sort of bizarre sacrifice? Yet why would she be clutching such an expensive rosary. And what about those fibers? Were they disguised? You know how they think, Le Bec, as well as I do." He watched as his assistant took an instrument from an inside pocket and ran it over the girl's head and neck. Straightening himself, Le Bec studied his readings, nodding occasionally as his instincts were confirmed.

The commissioner was giving close attention to the series of bloody marks leading away from the corpse to the front door of the apartment. Again he noted those initials on the back of the crucifix. "My God!" he murmured. "But why...?"

II. Monsieur Zenith: A Brief History

"I suspect our murderer had good reason to dispose of the corpse in this way," declared Lapointe. "My guess is that her face and body were both too well known for her to be simply dropped in the Seine, while the murderer did not wish to be observed moving her through the streets of Paris, either because he himself was also highly recognizable or because he had no easy way of doing what he needed to do. And no alibi. So, if not one himself, he called in an expert, no doubt a person already known to him."

"An expert? You mean such people understood about metatemporal tran-science in the 1820s?"

"Generally speaking, of course, very few of our ancestors understood such things. Even fewer than today. We are not talking of time-travel, which as we all know, is impossible, but movement from one universe to another where one era has developed at a slower rate in relation to ours. Needless to say, we are not discussing our own past, but a period approximating our own present. That's why most of our cases take us to periods equivalent to our own 20th or early 21st century. So we are dealing here with a remote scale, far removed from our own. Another reason for our murderer to put as alternative planes scales between our own and theirs."

Lapointe was discussing the worlds of the multiverse, separated one from another by mass rather than time. Each world was of enormously larger or smaller scale to the next, enabling all the alternate universes which made up the great multiverse to coexist, one invisible to the other for reasons of size. Not until the great French scientist Benoit Mandelbrot had developed these theories had it become possible for certain adepts to increase or decrease their own mass and cross from one of these worlds to the other. Mandelbrot had effectively provided us with maps of our own brains, plans of the multiverse. This in turn had led to the setting up of secret government agencies designed to create policies and departments whose function was to deal with the new realities.

Now almost every major nation had some equivalent to the STP in some version of its own 21st century, apart from the United States, which had largely succeeded in refusing to enter that century in any significant sense and was forced to rely on foreign agents to cope with the problems arising from situations with their roots in the 21st century.

"But you are convinced, chief, that the murderer is French?"

"If not French, then they have lived in France for many years."

Used not to questioning his superior's instinctive judgments, Le Bec accepted this.

As their electromobile sped them back to the Quai d'Orsay, Lapointe mused on the problem. "I need to find someone who has an idea of all the metatemporals who come and go in Paris. Only one springs to mind and that is Monsieur Zenith, the albino. You'll recall we have worked together once or twice before. As soon as I get back to the office, I will put through a call to Whitehall. If anyone knows where Zenith is, then it will be Sexton Blake."

Sexton Blake was the real name of the detective famously fictionalized as Sir Seaton Begg and Lapointe's opposite number in London.

"I did not know Monsieur Zenith was any longer amongst us," declared LeBec.

"There is no guarantee that he is. I can only hope. I understood that he had made his home in Paris. Blake will confirm where I can find him."

"I understand, chief, that he was in earlier days wanted by the police of several countries."

"Quite so. His last encounter with Blake, as a criminal, was during the London Blitz. He and his old antagonist fought it out on a cliff house whose foundations were weak. The fictional version of the case was been recorded as *The Affair of the Bronze Basilisk.* Zenith's body was lost in the ruins of the house and never recovered, but we now know that he returned to Jugo-Slavia where he fought with Tito's guerillas against the Nazis, was captured by the Gestapo before he could smoke the famous cyanide cigarette he always kept in his case and was found half-dead by the British when they liberated the infamous Milosevic Fortress in Belgrade, HQ of the Gestapo in the region. For his various efforts on behalf of the allied war-effort, Zenith was given a full pardon by the authorities and in his final meeting with his old adversary Sexton Blake, both men made a bargain–Blake would allow no more stories of Zenith to be published as part of his own memoirs and Zenith would not publish his memoirs until 50 years after that meeting which was in August 26, 1946. Both men have been exposed to the same effects which conferred longevity upon them, almost by accident. That 50 years has now, of course, passed."

"And Monsieur Zenith?" asked Le Bec as the car hummed smoothly under the arches into the square leading to their offices. "What has happened to him?"

"He has become a kind of gentleman adventurer, working as often with the authorities as against them and spending much of his time in tracking down ex-Nazis, especially those with stolen wealth, which he either returns in whole to their owners or, if it so pleases him, pays himself a ten percent 'commission.' He will now sometimes work with my old friend Blake. His adventures will take him across parallel universes where he assumes the name of 'Zodiac.' But he still keeps up with his old acquaintances from the criminal underworld, mostly through a famous London thieve's warren known as 'Smith's Kitchen' which now has concessions in Paris, Rome and New York. If anyone has heard a hint of the business here, it will be Zenith."

"How will you contact him, chief?"

Lapointe smiled almost to himself. "Oh, I think Blake will confirm I know where he will be later this morning."

III. Familiar names

A broken rosary, a silver crucifix bearing the initials "J.C.," a few coarse, brown fibers, some photographs of the corpse seen earlier at Les Hivers... One by one, Commissaire Lapointe laid the things before him on the bright, white tablecloth. He was sitting in a fashionable café, L'Albertine, situated in the Arcades de l'Opéra whose windows looked into a square in which a beautiful fountain

161

played. Outside, Paris's *haut-monde* strolled back and forth, conversing, inspecting the windows of the expensive shops, occasionally entering to make purchases. Across from him, sipping alternately from a small coffee cup or a glass of yellow-green absinthe, sat a most extraordinary individual. His skin was pale as alabaster. His hair, including his eyebrows, was the color of milk, and whose gleaming, sardonic eyes resembled the finest rubies. Dressed unusually for the age, the albino wore perfectly cut morning dress. A grey silk hat, evidently his, shared a shelf near the cash-register with Lapointe's wide-brimmed straw.

"I am grateful, Monsieur, that you found time to see me," murmured Lapointe, understanding the value the albino placed on good manners. "I was hoping these objects would mean more to you than they do to me. Evidently belonging to a priest or a nun–"

"Of high rank," agreed Zenith continuing to look at the photographs of the victim.

"We also found several long black hairs, traces of heavy red lipstick of fairly recent manufacture."

"No nun wore that," mused Zenith. "Which suggests her murderess was disguised as a nun. In which case, of course, she is still unlikely to have worn lip-rouge. It was not the young woman's?"

"Hers was from an earlier age altogether." Lapointe had already explained the circumstances in which the corpse had been discovered, as well as his guess at the time and date when she was murdered.

"So we can assume there were at least two people involved in killing her, one of whom at least had knowledge of the multiverse and how to gain access to other worlds."

"And at least one of them can be assumed still to be here. Those footprints told us that part of the story. And some effort had been made to wrest the rosary from her fingers after she had arrived in Les Hivers."

"The man–shall we assume him to be a priest?" Monsieur Zenith raised the rosary as if to kiss it, but then sniffed it instead. "J.C.? Some reference perhaps to the Society of Jesus?"

"Possibly. Which could lead us to assume that the Inquisition could have been at work?"

"I will see what I can discover for you, Monsieur Lapointe. As for the poor victim..." Zenith offered his old acquaintance a slight shrug.

"I believe I have a way of discovering her identity also, assuming she was not what we used to call a 'virtuous' girl," said Lapointe. "I have already checked the police records for that period and no mention is made of a society disappearance that was not subsequently solved. Therefore, by the quality of her clothes, the fairness of her skin, condition of her hair, not to mention her extraordinary beauty, we must assume her to be either of foreign birth or some kind of courtesan. The cut of her clothes suggests the latter to me. There is, in that case, only one place to look for her. I must inspect our copy of De Buzet."

Zenith raised an alabaster eyebrow. "You have a copy of the legendary Carte Bleue?"

"One of the two known to exist. The property of the Quai d'Orsay for almost 200 years. Of little value, of course, in the general way. But now—it might just lead us to our victim, if not to her murderers."

Monsieur Zenith extinguished his Turkish cigarette and rose to leave. "I will do what I can to trace this assumed cleric and if you can discover a reasonable likeness in La Carte Bleue, we shall perhaps meet here again tomorrow morning?"

"Until then," declared Lapointe, standing to shake hands. He watched with mixed feelings as the albino collected his hat and stick at the door and strolled into the sunlit square, for all the world a flaneur from a previous century.

Later that same day, wearing impeccable evening dress as was his unvarying habit, Monsieur Zenith made his way to a certain unprepossessing address in the Marais where he admitted himself with a key, entering through a door of peeling green paint into a foyer whose interior window slid open and a pair of yellow, bloodshot eyes regarded him suspiciously. Zenith gave a name and a number and, as he passed through the second door, pulled on a black domino which, of course, did nothing to disguise his appearance but was a convention of the establishment. Once within, he gave his hat and cloak to a bowing receptionist and found himself in those parts of the catacombs made into a great dining room known to the aristocrats of the criminal underworld as La Cuisine de Smith. Here, that fraternity could exist unhindered and, while eating a passable dinner, could listen to an orchestra consisting of a violinist, a guitarist, double-bassist, an accordionist and a pianist. If they so wished, they could also dance the exotic tango of Argentina or the Apache of Paris herself.

Zenith took a table in an alcove under a low stone ceiling that was centuries old and blew out the large votive candle which was his only light. He ordered his usual absinthe and from his cigarette case removed a slender oval, which he placed between his lips and lit. The rich sweetness of Kashmiri opium poured from his nostrils as he exhaled the smoke and his eyes became heavily lidded. Watching the dancers, all at once he became aware of a presence at his table and a slender woman, whose domino only enhanced her dark beauty, an oval face framed by a perfectly cut "page-boy" style. She laid a hand lightly on his shoulder and smiled.

"Will you dance, old friend?" she asked.

Although she was known to the world as Una Persson, Countess von Beck, Zenith thought of her by another name. He rejoiced inwardly at his good fortune. She was exactly whom he had hoped to meet here. He rose and bowed, then gracefully escorted her to the door where they joined in the rhythms of The

Entropy Tango, that strange composition actually written for one of Countess Una's closest friends. In England, she had enjoyed a successful career on the music hall stage. Here, she was best known as a daring adventuress.

Arranging their wonderful bodies in the figures of the tango, the two carried on a murmured conversation. When the final chords rose to subtle crescendo, Zenith had the knowledge he had sought.

At his invitation, Countess Una joined him, the candle was relit and they ordered from the menu. This was to prove dangerous for, moments after they began to eat, a muffled shot stilled the orchestra and Zenith noted with some interest that a large caliber bullet had penetrated the plaster just behind his left shoulder. The bullet had flattened oddly, enough to tell him that it was made of an unusual alloy. Countess Una had recognized it, too. It was she who blew out the candle so that they no longer made an easy target.

They spoke almost in chorus.

"Vera Pym!"

Who else but that ruthless mistress of Paris's most notorious gang would ignore Smith's rules of sanctuary, respected even by the police?

But why had she suddenly determined to destroy the albino?

Zenith frowned. Could he know more than he realized?

IV. Fitting the Pieces

Commissaire Lapointe was unsurprised by Zenith's information when they met at L'Albertine the next morning. Vera Pym (believed to be her real name) was the acknowledged leader of a gang which had in its time had several apparent leaders. Only Pym, however, had remained in control of the *Vampyres* throughout their long career. She was one of a small group capable (to one degree or another) of moving between the worlds and living for centuries. The rank and file of her gang, for all their sinister name, had no such qualities. Some did not even realize she was their leader, for she generally put her man of the moment in that position. Occasionally, she changed her name, though generally it remained a simple anagram of her gang's. And she had many disguises. Few were absolutely sure what she looked like or, indeed, if she was always the same person. Several times she had been captured, yet she had always been able to escape.

"She has been a thorn in the side of the authorities for well over a century," agreed Lapointe. "And, of course, she is one of the few we can suspect in this case."

"What's more," added Zenith, "she has recently been seen in the company of a man of the cloth. An Abbé by all accounts."

"My God!" Lapointe passed a photocopied picture across the table. "Tell me what you make of that!"

Frowning, the albino examined the picture. "Not much, I'm afraid. Is she?..."

"The likeness is remarkably similar to our victim. Her name was Sarah Gobseck, a Jewess better known in her day as La Torpille."

"A surprisingly unfeminine sobriquet."

"I agree. But at that time a torpedo was something which lay in the water, half-hidden by the waves, until hit by a ship. Whereupon it would explode and as likely as not sink the ship. She is most famous from Balzac's *History of the Courtesans*."

"Ah!" Zenith sat back, drawing on his cigasrette. "So that's our Abbé! Carlos Herrera!"

"Exactly. Vautrin himself. Which would explain the initials on the rosary. So he is here now with Madame Pym. Which also explains anomalies in his career as reported by Balzac. Vautrin is Jacques Collin, the master criminal, who vanished from the historical records at about the time our 'Torpedo' became an inconvenient embarrassment to more than one gentleman. Suicide was suspected, I know. But now we have the truth."

"No doubt Collin also vanished into the 21st century, since Balzac becomes increasingly vague concerning his identity or his exploits and appears to have resorted to unlikely fictions to explain him. He knew nothing of La Pym, of course!"

"But this does nothing to tell us of their whereabouts," mused Zenith.

"Nor," added Lapointe, "how they can be brought to justice."

For some moments, Zenith was lost in thought, then he glanced at his watch and frowned. "Perhaps you will permit me, Monsieur le Commissaire, to solve that particular problem."

Lapointe became instantly uncomfortable. "I assure you, Monsieur Zenith, that while I appreciate all your help, this is ultimately a Police matter. I would remind you that you are already risking your life. La Pym has marked you as her next victim."

"A fact, Monsieur Lapointe, that I greatly resent. Because of a promise I made to a certain great Englishman, I regret to say I have been forced to live the live of a bourgeois professional, almost a tradesman, and no longer pursue the life I once relished. However, in this case a certain personal element has entered the equation. I feel obliged to satisfy my honor and perhaps avenge the death of that beautiful young creature who, through no fault of her own, was forced into a profession for which she had only abhorrence and which resulted, at least according to de Balzac's history, in an unholy, early and wholly undeserved death."

"My dear Monsieur Zenith, if I may make so bold, this remains a matter for the justice system."

"But you are helpless, I think you will agree, certainly in the matter of Collin. He will evade you, as no doubt also will La Pym."

"If so, then we will continue to hunt for them until we can arrest them and prove their guilt or innocence in a court of law."

The albino bowed from where he sat. "So be it." And with that he got to his feet and, making a polite gesture, bade the Policeman au revoir.

Commissaire Lapointe immediately made his way back to the Quay d'Orsay where LeBec awaited him. He read at once the concern in his superior's face.

"What's up, chief?"

Lapointe was in poor humor and in no mood to explain, but he knew he owed it to LaBec to say something. "I'm pretty sure that Zenith has an idea of our murderers' whereabouts and intends to take the law into his own hands. He is convinced that he knows who they are and how to punish them. We must find him and follow him and do all we can to thwart him!"

"But, chief, if he can deliver justice where we cannot...?"

"Then all our civilization stands for nothing, LeBec. Already the Americans and the English have adopted the language of the blood feud in their foreign affairs, demanding eyes for eyes and teeth for teeth–but that is nothing more or less than a reversion to the most primitive form of law available to our ancestors. France cannot follow the Anglo-Saxons down that road and I will do all in my power to make sure we do not!"

"And yet..."

"LeBec, for 20 centuries, we have steadily improved our civilization until our complex system of justice, allowing for subtle interpretation, for context, for motive and so on, has become paramount. It is the law I live to serve. Zenith, for all he behaves with courage and honor, would defy that justice, just as he used to, and I will have no part in it. Though I lack his resources and knowledge–even, perhaps, his courage–I must stop him. In the name of the Law."

Understanding at last, LeBec nodded gravely. "Very well, chief, but what are we to do?"

"Our best," declared Lapointe gravely. "I suspect that Countess von Beck, your own distant cousin, is still helping him in this. For that reason, I put a man to follow her. If we are lucky, she will lead us to Zenith. And Zenith, I sincerely hope, will lead us to the murderers–to Vautrin and Vera Pym–while there is still a chance of our apprehending them."

"Where are they going, chief? Do you know?"

"My guess is that, since they failed to kill Zenith last night, they will attempt to return from whence they came. But how they will make that attempt remains a mystery to me."

V. Zenith's Resolution

Una Persson's car had been seen heading up the Boulevard Voltaire towards the Boulevard du Temple, carrying at least two passengers, so it was for the Marais that the Policemen headed in their own Citroen ECXVI, perhaps the fastest car in France, powered by three enormous super-charged batteries. The sleek, black

166

machine had them outside the Cirque d'Hiver within minutes, but from there they had to run towards the canal and down the steps to the great basin by now, at twilight, alive with dancing neon and neurotic music. There at last Lapointe caught a glimpse of his quarry and pointed.

Zenith, as was appropriate, wore white tie and tails, carrying a slender silver-tipped ebony cane, an astonishing sight to LeBec who had never seen him thus. "My God, we are pursuing Fred Astaire and Ginger Rogers!" joked Lapointe's assistant.

The Commissaire found no humor in this. "This could be a dangerous business, lad. There was never any profit in making that man one's enemy. He was once the most dangerous thief in Europe and Europe is lucky that he gave his word to an old friend to forsake his life of crime or he would still be causing us considerable grief!"

Suitably chastened, LeBec panted, "What is he? Some kind of vampire?"

"Only in legends. And not in any way associated with Vera Pym and her gang." Lapointe continued to push his way through the crowd as the evening grew darker. "At least, I have some idea now where he is heading. There must have been a gateway created by the murderers..."

Crossing the old wooden bridge over the basin, they saw what had brought the crowd here. It was a huge black barge of the kind once used in the canal folk's funerals, two decks high. "It came up out of there–not ten minutes ago!" said an underdressed young woman wearing garish face-paint. "It just–just appeared!"

Lapointe stared into the still-mysterious maw of the underground canal. "So that's where they've been hiding. A veritable water-maze," he muttered. "Hurry, LeBec, for the love of God!"

At last, they had forced a passage through the crowds, back to the tall looming house in rue Mendoza where the corpse of Sarah Gobseck had been discovered. As Lapointe had guessed, the two ahead of them had abandoned their own car and were hurrying towards the entrance of No. 15 into which they swiftly disappeared.

By the time Lapointe and his assistant had reached the door, it was locked and bolted. Much time was wasted as they attempted to rouse the residents and gain access.

Now, at the very top of the building, they could hear a strange, single note, as of an organ, which began to drown almost all other sound and made communication difficult. As they neared the fifth floor, they became aware of a violent, pulsing light filling the stairwell below. It seemed to pour through the skylight and have its origins on the roof. The air itself had an unnatural quality, a strong smell of vanilla and ozone which reminded Lapointe irrationally of the corniche at Bourdeaux where as a boy he had holidayed with his family.

Next, an unnatural pressure began to exert itself on the men, as if gravity had somehow tripled in intensity and they moved sluggishly with enormous effort up to the final landing where Monsieur Gris, an expression of terror on his features, was attempting to descend the stairs. Behind him, a ladder had been pulled down from the ceiling and now gave access to an open door in the roof.

They were at last straggling the ladder to the roof. There, amongst the old chimneys and sloping leads, stood four people—a vicious-looking woman whose beauty was marred by a rodent snarl and a tonsured priest whom Lapointe immediately identified as Vautrin—otherwise known as Jacques Collin, but here disguised as the Abbé Carlos Herrera!

Confronting Vautrin and his co-conspiratator Vera Pym were Zenith the albino and the Countess Una von Beck. All were armed—Vautrin with a rapier and Pym with a modern automatic pistol. Zenith carried his ebony sword-stick while Countess von Beck had raised a Smith and Wesson .45 revolver which she pointed at the snarling leader of the Vampires.

And, if this scene were not dramatic enough, there yawned behind Pym and Vautrin a strange, swirling gap in the very fabric of time and space which mumbled and cried and moved with a nervous bubbling intensity.

"Sacred Heaven!" murmured Lapointe. "That is how they got here and that is how they intend to leave. They have ripped a rent through the multiverse. This is not a gateway in the usual sense. It is as if someone had taken a sledge-hammer to the supporting walls of Saint Peter's! Who knows what appalling damage they have created!"

Then, suddenly, Vautrin had moved, his long, slender blade driving for Zenith's heart. But the albino's instincts were as sharp as always. Dodging the thrust, he drew his own rapier of black, vibrating steel which seemed to sing a song of its own. Mysterious scarlet runes ran up and down its length as if alive. He replied to Vautrin's thrust with one of his own.

Parrying, Vautrin began to laugh—a hideous obscenity of sound which somehow seemed to blend with that awful light pouring through the rift in multiversal space their crude methods had created. "Your powers of deduction remain superb, Zenith, even if your taste in friends is not. She was indeed 'La Torpille.' I thought I had driven her to self-destruction, but she failed me in the end. I struck her down, as you and the others have guessed, and then, to make sure the body was never discovered, and seen to be murdered, I employed the services of Madame Vera Pym here. She is an old colleague."

Now Lapointe had drawn his revolver and was levelling it. "Stop, Monsieur Vautrin. In the name of France! In the name of the Law! Stop and put down your weapon. On your own admission, I arrest you for the murder of Mademoiselle Sarah Gobseck!"

Again, Vautrin voiced that terrible laugh. "Prince Zoran, Commissaire Lapointe, your powers of deduction are impressive and I know I face two wonderful opponents, but you will not, I assure you, stop my escape. The multiverse herself will not permit it. And put up your weapons. You cannot kill me any more than I can kill you!" He used Zenith's given name, Zoran, which went with the title he had long-since renounced, almost challenging the albino to prove his humanity.

Then, perhaps goaded by this, Zenith struck again, not once but twice, that black streak of ruby-coloured runes licking first at Vautrin's heart and then, as she raised her pistol to fire, at Vera Pym's.

The woman also began to laugh now. Together, their hideous voices created a kind of resonance with the pulsing light and almost certainly kept the gateway open for them. Vera Pym was triumphant. "You see," she shouted, "we are indestructible. You cannot take our lives in this universe, nor shall you be able to pursue us where we are going now!"

And then, she stepped backwards into that howling vortex and vanished. In a moment, Vautrin, also smiling, followed her.

For a sudden moment there was silence. Then came a noise, like a huge beast breathing. The roof was lit only by the full Moon and the stars. Lapointe felt the weight disappear from him and knew vast relief that circumstances had refused to make Zenith a murderer and Countess Una his accomplice, for then he would have been obliged to arrest them both.

"We will find them," he promised as the snoring vortex dwindled and disappeared. "And if we do not, I expect they will find us. Have no doubt, we shall be waiting for them." He raised exhausted eyes to look upon a bleak, emotionless albino. "And you, Monsieur, are you satisfied you cannot be revenged on the likes of Vautrin?"

"Oh, I fancy I have taken from him something he valued more than life," said the albino, sheathing his black rapier with an air of finality. He shared a thin, secret smile with the Countess von Beck. "Now, if you'll forgive me, Monsieur le Commissaire, I will continue about my business while the night is young. We were planning to go dancing." And, offering his arm to Countess Una, he walked insouciantly down the stairs and out of sight.

"What on Earth did he mean?" LeBec wondered.

Commissaire Lapointe was shaking his head like a man waking from a doze. He had heard about that black and crimson sword cane and believed he might have witnessed an action far more terrible, far more threatening to the civilization he valued than any he had previously imagined.

"God help him," he whispered, half to himself, "and God help those from whom he steals..."

John Peel normally writes science fiction and fantasy, but for both his and our pleasure, he finds time to craft clever little period mysteries for Tales of the Shadowmen. *After the Count of Monte-Cristo and Rouletabille, his protagonist in this third volume is Isidore Beautrelet, the young amateur detective that nearly outsmarted both Arsène Lupin and Sherlock Holmes in* The Hollow Needle. *But in a twist characteristic of Peel's stories, the lackdaisical Beautrelet is here teamed up in an amusing Franco-British* Entente Cordiale *fashion with a legendary and earnest English hero of the times whose help becomes necessary to solve the intriguing mystery of...*

John Peel: *The Successful Failure*

Fontainebleau, 1913

The Police were still buzzing about the Musée du Château de Fontainebleau when Isidore Beautrelet ambled up to the entrance. Most of the men appeared bored, but were attempting to seem active. Beautrelet could tell, however, that they were studiously doing nothing of any importance. While he knew that sometimes persons entered the Police force with low aims, it was a trifle puzzling that so many of them should be concentrated in such a small area. It was even more puzzling when he discovered that they were there in the company of Commissaire Guichard, an efficient and uncommonly able officer whom Beautrelet had once had occasion to assist. It was not like him to tolerate such obvious inefficiency in his men. They were, however, efficient enough to refuse entry to Beautrelet, but sent word to the Commissioner.

"Beautrelet!" the Policeman called out a few moments later, hurrying to greet the young student. "I don't know how you managed to hear of this so quickly, but I am sorry to say that there can be nothing in this minor mystery that could possibly be of interest to you."

Beautrelet spread his hands. "In all innocence, Commissaire," he vowed, "I was not even aware that there *was* any mystery."

"Indeed? Then why does your arrival coincide with a bungled burglary attempt?"

Beautrelet smiled. "Simple chance," he said. "I am currently occupied at university with the study of art, and the Musée de Fontainebleau has an exceptionally fine collection of medieval icons. I am here purely as a member of the public, hoping to broaden my grasp on the finer points of such masterpieces."

"I must confess I am relieved," Guichard said. "For one ghastly moment, when I saw you striding up the pathway, I was certain that there was some dreadful crime that I was completely overlooking, and which you were already well upon your way to solving."

The young man laughed. "Nothing like that, at all. As I said, I had no idea that any crime had been committed."

"Technically, one hasn't," the Commissioner said. "The would-be thieves were disturbed and left the premises empty-handed. I am here merely in the attempt to see if they left any clues as to their identity behind. But the search has been unsuccessful–they were too professional to make such mistakes."

"Indeed?" Beautrelet now understood why so many Policemen were attempting to look useful without actually working–there was nothing to find, so little need to exert oneself. "Then I am sorry I caused you any consternation. Do you have any notion when the Museum will be opened to the public again? I have made a fairly strenuous trip out here, and would hate to be turned away without seeing the remarkable triptychs they possess."

Guichard shrugged, a gesture that involved moving much of his upper body; it was most expressive. "The general public–I do not know. But for you, I am sure I can arrange something. Come with me." He led the way inside the neo-Gothic building, where two worried-looking gentlemen were pacing impatiently. The Museum Director, an older man, with thinning grey hair slicked and precisely combed back, rushed with as much dignity as he was able to meet them.

"Commissaire," he said, urgently, "nothing was stolen, nothing was harmed. How much longer must we be inconvenienced by all of these brutish bluecoats clomping about my premises?"

"Monsieur Voisin," the Policeman said politely, "we are completing our investigation and will shortly be leaving. In the meantime, may I be permitted to introduce you to Monsieur Isidore Beautrelet? He is a student of art, and I would ask you to be kind enough to allow him to study whatever he wishes."

The second man had arrived by now, and at the name his eyebrows shot up. "Isidore Beautrelet?" he asked. "The celebrated young detective? You have called him in to consult upon this minor case?"

Guichard shook his head. "No, Monsieur Poitevin, he is not here in any capacity save that as a student of art. He wishes to examine your triptychs to aid him in his studies in school. I merely introduce him to you gentlemen in the hopes that you will be kind enough to extend him courtesies beyond that of the average member of the public."

"But of course, Commissaire," Poitevin agreed. "We would be most pleased." He turned to Beautrelet. "In fact, you have timed your visit just right–for today we are packaging the triptychs in seven cases for shipment to the Louvre Museum tomorrow morning, where they will be on display for several months."

"This is all very well," the Director complained to the Commissioner. "But when may we get back to normal? And when will you remove your suspect?"

"Suspect?" Beautrelet's eyes sparkled. "Come, Inspector, you made no mention of having seized a villain!"

"Hardly that," Guichard laughed. "He is merely a young boy who cannot account for his activities too well. I would not even call him a suspect–merely suspicious. He's a young Englishman who speaks remarkably good French, but who appears to me to be a trifle lunatic."

"You intrigue me," Beautrelet confessed. "A crime that is not a crime, and a suspect who is not a suspect? It seems a shame that there is no real mystery here then, all things considered."

"There's nothing to get your fertile little brain overly interested," the Policeman insisted.

"Quite," Poitevin agreed. "It was merely a botched robbery, and the thieves managed to steal absolutely nothing. The young Englishman was merely lurking about and unable to account for himself. I'm sure he's merely a simpleton, like so many of that island race."

Beautrelet sighed. "Then it is perhaps a bad thing that all of this non-mystery has excited my perhaps overly-active imagination. Might I be permitted to learn the facts of this non-case?"

"They are simply told," Guichard replied. "At 2 a.m., the night guards made their rounds and found nothing amiss. They retraced their steps precisely on schedule at 2:27 a.m., and discovered a door ajar. One of the guards sounded the alarm, and three men promptly fled through the gardens. The guards telephoned the police, the Director and Monsieur Poitevin. We all arrived here roughly together. While these two gentlemen examined for any missing objects, I and my men searched for clues. But the thieves were obviously professionals, and had left nothing to be discovered."

"And my assistant and I checked the collection thoroughly," Monsieur Voisin added. "We soon ascertained that nothing had been stolen. The thieves were obviously interrupted before they could steal anything."

The Commissioner nodded. "And one of my men, searching the general area, came across a young English boy who was not able to explain his presence here with any clarity, so he was apprehended."

"Interesting," Beautrelet commented. "There is nothing missing, and the guards say that the men were carrying nothing?"

"Nothing," Voisin confirmed.

"Might I perhaps be allowed to see the room in which they were disturbed?" Beautrelet asked the Director. After a moment, the older man shrugged.

"The Police have thoroughly investigated, but I can see no reason to refuse such a simple request. If you would follow me?" He led the way from the entrance hall into a side room.

Beautrelet noted that the walls were lined with paintings, none of which were of great value or of interest–minor works for the most part by French landscape painters. There were also some small statues on pedestals, including two which even his untrained eye could see were Greek originals, dating back to at least 300 BC. They appeared to be quite fine. "Curious," he commented.

"What is?" asked Director Voisin, frowning.

"Assume for a moment, if you are able, that you are an art thief. You determine to break into the Musée de Fontainebleau. What among the collection would you steal?"

"Why..." The older man spluttered a moment, and then scowled. "I would take the icons, I imagine."

"So, too, would I," Beautrelet agreed. "Yet, if I recall the floor plans for this Museum correctly, the icons are housed upstairs, are they not?"

"Yes," Poitevin agreed. "I imagine that the thieves intended to head there, but were startled and fled instead."

"Yes, I think most people would imagine that," Beautrelet agreed. "Is it not odd, then, that they took nothing?" He gestured toward the two statues. "Even if I were fleeing in fear from the guards, I think I would have the presence of mind to help myself to those rather valuable objects."

"Perhaps the thieves did not realize how valuable they are?" Poitevin suggested.

"That is always possible," Beautrelet agreed. "But you would imagine that anyone attempting to rob an art museum would know the value of what they are stealing."

"Unless they were focused in on stealing a certain set of items," Guichard offered. "They may have been specialists."

"Again, it is possible." The young man rubbed his hands together. "Now, what about your suspect? Pardon me, your non-suspect?"

The Commissioner laughed. "Whatever he is, I think you'll find him interesting."

He led his friend to a door marked *Privé*, and they passed into a rather crowded office. There was a desk and a set of filing cabinets, but a large portion of the room was taken up with a number of packing cases. Into what small space was left were crowded a bored-looking policeman and a teenaged boy who looked decidedly cross.

He was fair-haired, and appeared to be about 14–though, as he was small, Beautrelet decided he might just be a little older. He stood straight, and controlled his temper with obvious difficulty. Guichard gestured toward the youth. "This is Mr. James Big... Big..." He stumbled over the name and finally gave up, shrugging. "One of those impossible, unpronounceable English names."

"No matter," Beautrelet decided. "James will do nicely." He smiled at the youth, receiving another scowl in return. "Now, perhaps you can explain why you are found so close to a spectacularly unsuccessful robbery?"

"I know nothing about any robbery," the young man growled. "I was merely coming to the Museum to talk to the Director about his cousin."

"My cousin?" Voisin spluttered, confused. "Do you know him?"

"Not at all," James replied. "But I should like to. Is he not the man who, partnered with the redoubtable Monsieur Blériot, who constructed aircraft until quite recently?"

"Oh, that folly!" The Director sighed. "Yes, I'm afraid he is. It's all nonsense, you know. It will never catch on."

The youth glared at him. "This? This from a man whose country has invented the aerial show? It would seem that your career of glorifying the past has left you dwelling there also–the *airoplane* is the coming thing," he pronounced. "It will shape our very future. Mankind will no longer be bound by the shackles of the ground, but will soar to wherever his imagination can take him. And I aim to be in the forefront of those so soaring."

Beautrelet couldn't help chuckling at this statement, which earned him another of the boy's dark glares. "You are evidently an aero enthusiast," the young detective commented. "I find it difficult to believe you had anything at all to do with this robbery."

"That's what I've been trying to tell these idiotic Policemen for more than an hour now," James growled. "But they refuse to listen."

"We have listened now," Commissaire Guichard pointed out. He turned to Beautrelet. "My friend, I cannot simply release this youth until my investigations are complete. Perhaps I could impose upon you to keep an eye on him for me, and so free up the energies of my men?"

Beautrelet considered the proposal. There was something in this stiff-backed and stiff-necked young man that he found appealing. Truth be told, James reminded him of himself, but a few years back. And it might not be a bad idea if he had a hand in what he was already starting to plan... "Very well, Commissaire," he agreed. "If James is agreeable, I will happily take him into my custody."

"Are you another of these damnable Policemen?" the young man demanded.

"No; like you, I am a student. I merely dabble in detection as a sideline." He held out a hand. "My name is Isidore Beautrelet."

"James Bigglesworth," the other replied. After a moment's hesitation, he shook the offered hand.

Beautrelet could see why Guichard had faced problems attempting to pronounce such a surname! "Well, James," he said, "perhaps you'd be kind enough to accompany me? While the Commissaire clears up what details he can, I should like to have a chance to examine the triptychs I came to see, before they are packaged and shipped away. We do not have much time, it would seem."

The young man's face fell–he clearly had little interest in art, and wished only to get into his beloved aerial craft. Beautrelet had a little pity for the youth, but a little art education could hardly hurt James. Monsieur Poitevin took them up the wide marble stairs to the room where the icons were stored in cases that, he noted, were wired for an electrical alarm. James attended rather sullenly, but

Beautrelet found immense pleasure in examining the exquisite workmanship. From time to time, he pointed out details to the young man–the subtle workmanship of the gold leaf on one piece, the enameling on a second, or the subtle placement of jewels to enhance the scene on a third. Despite his initial sullen response, James soon began pointing out details without being prompted.

"You enjoy the artwork after all," Beautrelet commented with a slight smile.

"It's not as good at the work Monsieur Blériot manages on his rotary engines," James answered, "but there is skill of a kind here, and they are rather pleasing to the eye." He considered for a moment. "Are they very valuable, then?"

Beautrelet nodded. "I hesitate to use the word *priceless*, for each does have a price, but they are certainly irreplaceable–and much desired. There are collectors who would love to have these in their own hands, even if theft were involved."

"But the thieves apparently mucked the whole thing up," James said.

"So the Police believe," agreed the detective.

James didn't misunderstand the comment. "But you do not?" he asked, finally showing a little life.

"I do not," Beautrelet agreed. "The thieves, as the Police agree, were professionals. And yet they managed such a gross mistake as to not know the times the Museum guards made their rounds? Does that not sound like a contradiction in terms?"

"Yes," James agreed, thoughtfully. "If I were going to rob this place, that's one of the first things I'd want to discover. I'd need to know how long I had to swipe the stuff."

"And yet the Police would have us believe that these criminals were not as smart as two scholars, eh?" Beautrelet grinned. "Now, I don't know about you, but I find myself growing famished. Why do we not talk further over a plate in the local café?" And he steadfastly refused to be drawn on the subject of the robbery attempt until they were both seated and dining on a rather pleasant dish of chicken.

"Right," James said, his mouth rather full, "you don't buy this theory that the robbery was unsuccessful, then?"

"Not quite," Beautrelet answered. "I do not believe that it should be termed a robbery at all. The aim was never to steal anything."

James halted, his next fork load close to his mouth. "Then why break into the Museum at all?"

"Precisely!" Beautrelet beamed. "The Police, assuming the purpose to be robbery, do not consider any other possibility. I, on the other hand, approach the matter in my own way."

"You mean, you work like Mr. Sherlock Holmes–search out clues, and add them together to solve the mystery?" said James.

"I do not," Beautrelet replied, somewhat primly. "That sort of thing is all very well for Mr. Holmes, but it has little bearing on my methods. What I do is to examine the crime. I then form a theory as to how it is committed, and why, and then I go in search of the evidence necessary to prove me either correct or incorrect. Once I am certain I know how the crime has been committed, then I know what evidence must be there for my theory to be true. So!" He sat back from his meal and steepled his fingers together. "I begin with the idea that the thieves–we may as well call them that, even though they stole nothing–yet!–accomplished their purpose in breaking into the museum. Knowing the timetable the guards must follow, they allowed themselves to be seen and chased, empty-handed, from the premises. If they did not *take* anything from the museum, then, logically, their mission was to bring something *into* the place."

"Something in?" James was clearly confused. "Why would they want to do that?"

"That is the very essence of the problem," Beautrelet said, with some satisfaction. "When we know the answer to that, then we shall uncover the whole plot. So–their aim was not to steal, but to plant something in the Museum. Something that will make their intended target simpler to steal later, clearly. Their target *must* be the icons–aside from the fact that they are the most valuable items that the museum owns, we know that many of them are soon to be sent to the Louvre on loan for several months. The matter of the timing can hardly be coincidental. Now, as well-guarded as this museum is, the Louvre is so much more defended. Since the theft of the *Mona Lisa* from there two years ago, security has been increased and improved. The chance of stealing the icons from there must be minuscule. So, they are to be taken here."

"But they weren't taken," James argued.

"No, and why not? For the first reason, because it would take time to steal them. You were in that room with me, and saw the exhibits. All of the items are under glass, and there are electrical alarms affixed the cases. No doubt a moderately skillful thief could get around this problem, but it would take time. And time is what our criminals do not have. The guards make their rounds in such a fashion that the rooms are examined every seven minutes. That is clearly not enough time to steal the icons, no matter how expeditious the thief is."

"I see," James nodded. "But you said this was only the first reason; there are more?"

"One other," Beautrelet informed him. "Let us assume that the thieves did somehow manage to steal the icons and make their getaway. The alarm would be raised within minutes. Sleepy as the Police are in this town, even they would be able to respond in time, perhaps, to intercept the fleeing villains. And, in any case, even if the thieves escaped, everyone would know that the icons were missing, and a watch would be set for them. The icons are indeed beautiful and valuable, but there are not many places where they could be sold. Oh, the jewels and gold in them would be intrinsically valuable, but it is as complete works of art that they would fetch the most money–and once word of the theft was issued, the market for the icons would close."

James considered these points. "But you are making a case *against* stealing the treasures," he objected.

"Indeed I am," beamed Beautrelet. "And, in fact, the icons were *not* taken!"

"I must confess, I am getting extremely confused," James said with a frown. "You are arguing that no crime has been committed."

Beautrelet shrugged. "Well, there is the matter of breaking and entering, and criminal trespass–but, other than that, no crime *has* been committed–*yet*. What has occurred is merely the setting for the real crime–and a rather cunning one at that."

"But I'm blowed if I can see what the crime is yet!" James exclaimed in exasperation.

"That is because you were not present when the final clue was uttered," the detective consoled him. "I, however, was. Director Voisin mentioned that the icons would be sent to the Louvre in the morning, in seven packing cases."

James blinked. "Seven? But there were *eight* cases in the room." He smiled depreciatingly. "I don't normally count such things, but I was in there a while, and had little else to occupy my mind."

Beautrelet chuckled. "Yet you did note the one salient fact–seven cases are being sent out, but there are eight awaiting pickup." He examined his new friend with curiosity–did the English boy have the brains to work the rest out for himself?

After a moment, James's face lit up. "Of course!" he exclaimed. "The thieves brought in the extra crate... filled with replicas of the icons they wished to steal, no doubt. This crate must be marked in some way, so that they can tell it apart from the crate with the *real* icons... Then, when the crates are removed, the thieves will intercept the van carrying them and steal the crate that they want." He considered a moment further, then nodded with conviction. "They will set the raid up, like the raid on the Museum, so it will look as though they have failed again. There will, after all, still be *seven* packaging crates on the truck when they leave. The fakes will go on display at the Louvre. Sooner or later, someone will spot the deception, but by that point, the real icons will have been sold to collectors and the thieves long vanished."

Beautrelet beamed. "James, I do believe you have followed my thought processes almost exactly. We shall make a detective of you yet."

"Right," James said, putting down his utensils. "So we now tell the Police?"

"No, we do not," Beautrelet said sharply. "And that for two reasons. Firstly, because it is clear that there is someone on the inside working with the gang. This person must have supplied them with precise descriptions and photographs of the icons so that replicas could be forged, and must, clearly, be the one who is watching over the shipment. I do not have enough evidence to accuse any specific individual, so if the Police strike now, the truly guilty man will go free."

James nodded, understanding this. "And the second reason?"

"The Police have the same facts that we have; if they are not bright enough to follow them to the same conclusion we have, then I do not see why they should have the credit for the arrest of the thieves. Let the glory come to those who have worked for it."

The English boy's face lit up. "You propose that *we* capture the gang ourselves?"

"I do indeed."

James looked worried again. "Just the two of us? There may be many of them, and they may well be armed."

"Are you any good with a pistol?" Beautrelet asked him, casually.

"I'm a decent shot," James assured him. "I've had plenty of practice–I grew up in India, and did a lot of hunting."

"Fine. Then you shall carry my spare pistol, and I shall have one also. But I do not aim to get into a fight–I am sorry to have to say it, but I am not a terribly bold man. I prefer the cerebral arts to fisticuffs, and usually leave that side of things to the Police. No, I propose we arm ourselves simply in case of the unexpected. I propose also that we follow the delivery van, unseen, and then wait for the robbery. Once it is accomplished, we must then follow the thieves back to their hiding place, and the alert the local constabulary. They are professionals, and I am happy to leave the actual capture to them. I have, however, one small problem yet to overcome in my plan."

"And that is?" James prompted.

"How we shall be able to follow the thieves without being observed doing so by them. I shall have to think about it for a while."

James shook his head. "No, I do believe that I can work something out," he said. "The only problem is that what I have in mind isn't exactly legal."

Beautrelet made an airy gesture. "We shall be preventing a major crime–I should think my standing with the Police is good enough that bending the rules a trifle will be overlooked." He regarded James with amusement. "What do you have in mind?"

The English youth shook his head. "Let me plan it out before I tell you," he suggested. "Meanwhile, do you think we could manage some sort of disguise? It might be a good idea."

Beautrelet beamed; if there was one thing he enjoyed, it was in assuming a really convincing disguise. "I imagine that something of the sort might be arranged."

"It would help if you could make me look a trifle older," James suggested.

"A fake beard and moustache should do admirably," the detective decided. "And I shall become an itinerant painter–there are some sights hereabouts well worth a canvas or two, if I were only skilled enough."

"Right," James said, happily. "Then let's finish eating, and get to work."
He lay down his utensils.

Beautrelet smiled at his eager young friend. "I think we have time for a little pastry first..."

The following morning found Beautrelet at his easel two blocks from the Château, watching carefully whilst sketching the building. A large, noisy truck had drawn up earlier, and four workmen were engaged in loading the crates aboard. They were being watched carefully by several Policemen under the personal supervision of Commissaire Guichard. The good Commissioner had glanced over at Beautrelet several times with evident suspicion, but the disguise the detective wore–a goatee beard, a monocle and painter's smocks–served to hide his true identity from his friend.

All that was missing was James. The young man had vanished yesterday afternoon for a while in his own disguise, and had reappeared at supper time evidently rather proud of himself. He refused to explain how he had arranged for the truck to be followed, merely promising that they would not be observed. Then he had vanished after breakfast, and failed to reappear.

The rear of the truck was closed up, and there was a round of paperwork that was signed. Beautrelet was getting quite alarmed that his companion was still missing. It was starting to look as though his plans would crash and burn.

"Sorry I'm late," James apologized, hurrying up. "But I had the devil of a time getting petrol. Some of your countrymen are lazy beggars at this time in the morning. Am I too late?"

"No," Beautrelet informed him, considerably relieved. He gestured, though carefully–he did not wish to draw attention. "They are just about ready to leave."

"Then perhaps we should also," James said. "I'll give you a hand with your art supplies, if you like." Together, they packed everything away. They stopped at the café on their way, slipping the materials just inside the door, and then James led the way out of the town and into a large field.

Beautrelet stopped dead in his tracks, his face ashen. "What is that contraption?"

James laughed easily. "That *contraption*, as you call it, is one of the most advanced *airoplanes* in the world–the Morane-Saulnier Type L. There are only a half-dozen yet constructed, and I was lucky indeed to be able to borrow it. It isn't likely to be missed for a couple of hours yet."

"An aircraft?" the detective spluttered. "You propose that we use that... monstrosity to follow the van?"

"It's the best idea," James said, airily. "Those thieves will be looking behind them on the road for pursuit–not hundreds of feet over their heads."

"But... but... that machine must be very noisy!" Beautrelet protested.

"They won't hear a thing over the racket their own motor is making," James answered. "Besides, we'll be pretty high up–at least a thousand feet."

"A thousand feet?" the detective said, weakly. "In the air? My friend, you are insane! I told you before, I am not the most courageous of men, and I much prefer that my feet stay planted firmly on the ground. Besides, I do not trust these airplanes–they have a great tendency to crash."

"Not this beauty," James said happily, stroking the fabric of the fuselage. "It's got a very reliable Gnome Lambda 7 cylinder rotary engine, and it flies like a dream. I know–I had to fly it here this morning. Come on, you'll love it."

"I would hate it–if I were to try it, which I shall not!" The detective shook his head. "I am not getting into that death trap for anything this world has to offer!"

James sighed. "Well, then, I guess the crooks will get the better of us, because there's no other way to follow them without their knowledge." He sighed heavily. "I guess I'll just have to live with failure, then–the knowledge that they have beaten us."

Beautrelet was no fool, and could see immediately James's aim. But, at the same time, he had to confess his hand was well-played. If there was one thing Beautrelet would never allow, it was defeat. He knew it was stubborn pride and a touch of arrogance in his own character, and no doubt a flaw. But he would never allow himself to be beaten. Swallowing hard, he screwed up every last little bit of courage he possessed–and, as he had confessed, it was not a large supply–and he set his hand to the fragile craft.

"Help me aboard," he said through gritted teeth.

James helped him into the second seat, and then hopped cheerfully into the pilot's seat. "Engine's still warm and we shouldn't have much problem," he announced. The beastly machine roared to frightening life, and it took every gram of will-power the detective possessed not to leap, screaming, from the machine and back to the safety of the dear Earth.

Then James let out the throttle, and the plane taxied across the field, gathering speed as it went. It had to be going far faster than Beautrelet had ever traveled before–certainly more than 50 kph–and then it somehow managed to stagger into the air. Beautrelet was wishing sincerely he had not breakfasted so well.

The ground fell away below him, and he fought back panic that threatened to overwhelm his reason.

"This is the life, eh?" James laughed, his voice snatched away by the wind through the struts.

Life? This looked like death to Beautrelet! They were being suspended in the air only by the strength of a noisy, smelly engine and a large wing above their heads. At any second the whole insane contraption might fail, and they would plunge to their inevitable and grisly deaths... He strove to force this ghastly image from his mind.

180

James maneuvered the craft around, and a moment later he called out: "There's the road to Paris, and I can see the truck on its way. Take a look."

"You must be insane," Beautrelet complained. "I have no intention of staring over the side of this machine. I shall merely sit here and suffer."

"Oh, chin up, old man," James said cheerfully. "You'll get to love this in no time at all."

"You are quite correct," the detective agreed. "At no time at all will I get to love this. Keep your attention on the road, and I shall sit quietly here and panic until we are on the ground once again."

The journey was an absolute misery. Beautrelet sat as still as he was able, eyes screwed shut, attempting to breath regularly. Fear almost overwhelmed him, and it was only by shutting out the thought of what they were doing that he was able to remain seated. He allowed James to do the work, being updated by the young man from time to time.

"Ah!" James called, finally. "The truck has stopped! Some kind of a blockade." Beautrelet's stomach almost exited his mouth as the mad English youth dropped the plane down for a closer look. "A tree has been felled, which has forced the truck to stop. Ah, here's a second truck, blocking retreat–obviously the crooks we've been expecting. They have guns held on the workmen, and have started to unfasten the back of the truck. A couple of the men have gone in... and they're bringing out one crate and transferring it now... The workmen are being held in the cab, so they haven't seen it go... And here now comes the Police escort. They've seen the crooks, but the crate has been hidden."

"Naturally," said Beautrelet. "Now the thieves will allow themselves to be chased away, and when the shipping truck is examined seven crates will still remain. Once again, a successful failure on the part of these villains!"

"Right," James agreed, swooped their plane around again. "I'm now following the thieves' truck. This is all rather exciting, isn't it?"

"It will be if and when we return to the Earth safely," Beautrelet assured him. He was not at all assured that this was likely. He could picture any number of things going wrong with their flimsy craft, and see it spinning from the sky in his mind's eye and crashing back to the solid Earth, killing them both... He was on the verge of fainting from hysteria when he heard James call out again.

"The van's stopped at a large old house," he yelled over the howl of the wind and the pounding of the engine. "It's on the outskirts of this small town. I think we had best alert the Police now."

"And how do you propose to do that?" Beautrelet. "This infernal device is not fitted with a telephone."

"Drop a message," James said cheerily. "I wrote one before we started, and put it into a small pouch. We simply drop down low enough and lob it at the first Policeman that we find. It alerts him to follow us, and call in reinforcements."

Beautrelet had to admit that James was performing well in his detective duties. But the most important thing, to him, was their imminent landing, and his successful return to Earth. As soon as James had located a Policeman and dropped the message, he flew slowly back toward the house where the thieves had holed up. Then he looked for a field large enough to land in.

"Hang on tight," he called over his shoulder. "The landing's always the trickiest part."

"But you have done it before?" Beautrelet howled.

"Well–just the once. I've never been allowed in a plane on my own before this morning."

"What?" Beautrelet almost did faint that time. "This is the first time you have flown this craft?"

"The second–the first was when I borrowed it. In fact, it's only the second time I've flown *any* airoplane. But it's jolly easy, really–I haven't had any problems, have I?"

"He's insane," the detective muttered to himself. But it was probably a good thing he had not known this information earlier–if he had, nothing would have induced him to clamber into this Hellish contraption!

James took the plane down, and Beautrelet felt a distinct thump as the wheels touched the ground, bounced once, and then settled back. James cut the speed, and the craft gradually came to a halt. Beautrelet, with a cry halfway between thanks and terror, leaped from the craft, and fell onto his knees, kissing the ground.

"Never," he vowed, "never will I step into one of those Devil's devices again!"

"Buck up," James said, laughing, as he jumped lightly down. "That was the most awful fun. And we're safe and all in one piece."

"You are a maniac!" Beautrelet swore. He shuddered and pulled the tattered remnants of his courage together. "But now, let us meet the Police and go and capture the thieves."

That part of the adventure, at least, was simply effected. The local gendarmes, happy to show their big-city rivals how efficient they could be, raided the large house and captured the art thieves without a shot being fired. An hour later, Commissioner Guichard arrived, a surprised look on his face.

"But... there was no robbery!" he exclaimed.

Beautrelet, having regained his equanimity at last, laughed. "That's what they wished everyone to believe. But James and I knew otherwise."

Guichard gazed at the art treasures, half-unpacked from the shipping crate. "I shall have these returned to the Museum at once," he said.

"Not yet, please, Commissaire," Bernardine suggested. "We still need to capture the ring-leader of this little plot. He glanced at his pocket watch. "In an hour or so, the villain should arrive."

"How can you be so certain?" the Policeman asked.

"Because this is the half-day for the Château de Fontainebleau," Beautrelet explained. "And our mastermind will hurry here once it is closed to examine his haul. So, we have your men hide, and allow everything to look normal. And then we wait for our trap to be sprung." He glanced over at James, who was sleeping soundly in a comfortable chair. "Ah, the resilience of youth. You would hardly know, Commissaire, that only a short while ago, he and I were in peril of our lives a thousand feet above this house."

"I'm surprised he managed to get you into a plane," the Commissioner commented.

"No more than I am. But now–we wait."

Sixty eight minutes later, the front door opened and closed. A man's voice called out, and Beautrelet and Guichard both stiffened. James sprang suddenly awake, the loaned pistol in his hand.

The door to the room opened, and Monsieur Poitevin stepped through–and stopped, stunned, as three pistols were leveled in his face. "What does this mean?" he cried in shock.

"It means, my dear chap," James informed him, "that you've been well and truly nabbed."

Beautrelet beamed. "I could hardly have phrased it better myself. Commissaire, here is the ringleader of this gang." He turned to Poitevin and bowed slightly. "My congratulations, Monsieur–a very accomplished and creative crime. Unfortunately for you, it attracted my attention–otherwise, I am sure it would have been carried through most successfully."

He tipped his hat as the humbled man was led off by the Police. Then he turned to James. "Despite the affair of the aircraft, I wish to thank you for your assistance. You were of great help. And you have convinced me to keep my feet firmly planted on the ground in the future!"

"You'll be missing a lot of fun," James informed him. He handed back the borrowed pistol, and then held out his hand. "Well, Monsieur Beautrelet–thank you for a grand adventure!"

"And my thanks to you also, Mr. Biggles... Biggles..." He stumbled over the pronunciation of the foreign name.

James laughed. "Biggles will do just fine!"

Madame Atomos
by Cybele Collins (2006)

Joseph Altairac and Jean-Luc Rivera, both noted chroniclers of the fantastique *and the paranormal, used their expertise to explore the very origins of Madame Atomos and create an authentic-looking secret document that throws an unexpected light on her birth. They logically postulate that, after Madame Atomos' first strike on the United States in early 1963, some of the most shadowy players in the secret world of US intelligence were asked to investigate her and eventually discovered that, when it comes to Madame Atomos, the truth is indeed out there...*

Joseph Altairac & Jean-Luc Rivera: *The Butterfly Files*

Washington, 1963

The document printed below was originally classified Majestic Top Secret *and was released online by an organization known as the* Lone Gunmen, *that is, until their website was taken offline for reasons as yet unknown. We reproduce it here* verbatim *for our readers' enlightenment without vouching in any way for its authenticity. The footnotes (identified by arabic numerals) were part of the original document. The Lone Gunmen, however, have added three additional notes (identified alphabetically), attached at the end of the document.*

J.A. & J.-L. R

XF/AT/6 18 July 1963
From: Special Agent William Mulder, MJ-12
To: XXXXX, MJ-12 [a]
cc: J. E. Hoover, J. E. Evans, FBI ; Chief of Staff , US Army Intelligence; Prof. Tassilo von Töplitz, *Paperclip* (for evaluation).
Subject: Kanoto Yoshimuta, a.k.a. "Madame Atomos."

1. Acting upon a top priority request by J. E. Evans, the undersigned has launched an investigation into Subject. This investigation, code-named "Butterfly," was undertaken in Japan with the collaboration of the *Tokkoka*. [b] It has led to the discovery of a set of partially destroyed documents in an underground bunker located in the Shinjuku district of Tokyo. Special Agent Akamatsu of the *Tokkoka* has theorized that the bunker was one of Subject's very first bases, when she was still building up her organization.

2. The documents found are carbon copies of three letters printed on onionskin paper. Nothing else appears to have survived the blast when the *Tokkoka*, disregarding Agent Akamatsu's advice, affected a forced entry into the bunker. These letters are addressed by Subject to one Shiro Ishii, whom she affectionately calls "Uncle Ishii," then residing at an unnamed location in Pingfang, near Harbin, in Manchuria.[5]

3. In the first letter, dated October 1944, Subject thanks Ishii for the various samples collected from the *marutas* [6] which she now proposes to use for her own experiments. Subject establishes unambiguously that her experiments are based on protocols initially designed by Doctor Fu Manchu,[7] whose notes were found in his laboratory in Nanking after the Japanese invaded and sacked the city. It would seem that the capture of said laboratory was the veritable reason for their massive assault on that city.

4. In the second letter, which appears to have been written towards the end of May 1945, Subject inquires about Ishii's health and informs him that they are on the verge of beginning mass production. Subject remarks that the sacrifice of the *Yamato* and her 2,475 crewmen were not in vain. She reports that the first of the two submarines sent by Germany successfully avoided the American fleet and the 560 kilograms of uranium oxide it carried reached Nagasaki in time for her first experiments. The second submarine was forced to surrender in the North Atlantic on May 19, 1945. Subject adds that, despite the cowardice of the German crew, the two Japanese officers who were accompanying the shipment were given the right to commit suicide, thus preserving honor and, more importantly, the secrecy of her experiments. Ultimately, however, Subject concludes that, despite a succesful rate of mutation of the sample strains, her experiments have come too late to be used effectively by the Noborito Research Institute in their Fu-Go campaign.[8]

---

[5] This is likely Unit 731, a secret military medical unit of the Imperial Japanese Army based in Pingfang, which conducted research in biological warfare during the Second Sino-Japanese War and World War II.

[6] A special project of Unit 731 used human test subjects, dubbed *maruta* ("logs"), for their experiments. Whether this term originated as a joke, or from the fact that the official cover story was that Unit 731 was a lumber mill, is unknown.

[7] According to information obtained from Sir Denis Nayland Smith, we now know that the notorious Doctor Fu Manchu was also working on developing new strains of bacteria to be used as weapons of war at the same time.

[8] The Noborito Research Institute developed biological agents to destroy crops and plants using "Fu-Go" balloons sent to drift over the Western United States.

5. In the third letter, dated August 30, 1945, two weeks after Japan's surrender and three weeks after the bombings of Hiroshima and Nagasaki, Subject writes that the "Enemy" (America) has found the "Heart of the Dragon." [9] However, she adds that, thanks to her husband's forethought, she has succeeded in escaping with their most valuable secrets, and that she has now begun work on a plan to avenge their dead. Subject claims that she has already gathered a community of like-minded scientists around her and refers to a "Professor Aldridge" who has shared his blueprints for a new type of "flying object" with her, before the destruction of his own facility in Czechoslovakia. [10]

6. Finally, Subject writes: *"I shall carry the fight to the Enemy's heartland. Every day, I look at the new symbol of the battle that will occupy me for the rest of my life: this superb notebook that contains all the fruits of your* [Ishii's] *work and which your associates have delivered into my hands, as you instructed them to do. For it, I am eternally grateful, since the tattoed butterflies which adorn its binding will always remind me of..."* [11]

According to the results of this preliminary investigation, one is forced to conclude that, with respect to Subject, the truth is still out there.

William Mulder
Special Agent, MJ-12

A number of their scientists have come to work for us since the end of the war; a great number, however, have disappeared in unexplained circumstances.
[9] This may be referring to the fact that our experts found five Japanese cyclotrons, which could separate fissionable material from ordinary uranium, and six large separators. As you know, the cyclotrons were destroyed and dumped in Tokyo Harbor.
[10] This might help explain the mysterious disappearance of several prominent Japanese scientists mentioned in Note 4 above, and whose help would have been invaluable to our own Operation Nisei/731. As for Professor Aldridge, that name, and everything associated with it, is currently classified ATS-SCI and, therefore, cannot be discussed in this memo. See Documents X-F/3.9/95-11-24 and X-F/3.10/95-12-0. [c]
[11] The rest is illegible. We did find a fragment of what might have been that notebook amongst the charred remains of the bunker. Upon analysis, it appears to have been bound in human skin. The exact signification of the butterfly motif remains unknown; however, it is worth noting that many American G.I.s who fought in the Pacific Theater wore butterfly tattoos.

[a.] *All the recipients' names on the original document were blacked out, but we were able to restore most of them after careful analysis and comparisons with other known memoranda of the period.*

[b.] *The Japanese secret police, allegedly disbanded in 1945, but obviously still operate, albeit in relative secrecy.*

[c.] *This is clearly* the *Professor Aldridge, a key figure in the development of 20th century astronautics, whose biography was compiled by author W.A. Harbinson.*

Chris Roberson's tale is a bittersweet, moving story that revisits characters dear to our childhood through the merciless prism of modern-day light. Its layered structure delivers new insights upon each rereading. Like Paul DiFilippo and Brian Stableford's contributions, it is uniquely suited to Tales of the Shadowmen, *wonderfully embodying how our dearest literary figures can acquire a life of their own, transcending that given by their original creators. Just as the undersigned's "The Star Prince" in Volume 2 changed the way one may look at Saint-Exupery's* The Little Prince, *it is unlikely that you will ever look at Jean de Brunhoff's* Babar *in the same way after reading...*

Chris Roberson: *The Famous Ape*

Africa, Today

When the ape boarded the train in Comrade Olur Station, he'd given his name as Thomas Recorde. If the use of the surname, an antiquated pre-Republic custom, had raised any eyebrows, no one had seen fit to comment on it.

There were half a dozen other ape passengers on the mostly empty train, all in suits of clothes as threadbare as those Thomas wore, but they sat far apart from one another, not speaking, trying not to make eye contact. The only words spoken were exchanged with the elephant who made his ponderous way down the aisle, checking everyone's papers as the train steamed away from the station, leaving Olurgrad behind.

Thomas, for his part, kept his attention focused on the tarnished scrollwork on the cabin wall, studying it with the avid attention of one with nothing better to do. This had once been an imperial train, before the Animalist Revolution, and while it had been rechristened *The Glorious Battle of the Windmill* by the new government, its interior was still decorated with images of the Twelve Virtues. Thomas recalled the day at court, years before, when the old Elephant King had issued the decree that the Virtues should be emblazoned on all imperial property, commemorating a particularly portentous dream. The decree, of course, held as much weight now as any of the old King's numerous fancies, which was to say none at all, but while the images were faded, the figures themselves could still be discerned. This winged elephant, with his shield and saber, must represent Courage. This, with his saw, Perseverance, and this one Learning with his candle, and this Patience with his timepiece.

There were more, Thomas guessed, at the front of the car, but they were masked by the draped flag of Olurgrad, blazoned with a pair of white tusks on a field of green. There was some symbolism to that, Thomas was sure, the image of old imperial virtue being obscured by pious Animalist patriotism; but just what the symbol signified, he could not say, and did not much care.

Thomas had had his fill of piousness, and of patriotism. He had seen his first blue sky in years that morning, the horizons of his world for long decades limited by lifeless grey walls. But any joy he might have taken from his first impressions of freedom were marred by the noise of the parade. He and the other political prisoners had been cleaned up, dressed in the same suits in which they had been arrested years before, and marched out to Green Square to be put on display. It was Midsummer Day, the anniversary of the first Animalist Revolution. There had been a full martial parade, the ranks of the elephant army marching in time, the crowds singing *Beast of the World* in patriotic unison, if not entirely on key. The cannons of Fort Hatchibombotar were fired in salute, and then Comrade Poutifour had taken the podium. The first citizen of the nation, as well as the last surviving leader of the Revolution, the old elephant had been turned out with martial splendor, the ribbon of the Order of the Green Banner dangling from his left ear, his tusks polished to a mirror sheen. He delivered a rousing speech on the recent successes of the various Animal Committees, the minor victories of the Sharp Tusks Movement and the Clean Tails League, the advances of the Wild Comrades' Re-Education Committee to uplift the primitive elephants of the veldt.

Then Comrade Poutifour had turned the crowd's attention to Thomas and the other political prisoners. A great show was being made of this exchange with the Ape Republic, and while the text of Poutifour's speech spoke of it as representing an improvement in the relations between the two great powers, the clear subtext, thinly veiled, was that the apes were fast losing the long-standing cold war, and that the elephants would assuredly be the ultimate victors.

When the first citizen had concluded his remarks, as the day was ending, the ape prisoners were ushered unceremoniously to Comrade Olur Station, put on the train, and sent on their way.

Built in the days when both ape and elephant were ruled by Kings, the old railway line was once a vital artery of traffic between the two nations. Even when the apes ousted their King, and instituted the Republic, regular rail service was continued. It was only with the advent of the First Forest War that the trains stopped running, and after the elephants withdrew from the conflict, when the Animalists seized power, it seemed for a time that the trains might never run again. Now, it seemed, service had been resumed, however limited the basis. What that presaged for the future, Thomas was not sure. He had been out of touch with internal politics for some considerable time.

Thomas remembered the first time he'd ridden this line, when he'd gone as a young ape to Celesteville, and the court of the Elephant King. Now, a lifetime later, he made that trip in reverse, finally returning home.

The train rumbled along through the night, making its steady way through the Ituri Rainforest, skirting the border between Karunda and the Congo. It passed unnoticed through lands dominated by human tribes, first that of the Ba Baoro'm, and then the Bansutos, who did not sense the passing of the specially camouflaged train.

As dawn broke, the train finally approached its destination. Just east of the Omwamwi Falls, it entered a hidden tunnel, passed briefly through a midnight-dark tunnel, and came out the other side in the valley hemmed on all sides by mountains. There, before them, lay the sprawl of the Ape Republic, with Gorilla City at its center.

The other passengers seemed to come alive, as the train pulled into Monkeyville Station, their eyes widening, gradual smiles pulling at the corners of their wide ape mouths. Were they hoping to see family waiting to greet them? Friends? Or were they simply overcome by the emotion of returning home, after so long a delay?

Thomas knew that if anyone was waiting for him, it would not be family, and it would not be friends.

The train came to a stop, and the passengers queued to climb down to the platform. Thomas hung back, looking for any opportunity. The train's crew had readily accepted it when he'd identified himself as Thomas Recorde on boarding, and the elephant who checked their papers was too bored to notice the discrepancy, but Thomas knew that his imposture would not stand up under the close scrutiny of the Ape Republic's authorities. The fact that he used his birth name as an assumed identity, while perhaps ironic, did little to ensure that he would escape the inevitable consequences that would follow the discovery of the name under which he was better known. Famous, in fact. Or infamous, to be precise.

As it happened, he needn't have worried. Just as it came time for Thomas to disembark, one of the apes who had preceded him off the train went into a bout of histrionics on returning to his native soil, hooting loudly like one of their primitive cousins in the jungle, dropping to all fours, and kissing with prehensile lips the very flagstones of the Gorilla City pavement. While all eyes were on this rather dramatic performance, Thomas slipped away into the milling crowd of the train station, seemingly undetected by the uniformed officers waiting to receive the returned prisoners.

Thomas had a moment of brief panic, as he glanced back and his eyes met those of an ape in a wide-brimmed yellow hat, a yellow raincoat draped over his long forearm. From his position, and posture, it was clear that the ape in the yellow hat was some superior to the uniformed officers.

His heart pounding in his chest, Thomas willed himself to break eye contact. Passing a news kiosk, he stopped walking, reasoning that he would look less like someone attempting to flee if he was no longer moving. Forcing himself to act as calm and naturally as was possible, he picked up a copy of the *Gorilla City Gazette*.

"Is this even real?" asked the she-ape behind the counter, narrowing her eyes and looking close at the rumpled republic banknote Thomas had produced. She peered at the date. "This thing is older than I am."

Thomas gave a lopsided grin that didn't reach his eyes, and answered only with a shrug.

"Whatever," the she-ape replied with a shrug of her own, and rang up Thomas's change.

Sliding the coins in his pocket, Thomas tucked the folded paper under his arm, and casually glanced back over his shoulder. The attentions of the ape in the yellow hat were elsewhere, his back turned to Thomas.

As the pounding of his heart gradually slowed its pace, Thomas walked out of the Monkeyville Station, into a brief and clear Gorilla City morning.

It had been a lifetime since he had been back, and Thomas had no notion where to go. All he knew was that he wanted to be away from the station. He hurried to the cab stand on the corner, hopped in the backseat of the first car in line, and shut the door behind him.

"City Center, please," Thomas said.

The ape in the front seat, a weathered old silverback, glanced in the review mirror, his eyes narrowed beneath the brim of his cap. "You mean downtown?"

"*Oui*," Thomas said, and then cursed himself inwardly. "That is, yes."

The driver shook his head, but pulled away from the curb, merging into traffic.

Throughout the drive, not a word was exchanged between them, but at every stop the driver would stare intently through the mirror at Thomas, eyeing him with clear suspicion. Was he reacting to Thomas referring to a district of the city by a name not used since the days of the old King? Or to the Gallic accent which Thomas could not hide, having spoken nothing but the elephants' French for decades?

In silence, they reached the center of the city. Thomas paid the fare, his ancient bills eliciting the same response from the drive that they had from the newsvendor. His suspicions aside, however, the driver was happy to keep the change, and pulled away from the corner and back into traffic without a backwards glance.

The Sun had risen high enough in the east that the light now spilled between the close-packed buildings at the city's center. Thomas's shadow reached out an impossible distance before him as he walked, touching the buildings on the street's far side. His stomach grumbled, and Thomas realized absently that he had not had a bite to eat since leaving the prison in Olurgrad the morning before. He was unexpectedly famished.

In the shadow of a building that, in Thomas's youth, had been the Office of the Exchequer, but which now appeared to be an art museum of some stripe, was a small sidewalk café, tables under white clothes, straight-backed chairs with well-upholstered seats, shade umbrellas still folded from the night before. Thomas found a seat at the table farthest from the street, the stones of the building wall behind him cool through the thin fabric of his antique suit, and waved the waiter over.

Thomas ordered a pot of tea and a basket of fresh bread, doing his best to adopt the lost accent of his youth and failing. The waiter, though, subtler than the cabdriver had been, narrowed his eyes only slightly when confirming Thomas's order, and then left him with a tight, professional smile.

When his tea arrived, poured steaming into a delicate porcelain mug, Thomas spread the newspaper out before him, and read the news of the day.

President Solovar was up for reelection again. From what Thomas read, it appeared that the main opposition in the impending election came from two corners: Mohor's Anthar Primitivists on the one side, and the Force of Mind Party led by Grodd on the other. The article contended, however, that early polls indicated that Solovar would carry the day.

None of the names meant anything to Thomas. The last time he'd had reliable news of home, Huc had still been President of the Republic, and he'd never heard of the Anthar Primitivists or the Force of Mind Party, nor of Mohor or Grodd, whoever they might be. He might as well have been reading about some unknown, foreign country.

Which, in many respects, he was. It had been a lifetime or more since the death of God and the ouster of the old King, and the country had clearly changed in ways that the early Republic could never have guessed. When Thomas had left for Celesteville, sent to do Red Peter's bidding, General Huc was newly elected, the first President of the Republic. Now, the old General was surely dead, and an unknown set of players had taken to the political stage.

Thomas shut tight his eyes, remembering evenings at the Huc family home in his younger days. He had been betrothed to the General's daughter, Isabelle, when it came time for him to leave. But the General had felt his daughter too young to marry, and so Thomas and Isabelle had promised to wait until Thomas returned from his assignment in the elephant nation. When war had broken out, and Thomas's stay in the court of the Elephant King had been extended, he consoled himself in the knowledge that the war could not last forever, and that eventually his name would be cleared at home, and he and Isabelle would be reunited. Then the Animalists had overthrown the Elephant King, and jailed Thomas as a counter-revolutionary, and a lifetime had passed. For all he knew, Isabelle was dead as well, buried beside her father in the Huc family crypt.

Thomas's stomach roiled, and he angrily turned the page, looking for some relief from memory and politics. He sought solace in the entertainment sections, and failed to find it.

At the top of the page was a review of a new drama, entitled simply *Princess Flora*. The work of a rising young ape playwright, the drama was apparently based on rumors that the Elephant Princess, daughter to the old King, had survived the purges in the first days of the Animalist Revolution, and had emigrated first to Europe, and then to the United States. The reviewer called *Princess Flora* a masterwork, an uplifting story of the indomitable animal spirit, of perseverance in the face of overwhelming odds.

It was all nonsense. Nothing but fiction, whatever the playwright or the reviewer might think. Thomas knew first hand. He'd been there, had counted the bodies as they were dragged one by one from the King's summer home. There was no chance that any of the royal family had escaped that bloody retribution, not even sweet, simple, blameless Flora. She may have been possessed of an indomitable spirit, but when facing the overwhelming odds of a firing squad, even that brave young elephant had not persevered.

Not politics, nor entertainment, then. Perhaps in the pages of the editorials he might find some escape, some relief. But no.

The paper's back page was dominated by a single editorial, a lengthy missive excoriating the present government for allowing the return of the traitor Zephir to Gorilla City. There may have been implicit in the condemnation some message of support for one of the opposition candidates, either Mohor or Grodd, but such subtleties were beyond Thomas. He could only stare fixated at the name written so often in smudged black ink, and the atrocities and crimes so often attached to it. Zephir. The Traitor.

Eyes wide, Thomas looked up from the paper. On the far side of the patio, the waiter was in close conversation with a silverback ape in a fine suit, whispering in low voices while pointing in Thomas's direction. Suppressing the urge to panic, Thomas dropped a handful of rumpled republic notes on the table, and hurried from the café, his basket of breads untouched, his tea left still steaming in its mug.

Thomas walked at speed up the street, turned a corner, turned another corner, and promptly got lost. The city of his childhood seemed to have consumed and digested by another, and while bits and pieces could be matched to his memory, most was as unrecognizable as the names in the morning paper. Still he kept walking, aimlessly, as quickly as possibly without looking as though he were running. He resisted the temptation to look behind him, convinced that at any moment he would be recognized.

He walked down a narrow street, towering buildings crowding on either side, in deep shadows, the light of the morning Sun completely obscured. Then he turned a corner blindly, and found himself in a different world.

He had reached the geographic center of the city. Once known as Kensington Gardens, it had been renamed after the death of God as Moreau Park. Thomas remembered the dedication ceremony, as clear as though it had been the day before. Isabelle had stood by his side, hand-in-hand, and they'd wondered aloud what the future would bring, now that God was no longer among them. That was before the ouster of the old King, when Isabelle's father had simply been the head of the ape army, but even that, too, would soon change. It had been a strange, heady time, as all of the carefully crafted illusions so precious to the old order were one by one chiseled away, and a new, fresh-minted future revealed.

Thomas passed under the arch at the park's entrance, the bronze now tarnished a greenish-brown. A walking path stretched out before him, curving slightly to the west, while to his left stood an obelisk, with rows of cages arranged beyond. A zoo of some sort, it seemed.

Walking closer, Thomas was able to read the plaque set on the obelisk's face. Provided by the Gorilla City Humane Society, the plaque listed the names of all the mutants and sports which had been successfully reintegrated into human populations, with new identities and histories. Kaspa, Zembla and Ka-Zar. Nyoka, Sheena and Jann. The list went on and on.

Beneath the sign was a piece of weathered paper in a metal frame, a less grand notice. It said that in the cages beyond were those unfortunates who had not yet been "successfully retrained," and who remained on as wards of the state.

Thomas winced, despite himself. He knew what the notice meant, knew it had nothing to do with his past circumstances, but the resonances were too close to be ignored. Steeling himself, he rounded the obelisk, walking down the promenade, passing each of the cages in turn.

From time to time, the genetic engineering which granted the apes of Gorilla City intelligence and abilities in advance of their more primitive jungle cousins, went awry, leading to the birth of, to be charitable, "undesirables." Most of these displays commingled characteristics of an ape and the human from which the engineered genes had been drawn. Most often, these sports gave the appearance of being entirely human on the outside, while on the inside being as savage and unsophisticated as the most primitive jungle gorilla. These sad creatures belonged truly to neither world, human or ape, falling somewhere in between.

When Thomas had been a child, the order of the day was to eject these unfortunates from polite society, casting them out into the wilderness, like Spartans abandoning unwanted children to the elements. The hardiest of the sports, though, survived, taking refuge in the caves above the city. Thomas had heard campfire stories in his youngest years about these strange ape-men, and what became of them in the wild. In the years since, more forward-thinking citizens of Gorilla City had evidently objected to this admittedly cruel treatment, and sought other solutions to the problem. And it seemed that they'd had some measure of success, having found ways to reintegrate the ape-men into the human populations.

What remained in these cages, then, were those sports too primitive ever to be retrained, too much animal ever to pass as man, too much man ever to live among the animals. Thomas paused by one cage, inside of which hulked an ancient silverback ape-man, wrinkled and bent. A sign on the cage door indicated that his name was "Malb'yat." Thomas peered in, his heart going out to the sad, hunched creature in the cage, remembering the years he himself spent in a room no larger, no more amenable.

The old ape-man looked up, his watery eyes meeting Thomas's. He reached up a wrinkled hand, gnarled into a claw, and in a plaintive voice said, "Where? Where Balza?"

Thomas shook his head, sadly. He had no notion what a "Balza" was, nor had any confidence that the poor creature would understand the answer, if he had. He turned, and continued down the promenade.

Beyond the zoo, Thomas came to a statue atop a high pedestal. In cast bronze, it depicted a creature with the face of a man, and a body that intermingled aspects of man and gorilla, wearing an open shirt and loincloth. It was a familiar figure, and one which had haunted Thomas's dreams throughout childhood.

The strange man-ape depicted in the statue had insisted that his creations call him "God," and it had not been until after his death that the gorillas had learned the name by which he had once been known to his fellow humans. The apes of Gorilla City, like the elephants of Olurgrad and the rhinoceroses of Rataxesburg, all owed their intelligence to Francis Arnaud Moreau, as did the animals on whom he had originally experimented while still living in England, whose descendants on Manor Farm had originated the doctrine of Animalism.

It was unknown how God had come to resemble his fellow man so little, but it was rumored that his strange appearance was the result of self-administered gene therapies. The story went that he had once suffered near-fatal injuries on an island in the Pacific Ocean, before coming to Africa, and had been left for dead by earlier creations. The introduction of genetic material from healthy apes to his system had healed his injuries, but in time the gorilla genes began to breed true, and with each passing year he became less and less man, more and more ape. Like the unfortunate sports in reverse, in time he was little more than a man trapped in an ape's body.

Which, it could be said, was true of every ape in Gorilla City, to some extent. But most found it distasteful to dwell on the question of just where all the genes in their makeup originated.

Of course, only a generation after his passing, there were already those who questioned the existence of God altogether, dismissing any talk of genetic manipulation or design, and insisting that the intelligent species of apes, elephants, rhinoceroses, and others had arisen naturally, by process of evolution. But so far as Thomas knew, those who held such notions were still few in number, and regarded as no more than cranks and zealots by the scientific establishment.

Thomas continued on past the statue, following a tree-lined path that curved off to the right. The weather that morning was mild, though the sky was clear and the Sun was bright in the east. A she-ape in some sort of athletic suit jogged by, singing softly along with the music faintly audible from the large headphones over her ears. In the opposite direction came an older ape on a bicycle, a young chimp riding along beside, balanced precariously on a cycle still outfitted with training wheels. In the distance, Thomas could hear the sounds of a group of juvenile apes playing soccer in an open field, while a young she-ape and her mother could be seen flying a kite nearby.

Each time another ape passed, Thomas felt sure that he would be discovered, but no one seemed to pay him any mind. He was anonymous, it seemed, just another old ape in an ancient suit, like the vagrants rummaging through the trash bins, or asleep on the park benches. Is that where he would end up, after all this time? As another of their number, the faceless and anonymous street dwellers?

Hunger and fatigue worked at him. He had walked already this morning more than he had in years, and with no food in his belly, and having had only fitful sleep in the train car the night before, his energy was flagging badly. Finding an unoccupied park bench, he sat down to rest a moment. Sighing deeply, feeling the aches in his long underused muscles, he closed his eyes, thoughtfully.

When he opened them again, the quality of the light had changed. He must have fallen asleep without realizing it, the Sun climbing higher in the sky as he slept. More than that, though, he discovered that he was not alone, feeling the presence of another on the bench beside him.

Thomas turned his head, startled.

There, sitting beside him, was an ape of advancing years, wearing a yellow trenchcoat and matching wide-brimmed hat. Eye half-lidded, he puffed contentedly on the pipe clenched between his teeth, elbows draped casually over the back of the bench.

It was the ape that Thomas had seen at the train station that morning, directing the movements of the uniformed officers.

Thomas's heart pounded in his chest. He was too frightened even to move. He had been discovered, clearly. Could he run? Was there any point in trying? Where would he go?

"Look there," the ape in the yellow hat said casually, still not looking in Thomas's direction. He took the pipe from between his teeth, and pointed with its stem to a point above the tree line. Thomas, swallowing hard, looked in the direction indicated, and just visible over the treetops could see the ramparts and towers of an imposing structure hulking over the city, styled as a medieval castle. "Do you recall when, as young apes, we'd whisper behind our hands, referring to that monstrosity as the House of Pain? You might find it amusing to learn that, with God long dead and the castle remade into the Presidential Palace, there are many who feel it deserves that childish name better than it ever did before."

Thomas narrowed his eyes, looking at the other ape carefully. There was something about the curve of his jaw, something about the quality of his voice that was hauntingly familiar. As if...

"George?" Thomas said, recognition dawning.

"Hello, Zephir, my old friend." The other ape turned to him, smiling. "It's good to see you again."

Confused emotions swirled in Thomas. A smile came unbidden to his lips, but within he still felt the fear of discovery, the vertiginous tremble of uncertainty.

"I would have thought you were still in America," he replied, at length.

George returned the pipe to his mouth, puffing deeply. Then, the smoke curling from the corner of his smile, he chuckled. "No, I grew weary of adventures, I'm afraid. A young ape named Bonzo was given the task of watching the Americans, and I was brought home." He paused, and a cloud passed momentarily across his features. "Too late to see our old teacher Red Peter again, but not too late to be offered his vacated seat at the head of the intelligence services."

Thomas nodded, appreciatively, lips pursed thoughtfully. "So you're the head ape, now?" He was genuinely impressed. "And the intelligence services still persist, as they did when we were young?"

George inspected the contents of his pipe's bowl, and then overturning it tapped out the ashes onto the ground between his feet, knocking the pipe against the palm of his hand. "There is a remarkable inertia to such systems, my friend. There have been precious few changes made to the spy apparatus since it was first instituted by Wolsey under the old King, as I'm sure you'll recall. When Colonel Aristobald took charge under the new Republic, he did little more than change the names and titles on the doors. And when Wolsey's first operative and protégé Red Peter returned from the field to take charge upon the death of Aristobald during the First Forest War, he reversed the few changes that Aristobald had made. When I took control, I saw no reason to muddy the waters with unnecessary changes."

"Hmph." Thomas shook his head, ruefully, the smile fading from his lips. "Red Peter," he repeated. "That old bastard."

"That he was," George agreed, pulling a pouch of tobacco from a pocket, and refilling the pipe's bowl. "And the finest mind I've ever encountered."

"I don't recall you speaking of him so highly when we were his pupils," Thomas snarled momentarily, and then his expression softened, as he remembered fonder memories. "In fact," he went on, smiling, "I distinctly recall you mocking Emily mercilessly for praising him on rare occasion. If she hadn't been sent on assignment to England when she was, I was sure you'd murder each other. Or fall in love. One of the two."

George damped down the tobacco into the pipe with the tip of his thumb, and smiled. "It is a thin line, to be sure."

"Whatever became of Emily, anyway?" Thomas asked.

George's smile froze, and he was silent for a moment, striking a match and sucking its flame into the pipe. When the tobacco began to burn, he shook out the match, and in somber tones, replied. "She fell in love with a human. It... ended badly."

Thomas nodded. "Such things usually do." He paused. "And what about...?" He broke off, and swallowed hard. "What about Isabelle?"

George glanced over, blowing out a stream of smoke. He opened his mouth to answer, but Thomas interrupted before he was able to speak.

"No, don't tell me," he said, hurriedly. "I... I'd rather not know, I think."

George nodded, and returned the pipe to his mouth.

"So," Thomas said, brightening slightly. "You're the new spymaster, are you? I assume you've a new crop of intelligencers you're carefully cultivating, eh?"

"Of course." George smiled. "You'd scarcely believe how young these apes seem, when they come to me. I recall you, Emily and I were most fully grown when Red Peter recruited us for the intelligences services, but if we were anything like as old as Chim-Chim, Magilla, Bear and Grape, we must have been scarcely babes in arms."

"These are their names, your young protégés?" Thomas's eyes bobbled. "They sound more like circus performers than civilized apes."

George chuckled. "Ah, but were those of our generation any better? Back when God was in his castle, Henry still on his throne, and this city was still called London, I was George Boleyn, Emily was Emlia Bassano..."

"And I was Zephir."

"I suppose." George chose not to remark on the interruption. "But only among friends, Thomas."

It was true. Even before the ouster of the old King, it had never been Thomas, only Zephir; his father, Robert Recorde, had four sons and five daughters, who were seldom if ever called by their given names, but instead known as the Four Winds and Five Wandering Stars. With the coming of the Republic, and the abolition of the names bestowed by God, he had simply made it official, and Thomas Recorde became Zephir.

He wondered what had become of his three brothers, and of his five sisters. He had heard from his mother once, in the days of the First Forest War. His seeming betrayal of the Republic, siding with the elephants, had broken his father's heart, she said. So far as the family as concerned, the letter had read, brother Zephir was already dead.

"My parents are dead and buried, I suppose," Thomas said aloud, musing. "I'd always hoped to square things with them, to let them know that their son wasn't really a traitor. But then..." Thomas trailed off, his eyes unfocused.

"I was in America when I heard about the Revolution, and about your being imprisoned. It... It just made me sick that I wasn't able to do anything to help back then."

Thomas took a deep breath, and gave a limp shrug. "You shouldn't blame yourself. I suppose it isn't anyone's fault but my own. I should have known something was in the wind when the Old Lady was assassinated by the cabal of Fandango, Capoulosse and Podular. They hoped to rid themselves of her influence over the King, you see, taking her place in the King's favor. But it was only a short while afterwards that Hatchibombotar, Olur and Poutifour sprung their Revolution. If I'd been any sort of spy, I'd have seen it coming, but I'd allowed myself to get too close to the royal family, and saw nothing of what was happening with the common elephants outside the palace walls." He paused, his lips drawn into a tight line. "More's the pity."

"There was a war on, Zephir," George replied. "And you were doing your duty. When the Elephant King and the Ape Republic went to war, you were perfectly positioned to act as our eyes and ears in the enemy court."

"Yes, but only by posing as an enemy myself, a traitor to my own people."

"You were an invaluable source of information during the First Forest War. I've seen your reports myself, since taking Red Peter's job. The Republic might well have lost the war to the elephants in those early days, if not for you."

"Yes," Thomas said hotly, eyes flashing, "and what was my thanks for it? A lifetime rotting in an elephant jail."

George reached out and placed a hand on Thomas's shoulder, his expression grave. "Zephir, you must know that was one of the hardest decisions that Red Peter ever had to make. But for the gorillas to claim you as one of their own, to prove your innocence, would have been to expose our entire network of informants. The elephants had to believe you were really a traitor."

"And our own people, George?" Thomas tugged the folded newspaper from his pocket, brandishing it at the yellow-hat wearing ape. "They had to believe it still, as well?"

George lowered his gaze. "I'm sorry, Zephir. There just wasn't any other way."

Thomas threw the paper to the ground, and leapt to his feet. "I was abandoned, George! Left to the tender mercy of the Animalists! And now freed only because the elephants have found some use for me as a bargaining chip, tossed in with a bunch of other anonymous political prisoners."

George looked up at him, surprised. "You mean, you didn't know?"

Thomas narrowed his eyes, arms crossed over his chest. "Didn't know what?"

George shook his head, sadly. "Oh, Zephir. It was at my urging that Solovar arranged for the release of the apes held by the elephants. We had to offer Olurgrad a raft of political concessions to close the deal, but I knew that no price would be too high. Not when the bill had come due, all these years later."

Thomas opened his mouth, and closed it again. His eyes widened. Finally, he said, "You did this?"

"Zephir," George sighed, "I've been laboring ceaselessly since I took office to get you released. In fact, I've done little else for the last few years but investigate every possible angle. This was just the first to bear fruit."

"But... but..." Thomas was taken aback.

"Unfortunately," George continued with remorse, "I've been unable to convince Solovar that your name should be cleared publicly. At least not yet. All of Red Peter's files from those days have been sealed, by the President's order, until the end of the century. His position–with which I disagree, but my voice carries little weight–is that with tensions easing with the elephants, and hope for reconciliation on the horizon, it wouldn't do to reopen old wounds, and to remind them that relations between our two countries were not always so genial."

Thomas set his jaw, eyes narrowed. "So I'm to remain a traitor." It was a statement, not a question, demanding no answer. "Hated by my countrymen."

"I'm afraid that those who remember the name of Zephir, yes, will likely hate his memory." George paused, and gave a sly smile. "But who remembers that there was ever a Thomas Recorde, my friend? I doubt there's more than a handful still living who remember that the famous Zephir was once called by that name, and one of them stands before you."

Thomas shifted uneasily, averting his gaze. "This is not how I foresaw my homecoming, when I left for Celesteville, all those years ago."

George climbed to his feet, slipping his pipe into his pocket. He stepped to Thomas's side, and put a hand on his shoulder. "Come work with me, friend. There's a place for Thomas Recorde at the intelligences services, even if there isn't one for Zephir. I can use someone with your experience to help train my students, to increase their chances of surviving in the field."

"I don't know..." Thomas began, uneasily.

"You don't have to decide right away," George hastened to add. "We will discuss it further over dinner tonight. I've invited someone to join us, by the way. Another of those who remember the name of Thomas Recorde, but who hold no grudge against the name Zephir, for all of that."

Thomas looked up and met George's eyes, confused.

"Have you forgotten, old friend?" George asked. "Isabelle was a young ape with us, too, and has never forgotten the name to which you were born."

"I-Isabelle," Thomas repeated, his tone breathless.

George tightened his companionly grip on Thomas's shoulder, and nodded. "She waited for you. All of these years. She waited."

Thomas tried to reply, but couldn't think of the words to say.

"Come on, Thomas Recorde," George said, taking him by the arm. "It's time to go home."

Judex
by M. Gourdon (1956)

Bob Robinson knows Judex *because he wrote a screenplay for an updated remake of the renowned serial. Louis Feuillade's* Judex *was a way to redeem the author for his virulent paean to supervillainy in both* Fantômas *and* Les Vampires, *two previous serials brimming with undisguised cynicism and thinly-veiled attacks upon the bourgeoisie.* Judex, *on the other hand, in Feuillade's own words, was meant to "exalt the finest sentiments." But, in reality,* Judex *is anything but tame; Robinson's* Judex *highlights the merciless side of the character, never as evident as when the Parisian avenger teams up with another hunter as fierce as he is...*

Robert L. Robinson, Jr.: *Two Hunters*

Paris, 1915

The sounds of the Parisian streets trickled through the slightly opened windows in the main office of the Banque Favraux, as street vendors, strolling lovers and the honking horns of new motorists created an opera of sorts. The sweet cascading scents of perfumes, pastries and cigarettes mixed in the air as they formed a new smell, unique to the City of Lights. Within the marble walls of the building, the hum of commerce filled the air as men diligently followed the financial markets in Europe and abroad.

Entering the magnificent building of the bank, in a brisk walk, his large frame covered in a fine overcoat and hat, with the brim over his face, was a man with eyes like those of a beast. They blazed mercilessly at all who met his glance. For weeks, he had lived in the shadows; those who knew him thought him dead. But the time had come for his return. The time had come when justice–or so he believed–must be served. Or more precisely, vengeance would serve in lieu of the justice he craved.

Coldly, the man approached a receptionist, a proud-looking woman who sat behind a desk. Her hair was tightly pulled back in a bun, her face expertly wore the latest in makeup, enhancing rather than detracting; she sat there in her tailored blue dress, her stern, yet beautiful, appearance complementing the décor of the office. She looked up at the man and was not put off by his eyes, as she had seen those kind of eyes almost every day for a year.

"I am here to see Monsieur Favraux," announced the stranger, handing her his calling card. "I have an appointment. My name..." The man suddenly paused; he had kept his name silent for months. Then, he announced with arrogance: "My name is Nikolas Rokoff."

The receptionist took his card and placed it on a silver tray, its edges wonderfully ornate, then signaled to an office boy. Upon the simple wave of her hand, the boy–no more than 12–ran over to stand before her.

"Louis," she ordered the youth, "bring this to Monsieur Vallières. At once."

The boy walked quickly away.

"You may have a seat, Monsieur Rokoff. It shall be a few moments."

Rokoff removed his hat and sat in a chair, his eyes always scanning the room, never once stopping. After a short time, the boy came back down. He nodded to the receptionist, who looked at Rokoff. "Monsieur Vallières will meet you upstairs," she said.

Rokoff rose and followed the boy to the elevator cage.

The boy held the gate open, waiting for the larger man to enter. Once inside, his hands skillfully manipulated the levers, operating the car as they rode together to the top floor of the building.

Neither spoke during the ascent, the boy enjoying the wondrous ride as if it were its first again, Rokoff quitly anticipating the meeting at the top. As they came to a halt, the boy again opened the gate, revealing a gentleman standing before them. His hair and beard betrayed his age as they sparkled shining silver. For an elderly man, he was tall, although slumped over from age; his eyes shone with signs of the youth he once had been. Rokoff exited the elevator. The boy smiled at him before manipulating the levers to bring the car back to the ground floor.

"Monsieur Rokoff," began the man as he extended his hand, "welcome to the Banque Favraux. I am Monsieur Vallières, personal secretary to Monsieur Favraux. Please, come with me." The elderly man led Rokoff down the hall to the outer chamber of an office. Knocking once, then opening the door, Vallières entered, with Rokoff following, into the office of Monsieur Favraux.

The huge corner office was one of opulence, fine art and comfortable furnishing filling the room.

"Monsieur Rokoff," said a voice from behind a large marble desk. "I don't often meet with strangers."

Rokoff walked towards the desk. "It is in both of our interest for you to do so, Monsieur Favraux," replied Rokoff.

"Please sit," said the banker as he motioned to the chair before his desk. Vallières took the seat beside Rokoff, then opened a leather-bound portfolio to take notes.

"I was under the impression that we would speak alone," began Rokoff as he glanced at the secretary. "What I have to say is most confidential."

"Monsieur Vallières is my right hand," said the banker. "If you want to work with me and make use of my resources, you must learn that he is amongst my most treasured ones. It is that simple. Now, what do you have for me?"

Rokoff rubbed his bald head for a moment as he decided which course of action he would take. He had come too far to back out now. "I believe that there's an absolute fortune to be found in Africa."

"That is nothing new. Men every day travel to the dark continent to find their fortunes."

"Listen to me, Monsieur Favraux, and listen to me well. I'm not a man to be trifled with, nor dismissed casually. I've come to you for a simple reason: I need the funds to accomplish two things. Mount an expedition to a city called Opar, and get the services of a certain English Lord to guide us."

"Then why ask to speak with me? There are men in my employ here who could evaluate your project and make a decision."

"It's not that simple. First, only one man knows where Opar is located. I believe that it is the reason for his fortune. And he won't be easily persuaded. Second, and this is more important for you, the pay-out for this is beyond anything you might imagine. Gold, gems of untold value... We could fill ten ships and still not have dented this treasure."

Favraux rose from his desk and walked to a bar located along the wall. He reached in and took out a bottle of brandy, of which he poured two glasses. Walking back, he handed one to Rokoff. "Why haven't you already made this English lord some kind of offer then?" Rokoff raised his glass in thanks to Favraux, and then drained the contents in one swift sip.

"Why? This man is not like you or I. He is a demon, with the strength of ten men. Believe me when I tell you this. I've had my hands on his throat, and he's had his on mine, and we've looked into each other's eyes with hate. I know for sure, he is more beast than man."

"I wasn't told you were a madman, Monsieur Rokoff. Our mutual acquaintance, Alexis Paulvitch, said you were a man to be listened to."

"Then listen to me, you pompous ass. Lord Greystoke is no normal man. He was the son of an English lord, born in Africa and raised by apes. Do you understand what I am saying? He was not raised by men, suckling on the milk of his proper English mother, but at the tit of a hairy ape. He ruled a herd of them, along with a tribe of natives. In the jungle, he is seen as some mystical god... a warrior of unequalled skill and strength. They call himTarzan."

"My God," said Favraux. "I'd heard that story, but I thought it was legend."

"It is not. I know this man. We're sworn enemies, but each time he returns from Africa, his estate grows. I paid his banker for information, a man in Switzerland, and he told me that Greystoke's deposits are all in gold and jewels. And each one larger than the one before it."

"If this jungle man is your enemy, then how will you get him to lead you to this fortune?"

Rokoff walked to the bar and refilled his glass. "Ah," he exclaimed, "there is only one thing that makes Greystoke a man and not a beast. His woman. He has a wife and a son. And they're in Paris as we speak."

Favraux rubbed his chin, and then looked at his secretary. *It was tempting,* he thought, *but fantastic.*

"Monsieur Rokoff," asked Vallières, "if this man hates you, why would he help you?"

"To regain what he wants," said Rokoff.

"And that would be?" said Vallières.

"His family. I will take his family. You will keep them hidden, until we return with the treasure."

Favraux stood up. "You ask me to commit a crime, Monsieur Rokoff? Kidnapping, coercion, possibly more. Are you mad? I run a bank!"

"You run more than a bank, Monsieur Favraux. Do not think that I do not know your business. Your fortune was made by stealing from others, throughout Europe. You've blackmailed officials, embezzled millions, help the Vampires launder their loot... Yes, you're more than a banker. But all that doesn't matter now... the kind of fortune I'm talking about will erase your past, make you as respectable as the families you've ruined."

Vallières' eyes blazed as he listened to the two men, but he said nothing.

Favraux laughed out loud as he took the bottle from Rokoff's hand. "Good, we understand each other. Now, where is this ape man?"

Across the City of Lights, at the Royal Palace Hotel, two men stood on a balcony looking out at the skyline. The smaller of the two wore the uniform of the French Navy. His name was Paul d'Arnot. A slim cigarette in his left hand twirled to and fro as he spoke, like the baton of an orchestra conductor. He held a glass of Burgundy in his right hand. Beside d'Arnot was a bronzed god, a full head and half taller, with a body that would rival the sculptures of the Louvre. That was his friend, John Clayton, Lord Greystoke. Paris was a regular stop on the annual trips he took with his wife. "This is a jungle of a different sort, eh, John?" Paul asked his companion. "The predators that come after a man here, come with a smile and a desire unknown to all but them."

"My world was simpler before I met you," said Greystoke. "My enemies were so for no other reason than I was a meal to them, or they were a meal to me. It was easy. No anger, no hatred. Since becoming a civilized man, I have discovered emotions that my brothers, the Great Apes, would find humorous."

"Ah, this is true, but would you have known the wonders of love? To see a rare beauty and know that she is the one for you. Do you think your ape friends know that?"

Greystoke looked out over Paris with his grey eyes, and thought back to his youth, to a love named Teeka, but chose not to mention her. Paul, while he accepted much of his life prior to their friendship, would never understand his love for this beautiful creature. The female who filled his heart with longing, until the day he first saw the golden tresses of the one who would become his mate, his wife, Jane Porter. "No Paul," he replied. "They don't. But neither do you, calling on a different lady every night."

The two men laughed, then sipped their wine in a moment of silence.

"Your wife took your son shopping in Paris," said d'Arnot. "There goes that amazing fortune of yours." It took Greystoke a long time to understand the value of wealth and the importance that other men put on it. He only saw that the jewels of Opar provided him and his family with security.

"Jane should return shortly with her litter carrying her treasure," he laughed. "She loves to hunt in the shops of the Left Bank as I in the jungle. But she left Jack here, with his nanny."

"What a quiet child," said the French Lieutenant. "I did not even know he was here."

"From what I understand, it is common trait among men of my bloodline. My mother told me I never cried as a baby."

"Your mother?" exclaimed d'Arnot. "But I thought she..."

"Kala," said Greystoke gently. "The mother who raised me."

Suddenly, the Jungle Lord turned his head. His eyes narrowed as he tried to identify the source of a sound he had just heard.

"John..." started d'Arnot before a quick hand signal from Tarzan silenced him. Without a word, the civilized man the world knew as Lord Greystoke vanished as the creature called Tarzan of the Apes hurtled off the balcony skyward, scampering towards the rooftops.

He jumped across the span of the boulevard to the roof across the way where a man in black stood tall. He was an imposing figure, as tall as the jungle lord, dressed all in black, with a matching hat covering his face.

"I mean you no harm, Lord Greystoke," said the man in black.

"Who are you?"

"My name is Judex. I'm here to help you. A man whom you believe to be dead is alive, and at this moment, he has taken your wife as his prisoner."

"Rokoff!"

"Yes. Unfortunately, I arrived too late to stop him..." Judex watched Greystoke sizing him up, deciding if he was telling him the truth or not.

"They could be holding her anywhere," muttered Tarzan to himself.

"True," said Judex. "But in this case, they're not. They've taken her to a building near the Moulin Rouge. We must hurry. My car is down there."

The two men swiftly made their way to the street and entered Judex's large, black sedan. The crime-fighter wove his way through the bustling streets of Paris just as Tarzan wove his way across the branches high above the ground of Africa.

"I should have made sure Rokoff was dead," said the Jungle Lord. "Until one of us is dead, he will always threaten my family."

"His goal is two-fold," said Judex. "Your death, but only after you show him the location of the lost city of Opar."

"How do you know this? No one knows of Opar."

"Rokoff does. A man as evil as he named Favraux now does too. But don't worry, your treasure is your own. I only serve Justice."

"I care nothing for gold and jewels, only my wife."

"Then, let us make haste," said Judex as he drove even faster.

In silence, the two avengers rode, as if on the wings of a chariot to the field of battle. The stars came out as the car slowed behind a warehouse. Judex pointed to a building with a windmill on it. "She is in there. It's a club with song and dance, which is good for us, as it will cover the noise. Once, it was the center of all society in Paris; now only those chasing a dream go there, and become lost in absinthe. We must go quickly."

Inside the building, Jane Porter sat in a large room, her arms bound behind her, a blindfold over her eyes. "Where am I?" she had pleaded for the length of time she had been held captive. But no one ever answered. No one, until now.

"You are my guest Lady Greystoke," said a booming voice which she thought she recognized.

"You!" she gasped. "But you're..."

"Dead? Hardly. It takes more than an ape man to kill Nikolas Rokoff."

"Why? We meant you no harm. Will this nightmare never end?"

"When the treasures of Opar fill my coffers, and the head of your husband hangs over my fireplace, like a wild beast, then it will be over."

Rokoff walked over to the bound woman and pulled off her blindfold. They glared at each other, eyes locked in hatred. "When John finds me..."

"Finds you!" shouted Rokoff. "He will find you only when I choose to let him find you, and that will only be so you can watch as I take his life before your eyes. But only after he has shown me the secrets of Opar!" Rokoff ran his hands through Jane's golden hair. "And then, I will decide if you will become my mistress." Jane spat at him as he laughed and walked to the door. He called one of the five men who were waiting in the other room. "Go to the hotel where Greystoke is staying. Give him this note," he instructed, handing the man a slip of paper.

Walking away from the building, the apache whistled a popular tune, unaware of the two men coming towards him. As he walked past them, Tarzan stopped and sniffed the air. In a single lunge, he turned around and grabbed Rokoff's henchman, his hands squeezing the apache's throat.

"My wife! Where is she?"

The man could barely speak, his eyes bulging in horror. His shaking hand pointed to the building. Judex knocked the apache unconscious as Tarzan growled at him. "If she is harmed, you will be the first to die."

They entered through the back way. Judex smiled as he pointed out a high window to Tarzan. The jungle man took a prodigious leap and vanished. Then a strange sound was heard through the building. A roar in the night. The war cry of the Great Apes.

Inside, Rokoff stopped in his tracks, sweat breaking out on his brow. "Impossible. He can't be here." He took a look at the outer room. The men had pulled their pistols as a bronze blur entered. Before they could react, Tarzan was on them. Shots rang out, blasting holes where the ape man was.

Rokoff retreated from the carnage and looked for Jane, but she was no longer there. He looked in absolute fear at the empty chair that had once held his prisoner–but no more. He had to escape before Tarzan could find him. Running into the hallway, he made his way outside but stopped as a dark-clad figure sprang before him.

"You have sinned against this man and his family, Rokoff," said Judex. "It is time to face Justice."

Rokoff's answer was an explosion of gunshots as the villain fired madly at the spot where his enemy stood. But before he realized, the figure in black had vanished in the night, his laughter left behind. The alley was empty, filled only with the empty clicks from his gun and, from inside, the sound of Tarzan finishing off his men.

Suddenly, a body crashed through the wall, followed by the Ape Man, his shirt shredded, his steel body glistening in the dim light.

"Rokoff!" challenged the Jungle Lord. Rokoff snapped a switch blade open and charged. His knife slashed frenetically but kept missing Tarzan, who eventually caught him with a massive fist across the jaw, breaking it in two. Roaring in pain, mad with blood lust, Rokoff came on harder, trying to plunge his blade into his foe's body, but it was not to be. In one, swift movement, Tarzan lifted the villain's huge frame and brought him crashing down on his knee, breaking the back of his mortal enemy, killing him.

Judex stepped out of the shadows. "He is dead. Justice is served."

"My wife..."

"I have her. While you attacked Rokoff's men, I went to get her. Desperate men do desperate things and I did not want any harm to come to her."

Judex led Lord Greystoke around the corner where Jane rushed into his arms. Neither could speak as they held each other. "We must hurry," said Judex. "The gunshots will have alerted the police and while they move slowly, they move surely."

The black car raced off into the night, returning Tarzan and Jane to their hotel where d'Arnot waited with young Jack and his nanny. As they left the sedan, Tarzan turned to Judex. "You have my thanks, Judex."

"And you have my friendship, Lord Greystoke. If we can't protect our loved ones, justice will be replaced with revenge. Farewell."

The black car sped off into the Paris streets.

The next morning, at the Banque Favraux, the banker was having his morning coffee. Vallières sat before him, going over the reports from the financial markets in America when he stopped short. A tall stranger had just appeared in the halls of the top floor and walked into the office unannounced.

"Who the hell are you and how did you get in here?" demanded Favraux.

"The window was open. I am Lord Greystoke."

"Greystoke..." stammered the banker. "What do you want?"

"You allied yourself with my enemy in his quest for Opar. He is dead. If my family is ever threatened again, you will become my enemy and incur the same wrath. Do you understand?"

"I do," said Favraux.

"Never forget that. There is no place on Earth I wouldn't hunt you down."

Vallières rose from the chair, his old bones making it a slow task for him. "Please, Lord Greystoke," he said, "allow me to show you to the elevator... It is easier than the window, I assure you."

Greystoke followed the old man out.

"Again, my thanks," he said, before taking the elevator.

"You know it is me?"

"Despite your disguise, your scent is known to me. Why you serve that man, I don't know, but you must have your reasons."

"I do. But the time for my justice is coming. So, I wait and learn."

"Then may your hunt go well, my friend," said Tarzan extending his hand.

"And may peace find you and your family," said Judex, taking his hand in friendship.

Both men smiled at each other as Greystoke entered the elevator, to ride the cage down to the street. Vallières returned to a shaken Favraux. "He has left."

"Thank God," said the banker. "A crazed madman like that, I don't need. Not when there is other, easier money to be made."

Judex looked at Favraux and smiled faintly.

We began this third collection of Tales of the Shadowmen *with Matthew Baugh's homage to Paul Féval, and, appropriately, we close it with Brian Stableford's mammoth and expanding contribution to the Féval "universe," the second installment of his very own* roman feuilleton: The Empire of the Necromancers...

Brian Stableford: *The Child-Stealers*

(Being the second part of
The Empire of the Necromancers)

The Story So Far

In Paul Féval's classic roman feuilleton John Devil—*whose principal action is set in the year 1817—the eponymous legendary pseudonym is adopted by the ambitious Comte Henri de Belcamp, along with many other names, in the course of pursuing his various projects. These include the rescue of his mother, Helen Brown—a notorious English thief—from an Australian prison camp and the construction of an unprecedentedly powerful steamship with which he intends to rescue Napoleon from St. Helena and conquer India.*

 In order to pursue the latter plan, Henri makes use of the secret organization: the Knights of the Deliverance. To protect the secrecy of this alliance he—or his evil half-brother Tom Brown, who is almost certainly another of his alter egos rather than a separate individual—murders a potential traitor within the London branch of the organization, Constance Bartolozzi. This brings him into direct conflict with Gregory Temple, the senior detective at Scotland Yard, whose pioneering methods he has been studying at close range in the guise of junior detective James Davy.

 Henri's role as James Davy allows him to frame Temple's former assistant, Richard Thompson—who is secretly married to Temple's daughter, Suzanne—for the murder and to persuade Thompson to flee to France, where Suzanne is a guest at his estranged father's château near the village of Miremont. Henri is assisted in London by his long-term companion Sarah O'Brien, the daughter of another of his (or Tom Brown's) victims, who was killed in Germany while John Devil was studying there under the name George Palmer. Sarah rents the so-called "new château" on the Marquis de Belcamp's former estate as Lady Frances Elphinstone when Henri finds it politic to reconcile with his father, partly in order to set up an alibi for the commissioned murders of his mother's wealthy brothers. There is, however, an obstacle to the fortune Henri intends to collect by this means: Constance Bertolozzi's daughter, Jeanne Her-

bet, who is the designated heir of both brothers (neither of whom knows which of them is her father), and also happens to be a resident of Miremont.

Henri's first act on arriving in Miremont is one of spontaneous heroism, which saves Jeanne's life–after which he falls in love with her and decides to marry her fortune rather than murdering her. He eventually does marry her, although he has to do so in the guise of English entrepreneur Percy Balcomb because he is supposedly in jail. He is there because the obsessive Gregory Temple, having failed to prove that Henri murdered Maurice O'Brien and Constance Bartolozzi and commissioned the murderers of Helen Brown's brothers, has found out where the actual murderers of the brothers have been buried, on Henri's orders. Temple achieves this by tricking the mistress of the vertically-challenged Ned Knob, who was a witness and accessory to their disposal.

After a tense climax in Newgate Prison–where Henri beats Temple to the punch in rescuing Richard Thompson from the hangman, and is thus able to confront his nemesis in the condemned cell, attempting to drive him mad by telling him that Tom Brown is actually his son–Henri learns that the Brotherhood of the Deliverance has been betrayed, and that his new steamship has been destroyed on the slipway by rebels in the African country where it was being secretly built. He then finds it politic to shoot himself in the head in front of his father, supposedly bringing down the curtain on the entire affair.

The Empire of the Necromancers is based on the premise that Henri faked his death–a deception well within his capability and entirely in character–and that his epic struggle with Gregory Temple was always bound to be renewed.

In Part One, "The Grey Men," published in Tales of the Shadowmen 2– which is set in November 1821–Ned Knob is unexpectedly confronted with one of his former associates, "Sawney" Ross, who has been hanged but now appears to be alive again, though somewhat slow-witted. The reanimated man is collected by a physician named Germain Patou (a character who previously appeared in Féval's The Vampire Countess), and Ned follows them to the bank of the Thames, where they board a boat and are met by a man in a Quaker hat– the symbol of identity Henri always wore in his guise as John Devil.

He is hit over the head and wakes up in Newgate, where he is interrogated by Gregory Temple, now working for the secret police. Although Temple is investigating a series of body-snatching incidents, his attention has inevitably been caught by the Quaker hat. Once released, the ingenious Ned tracks Patou to a house in Purfleet, where he renews his acquaintance with Henri and witnesses the resurrection of a man from the dead using an elaborate electrical technique recently discovered by an as-yet- unnamed Swiss scientist.

The inhabitants of the Purfleet house have to race to the docks when their ship, the Prometheus, is attacked by a rival group commanded by the only one of the reanimated grey men to have recovered all his faculties–a person who now styles himself General Mortdieu. The Prometheus is destroyed and Mortdieu's hirelings seize the electrical apparatus from the house, taking it to their own *ship, the* Outremort. *Ned is arrested again, but makes a deal with Temple and they go together to Greenhithe, where the* Outremort *is about to depart for an unknown destination. Henri and his supporters arrive too, and a three-cornered battle develops, which eventually arrives at an impasse. Mortdieu sails away, taking Patou with him, while Henri and Temple are left to lick their wounds– and, of course, to pick up their old rivalry where they left off in 1817... Now read on...*

London, Miremont, 1821

Chapter One
Gregory Temple's Sleeplessness

Gregory Temple had never been a sound sleeper, and his restlessness had not decreased with the years. There had been many a night when he had tossed and turned for hours on end without ever seeming to sleep at all, even without the excuse that he presently had for the return of his most disturbing obsession.

It seemed to him now that he had not slept for a single minute in the previous 72 hours, since he had first renewed his acquaintance with that ridiculous little man, Ned Knob. Master Knob had brought his obsession back to life, by leading him to his nemesis, John Devil–who had come back from the dead without the seemingly-dire inconvenience of becoming a grey man.

Master Knob had added vile insult to cruel injury by claiming that he was intimately acquainted with Suzanne and her new family, but that should have been a minor irritant by comparison with the news that Comte Henri de Belcamp had not, after all, splattered his brains all over the gloomy walls of the Château de Belcamp. Alas, once lack of sleep began to bring delirium into Temple's waking life, even minor irritants could be temporarily blown up out of all proportion, augmenting his fundamental distress.

It should have been the monstrous thought of John Devil's continued freedom that was keeping Temple awake now, as it had for two nights before, but it was not. He should have been cudgelling his brain in the attempt to figure out a way of finding the bandit again, or at least berating himself for not having succeeded in capturing the bandit at Greenhithe when they had been forced to quit the *Outremort*. Instead, he was berating himself for something else entirely, and calling himself a monster worse than any mindless grey giant or any phantom in a Quaker hat. He was drowning in regret for his own foolishness in somehow having contrived to put it completely out of is mind that he had a daughter, and that his daughter had a husband and a son.

He had been ill, of course, and mad too–but what kind of excuse was that, for a man like him? He was no more than slightly ill now, nor was he much more than slightly mad. He was a trusted agent in the King's secret police, charged with maintaining the peace and security of the realm–but how could he trust himself to do that, when he had not even been able to maintain the peace and security of his own family?

I am a man of great intellect, he told himself, repeatedly. *I am a diehard enemy of evil. How can I be such a stupid wreck of a human being?*

He would have sworn on the Bible, sincerely, that he had not slept for an instant–but he had closed his eyes in the attempt to rest, and he must also have muffled his ears, else he would surely have heard the door of his room open and close. How else could he explain the fact that he had no inkling that anything was wrong until the point of a rapier actually touched his throat?

"Be still, Mr. Temple," a voice advised him. "I am very anxious not to hurt you."

A phosphorus match spluttered then, and a flame lit up. It was applied to the candle on his night-stand, which lit in its turn."

"A miracle of scientific enlightenment," John Devil commented, as he blew out the match. "So much more effective than flint and German tinder. We are living in exciting times, Mr. Temple, when anything and everything seems possible." He looked around the room as he spoke; although he said nothing, Temple knew what he must be thinking: that this was a direly shabby apartment for a man who had once lived in a good house, with a wife and daughter and servants.

Temple could not raise his head from his pillow without endangering his throat. "If you are so very anxious not to hurt me, John Devil," he said, bitterly, "why do you come into my room with a naked blade?"

"Because I am equally anxious to ensure that you do not hurt me, Mr. Temple. I did not shoot you when I held a gun to your head at Greenhithe, even when you refused to obey my instructions. I'm not so sure that you'd have done me the same courtesy, had the roles been reversed. I need you to sit quietly for a little while, so that I can explain to you why we must make a truce–and more than that, become allies for a little while."

"Because of the challenge of the dead-alive?" Temple said, with a sneer. "The protectors of His Majesty's government do not need your advice to make policy on that issue."

"I am not even certain that this concerns the dead-alive, Mr. Temple–although it would be a bizarre coincidence if it did not. I am certain, however, that it does not concern your stupid secret police. This is personal, Mr. Temple. Will you read this letter, please?"

John Devil, who was not wearing his Quaker hat, held out a single sheet of paper, folded in two. Temple took it. It was not until he had opened it and read the name of the addressee and the signature that the blond man withdrew the point of the rapier, allowing Temple to raise his head.

Temple was able to look his persecutor in the face then–and was astonished to see that the handsome features were contorted by anxiety and dread. When John Devil had been James Davy, he had occasionally feigned anxiety, but dread had seemed to be beyond his emotional range, even then.

There was a pistol in the drawer of the night-stand, but Temple made no attempt to reach for it. The letter was addressed to "My Dear Ned", and it was signed "Suzanne"–in the context of his recent delirium, those words seemed unusually pregnant with horror and distress. Temple blinked twice to clear his eyes, and then he read the body of the letter.

My dear Ned, the letter said. *We are in desperate trouble, and we need your help. We also need my father's help, if he is alive and sane and willing to offer it. I do not know whether you will know how to find him, or whether he will see you if you go to him, but I beg you with all my heart to try. My darling Richard–my son, that is–has been kidnapped from the garden at the Château de Belcamp, and two younger children with him: Jeanne's son, and the son of Sarah, Countess Boehm. Since Count Boehm's death, Sarah has returned to live at the new château, and the children very often play together; they were all playing in the garden this morning, watched over by their nurse and Pierre Louchet, when a number of armed men wearing masks came in and took them away. Pierre tried to stop them, but was struck down–he is not badly hurt, thankfully, save for his pride. One of the masked men told the nurse that we should gather gold to pay a ransom, that we would be given instructions for its delivery in due course, and that we must not contact the police. No communication has come as yet, but Jeanne and Sarah are both making efforts to assemble as much gold as they can. We do not know how large the demand will be. We dare not contact the Prefecture of Police in Paris, but we desperately need the advice of someone who knows about such matters. If you can get this letter to my father, I beg you to do so. Please try as hard as you can. Your loyal friend, Suzanne.*

Temple looked up at John Devil, feeling the wrath build inside him. "How do you come to have this letter, Monsieur de Belcamp?" he asked, seething with anger.

"Because Ned brought it to me," John Devil replied, "and entrusted it to me so that I might bring it to you, while he set off for the château without delay. You will understand the logic of the situation, of course–had he brought it to you first, you would not have known where to find me, even if you had consented to show it to me."

"So far as any of the mothers knows," Temple said, sourly, "neither one of us is alive, else they would doubtless have written to us directly. Are you prepared to let your wife know, now, that she is not a widow after all?"

"She is a widow," John Devil said. "But we have learned of late that the dead can no longer be relied on to be as quiet as they used to be. Dead or not, I will help my son if I can, just as you will help your grandson. Together, Mr.

215

Temple, we might be a force to be reckoned with. We are allies in this, whether it pleases us or not, and we must put our differences aside."

Temple let the sheet of paper fall on to the coverlet. He did not doubt that his own features were contorted, probably more hideously than his interlocutor's "Is Mortdieu behind this?" he demanded, hoarsely. "Is he trying to raise funds to defend his empire of the dead-alive?"

"It's possible, but not likely. He cannot be everywhere at once, and he needed all his forces to destroy the *Prometheus* and steal my apparatus. It might well be someone else anxious to acquire the secret in a hurry, who imagines that I know even more than I do—but we must not neglect the possibility that this is the work of perfectly ordinary men possessed of a perfectly ordinary greed."

"Jeanne and Sarah Boehm are both rich," Temple said, thoughtfully. "Either of their children might have been a prime target—to catch both at once would be a rare coup for any gang of kidnappers. It's a pity, though, that my poor grandson should chance to be with them when they were seized. Suzanne and Richard haven't a farthing, alas—I don't know what their exact status is at the Château de Belcamp, but they must be servants in all but name. Friedrich Boehm told me once that he was mixed up with a relic of the *vehmgerichte*—might this be an extension of the feud that killed his brothers, and would doubtless have procured his own assassination had he not been condemned to death by tuberculosis?"

"It's possible," John Devil repeated, "but again, not likely. I knew several self-styled knights of the *vehm* when I was studying in Germany, although I was not supposed to be privy to their secret lives. They all prided themselves on being men of strict honor, and even though there was a measure of self-delusion in their pose, I doubt they'd stoop so low as to imitate Corsican bandits."

"Corsican, you say? Do you suspect the *Veste Nere* then? It's rumoured that a nest of them has lately taken up residence in Paris."

The former James Davy smiled, grimly. "I believe that it was me who whispered that rumor in your ear, in happier times," he said. "And it was Tom Brown who whispered it in James Davy's. Again, it's possible—but not likely. We're wasting time, Mr. Temple. We have plans to make, and must be under way by dawn. We have a long journey ahead of us. I did it once in less than a day, when I was Percy Balcomb, but I had to make careful preparations. We'll be lucky to arrive in two—and I do not know whether or not to pray that nothing will happen before we do."

Temple caught the implication of that remark easily enough. If nothing happened until he and the late Comte de Belcamp arrived, that might be because they were expected and awaited—in which case, the affair might be more complicated than any simple demand for ransom. He looked down at the letter again.

John Devil anticipated his question. "The messenger who brought it came with all possible speed," he said, "but it required 48 hours to get it into Ned Knob's hands. There is every possibility that the man was followed, and it is not impossible that the letter itself has been read. Ned says that he was not followed when he brought it to me, and he is usually trustworthy in such matters, but your intervention might be expected. For that reason, we must make our way to Dover separately–you must take the early morning coach from the Post Office–and we must be careful aboard the packet-boat. I dared not take the risk of our being unable to obtain a seat on the mail-coach from Calais to Paris, so I instructed Ned to reserve two when he passed through, in the names of Gideon Markwick and Henri Moreau–you are, of course, Markwick, and I have taken the liberty of making up false papers in that name."

John Devil took a sheaf of papers from his pocket and threw them on to the coverlet beside the abandoned letter, but he did not pause in his discourse longer than was needed to draw breath. "If you are followed," he went on, "they are bound to suspect that we are traveling together, even if we do not speak to one another–but that will not matter, provided that we are discreet. In Paris, we will separate. I will slip away from anyone who follows me, while you need take no such precaution in going on to Miremont. What you do when you get there will depend on the situation you find; I will contact you as and when I can, but you may be sure that I shall be busy. Given your status, you might be tempted to make contact with the Prefecture of Police in Paris, but I assure you that such a move can only make matters worse–Monsieur Vidocq's so-called *Sûreté* would be far more interested in the gold than the children, and we undoubtedly have enough enemies to deal with already."

"By what right do you expect me to follow your orders meekly?" Temple demanded.

"We have set that game aside, Mr. Temple. We are united now, while we have a common purpose. I have had a little time to think about this; you have not. I have applied the same reasoning to the problem as you would yourself, and we must both follow its dictates. You must get dressed now, and pack in haste. You must be at the Post Office in time to catch that coach–and if you must travel on top, at the risk of freezing to death, you must do it. I must go now, to complete my own arrangements. I shall see you on the packet-boat, but if we find an opportunity to talk during the crossing, we must be very careful."

John Devil did not prolong his farewell. He opened and closed Temple's bedroom door as quietly as he must have done when he came in, and Temple could not help envying the steadiness and delicacy of his enemy's hand. He got dressed as rapidly as he could, and then packed a bag. The first thing he put in it was his revolver. He hesitated over his makeup kit, but left it aside; his own face was no longer as recognizable as it had been four years ago, and no one in Calais was likely to challenge the supposition that he was Gideon Markwick, provided that the papers made out in that name were in order.

He checked the sheets of paper that John Devil had casually thrown on the bed, and found them to be as expertly forged as the stock of false identities he maintained on his own behalf. He tried to find some consolation in the thought that this was one name John Devil would never have the opportunity to adopt for himself.

He managed to find a cab to take him to the Post Office, and got there in time to buy a ticket for the coach. Had it been high summer, he would not have been able to obtain a seat so shortly before departure even on the rotunda, but it was November, and he was able to secure an inside berth. Fortunately, the roads had not yet been so badly churned-up by autumnal rains as to cause any substantial delay en route; he was reasonably confident that he would arrive in time to catch the packet-boat.

It was during the few minutes that he had to wait before the coach's departure that it struck Temple, with forceful impact, that he would be forced to confront his daughter, and all the bitterness that had somehow accumulated between them. He not only had an excuse for doing so, but a golden opportunity to make amends. Compared with that, the necessity of calling a truce in his eternal feud with John Devil seemed far less important than it might have.

But what if I fail? Temple thought, as the vehicle drew away, its harness jangling. *What if I fail?*

It was not warm, even inside the vehicle, and Temple kept his overcoat buttoned to the neck and his scarf wound tight. He pulled his old felt hat down so that the lining protected the tips of his ears while the scarf warmed the lobes, even though he knew that the combination must make him look as furtive and sinister as any chapbook villain. None of the other passengers did anything different, even though two of them appeared to be the kind of dandy who would normally place the priorities of appearance far above those of comfort. The others were all men of business–as might be expected given the season.

By the time they had reached Dartford, Temple had ascertained that the apparent dandies were, in fact, literary men rather than true gentlemen, following the sartorial example of Lord Byron as best they could on a meager budget. They were speaking in low tones because there appeared to be some dispute between them, regarding an item of fiction one of them–or perhaps his wife–had published anonymously, based on a manuscript provided by the other. There was mention of the North-West Passage and a ship becalmed in ice, and some unusually-vituperative discussion of the necessity of providing an aesthetically-satisfactory ending in a published story, even if it required some bending of the truth. Temple tried as hard as he could not to listen, so that he could concentrate on more urgent matters.

It was even easier to ignore the desultory conversation of the businessmen, who felt compelled to maintain near-silence apart from a desultory flow of conventional inquiries, acknowledgements and apologies, even though some of them clearly knew one another by sight. Thirty years before, it was rumored, mail-coaches had been rich sources of wit and gossip, but that was before the etiquette of English travel had been brought to its full maturity. Things might have been different had there been one or more ladies aboard, but there was no cause for effusive gallantry here, and Temple judged that he was not the only one grateful for the fact.

Temple did not even attempt to sleep, in spite of his success in shutting out his surroundings because he needed to catch up with the reasoning that had put him on the coach. By the time he reached Dover, he had to be sure that John Devil was no longer one step ahead of him in matters of calculation.

In his days as a detective at Scotland Yard, Temple had been involved in more than a dozen kidnapping cases, and had been the senior officer on more than half of them. The tactics of handling such cases were always the same; the first priority was to secure the release of the victim, even if that meant paying a ransom–but every effort was made to follow the kidnappers from the point at which they collected the ransom, with a view to recovering it as soon as possible and apprehending the guilty parties. Sometimes, the bandits were captured; sometimes they got away. More often than not the victim was returned unharmed, but in the minority of cases...

This case would not be an easy one to manage, Temple knew, because it would be on foreign ground. Although he had played the part of Comte Henri de Belcamp more assiduously than any other, John Devil had probably spent less time at the château than Temple had, as a guest of the late Marquis, so it was unfamiliar territory to him too. On the other hand, John Devil might have forces to draw upon in Paris, and it appeared that Pierre Louchet, who had lived most of his life in the forest near Miremont, was now part of the Comtesse de Belcamp's household staff. Then, there was Ned Knob, who seemed to have grown devilishly clever as well as devilishly bold since he had been recruited to Tom Brown's gang four years before, and Richard Thompson, who had shown promise as a detective when he had been in Scotland Yard's employ. When he arrived at the château, he would not be entirely without resources–but everything would depend on the timing of the ransom demand and the instructions it contained.

If the kidnap had taken place three days ago, Temple reasoned, then the mysterious General Mortdieu, the would-be emperor of the dead-alive, could not possibly have been directly involved. He had been in London, planning and executing a very different criminal project. Nor could the masked men who had carried out the abduction have been grey men, else their condition would have been noticed by Louchet or the nurse. On the other hand, the coincidence of timing was so striking that it was difficult to believe that there was no connection at all between the parallel events in Miremont and London. How long, he wondered, had John Devil and Germain Patou been in London? More to the point, how long had they been working in Portugal before that? How had the two of them acquired the secret of resurrecting the dead? How many other people knew that secret, or knew that there *was* a secret?

The last question, he decided, was the vital one. Mortdieu had known that Patou and John Devil could resurrect the dead because they had resurrected him.

At the house in Purfleet and aboard the *Prometheus*, they must have had at least 40 hirelings, many of whom must have known what their business was and all of whom would have been able to find out without taking overmuch trouble–and to that number would have to be added Jack Hanrahan and the other body-snatchers who supplied their raw materials.

Even if Patou and John Devil were the only two who knew what the secret was, there must be dozens, if not hundreds, of people who knew that they possessed it. One of the reasons that Mortdieu had been so desperate to make his own play was he knew full well that time was of the essence. There might be only a handful of men apart from Patou and John Devil who knew how to bring the dead back to life, but there must be many more who were determined to possess the secret with all possible speed.

On the other hand, Temple thought, anyone who believed that kidnapping the Comtesse de Belcamp's son might provide a way to acquire the secret of resurrection would have to know that the man who had it was, in fact, the Comte de Belcamp–and even Jeanne de Belcamp did not know that her husband was alive, let alone that he had somehow acquired the secret of a strange immortality. Was it not far more likely that Jeanne's own fortune, which was no secret at all, had been a lure attracting common criminals? Would not that natural magnetism have been redoubled by the fact that Sarah Boehm, whose inheritance must also be common knowledge, had recently moved into the new château, literally next door, with a child of almost exactly the same age as Jeanne's?

He needed to know far more. He needed to know, at the very least, what John Devil knew–and he was determined to find out, no matter how careful and discreet he had been commanded to be on the ferry that would take them both to Calais. Alas, John Devil was not waiting in Dover when the mail-coach arrived, nor had he put in an appearance by the time the packet-boat was due to set out. When the boat left the harbor–without a moment's delay, for it was a brand-new steamboat, which had no need of any generosity from the wind or the tide–Temple had not caught a glimpse of his supposed ally.

Two possibilities sprang to the detective's mind: firstly, that the other man was on board but in hiding, having found a means to keep out of his way; secondly, that the other man had always intended to travel by a different route, at least to Calais, and perhaps all the way to Paris. The second alternative seemed more likely, if only because it fit in with the man's essentially devious character. The combination of the Dover coach and the packet-boat was not necessarily the best or the fastest way to get to the French shore from London; John Devil might as easily have gone to London Bridge to pick up a ship that would sail–or, more likely, steam–all the way around Kent. If the other had taken that route, he might get to Calais first–or he might not go to Calais at all, preferring some other port of entry.

Damn the man! Temple thought, as the ferry began to rock and lurch in the choppy autumnal sea. *Even as an ally, he's the most treacherous snake an honest man could ever dread to encounter.*

Chapter Two
John Devil's Lateness

Temple cursed John Devil a hundred times more while the steamboat made its way across the Channel, across a relatively calm sea. Even as he cursed, though, he recognized the possible logic of the course of action. If there was more to the kidnap than simple banditry, the child-stealers would probably know that Suzanne had written to Ned Knob, and would therefore be expecting Temple's arrival in Calais. If so, it might be unwise to let them know that Henri de Belcamp had also been alerted by the same missive, and had entered into an alliance with his old enemy. But why, if John Devil had never intended to travel with him even for part of the journey, had he implied that he would? Why had he not simply told the truth? Perhaps he was incapable of it, even in—or especially in— circumstances that compelled him to work in association with his old adversary.

It occurred to Temple to wonder whether the letter might have been a carefully-fabricated contrivance to get him out of England—that there might not have been any kidnap at all—but he could not believe it. John Devil was more than capable of playing such a foul trick, but, had he wanted to get Temple out of the way for any considerable length of time, he would surely have chosen a deception that would not be so soon uncovered.

Temple did not go up on deck during the crossing, but contented himself with searching the crowd of passengers below decks with his eyes. He was satisfied soon enough that John Devil was not among them—and was not disguised as a crewman either, unless he was the kind of crewman who spent his time at sea confined to the engine-room. He was also in search of any indication that he was being followed. Five of his fellow passengers from the mail-coach had taken the ferry—including the two literary men—but none of them had shown the least flicker of interest in him since they had got down from the coach. If anyone else on board had been looking out for him, they gave no sign of it.

He was able to take a late breakfast on the packet-boat, and to drink a pot of coffee, but he arrived in Calais neither satiated nor fully alert. Once his papers had been inspected, and handed back to him without hesitation, he made his way to the booking office for the Paris coach and asked whether there was a ticket waiting for Gideon Markwick. There was, and he only had to show his documents again to claim it.

"Has Monsieur Henri Moreau collected his ticket yet?" he asked, in French.

"Non, Monsieur," was the reply.

"But you do have a ticket awaiting collection by the gentleman in question?"

"Oui, Monsieur."

Temple checked his watch. If "Henri Moreau" was going to catch the Paris coach, he had only a quarter of a hour left to pick up his ticket. He stayed close to the booking office while he waited, but no one came. When the coach got under way, there was an empty seat inside.

"This is a rare stroke of luck," one of Temple's fellow passengers said to him, in faintly-accented English, as they settled in to their places. "For once, we may be comfortable. They cannot take on an extra passenger before we reach Amiens, you see, in case the missing man is waiting at one of the stops where we change horses. My name is Giuseppe Balsamo, Monsieur–I'm pleased to make your acquaintance."

Temple suppressed a sigh; he was in France now and the etiquette of English travel no longer applied. He shook the hand that had been offered to him, and said; "Gideon Markwick. Your English is very good, sir–far better than my Italian, I fear."

"I have been away from my native land for a very long time," Balsamo told him, with a slightly theatrical sigh. Temple was sure that the man had not been on the packet-boat, but that might only mean that he had arrived in Calais on another vessel, or that he had been there on business. Balsamo seemed to be some 20 years younger than Temple–certainly no more than 40 years old, and probably less–so his reference to "a very long" time seemed slightly odd.

"We have been living in turbulent times," Temple commented, in a neutral tone. "Many men have been displaced from their homelands, only to find them unrecognizable on their eventual return."

"That is always the fate of the wanderer," the other man agreed–and then withdrew slightly, as if to end the conversation. Temple was not at all displeased by that–except that he suddenly realized, as the man took a French newspaper from his overcoat pocket and began to unfold it, that he had heard the name Balsamo before, coupled with the forename Joseph–which was, of course, the English form of Giuseppe. He had to rack his brains for several minutes before he dredged up the memory, but it came to him in due course.

Many years before, when he had been one of the earliest recruits to the Metropolitan Police's detective division, the complex entanglement between politics and crime had had a very different complexion, more concerned with foreign espionage than domestic radicalism. The new division had inherited a stock of dossiers compiled on hundreds of foreign nationals reputed to operate as spies, including many of wide repute. One of those dossiers had concerned a poseur named Count Cagliostro–whose real name, the reports alleged, had been "Joseph" Balsamo.

Temple had never had the slightest involvement with the man, but he had read the dossier because of its melodramatic quality, as a kind of modern legend.

He recalled now that Cagliostro had cultivated a reputation as a magician, and had been exiled from France after his alleged involvement in the scandal of a necklace supposedly commissioned by Queen Marie-Antoinette, but actually obtained on false pretenses by a band of tricksters. Cagliostro had spent some time in England thereafter, and had been briefly imprisoned in the Fleet–but this could not possibly be the same person, who must have been 50 or thereabouts when he was in England then, and would therefore be 80 now. It might, perhaps, be the other Balsamo's son... or the name might be a pure coincidence.

On another occasion, Temple would have let the matter go–but he was, at present, very sensitive to the potential significance of coincidences. When the other man finally put his newspaper away, and Temple was able to meet his eye again, he took the opportunity to say: "I believe I knew a man named Balsamo once, in London–but he was quite old and I was very young. Perhaps he was your father?"

"My father never left Italy," the other said, mildly, "and Balsamo is not an uncommon name there. Your man might, I suppose, have been a distant relative. I have visited London myself on many an occasion. Things go well there, I hope?"

"Tolerably well," Temple replied. "The war was costly, of course, and we are still paying the price in social unrest, but we are making progress."

"Progress?" Balsamo echoed. "A French idea, is it not? Did you not fight the war to prevent progress?"

"In England," Temple told him, only a trifle stiffly, "we did not consider the Revolution or the Napoleonic Empire to constitute political progress–but when I used the word, I was thinking of an altogether different sort of progress than the merely political."

"Perhaps I am mistaken," Balsamo said, "but I was under the impression that the core of the philosophy was that there is only one sort of progress–that technical progress and social progress march hand-in-hand, each nourishing the other. Or were you thinking of the doughty puritan's *Pilgrim's Progress*?"

"No," said Temple, suppressing a surge of annoyance at what seemed to him a deliberate misunderstanding of his meaning. "I meant that the nation is making progress in returning to normal–to harmony and prosperity."

"Indeed?" Balsamo queried, cocking an eyebrow. "I never had the impression that harmony was normal in England–nor prosperity, for all but the favored few. On the other hand, I believe that your country is in the forefront of technical progress. You have nurtured several important pioneers of the new science of electricity, have you not? Humphry Davy and Michael Faraday are famous throughout Europe. My own compatriots, Luigi Galvani and Alessandro Volta, have made considerable contributions to the same great work, which I find very exciting. It will favor social progress too, I think–it has the potential to bring about a social revolution far more profound than the one wrought by France's

Jacobins. It was most unfortunate that they sent their own native genius, Monsieur Lavoisier, to the guillotine."

Temple was slightly surprised by the turn the conversation had taken, but not disturbed. Perhaps it was significant, and perhaps not–but it was, at any rate, not uninteresting. "What kind of social revolution do you mean, Signor Balsamo?" he asked, curiously.

"The second wave of the industrial revolution, of course," Balsamo told him. "Steam is supplying the power to a vast new generation of machines, including traveling engines of various kinds. It is already revolutionizing manufacturing processes, and will surely increase our mobility tremendously. Mechanics is only the beginning–when the capabilities of electricity are added to the skill of new machinery, there will be a further increase in its ingenuity. What a future we would have to look forward to, Mr. Markwick, if only we were not fated to pass on to another world at a mere threescore years and ten!"

"It is certainly becoming easier to clothe ourselves," Temple agreed, judiciously, "but there is only so much land, which can only yield so much wheat to make bread. There are limits to ambition, Signor Balsamo."

"Ah!" said Balsamo. "You are a Malthusian, of course, Mr. Markwick. You find it difficult to believe in my kind of progress because you find it easy to believe in the inevitability of the Malthusian checks: war, famine and disease. The horsemen of the apocalypse, who never rest–with Death himself as their constant companion. Are you so sure, then, that there is so little prospect of progress in diplomacy, agriculture and medicine... or even the fight against Death itself?"

By now, Temple was perfectly certain that the conversation was significant, although none of their fellow passengers could have guessed it, no matter how carefully they were eavesdropping. "The Balsamo I knew in London," he said, casually stretching the truth, "thought something similar. He was an alchemist of sorts, in quest of the philosopher's stone."

"In that case, I do know the Balsamo to whom you refer," the other man said, mildly, "perhaps rather better than you do. He is not a relative. If there were a philosopher's stone, it would probably be electrical in its nature and effects, don't you think? A distillate of the fire of Heaven, which Prometheus stole for the benefit of humankind. His work goes on, of course, despite its early interruption and his cruel punishment. By a curious coincidence, I believe I saw an English poet in Calais today who recently published a wonderful celebration of *Prometheus Unbound*. It came out just a few months ago–have you had a chance to read it?"

"I have not read it," Temple confessed. He only hesitated briefly before adding: "I did notice, though, that there was a ship named *Prometheus* that was burned in Purfleet Harbour only two days ago."

"Was there, indeed? The idea is in the air, you see. We live in a Promethean age. There was another literary work in English, I think, titled *The Modern*

Prometheus–an account, disguised as fiction, of work done in Switzerland a few years ago. That was based on a different version of the myth, I think–or perhaps a gloss on Shakespeare. You remember Othello's lament, no doubt, when he contemplates poor Desdemona's corpse, and plaintively regrets the want of some *Promethean heat* to restore its warmth?"

"I have never been much of a playgoer," Temple said, with a slight hint of resentment at the manner in which the other man seemed to be teasing him for a lack of erudition. "I'm a practical man, alas, with little time for literary flights of fancy."

"Now, there you have the advantage of me," Balsamo said. "I, alas, am a rather impractical man, with far too much time for flights of fancy. My father always told me that it was a curse, although I have always insisted, perversely, on reckoning it a gift. If you do not know Shakespeare and Shelley, you will certainly be unfamiliar with Ludovico Ariosto and Torquato Tasso, but I would like to think that theirs is the spirit that flows in my veins–epic, magical and boundless. That is why I am so glad to have some extra space on the journey, thanks to the man who reserved a seat but never arrived to take it. I do hope, though, that no misfortune has overtaken him. I would not like to think of a man suffering serious inconvenience merely to reward me with a little elbow-room."

"We have lived in turbulent times these last 30 years, as I said," Temple observed, with a slight hint of acid in his voice. "Misfortune has been all too common. The blood in my veins is more prosaic in its inspiration. To me, Signor Balsamo, the establishment of peace and prosperity is progress–the only true progress that there is."

"That's an old man's opinion, Mr. Markwick, if you don't mind me saying so–and I mean no insult by it, because you don't appear to me to be a man who is ready to settle for retirement and a graceful fade into oblivion. If you had the chance of a second lease of life, I believe you'd take it, no matter how turbulent the times might be in which you'd have to make use of it."

"Would you take such a chance, Signor?" Temple asked, point blank. "If there were some risk about it, that is."

Balsamo laughed. "Oh yes," he said. "Once, twice, and as many times as I might, regardless of risk. I have no fear of eternity in *this* life." He left it un-stated as to whether he had any cause for anxiety regarding eternity in the other, but Temple took the inference that he might.

"Have you some message for me, Signor Balsamo?" Temple asked. "Or some demand to make, perhaps?"

"Why, no," Balsamo said. "I am merely making conversation, to while away the time. I am impatient for the advent of the steam-powered coach, which will hurtle along the road at 20 or 25 miles an hour–although the road might have to be remade to accommodate such reckless progress."

"Do you really believe that you or I might one day have the opportunity of a second lease of life?" Temple asked.

The Italian shrugged. His round face was configured to accommodate an unusually capacious smile, and now he smiled as broadly as he could. "I don't know, Mr. Markwick," he said, "but I would certainly count it as progress–and I can understand the appetite of those men who are ardently desirous of finding the secret of vital force in the mysteries of electricity. Men who have lived through turbulent times, and have borne witness to so much death and destruction, cannot help but be hasty in trying to seize such opportunities. Peace and prosperity are shallow goals, if they can only be attained briefly, by men long past the vigor of youth."

"Haste is one thing," Temple said. "Crime is another."

"Not all men think so," Balsamo said, his gaze suddenly fixing itself on the narrow empty space where Henri Moreau would have taken up far more room than the actual passengers had left.

Temple did his level best to give nothing away, but his heart sank as he guessed that the cat must already be out of the bag. The mere fact that Ned Knob had reserved two seats had given the game away. He tried to take what comfort he could from the thought that Giuseppe Balsamo must be even more troubled than he was by the fact that Comte Henri de Belcamp, resurrector of the dead, had not arrived to claim his ticket.

Because the journey from Calais to Paris was more than twice that between London and Dover, most passengers on the route made an overnight stop. The coach that Temple had boarded was scheduled to make that stop in Amiens– where it arrived shortly before midnight, according to local time. Those travelers with a greater sense of urgency had the option, however, of transferring to another vehicle in order to continue their journey with less delay that was routinely incurred in changing horses. By exercising that option, Temple knew, it ought to be possible to reach Paris not long after dawn, where he could either hire a carriage or take the local *patache* to Miremont. That was what he did–and honestly did not know whether to be glad or anxious when the mysterious Giuseppe Balsamo declined the opportunity.

"I fear that I need to sleep in a bed nowadays," the Italian explained, when they parted company. "In a lifetime of traveling, I have already spent too many nights attempting to sleep in carts and carriages. French highways are in better condition now than they once were, but the long summer's traffic has left a dire legacy of ruts and potholes, and such repairs as were carried out in the early autumn were superficial. I hope we meet again, Mr. Markwick–you have been an uncommonly entertaining traveling companion."

"That ought to be unlikely, Signor," Temples said, dryly, "unless fate has somehow contrived to tangle the threads of our lives together."

"Who knows what the future might hold?" was Balsamo's reply to that. "As a man of science, and a visionary, I'm bound to say that fate has nothing to do with such things–it's motive and circumstance that tangle men's lives together. We may well meet again, Mr. Markwick, if it transpires that we have goals in common."

Balsamo was right, of course, about the difficulty of trying to sleep on the coach that carried Temple forward in his journey–which had no empty seats, as Monsieur Moreau's reservation was not transferable. He wedged himself into a corner, giving himself the option of leaning his head on the wall beside the *portière*, but the temporary comfort offered by that option was an illusion; as soon as either front wheel hit a pothole, the resultant bump was likely to cause a severe headache and a swelling bruise.

Starved of sleep as he was, Temple was used to falling into a state halfway between a daze and waking delirium, so he contrived to remain relatively still and relatively calm, but the obsessive worries that mingled with his fragmentary dreams were alarming.

Whether John Devil had always planned to let him make the journey alone or not made little difference to the reality of his situation; even the plan that he had stated aloud required Temple to arrive at the Château de Belcamp alone, in advance of any rendezvous. He had been faced all along by the prospect of a painful meeting with Suzanne, and a difficult meeting with Jeanne, both of which he would have to negotiate unaided. While he had still been in England– and even more so while he had been conversing with Balsamo between Calais and Amiens–he had been able to distract himself with other concerns. Now, the question of what he might and ought to say to the two young women was becoming increasingly urgent.

To Suzanne, he owed a thousand apologies, whose profuse offering would at least give him time to think–but what was he to say to Jeanne? Must he tell her that her husband was alive, or should he–could he–procrastinate until the former Henri de Belcamp chose to make his own entrance? What would Ned Knob have told her, given that he was bound to arrive in Miremont first?

The situation was not improved when the journey–which had been pleasantly untroubled until then–was suddenly interrupted by one of those frequent accidents that were the bane of carriage travel. It was only a broken wheel, not a broken axle, but the wheel broke suddenly rather than giving due warning, and the subsequent upset injured two of the horses. Because it happened an hour before dawn, some distance from the nearest stop, there was no prospect of getting immediate help. The postillion dutifully rode off on one of the uninjured animals, but Temple knew that the vehicle would not be back on the road for several hours. He decided that he would probably get to Paris sooner if he hitched a ride to a coaching inn on one of the carts that were passing along the road, heading for the Parisian markets with all the velocity their plodding dray-horses could muster.

He had no difficulty in buying a cheap passage before dawn broke, but the morning was bitterly cold and there was no protection on the cart from the wind. The journey to the next coach-stop was not long, measured in miles, but it was not rapid either, and it dragged on for two hours. When he reached the inn, there was no carriage immediately available for hire, and another hour passed before he was able to resume his journey. By the time he finally reached Paris, it was afternoon, and by the time he had found another vehicle that would take him as far as Miremont, the Sun was sinking rapidly in the western sky. The increasing unease he felt as he drew closer to Miremont was further amplified by the fact that the carriage was being followed, not very discreetly, by a lone rider in hooded traveling-cloak.

The twilight was not quite gone when Temple dismounted at the *étoile* crossroad, but the rider was no longer visible. He must have turned off the road a minute or two before Temple got down. Temple watched the carriage rumble on, bound for Pontoise, then pulled himself together. It would be dark by the time he had climbed the hill to the château, whether he went through the village or risked one of the smaller paths that followed a more direct route, and he had no lantern with him.

Fortunately, he did not have to make a decision. Almost as soon as he had picked up his bag again, the silhouette of a man materialized at the entrance of one of the smaller paths leading away from the signpost.

"Wait a moment, Mr. Temple!" a voice called. "I'll light my lantern."

It was a voice that Temple remembered—that of Pierre Louchet, who once had worked for him briefly in London, after being stranded there, having served as a messenger. In those days, he had been a woodcutter, but now he was evidently employed at the château.

Lighting the lantern took time; Louchet was still dependent on flint and amadou to strike a light.

"How long have you been waiting for me, Pierre?" Temple asked.

"Not long, sir," Louchet assured him—although Temple deduced that he must have been loitering nearby for several hours, at least, if Ned Knob had assumed that his journey from Calais would go without a hitch.

"Is there any news?" Temple asked, as they fell into step.

"None, sir," Louchet told him. "No communication has been made as yet. Madame la Comtesse has raised 15,000 *livres* in gold and silver, and Madame Boehm has probably been able to gather a similar amount, but we do not know whether that will be enough. The waiting is the worst of it, sir. Mr. Richard and Madame Thompson have been out of their minds. They'll be very glad to see you."

"There's very little I can do, Pierre—at least until the ransom demand arrives. Even then..."

"I understand, sir—but your being here will make a big difference, at least to Madame Thompson. Did you know that their son was once confined to my care for a while, when he was a babe in arms? I was in my cottage then, and the circumstances were strange, but I learned to love him as if he were my own. I never knew, sir, when I worked for you in London, that he was your grandson, or..."

"I know, Pierre. I didn't know of his existence then, let alone his whereabouts. I've been the very worst of grandfathers ever since, and have not known how to set about repairing that fault. Now..."

"It's not too late, sir," Louchet said, as he hurried along the narrow bridle-path that provided the most direct route to the château. "She has longed to see you, sir, but... she had no news, no address. I think she would have asked Master Ned to find you long ago, if she could have thought of a good reason."

"She did, once," Temple said. "I came while the old Marquis was still alive–but I did not see her then. She was not yet in residence–I think she was in Paris, with Jeanne. I could have... but no matter. Tell me–is there any information at all regarding the kidnappers? You've questioned the villagers, I dare say?"

"Nothing's known in Miremont, sir–and nothing escapes the eyes of those gossips unless it's truly invisible. Whoever they were, they came across country and not by road. They knew the terrain well, and they picked the season well enough–there was no one abroad in the fields that day, for the weather was too cold. The livestock has been gathered in for the winter. I saw four, but there must have been more. I couldn't see their faces but they were strongly-built and purposeful–former soldiers, I'd judge. But who isn't a former soldier nowadays? They weren't the Emperor's men, I hope–but who can tell to what depths the poorer remnants of a humiliated army might sink? I never thought to cry *à l'avantage*, but it would have made me weep to receive a reply. Madame Boehm asked me whether they might have been Germans, but the one who spoke seemed French–Belgian French, mayhap, but French nevertheless. Mr. Knob asked me whether their skin was at all discolored, but I have no memory of any such thing. They were pale, not bronzed like southerners, but I couldn't tell whether they were Normans."

"They were mere mercenaries, Pierre. Even if we knew such details, it wouldn't tell us who sent them, or why. Until we know exactly what they want, we shall have no real idea what we are up against. If it's only the money..."

"Madame la Comtesse says that she is willing to pay. Madame Sarah is very angry, but she has agreed. If it's just the money they want, they'll release the children, won't they, sir?"

"I believe so. The children are too young to identify them in court, or give information that might lead to their capture; there's no profit in hurting them, and it always make good business sense to keep such vile bargains, for it encourages cooperation on the part of future victims."

"Madame Thompson is afraid that they might hurt young Richard, merely to put pressure on the Comtesse and Madame Boehm."

"That's unnecessary, and hence unlikely," Temple assured him–although he was far from certain that he was right in that estimation. If little Richard really were surplus to their requirements, the kidnappers might well think him useful for demonstrative purposes–and he had to be surplus, had he not? It was surely unthinkable that the real target of this whole insidious plan might be Gregory Temple, and not the Comtesse or late Comte Henri de Belcamp at all."

Louchet had the key to the main gate of the château in his pocket, and he locked it behind him when they had gone in. They went into the house by the main door, which the servant also locked behind them. Another Pierre–the Marquis de Belcamp's old manservant–hurried to meet them.

"Madame Thompson has fallen asleep," he said, in a whisper. "Mr. Thompson is with her, but Madame la Comtesse asked that you be taken in to see her before you see anyone else. Is that agreeable?"

"Of course," Temple said. "Lead on."

Chapter Three
The Comtesse de Belcamp's Distress

The drawing-room was lit by two candelabras, one of which was on the mantelpiece while the other stood on a small table set beside the armchair in which Jeanne, Comtesse de Belcamp, was waiting. She got up when Gregory Temple was shown in, and came towards him. He bowed politely.

His eyes darted around the room, taking its appearance in at a single glance. The décor was much as he remembered it, although the portraits had been rearranged. The late Marquis now had pride of place above the mantel, while his miscreant wife's portrait had been added to a recess beside the chimney-breast.

Temple was tempted to pause and study the portrait of Helen Brown at his leisure. When he had had been confronted by John Devil in the cell in Newgate where he had expected to find Richard Thompson, John Devil had told him a fantastic story concerning the locket he sometimes wore around his neck, claiming that the woman whose portrait was within it had been Helen Brown, and that the outlaw Tom Brown had been the result of her brief pseudonymous affair with Temple. The latter part was nonsense, of course–but as to the former, Temple had never been entirely sure. He resisted the temptation, knowing that contemplation would only add to his uncertainty, and hence to his torment.

"It's good to see you, Mr. Temple," the Comtesse said, a little hoarsely. "Last time we met, circumstance made us adversaries, but things are very different now. You are welcome in my home. Please sit down."

Temple waited until the Comtesse had taken her own armchair again before sitting in the one facing it. Once she was seated again, the light from the candles shone directly on the Comtesse's face. The last time Temple had seen her, in 1817, Jeanne had seemed an exceedingly young woman, little more than a child. In the intervening four years, she had aged a great deal. She was a woman in her prime now, and a mother; she was very beautiful, but her beauty was sorely distressed by pain, some of it recent and acute but some of longer duration and chronic. She seemed ten years older than she really was.

"I never considered you as an enemy, my lady," Temple assured her. "You may rely on my friendship now, if there is any way I can be of service."

"I'm glad to hear that," Jeanne said. "You'll forgive me, I hope, if I don't ask my servants to wake Suzanne immediately, but I wanted to see you alone first."

"I have not had any contact with Suzanne in four years," Temple said, grimly. "Another hour will make no difference."

"I have always thought that your refusal to communicate with Suzanne must have much to do with her intimate friendship with me," the Comtesse said. She did not phrase it as a question, but it was a question, and Temple knew that it demanded an explanation—one that he was unready to give.

"No, milady," he said. "That was not the reason. Have you any more news to add to what Pierre Louchet has told me?"

"Alas, no. Do you think that you will be able to help us, Mr. Temple?"

"I don't know," Temple confessed, frankly. "Until the kidnappers make contact, we shall not know exactly what they want, and even when we know what their demands are, it will be difficult to estimate whether they intend to play fair. Unless you intend to involve the Prefecture of Police, we have no alternative but to do as we are instructed and hand over the ransom. If we can get the children returned safely, we might then be able to make plans for its possible recovery, but I cannot be optimistic on that score. I shall act as your intermediary in the negotiations, if I may, and will do my utmost to make sure that the children are returned safely. In all probability, the best we can hope to achieve is that we shall be able to set someone to follow the money once it is handed over— but the kidnappers will expect that, and it will not be easy. Ned Knob is, I'm told, an accomplished bloodhound; I'm sure that he will do his best."

"And is Ned Knob the only assistant you have, Mr. Temple?" the Comtesse asked, with brutal directness.

Temple hesitated a moment, then sighed. "Madame la Comtesse," he said, "I am an honest man, although I am sometimes required by the necessities of my employment to practice deceit and dissimulation. I do not know what Ned had told you, or has refrained from telling you, but I must make my own judgment in any case. To be perfectly frank, milady, I do not know whether I am alone in having rushed to your aid. Another man was supposed to travel with me from Dover to Paris, but he did not appear to be on the packet-boat. Perhaps he was merely delayed, or perhaps he always intended to make his own way here—in which case, given that I was delayed on the road, he might have arrived in Miremont ahead of me. I dare not call him my assistant, and he has no right to think of me as his, but in this instance, if in no other, we are working to the same end. I do not know what resources he has to deploy, but I am forced to admit that he is a more ingenious man than I am, with a far greater capacity for working apparent miracles. Whatever little I can do to assure a successful outcome to this tragic business, he will more than double–but exactly what he will do, and how, I cannot tell."

"Who is this man?" the Comtesse asked.

"Your husband, milady," Temple told her. "Comte Henri de Belcamp, alias Percy Balcomb."

She did not show any obvious sign of shock or disbelief, but Temple judged that she had not had the news already from Ned Knob. The little man seemed more inclined to honesty now than he had been in 1817, but it seemed that his first loyalty was still to John Devil. It was, after all, to John Devil that he had taken Suzanne's letter in the first instance.

There was a long pause before the Comtesse spoke again, but when she broke the silence, her voice was almost steady. "I would be a liar if I said that I had always known," she said, softly, "but I had always felt *something* that would make such news, if and when it came, seem reasonable and expectable. I would be a liar, too, if I said that I had hoped–for how could I hope that the man I loved was withholding himself deliberately, refusing even to let me know that he was still alive? And yet... strangely, I do not feel betrayed. I think I came to understand what kind of man he is during our few precious days together. He warned me often enough that things might go badly awry–that he would be called murderer, traitor, madman–and that the path of our love might run anything but smooth. I do not know how he could bear to be alive and not to see his wife or his son, but I do believe that he has not found it easy, and must have thought it a necessity. But he will come now, will he not? Nothing will prevent him but actual death."

"He believes it to be possible, milady," Temple told her, thinking it best to put everything out into the open, "that he may be the real objective of this vile affair–that what the kidnappers want might not be limited to money. He has a secret, which might be reckoned valuable."

"He has a secret!" Jeanne de Belcamp echoed. "How can I be surprised by that? Secrets have always been his chief stock-in-trade. How could it be otherwise?" Her eyes flickered sideways, towards the portrait of the late Marquis, from whom the young Henri had had to keep the terrible secrets of his own identity, and his mother's fate.

"As yet, we have no way of knowing for sure whether he might be right," Temple went on. "It may be, though, that the reason he did not catch the packet-boat from Dover to Calais is that he was certain that I would be followed and did not want to be seen with me. I *was* followed–and something more insidious than that occurred on the coach between Calais and Amiens, where I believe that I may well have made contact with one of the people behind the kidnapping."

This time, the Comtesse did seem startled. "Morbleu!" she exclaimed, in a fashion that was not entirely ladylike. "Who?"

"He called himself Giuseppe Balsamo, but I think that was a teasing lie, intended to be suggestive. He judged that I would recognize the name as that of the self-styled Count Cagliostro, who made such an impact in pre-Revolutionary France as an alleged magician and alchemist."

"Magic and alchemy? Does he think that Henri has the secret of the philosopher's stone, then?"

"No, milady–but he may well believe that your husband has the secret of resurrecting the dead. The Comte de Belcamp certainly convinced Ned Knob that he has that secret, and, no matter how much I would like to doubt it, I have to admit that he almost certainly does. I have seen the results of his work. They are more horrible than hopeful, at present, but it seems that he and his associate–a Parisian physician named Germain Patou–had barely begun their research. Re-animating the body is, it seems, far easier than reanimating the mind. Most of his reanimated corpses were mindless idiots–but some were not, and he seems to have been exploring means to help the others remember who and what they had been, with some limited success. His work in London was cut short–but not, it seems, before attracting attention from more than one interested party."

"I do not want to be indelicate, Mr. Temple," the Comtesse said, "but there have been persistent rumors since the beginning of 1817 that you had gone mad. This story is not likely to dissuade its hearers from wondering whether the rumors might be true."

"The rumors may well be true," Temple said, flatly, "but my madness is an obsessive one, not a delusional one. If I am forced to believe and say things that are incredible, it is not because I have lost touch with reality but because the reality that has caught me in its web is one that presents a stern challenge to the imagination of ordinary people. No matter what you think of me, and no matter how this unfortunate business develops, you will discover before very long that the dead *can* be reanimated, after a fashion–and that the world of the future will be very different from the world of the past, no matter what the limitations of the process eventually prove to be. Ned Knob can tell you more about it than I can, for he has seen a resurrection accomplished, and has talked to a close friend who had been hanged. Your husband can tell you far, far more... if he will deign to show himself and dare to face you."

"My husband never lacked daring, Mr. Temple," Jeanne de Belcamp said. "No matter what you think of him, you cannot deny that. Whatever his reasons have been for letting me think that he was dead these last four years, a lack of daring was not among them."

"No," Temple conceded, "it was not. His madness is a more reckless sort than mine. Young Ned is not mad, though. I do not like the man, or his politics, but I cannot call him mad. With his sanity to support us, our history compels belief."

"You think, therefore, that when the ransom demand comes, it will not demand money?"

"Oh no, milady–I'm perfectly certain that it will demand money. I doubt that it will mention anything else, at least to begin with. On the other hand, I think it quite possible–and perhaps likely–that a snare is being set. While your husband works to recapture your children and the money, Signor Balsamo's friends may be working to capture him–which raises, I think, an important question.

"For myself, I am only concerned with the children. I confess that any money you and Sarah O'Brien might lose in consequence of their safe recovery is a matter of scant importance to me, although I always do what I can to see justice served and criminal enterprise thwarted. As for your husband, I do not care in the least what may happen to him. If the true price of recovering the three children were to hand him over, in order that his secret might be extracted from him–by whatever means–then I would do it without a moment's hesitation. You might think otherwise. If so, I need to know. I make no promises, but I will take your opinion into account."

The Comtesse de Belcamp frowned slightly as she considered the question. Temple was interested to know what her reply would be–but he had no chance to find out immediately, for the drawing-room door opened at that moment and Suzanne Thompson raced in, followed by her husband. Evidently, Suzanne had awoken without being roused, and her very first thought had been to ask whether her father had arrived.

Temple had expected some stiffness, some reproach, some reserve–but there was none. His daughter hurled herself upon him, and threw her arms around him. She was sobbing, but she contrived nevertheless to say: "Daddy, oh Daddy, I'm *so* glad you're here."

Temple hesitated, but then he returned the embrace, leaning over to kiss his daughter on the top of her head. "I'm sorry, child," he said. "So very sorry– for everything."

There was a long pause then, while the other people in the room had to wait.

Eventually, Temple disengaged himself from the embrace, and stepped towards Richard Thompson, extending his hand. "It's good to see you again, Richard," he said, adding–after only the merest hesitation–"my son."

Thompson gripped his hand gladly, and shook it vigorously. "It's good to see you, sir," he said. "We're in dire need of your quick mind and wise counsel."

Temple pulled himself together. "It might be best," he said, "if we were to assemble all the interested parties in one room, so that we may all know what we're about. Is it possible to summon Countess Boehm from the new château? And where is Ned Knob?"

It was Richard Thompson who answered. "Ned is watching the gate," he replied. "If any messenger comes, Ned intends to follow him when he departs.

234

Sarah knows that you were coming–she will be waiting to be summoned. Surrisy is with her. Do you remember Surrisy?"

Temple did remember Robert Surrisy, and could not help darting a glance at the Comtesse. Robert Surrisy had been in love with Jeanne Herbet before Comte Henri de Belcamp had made his spectacular entrance on the Miremont scene, and had only dallied thereafter with the woman he knew as Lady Frances Elphinstone because Jeanne had rejected him. Sarah O'Brien–alias Lady Frances–had rejected him too, and Temple had half-expected that Surrisy would renew his suit with Jeanne once Henri had been declared dead. He knew that the two of them had undertaken a voyage on the *Deliverance* with two committed couples–Richard and Suzanne, and Friedrich Boehm and Sarah–but it seemed that their brief alliance had not matured into anything richer. Perhaps that was as well, given that Henri was still alive.

"I'll send Old Pierre to the new château," the Comtesse said. "Sarah and Robert will come. Should I ask him to search for Ned?"

Temple considered the matter briefly, then said: "No. I was followed from Paris by a rider. The kidnappers must know that I'm here. If that's what they've been waiting for, their demand will arrive tonight. Let Ned stay where he is, so that he can follow his plan through."

"Should we wait a little while before holding our council of war, in case the messenger–or someone else–puts in an appearance?" the Comtesse asked.

"No," Temple said without hesitation. "When you, Suzanne and Sarah O'Brien are all gathered together, I shall be able to say what I need to say to the people who need to hear it. We must make our own plans, without regard to anyone else–but if a messenger does come, so much the better, We shall all be together to hear what demands are being made."

The Comtesse de Belcamp picked up a handbell from the table in order to summon the two Pierres, but before she had a chance to ring it, her hand froze. Another, more distant bell had sounded. Temple recognized it immediately as the bell suspended beside the main gate.

"I'll go," he said, immediately–but he was not as quick off the mark as Pierre Louchet, who had already gone out through the front door, with a lantern in his hand, by the time Temple reached it. Nor could Temple match the former woodcutter's stride as they crossed the courtyard. By the time he caught up with the other man, Louchet was already staring through the bars of the gate saying, in a scornful tone: "What do *you* want?"

"Who is it, Pierre?" Temple asked, placing a calming hand on the former woodcutter's shoulder

"It's the Besnard boy, from the village," Louchet said. "The one they call Don Juan–ironically, of course."

In the meantime, the offended individual had stretched out his hand, bearing a sealed envelope. "You should not speak in that fashion to a man who is attempting to do you a service," Besnard said. "I was asked to deliver this note by hand, and generously agreed to do it. I did not expect to be insulted for my trouble."

Temple reached through the bars and took the letter. He did not bother to ask how much the young man had been paid, but merely said: "You have my sincere thanks, sir. Who gave you the message, my friend?"

"I have never seen him before," Besnard replied. "He did not give me his name."

"Please describe him as carefully as you can," Temple said. "It's a matter of some importance."

Besnard shrugged. "He was much older than me," he said, "though not quite as old as either of you. He was a little stout, I suppose, but seemed very healthy. His face was rounded, his hair and eyes dark. Well-dressed, though somewhat travel-stained."

"What about his voice–his accent?" Temple asked.

"He was certainly French, but not local. A southerner, perhaps–there was something of the Languedoc about his pronunciation."

"And where did your encounter take place?" Temple wanted to know.

"At the inn–or, rather, outside its door. He did not come in, but met me as I was coming out. He said that he needed to get a message to the Château de Belcamp urgently, but did not know his way around and was in any case in a hurry to get back on the Pontoise Road. He offered me a *louis* if I would help him out–although it was not the money that made me do it, you understand, but kindness, to the stranger and Madame la Comtesse alike."

"You fool...!" Pierre Louchet began–but Temple silenced him with a curt gesture.

"We're much obliged to you, sir," Temple said. "Thank you, and good night." As he pulled Louchet away, he glanced left and right into the darkness. There was no sign of Ned Knob, but he trusted that the little man had heard every word, and would make every effort to catch up with the mysterious stranger–or at least to discover which way he had really gone.

"Will you run to the new chateau, Pierre, and fetch Countess Boehm?" Temple said. "This is what we have all been waiting for, and we must all know what it contains."

Louchet nodded, and let himself out by the small gate beside the main one. He took his lantern with him. Temple had to carry the letter back to the house to read what was written on the envelope. It was not very revealing, saying only: *To the Comtesse de Belcamp.*

Temple took it into the drawing-room. Instead of waiting for Sarah Boehm, he carefully broke the seal and took out the piece of paper folded within. He scanned its contents quickly, but then raised his hand to prevent the Comtesse from snatching it from his hand. "I will need to examine it more closely," he said, by way of explanation. "I shall read the message. It says: *Bring 10,000 livres to the eastern extremity of Little Switzerland at midnight. The first child will then be released. The money must be delivered by one of the parents, accompanied by no more than one man. If any attempt is made to interfere with us before the exchange, the first child will be killed; if we are pursued or harassed thereafter, the other children will be killed.*"

He paused, so that his listeners would know that he had stopped reading. Then he added: "It appears that the affair is to proceed by stages, and that we have a very short deadline to complete the first phase. The complexity is tiresome, and the short deadline leaves us no time to make preparations. On the other hand, the fact that Little Switzerland is nearby–I believe that is the nickname of the plateau on top of the hill that overlooks the château and the valley– implies that our adversaries must be close at hand, and ought to have at least one of the kidnapped children with them. Do you have 10,000 *livres* in gold ready to hand, my lady?"

"Yes I do," the Comtesse confirmed. "I shall make up a package. Which of us should go to make the exchange?"

"Suzanne will go, with me," Temple said. "I shall do my very best to make certain that the child is handed over before I surrender the money."

He had to repeat the contents of the note then, because the former Sarah O'Brien had just arrived, escorted by Robert Surrisy. He also repeated his assertion that he would go with Suzanne to deliver the money. "Monsieur Surrisy," he said, "you must give us half an hour before following us, if we do not return– but if you hear a gunshot, you must come immediately, as quickly as you can, with Richard and Pierre Louchet–but you must make sure that the château is not left unguarded."

"I wish you would let me go in your stead, sir," Surrisy was quick to say. "I am a lawyer now, and my soldiering days are behind me, but I know how to use a sword and a pistol, and I can ride very well."

"No," said Richard Thompson. "I should be the one to go. Suzanne is my wife."

"If I were not here, either one of you would doubtless make an excellent job of it," Temple said, "but it's me they expect, and it may be that they want me as well as the gold. It was no coincidence that this letter arrived so soon after my arrival. They've been watching out for me since I left London, and have even taken the trouble to sound me out. I was careful to conceal the extent of my knowledge regarding the secret of electrical resurrection, but they undoubtedly know that I am in the employ of His Majesty's secret police, and may imagine that I know far more than I do about the recent events in London. That might work to our advantage–if they are willing to hand over a child in order to persuade me to surrender to their custody, it is an exchange worth making."

Sarah Boehm stepped in front of Surrisy then to say: "What events in London? What secret of electrical resurrection?"

Again Temple had to repeat himself, informing the entire company that Henri de Belcamp was still alive, and had recently been involved in a violent struggle along the banks of the Thames for possession of a company of the dead-alive, and the means to revive more.

"Impossible!" was Sarah Boehm's response. Temple did not know whether she meant the resurrection of the dead, or the fact that her friend and longtime companion had played dead for so long without letting her know that he was still alive and still scheming to turn the world upside-down.

Surrisy, who evidently assumed that she meant the former, said; "There have been rumors abroad in Paris..."

"What rumors, Monsieur Surrisy?" Temple was quick to ask. "Have you heard mention therein of a man named Germain Patou?"

"The little physician? I know of him, yes–but not in connection with these rumors. I paid them little heed, to tell you the truth, for they seemed stale as well as silly. Have you heard of the Comte de Saint-Germain?"

"Yes I have," Temple said. "A poseur–a magician and pretended immortal, of the same stripe as Count Cagliostro, likewise not heard of since the Revolution, or at least since Napoleon's ascent to power. Is he said to have reappeared?"

"So rumor has it–and it's also said that he's on the track of some great secret, as valuable in its way as the elixir of long life that he already possesses. It's said that he's a member of an ancient secret society–but everyone in the world is nowadays said to be a member of some secret society or other, and every such society that is actually formed claims roots in deepest antiquity."

"I can well understand," Temple said, with a sight trace of sarcasm, "that a stalwart of the Brotherhood of the Deliverance would know far better than to pay any heed to silly talk of secret societies. What say you, Sarah O'Brien? Your husband was intricately involved with some relic of the *vehmgerichte*, I understand?"

"I was a very active member of the Deliverance myself, Chief Inspector Temple," the Irishwoman retorted, with more than a hint of vitriol, "under more names than one. Are you bearing grudges still, to speak to me in that tone?"

Temple recalled the night on which he had surprised Sarah O'Brien and Richard Thompson together, riding the Russian Mountains at the Colisée, thus slotting the last piece of James Davy's intricate jigsaw of deception into place–but that belonged to another life now, and another world. "I beg your pardon, Countess Boehm," he said, humbly. "I had no right to be rude–and I bear no grudge. In this matter, we are all on the same side–even John Devil himself. I hope, now that he was able to arrive ahead of me, for I'd be prepared to wager that he would have seen the stranger accost young Besnard in the village, and might even now be watching from the ridge of the hill. We cannot rely on that, though–it is more likely that he is still in Paris, if he is in France at all. We must be prepared to handle this ourselves. I will do my utmost to secure the freedom of whichever child they bring to the meeting-place, if they bring one at all, and I shall not fire on them unless there is some treachery. If I can simply exchange the money for the child, I will. Then, I suppose, we shall have to await a further communication. If things go wrong... well, we shall have to re-evaluate the situation. Are we all agreed on what will happen at midnight? It's not far off, I fear."

"I cannot see why you should automatically assume command, Mr. Temple," said Countess Boehm. "I understand why your daughter sent for you, but it is not your money that is at stake."

"He has assumed command because I have asked him to do so, Sarah," the Comtesse de Belcamp stated, flatly. "Tonight, at least, it is my money that is at stake. Who else should be in command, do you suppose?"

Sarah Boehm did not reply. Robert Surrisy hastened to fill the silence. "Mr. Temple has far more experience in this sort of matter than anyone else, Sarah," he pointed out. "Richard has been a policeman too, but I dare say that he is perfectly willing to follow the advice of his old senior officer. I was a Knight of the Deliverance, and am proud to have served in that capacity, but the mothers of kidnapped children surely ought to look to a man like Gregory Temple for expert assistance."

Temple bowed to Surrisy, but Countess Boehm still seemed inclined to rebellion. "That does not mean that Temple's daughter should go with him," she objected. "Why should I not go–or Jeanne since she is determined to part with her money while I hold mine in reserve?"

"It is precisely because the two of you are the ones with the money that Suzanne should go," Temple said, flatly. "If I am to be trusted to handle the affair, the matter is not negotiable. Now, Monsieur Surrisy, may I question you further regarding these rumors? Was there, by any chance, any reference to a man named Giuseppe Balsamo?"

"That was Cagliostro's real name," Surrisy said, immediately. "No, I have not heard it spoken–but if there were a secret society of magicians that included the Comte de Saint-Germain, how could Cagliostro not be a member of it? He's said to be dead of course–but we know what rumors of *that* sort are worth."

"What about the *Veste Nere*?" Temple asked.

Surrisy's expression shifted. "I've heard that term, and its French equivalent, the *Habits Noirs*, bandied about the Palais de Justice," he admitted, "but that's another matter, somewhat less fanciful in essence. There's a world of difference between bandits who ape gentlemanly dress, and aristocrats who wear it with the entitlement of centuries. The *Veste Nere* are common criminals; these others–if they exist–are more likely to be madmen."

"That seems only too likely," Sarah Boehm put in, acidly, "If we are to discuss rumors while the clock ticks, did I not hear a rumor to the effect that Gregory Temple is now a lunatic, who cannot be trusted in anything?"

"That's a lie!" Suzanne protested.

"I liked your late husband, Madame Boehm," Temple said. "Indeed, I offered to sell you to him once, for the price of a steamboat engine–but I sold the bearskin before I had the bear, and the engine went to a trader who matched my price with slightly greater immediacy. All that is water under the bridge now, and I have said that I bear no grudges; it would be as well if you could set yours aside, at least for tonight. Even an old lunatic can carry a bag full of gold to the top of a hill and complete the purchase of a child–and if there's some trickery afoot, a madman of my sort might be as useful as a sane man. I am, if nothing else, expendable."

Sarah Boehm hesitated, but then she nodded. "Why not?" she said, presumably meaning: *If someone has to risk his neck, why not you?* Suzanne must have understood that, because she put her arms around her father's neck again, and said: "I'm sorry."

Temple was astonished to find tears in the corners of his own eyes as he replied: "I am the one who should be sorry."

Chapter Four
The Child-Stealers' Enterprise

The route from the Château de Belcamp to "Little Switzerland" and a hunting-path that diverged from the bridle-path that Temple had already followed in company with Piere Louchet, going uphill instead of down before looping back to make its separate way to the *étoile* where the road to Miremont quit the highway. The region's nickname was ironic, because there was nothing mountainous about the region at all; most of the plateau was wooded, but at the eastern extremity to which the ransom note had referred was a small heath, which culminated in a viewpoint from which one could see the entire valley of the Oise, including the full extremity of what had once been the Belcamp domain.

Temple assumed that he and Suzanne would be required to cross the heath and stand on the viewpoint itself, fully exposed beneath the Moon and stars to anyone watching from a semicircular arc of woodland that measured at least 200 paces from end to end. They would be watched from some covert there, and someone would eventually come to meet them. With this prospect in mind, they set out from the château some 25 minutes before the appointed time.

"You have not really been mad, have you, Father?" Suzanne asked, as they trudged through the grounds to the commencement of the path. The gold, packed into a single satchel, was weighing very heavily on his right arm.

"Have I not?" Temple replied. "I believe I was, at least for a while–but I am making progress." His mouth twisted into a grimace as he used the word–by which he meant, yet again, the restoration of normality and harmony–but Suzanne was holding her lantern in such a way as to light their path, and she could not have seen the expression.

"Is that why you did not write to me?" she asked. "I thought that you were angry with me–that I had betrayed you in so many ways. Richard... the baby.

When I helped Henri de Belcamp, I was acting under duress, but I know that's no excuse... not what you would expect of your daughter."

"I should never have made the stupid declaration that Richard was no fit husband for you," Temple said. "I was to blame, not you. As for your being here when Henri de Belcamp came home, and being caught up in his machinations–I understand how desperate you were, and how helpless you felt. It was none of your doing that prevented me from writing to you, but my own shame. I was angry with myself; it was I that felt unworthy of contact with you. I was a fool. I had put it completely out of my mind until Ned Knob reminded you–and I immediately became angry with him, and called him all manner of ugly names, for which he was right to chide me. I should have done everything I could to clear Richard's name and open the way for the two of you–I mean the three of you–to return to England, but I did not, because I could not face him. If only I had got to his cell in Newgate before John Devil, instead of after... but that, again, was my fault, not his."

There was a pause while she digested this, and then she said: "Did you mean what you said about the kidnappers wanting you as well as the gold?"

"It's possible," he said. "They've been dogging my footsteps since Calais, at least, and could have seized me by force at any time, but they know that if they want my full cooperation, they'll have to play a craftier game. It's Henri they really want–he's the one with the secret–but they must be afraid by now that he'll stay away, or at least in hiding, for exactly that reason. They might regard me as a mere morsel to give them something on which to chew until Henri is prepared to show his hand."

On the other hand, Temple thought, but dared not say aloud, *they might need someone to kill, in order that John Devil may be challenged to bring him back alive.*

"Sarah and Jeanne are at odds," Suzanne told him, after another brief pause. "They were never the best of friends, for they began as rivals, but this business has driven them much further apart."

"So I observed," Temple said. "It will not matter. Circumstances will force them to work together, to the same end."

"If all the children were all released together, that would be true," Suzanne agreed. "But that is not the case. If Sarah's boy were the one returned tonight... I'm not so sure that she'd be ready to give her money for the release of the others."

"I think you underestimate her," Temple said. "In any case, it will be little Richard who's released tonight. He's the least valuable of the three."

"Do you really think so, Daddy?"

"I'm almost certain–but hush now. We're getting close to the rendezvous, and we're almost certainly under close observation."

Suzanne obeyed immediately, falling silent and lifting the lantern higher. Not for the first time, Temple shifted his satchel from one hand to the other, bring temporary relief to one of his overstressed arms. He had not anticipated, although he should have, the state of extreme exhaustion that he would be in when he had climbed the hill. He had not rested properly since he set off from London, nor for three days before. No matter how little resemblance the hill above Miremont bore to a Swiss Alp, the steep climb was as hard on his tired legs as the gold he carried was on his shoulder muscles.

By the time they reached the bare land at the eastern extremity of the ridge, Temple was very glad of an opportunity to pause and draw breath. The sky was hazy and such moonlight as there was seemed quite impotent, but it was possible to see that the patch of heath was utterly deserted. No one was waiting there.

Suzanne looked at him fearfully, and he put his spare hand on her shoulder in what he hoped would pass for a gesture of reassurance.

"They'll be watching from cover," he assured her. "We must go to the edge, where the drop is sheerest, so that they can see that we're alone and have nowhere to run." He stepped forward again, taking a deep breath as he did so. The night air was cold enough to slice into his lungs like a razor, but it carried the oxygen he needed to replenish him.

When he and Suzanne had reached the limit of the ridge, where the ground fell away almost vertically, Temple set the bag that contained the gold down on the ground, positioning it carefully. He instructed Suzanne to keep the lantern elevated, displaying their faces plainly to any watchers in the bushes on the edge of the forested section of the ridge.

He was fully prepared to wait, if it should prove necessary—but they did not have to wait long. A lone man came out of the bushes, just about visible although he had no lantern in his hand. He did not have a child with him either.

"Step away from the gold, if you please, Mr. Temple," a voice said, in very good English, spoken with a mild continental accent. "Then take your pistol out of your pocket, very carefully, and throw it over the edge, hard enough to ensure that it will fall for ten or twelve times a man's height before it hits the ground."

"I will do nothing until we see the child," Temple said. "Indeed, I want the child safe in Suzanne's care before I step away from the gold. I shall keep my revolver, but you may watch us depart in company with the child, leaving the gold behind. That way, we shall both be sure of getting what we want."

"How do we know that the bag contains gold?" the other asked.

"You still have two children captive," Temple pointed out. "We would not put them at risk by playing false. Shall I throw you a coin or two by way of demonstration?"

"What would that prove?" the kidnapper asked—but he had the luxury of sounding amused, knowing that he had the upper hand.

"As much as your returning one child proves regarding the well-being of the others," Temple retorted. "Next time, I shall insist on seeing both before I hand over any money—and before you waste time in pointing out that you could shoot us down from ambush and simply take the gold, may I point out that the slightest nudge from my foot will send the bag skidding down the slope, scattering its contents far and wide. No one will disturb us if no shots are fired—but if you fire on us, you will not have time to gather your plunder before others come running."

"The brave soldier of Napoleon, the former apprentice detective and the old woodcutter?" the other countered. "We are men of peace, who abhor violence, but I think we could take care of them were the need to arise. Your midget, by the way, is off on a wild goose chase just now. Your other friend has not shown up at all—which is a deep disappointment to us, though not entirely a surprise. Do you know how to contact him?"

"Who?" Temple asked. The other man was close enough now for his face to catch a glimmer of lamplight. It was not the man who had called himself Giuseppe Balsamo, nor did he fit the description given by young Besnard. This was a tall and slender man with a goatee beard. He was wearing a black coat beneath his traveling-cloak, but he seemed no more reminiscent of a member of the *Veste Nere* than a medieval alchemist who had outlived his natural span. The cloak was hooded, but the hood was not up.

"Don't play games, Mr. Temple," the kidnapper said. "You know the stakes we are playing for—but we do need the money; this promises to be a very expensive campaign. We are honest brokers, though, and not averse to sensible compromise." He lifted his arm and beckoned.

Temple could hardly see the gesture, and he was much closer to his interlocutor than the bushes from which the bearded man had come, but someone there with good night vision was ready to respond to the summons. Two other people stepped out of the thicket—one of them a little child, perhaps four years old.

Suzanne must have had good night vision herself, or a mother's instinct, for she immediately ran towards them, crying: "Richard! Richard!" The flame of the lantern flickered wildly as she ran, but it did not go out.

Temple bit his lip, wishing that she had waited for the child to come to them but not wanting to call her back.

"We will need proof that the others are alive and well," Temple said, grimly, to the dark shadow confronting him. "This is an earnest of our intent, but we will not hand over any more money unless we are convinced that the younger boys are well."

"Very well, Mr. Temple," said the man with the goatee, with suspicious alacrity. "You are very welcome to come with us, and see for yourself."

Temple had half-expected that, but he was still somewhat uncertain of what he might be letting himself in for. It seemed an opportunity that might be too good to be missed—but he knew that it would also be a dangerous move, and that it would leave Jeanne de Belcamp with no more help and support than she had had before his arrival.

"Suzanne," he said. "Take little Richard with you and go back the way we came. I'll stay here to make sure that you're safely on your way home, and then I shall go with these men, to make sure that... the other children are safe." He stumbled slightly in his discourse when he suddenly realized that he had not asked the name of Jeanne's child, or of Sarah's.

Suzanne opened her mouth to protest, but he cut her off abruptly. "Don't waste time, Suzanne!" he commanded. "Go–take the lantern with you, and hold it up so that I can measure its progress."

She did not hesitate any further. She had her son and the opportunity to make him safe. She hurried him back to the point where the path disappeared into the trees, drawing him along by the hand, and soon vanished from sight. The boy had not looked at Temple, even when he spoke, and presumably had no idea that he had just met his grandfather for the first–and perhaps the last–time.

"You knew, of course, that my grandson was the least valuable of the three," Temple said, in a low voice. "Thus far, you've given away very little and received 10,000 *livres*. You must not raise the stakes too much–and you ought to play fair with me, for I'm the best hope you have of making everything go smoothly."

This time, the man with the goatee laughed in the near-darkness. "It's not in our interests for anyone to die," he said. "At least, until we can be sure that we can bring them back. I hope you can assist us with that, Mr. Temple–or at least in locating your old adversary. We were hoping to see him on the coach from Calais, and were sorely disappointed when he missed it. Please pick up the gold and step away from the edge."

Temple waited a little while longer, for Suzanne's sake, but as soon as his shadowy interlocutor took another step forward, he did as he as he had been told, and picked up the gold. He stepped forward, and handed it to the bearded man, who fumbled as he took it because he could not see what he was doing.

"Lead on," Temple said. "I'll do my best to follow, in spite of the gloom."

"I think it best if there's no delay," the other said. "Give him the flask, Brother."

Again the darkness made it difficult, but Temple eventually contrived to accept a small stoppered bottle from one of the two men who had brought little Richard out of the bushes.

"Drink it all," the leader instructed.

Temple did not hesitate. He took the stopper from the bottle, raised it to his lips and drained the vessel. He might have tried to tip the contents into his sleeve, or hold them in his mouth in the hope of an opportunity to spit them out, but the advice he had given the kidnappers held good for him too: at this early stage of the game, it was best to attempt no trickery.

He did not even dare to pretend to fall unconscious before the draught actually took effect–which gave him time to consider its taste very carefully. The drug was not one that he recognized. It was not bitter, but it did not seem to have been sugared or mixed with liquor to make it more palatable. It was certainly not laudanum.

"The secret of the philosopher's stone *and* a better sleeping draught," he murmured. "You seem well-supplied with secrets already. I apologize for my awkward size–it won't be easy to carry me to..."

He could not complete the sentence, and was in any case regretting that he had not thought of something wittier to say. He felt his knees buckling as his senses reeled–and was oddly grateful to surrender his effortful grip on consciousness. He had, after all, been extremely tired for a very long time.

Chapter Five
The Alchemists' Masquerade

Gregory Temple woke up gradually and reluctantly, extricating himself by slow degrees from a dream whose joy and comfort were based in lack of meaning, absolute inconsequentiality and a profound sense of well-being. He had not been able to escape himself to such a remarkable degree for many years, and he could not help but struggle against the compulsion to return to himself and put on all his troubles once again.

The physical necessities that finally forced him back to the awful pattern of his life were thirst and a need to urinate. The windowless cell in which he found himself, lit by a single candle that had burned very low on the wooden table set beside his pallet, fortunately provided the means to satisfy both needs. He drank directly from the pitcher set beside the candle, and drained it to the dregs. Otherwise, he felt quite well; there was no trace of the headache he would have expected to feel had he been rendered unconscious by any conventional means.

The cell was small–when he stood in the center he only had to lean slightly to one side or another to touch all four walls, three of which were made in grey brick and one of solid stone–but it was not unfurnished. In addition to the bed and the small table, there was a writing-desk bolted to the wall, with a long-legged chair. There was paper on the desk, and the inkwell was full. The nightstand had a cupboard, but all it contained was a bundle of candles–perhaps enough to light the cell for a week. There were no matches, however; Temple made a mental note to be sure to light a new candle before the old one burned out.

The door of the cell was made of wood, without any cast-iron reinforcements, and the inspection hole set at head-height had a wooden shutter rather than a wrought-iron grille. There was no flap at the bottom through which trays of food could be passed without the necessity of unlocking the door. It was, in consequence, more reminiscent of a monk's cell than a dungeon–but the door *was* locked, presumably by means of an external bar. Temple estimated that it would only be the work of ten or twelve minutes to break it down–but he could not do that without making a good deal of noise.

It was easy enough to push the shutter back and look out, but the corridor beyond was unlit.

"Hello!" he shouted. "Is anyone there?"

His ears–which were still keen, despite his age and his failure to hear John Devil enter his bedroom in London–caught the sound of movement from what he guessed to be a cell next to his own, but no one replied.

"Hello!" he called again. "My name is Gregory Temple. My daughter Suzanne is the wife of Richard Thompson, and the mother of another Richard, who was returned to his home last night."

There was no evident reply from the next cell, but his raised voice had attracted attention from elsewhere. The radiance of a flickering candle-flame, approaching from some distance away, shed some little light on the wall opposite his cell, which was grey stone, as solid as the opposite wall of his cell. The reflections brightened as the candle came nearer, until the flame was held up so close to the hole in the door that he could not see through it, at first, to the man who was holding it. Eventually, though, it was moved aside, deliberately displaying the carrier.

The man's face was invisible, completely hidden by a ornate mask carefully molded in the form of a death's-head. There must have been real eyes within what appeared to be empty sockets, but they were not visible; they must have been obscured by something resembling smoked glass–although it must have been very difficult for the masked man to see by feeble candlelight with his eyes screened in that fashion.

"You have slept for a long time, Monsieur," said a voice he did not recognize, in French. "You must have been in dire need of it. You owe us a debt for your healing, as well our generosity in granting your request."

"My request has not been granted," Temple replied, in the same language. "I have not seen the children yet." It occurred to him then that he had called out before in English–a language in which neither the three-year-old Marquis de Belcamp, nor the three-year-old Count Boehm, could be expected to regard as their first. Even the four-year-old Richard Thompson probably spoke French far more often than English, although he must be fluent enough in both languages.

"That is easily remedied," the masked man said. "But you must swear an oath that you will be peaceful and obedient. This is a convent, after all."

"Is it?" Temple countered. "To judge by the cold and the quality of the air, we are underground. Are we in a crypt, then? Or are we in the catacombs beneath Paris, where the bones of past generations are stored for want of burial-grounds?"

"The Council will be glad to find you in an inquisitive mood," the masked man said. "I do need your solemn oath, sworn on the name of almighty God, that you will obey the instructions given to you, and that you will do no violence to anyone while you are here."

"I swear by almighty God," Temple said, speaking in English so that he would not fall victim to any careless or inept expression, "that I will do no violence to anyone while I am here unless I am compelled to defend myself or the children you have stolen. I similarly swear that I will obey the instructions I am given to the best of my ability, so long as they are not in conflict with previous oaths I have sworn and the duties that I fulfill as a servant of His Majesty King George of England."

The masked man laughed. "We have nothing against King George, at present," he said, continuing to speak in the tongue with which he was more comfortable, although he seemed to understand English well enough. "We have not been in sharp conflict with an English King since the 16th century–but more than one of England's recent enemies has been our adversary."

"Times change rapidly nowadays," Temple reported. "Yesterday's enemy of England may be today's ally. May I see the children now?"

"You may." Temple heard the sound of the bar being withdrawn, and then had to step back as the door opened inwards. The masked man stood aside, and bowed slightly as he let his prisoner out.

Temple immediately went along the corridor to the next cell, and removed the bar blocking its door. He pushed the door carefully, in case the children were huddled behind it listening–but they were both sitting on the bed, huddled close for mutual comfort but without either one placing his arm around the other's shoulder. They seemed very small, although Temple did not know what height a three-year-old boy might be expected to attain. They were very similar in stature and in appearance, although one had dark hair and one was blond.

"Am I in the presence of the Marquis de Belcamp and Count Boehm?" Temple asked, speaking slowly, in French. "I am here on behalf of your mothers, who asked me to make sure that you are well."

The blond boy relied first, saying "I am Armand de Belcamp, monsieur."

"I am Friedrich Boehm," the other said, also in French. He added: "Have you come to take us home?"

"Now that I have met your captors," Temple said, "I am convinced that they mean you no harm, in spite of their attempts to seem fearful. They seem to think themselves a cut above the ordinary run of bandits, and will doubtless treat you politely in consequence. You must stay here for a little longer, but I will talk to them, and will try to work out a means of getting you both safely home." He was not certain that boys so small could follow the logic of this overly florid speech–which was intended as much for his captor's ears as for theirs–but the blond boy nodded, and said: "Thank you, sir," in English.

Temple reached out a hesitant hand to touch Armand de Belcamp on the top of the head, and the young Marquis reached up to grip his wrist, almost as if he were the one doing the reassuring rather than the one being reassured.

"You're brave boys," Temple said. "Your fathers would be proud of you."

Friedrich Boehm's dark eyes–his mother's eyes–welled with tears then, but the little boy hastened to wipe them way. He had obviously been old enough to be conscious of what was happening while his father died. Armand de Belcamp released Temple's wrist and put his arm round his friend. There was no reflection here of the tension that had sprung up between their mothers.

Temple stepped back, and allowed the masked man to secure the door. "Very well," Temple said, in French, when the task was complete. "Let us proceed to my audience with the Comtes de Saint-Germain and Cagliostro. I am eager to hear what your brotherhood of alchemists and magicians has to say to me."

"You are a fortunate man, Monsieur Temple," the other replied. "It has been 40 years and more since such a council as the one which will interrogate you has been summoned. I hope that you are sensible of the privilege. The world has changed a great deal in the interim–but that is nothing compared with the changes that the next 40 years will bring, if we cannot contain this demon electricity."

"A demon, is it?" Temple retorted. "Your friend Balsamo spoke of it quite affectionately. I do hope that he was not misrepresenting his ideas in the hope of teasing some indiscretion from me–that would not be a gentlemanly way to behave."

"After you, Monsieur Secret Policeman," the masked man said, in English, pointing the way that his prisoner should go.

Temple was as obedient as he had promised to be. He judged by the condition of the corridors along which they walked that they were most certainly underground, and that they were not about to return to the surface. The chamber to which he was taken was a rounded cavern some 30 paces in diameter whose ceiling was a vault of grey rock. The walls were lined with a series of elaborately carved wooden compartments, many of which were equipped with benches and some with writing-desks, while the humblest had the kind of half-seats that were called *misericordia* by the Romanists–mercy seats, to which the weak might go to the wall for support when the long masses of Medieval times became too burdensome. Temple, not much to his surprise, was shown to an individual chair placed in the center of the near-circle, at the focus of everyone's attention.

Less than half the seats were occupied when he was ushered in, but that was because the council had not yet gathered in full. While he sat patiently in the center, a dozen more came in one by one, making 31 in all. Every one of them was wearing a black monk's habit and a carefully-made death's-head mask. Had they raised their hoods and taken up scythes, they could have passed for Death himself, multiplied 30 times over–as Death must surely be nowadays, in order to cope with the incessant demands of the present population of Christendom.

Temple waited until he was spoken to, observing as much as he could his self-appointed judges–which was, for the most part, their hands. It was difficult to be sure, but he suspected that at least five of the 31 were women. There was not a single pair of hands in the entire ominous circle that was as gnarled and wrinkled as his own–but he was reluctant to take that as good evidence that no one else here was as old as he was. Indeed, he had begun to suspect the opposite. If the scene was reminiscent of the Inquisition of the 17th century, he thought, that was probably not entirely by coincidence, nor the result of the careful mimicry of some ancient woodcut.

Eventually, his examination began. The acoustics of the chamber were odd, making it difficult to determine exactly which death's-head was speaking. Without the sight of moving lips to prompt him, he could only determine the approximate direction from which each voice came.

"Thank you for the oaths that you have given, Mr. Temple," said a voice which might have been that of Giuseppe Balsamo, in English. "We have taken due note of their exactitude, and we are as acutely aware as you are that some of our questions will touch on information that you must have learned in your capacity as a policeman. I repeat, however, that we are not enemies of England, and have nothing against you personally."

"As to whether you are enemies of England or not, I cannot judge as yet," Temple replied, "but there is certainly a matter of personal enmity between us. You have kidnapped my grandson, and two other children who are his closest friends, and have offered them for ransom. That is a despicable criminal act, and no amount of mummery will dignify it. If I can do so, I shall deliver you all to the judgment of the law–but first, I must see the children safe, and it is for that reason that I am here. Let us discuss the terms for the ransom of the two remaining boys."

"The matter is not so simple, as you well know," another voice said, also in English, but more heavily accented. "The most important issue of personal enmity at stake here is that between you and the man who once styled himself the Comte de Belcamp."

"That is irrelevant," Temple said, flatly. "I am here as the representative of the widowed Comtesse Jeanne de Belcamp."

"But she is not a widow," another voice put in. "Let us not waste time with pretense. You were expecting the Comte to join you on the coach from Calais. He did not. Where is he now?"

"I have no idea," Temple said. "I can only suppose that he is making his own arrangements, probably in Paris, to hunt you down."

"He has no army to bring to bear," said a voice from the left, again speaking English, seemingly not as a native tongue. "He has no claim on the Deliverance now, and could not muster them if he had." There seemed to be no president or appointed spokesman in the circle, but neither was there any apparent contest as to who should speak next, nor any obvious system determining the pattern according to which they took turns.

"I had not seen the man for more than four years, until three days ago or thereabouts," Temple said. "I know nothing of his resources."

"You know his work."

"Do I? I have been presented with a bizarre patchwork of evidence and rumor, but I know nothing for sure. He claims to know how to restore the dead to life–but from what I've seen, it's a futile pursuit even if the claim is true. Nor is he the only one who knows the secret. If, as it's claimed, the method is a matter of science and not of magic, it will be common knowledge soon enough. Even if that were not the case, kidnapping his son in the hope of making him surrender it is a foolish as well as a vile thing to do. If, as rumor has it, you represent yourselves as alchemists and magicians, you are doubtless long practiced in deceit, but I would have thought you capable of greater wisdom. Since you obviously cannot make gold, but must steal it like any other bandit troop, why can we not discuss *that* business, instead of wasting time with idle fancies."

"You have not sworn an oath to tell the truth, Mr. Temple," said yet another voice, "but it will save us all time if you do. The longer you seek to delay us with your policeman's tricks, the longer it will be before those two children are returned to their anxious mothers. As a matter of fact, we *can* make gold–but the process is expensive as well as troublesome. Magic is not wish-fulfillment, Mr. Temple, but labor as hard as any other. Nothing is free–especially the ability to live longer than the normal human span. The resurrection of the dead cannot be expected to be different; it will doubtless be a difficult and tiresome business, requiring hard-won skills and carefully-stored wisdom."

"So it seems," Temple agreed, softly. "You might have done better not to wait for my arrival. Had you sent your note a little earlier, you might have snared a man who knows far more about the dead-alive than I do."

"Don't lie to us, Mr. Temple." This voice was as calm as all the rest, but it had an edge of exasperation in it. "Edward Knob knows only what he saw. You have access to everything that King George's police forces know."

Temple felt a slight sinking feeling, as he realized that these masqueraders really did think that he knew far more than he actually did. They had assumed that King George's police forces had been watching the mysterious Arthur Pevensey since the *Prometheus* had first docked at Purfleet, and that they had kept close watch on the *Outremort* too. Perhaps there were European nations where foreign ships were monitored as closely as that, but England had too may radicals of her own to deal with, and was obsessed with the danger that her own people might revolt as the French and Americans had.

Temple and his fellows had been far too busy hunting Tom Paine and suppressing *The Rights of Man* to take any note of the likes of Pevensey and Mortdieu, whose adventure would have been written off as a mere ghost story had any word of it reached the ears of Temple' fellow agents. Not a word had been committed to any official dossier until Temple had made his own report of his official interrogation of Ned Knob and the subsequent events at Greenhithe. If his calculatedly-tentative statements concerning Mortdieu had been believed by his superiors, their only response would have been relief that the *Outremort* had sailed, thus taking the problem away from the troubled English shore. Unless and until he returned to London–or more grey men began to appear in evident profusion–no clerical functionary working for the English government would inscribe a single line to ensure that the matter would be pursued.

"There may be men in England who would be intensely interested in Ned Knob's story," Temple said, dully, "but they are not working for His Majesty's Government. From the viewpoint of Lord Liverpool, and everyone working in his administration, it would qualify as Jacobin science, to be parodied and suppressed. No Parliamentarian in England has the imagination to see what difference the resurrection of the dead might make to the condition of the world, and none would sympathize if they could. Their response to the notion would be to condemn anyone who espoused it as an enemy of the state, to be pilloried, imprisoned or transported."

"Do you have the imagination, Mr. Temple?" someone–who might have been Balsamo–asked.

"I doubt it–and if I had, it would be better for my career were I to suppress it rigorously," Temple replied.

"You're too modest, Mr. Temple. Were you a man who put his career before his principles, you would not be here."

"The reward for such meager imagination as I have," Temple told them, "is I am considered a madman, tolerated but not trusted. My past achievements, and the skills that forged them, are grudgingly respected, but I have no friends among those in power, or even positions of petty authority. But that is not the issue. I repeat: I had no idea that the former Comte Henri de Belcamp, alias Tom Brown, was still alive until three days ago. The first conversation I had with him lasted no more than a few minutes, and mostly consisted of threats uttered while he held a gun to my head. The second was solely concerned with the matter of the kidnapped children, which forced us to set aside our differences and make an alliance. I did expect to meet him on the packet-boat from Dover, and to travel with him to Paris thereafter. I do not know why he did not follow his own plan– assuming that plan was any more than a device to manipulate me. All I *can* do, gentlemen, is to negotiate the release of the two children. That is the only reason why I am here. I strongly suspect that you know far more about this business of resurrection than I do. I am sorry that I cannot tell you more, but it is not my duty to the crown that prevents me from doing so–it is simple ignorance."

There was no interval in the séance, nor any whispered conference– merely a few moments of silence while each of the people in the death's-head masks decided whether they ought to believe him. The one who eventually spoke was not Balsamo, nor the man with the beard he glimpsed in Little Switzerland. It was a voice that spoke with a measure of natural authority.

"Your achievements and the skill that forged them are respected here, Mr. Temple, and not grudgingly. We have always thought of you as an ally of our cause, even though you probably had no idea we existed, or what our cause might be. You have called us common bandits, and we are certainly outlaws, although we could never concede that we are common; even so, we are entirely in sympathy with the campaigns you have waged against men like Tom Brown—and, for that matter, Tom Paine. We preferred Napoleon to the National Convention, but only as the lesser of two evils, and we had no love for the *Ancien Régime*, although we thought it the least of the three evils. We do not like Napoleon any better *now that the Deliverance has done its belated work*, and we are urgently desirous of acquiring the secret of resurrection in order that we might begin to use it in a manner that befits its delicacy as well as its power. We would like you to help us, if you will."

There were two important revelations contained in that speech, which Temple was both astonished and glad to learn. He closed his eyes momentarily, trying to summon up the image of a grey face, and cursed himself roundly for not having realized immediately *who* General Mortdieu must have been when he was alive. Even Ned Knob had guessed, it seemed—although he had kept the information to himself, save for one teasing hint. Temple understood, too, why men like these might be consternated by the former Comte de Belcamp's choice of resurrectees. Apart from the self-styled Mortdieu, formerly Napoleon Bonaparte, the only one who had so far recovered a significant portion of his former identity was Alexander Ross, popularly known as Sawney, the master of a "puppet tribunal" that had made mock of English justice, and the leader of a troupe of false witnesses, ever-ready to provide alibis at the Assize Court on payment of a fee.

"You say that you have the philosopher's stone," Temple said, slowly, ignoring the question that he had been asked. "You can make gold, and live far longer than common men—but not without cost. The gold you make is too expensive, and the longevity you have falls far short of immortality. You want the secret that Belcamp has so that you might reincarnate yourselves, and further increase your superiority to the common men to whom you concede no rights—and you want to reserve it for yourselves, if you possibly can. Will you assassinate men like Michael Faraday and Luigi Galvani, or will you try instead to recruit them to your pantomime?"

"We have never had to persuade men of that sort to join us," someone told him. "They have always done their utmost to beat a path to our door, as soon as they suspected that we might exist."

"And those who have not succeeded have done their very best to imitate us," another supplied. "The Rosicrucians are only the sincerest of our flatterers."

"And now, Mr. Temple," the man with the authoritative voice said, "you know that we exist, even if you only suspect who and what we are. What is your answer to our question? Are you prepared to help us obtain the secret that we seek?"

"I'm not even prepared to consider the matter until the two children you have stolen have been returned to their homes," Temple retorted, immediately.

"Yes, of course," the other countered. "But you are not such a prisoner of obsession as to be unable to think of the day after tomorrow. You know exactly what I am offering in return for your loyalty. Are you determined to die, or are you prepared to seek a better redemption that faith has to offer? If the latter is the case, will you curry favor with your former enemy, in the presently-frail hope that he might bring you back from the dead as something better than an imbecile–or would you rather ally yourself with wiser men? Men, that is, who have means of preserving you much as you are while you wait for the most disciplined scientists in the world to perfect the process of resurrection, and will do their utmost to guarantee you an afterlife in which your faculties will not be diminished in the least. You and I both know that it is possible, do we not? And it is, as you have remarked, a matter of science, not of magic."

"I'm flattered by the invitation," Temple said. "Will I be a full member of the brotherhood, or merely an employee, like your methodical kidnappers?"

"We are not offering membership," the authoritative voice replied, frankly. "We very rarely issue invitations of that sort, and you have done nothing to deserve one. We are merely pointing out the logic of the situation–which is that your wisest course of action by far would be to commit yourself to our cause."

Gregory Temple nodded his head slowly, to imply that he could indeed see the logic of the situation. He wondered if John Devil would see it as clearly, if he were sitting here–and how John Devil might react to that logic, when the time came for him to do so. "First," he said aloud, "the children. When the children are both safe, there will be time to consider other matters. Until then–and afterwards too, if you have sold them for three satchels full of gold–you are merely common criminals, too despicable to warrant the consideration of an honest man. My answer is no."

He thought that he heard the slightest of sighs disturb the silence that followed but it might have been a draught of air from one of the corridors disturbed by some obstruction.

I'm a fool, he thought. *I should have lied, and played along–but at least I'm still an honest man.*

"English stubbornness," said a voice from the left, in an accent more heavily accented than most. "We've met *that* before. We still need the other–and we need him now."

There was a sound then–not of a sigh but of a muffled hiss of disapproval.

"Take him back to his cell and tell him what to do," instructed the commanding voice. "We proceed with the plan."

Chapter Six
Giuseppe Balsamo's Overtures

After eating a meagre meal, Gregory Temple began to write a letter that he had been asked to produce on his captors' behalf.

My dear Suzanne, it read, *I have seen both Armand and Friedrich, and can attest that they are both well and are being cared for with all possible diligence. I am convinced that their captors have no intention of harming them, provided that the remaining two thirds of the ransom are paid. Tonight, at midnight, the Comtesse de Belcamp must take a further 10,000 livres to the bridge by the mill, where the Comte de Belcamp once saved her life. She may take Pierre Louchet with her, but no one else. The second child will then be surrendered. I will write again to give instructions for the third exchange. I too am quite safe and well, and will return to you when this business has been completed.*

He signed it *Your loving father, Gregory Temple*, and gave it to the masked man who was waiting to read it. When it was given back to him, he sealed it in an envelope, which he addressed *To Madame Suzanne Thompson, Château de Belcamp*. Before handing it over to the man who was waiting for it, he said: "When you have taken the second child away, the third may be afraid. Might he be allowed to share a cell with me so that I can reassure him?"

"Perhaps," was the only reply he got.

He surrendered the envelope, and went to lie down on his bed while the bar was replaced on the door of his cell. He did not feel tired; indeed, he felt quite well. He had no idea how long he had been unconscious, or to what particular day the "tonight" written in his letter might refer, but even if he had slept for 24 hours, it seemed to him that his current feeling of well-being was unexpected. The meal he had been given had satisfied his hunger despite its simplicity—which supported the hypothesis that he had not, in fact, slept around the clock—but he had only been given water to drink, so he had not been dosed with any obvious medicine since waking up. Whatever the kidnappers had given him to make him fall unconscious in Little Switzerland had not done him any harm, and apparently quite the reverse. Was that, he wondered, supposed to be a subtle demonstration of the extent and efficacy of their esoteric knowledge?

He wondered whether the fact that he had been asked to instruct the Comtesse de Belcamp to make the second ransom delivery meant that her son would be the second to be surrendered. If the conspirators' chief objective was to lure Henri de Belcamp out of hiding, they must be hoping that it would bring him hurrying to the bridge by the mill. It seemed a risky strategy, though. If he had not reached Miremont yet, the second exchange would doubtless proceed as ostensibly planned. What then?

It occurred to Temple that the demand that Jeanne de Belcamp should make the second exchange might be a feint, and that the child she would obtain in return would be Friedrich Boehm. But that seemed an unnecessary complication. Perhaps the alchemists believed that the order in which the children were returned would make no difference to Henri's inclination to intervene. They might well expect–and rightly so, in Temple's view–that pride would compel him to make just as much effort on behalf of Sarah O'Brien's child as Jeanne's. Sarah had, after all, been his close companion–and presumably his mistress–for far longer than Jeanne Herbet.

On the other hand, Temple thought, the kidnappers might have some way of knowing that the first installment of the gold had been provided by Jeanne, and were anxious that Sarah might hold back her share if her son was released before Armand. Was that likely? Temple had only met Sarah O'Brien while she was playing other parts–Sarah O'Neil in London, then Lady Frances Elphinstone in Miremont–and he could not claim to have the measure of her, but if she and Jeanne really had fallen out, despite the fact that Sarah must have moved back to the new château following her husband's death in order to be near her, her response to an appeal for help might be difficult to predict.

Temple was conscious of the fact that he was concentrating very narrowly on the immediate matter in hand, and ought perhaps to be devoting more thought to the question of exactly who his captors were and what their grander plan might be. He was first and foremost a policeman, though. He was no longer attached to Scotland Yard, because the King and Lord Liverpool apparently thought that his talents as a detective were more useful in another context, but he was still, in his heart of hearts, a diehard opponent of *crime*. His vocation was to catch robbers and murderers, coiners and cut-throats, kidnappers and fraudsters– anyone, in fact, who threatened to disturb the peace of law-abiding citizens.

Many attempts had been made to bribe him, and he had rejected them all, because his was a calling that could not be corrupted without being utterly betrayed. He had been accused of breaking the law himself–and had done it, too, most of all when he cheated his way into Newgate Prison with the intention of liberating a wrongly-condemned man–but he had never betrayed his calling, always acting in favor of innocents and against malefactors. That was his duty and his sole purpose now, no matter what fantastic lures might be laid out for him.

For that reason, he maintained the concentration of his thoughts on his future course of action in respect of the captive children–or, in a matter of hours, the captured child. His only objective, for now, was to keep that child safe. If there was a possibility that he and the child might escape safely, then he must try to do so–but in order for that possibility to come about, he would need to find out a great deal more about where he was being held and exactly how it was guarded. Might his captors consent to their prisoners taking a little exercise in the open air? Probably not–but he would ask anyway. If no escape proved possible, then he must think instead in terms of protection and defense–but he no longer had his revolver, or his knife. Both had been taken from his person while he slept, along with his watch, his pocket-book and most of his other trivial possessions. He had no weapons but his hands and his wits

No matter how insistently he told himself that he was not impotent, while he was sound in brain and limb, his opportunities for action seemed direly limited.

After what seemed like two hours, he heard noises in the corridor. He went to the door of his cell, opened the hatch and tried to see what was happening, but the angle was too narrow. It was his ears that told him that one of the two boys was being taken from the cell next door. Their youthful voices, raised in distress, told him that it was indeed Armand, not Friedrich, who was being taken away to be sold. He called out to Friedrich in very poor German to tell the boy not to be afraid, and then renewed his pleas in French to be allowed to have the boy in his own cell, so that he might soothe the child's fears—but the only reply he got was: "Later, perhaps."

He inferred from this that his captors had something else in mind for the interim, and so it proved. After the lapse of a further half hour or so, his cell door was opened and an unmasked man came in. It was the man with whom he had conversed on the coach between Calais and Amiens. The door was closed and barred behind him by someone in the corridor.

"Have your 30 comrades delegated you to make a further appeal, Signor Balsamo?" Temple asked. "There is no point, you know, until all three children are safe at home."

"There will be no further appeals, Mr. Temple," the other said. "We are satisfied that if you know any more than you were prepared to tell us in the star chamber, you will not yield it voluntarily. Personally, I believe you, and I made no secret of my confidence."

"Have you come to gossip about the wonders of electricity and the meaning of progress, then? I thought we had exhausted those topics on the coach. Shall I continue to address you as Signor Balsamo, by the way, even though that is not your name?"

"It would be convenient," the pretended Italian told him. "Are you so certain that I am not who I claim to be?"

"Perfectly certain. I saw the logic of the situation when your comrade mentioned the Rosicrucians and other flattering imitators. It is a matter of cryptic coloration. In pretending to be members of your brotherhood, poseurs like Cagliostro and the Comte de Saint-Germain provide you with a series of perfect disguises. By offering yourselves as defunct poseurs, layering folly upon folly, you augment the impression that there is no reality behind the sham. What better disguise could there be for a true secret society than to masquerade as a false one? The devil's greatest asset, it is said, is the inability of people to believe in him."

"We are not the devil's men, Mr. Temple," the false Balsamo said. "You have encountered us in strange circumstances–but that too is a kind of imposture."

"I disagree," Temple said. "I, a policeman, have disguised myself on occasion as a criminal, in order to eavesdrop on other criminals–but I have never gone so far as to collaborate in their crimes. Had I done so, I would have ceased to be a policeman in disguise, and become a common criminal myself."

"I take your point. We have honest ways of making gold, of course, which were adequate to our limited needs for centuries–but times are moving much more swiftly nowadays, and our needs have increased. Our worst misfortunes are far behind us, but we have had our difficulties during the recent wars, just like everyone else. We have always been firm adherents of the principle that the end justifies the means–including means like hostage-taking, and others of which you would disapprove wholeheartedly. It was once a common form of bargaining between powerful men, and we are great adherents of tradition. Are you so sure of your own moral ground, when your own upholders of the law hang so many men, woman and children, and transport so many others to hell-holes in Australia, in futile support of your own less-than-ideal ends? Your friend Ned Knob would not agree with you, I think."

"He's not my friend."

"He's a better friend than you imagine, Mr. Temple. He has confirmed your testimony and proclaimed your innocence loudly."

"Is he here, then? How did you capture him?"

"As my friend told you last night, he went chasing wild geese–and they caught him. He seems a good deal more interested in our temptations than you did, Mr. Temple. He offered to work for us with great alacrity, and swore to be our loyal servant for as long as we might need him."

"Then you would be well advised to make full use of him," Temple said. "He's a man of many talents, despite his size. If anyone can discover where Mortdieu went, he's the one."

"I don't doubt it. He probably swore eternal allegiance to Mortdieu with the same alacrity that he swore it to us, not to mention Henri de Belcamp. Still, such a man might be useful to us–more useful, it appears at present, than a man like you."

"Agreed," Temple said. "And yet, here you are, talking to me like a man in need of friends. Would it be possible, do you think, for me to take young Friedrich outside for a breath of fresh air? It's not good for a child of his age to be locked away underground for days on end. The air down here is terribly stale."

"On the contrary," the false Balsamo replied, calmly. "The corridor is uncommonly well ventilated, for a convent whose bowels have been slotted into natural fissures in the rock. Monks have ever been an ingenious breed, you know."

"Apparently, some monks have been more ingenious that anyone knows," Temple retorted. "That's where your secret society must have begun, I suppose, in the days when monasteries were havens of peace in a turbulent world, and the sole custodians of learning. There's an unmistakable Catholicism about your procedures and philosophies–the whole idea of a covert elite deciding what the multitude might be allowed to know, and hence to do, is Romanist through and through."

"We have a few ostensible protestants in our ranks," the other told him. "We have attempted to transcend the squabbles of the Reformation as we transcended other schisms, with a measure of success. You are correct, of course, to judge that we have long been formulated as a monastic order, but we have never taken our orders from Rome–not, at least, from the papal throne. In better times we were sometimes able to put our own people *on* the papal throne, but that was never easy. The college of Cardinals was always a difficult institution to influence, let alone control. Fortunately, its habitual introspection makes it easy to avoid."

"And I suppose that you have sometimes been able to put your people on other thrones?"

"No, Mr. Temple–that is one aspect of the game that we have let well alone, although we have sometimes had occasion to ensure that secular thrones fell vacant. It is a fundamental aspect of our philosophy that the quarrels of petty barons and their armies are irrelevant to the true pattern of history, which is the growth of knowledge and its careful application to the cause of progress–in the meaning that *we* attach to the word."

"You spent a good deal of time criticizing my use of the term," Temple told him, "but I confess that I still do not know exactly what you mean by it. Somehow, having sat through your star chamber as well as your subtle interrogation on the coach, I cannot see you as Godwinian Utopians committed to the ideals of universal liberty, equality and fraternity."

"No, Mr. Temple, we are not Utopians. We are, I suppose, dedicated Malthusians–although we have less affection for the negative checks than you might have supposed, on seeing our costumes. We believe in liberty and fraternity for the few and discipline for the many, and in a strictly ordered social hierarchy."

"Did you tell Radical Ned Knob that before he swore eternal loyalty to your cause?"

"I was not present, but I dare say that my comrades mentioned immortality for the few and mortality for the many, and pointed out the logic that would lead any other situation to hellish chaos."

"I would have to give that matter a great deal of thought," Temple said. "Even Ned Knob, I think, might hesitate to jump to that conclusion too readily."

"I agree entirely that you should give the matter a great deal of thought, Mr. Temple–and I trust your logic to reach the right conclusion in the end. We really are men of science nowadays, you know, even though we retain certain attitudes and rituals that were more appropriate to the alchemists, astrologers and diviners we once were. There was a time our organization included the only true men of science in Europe–but that was before the invention of the printing press. We underestimated its danger–perhaps the worst of all our many miscalculations, the Great Catastrophe notwithstanding. Attempting to manage history is a direly difficult business, as you can imagine."

"If history was ever manageable," Temple retorted, "it is no longer. Any attempts you have made in recent times must have demonstrated the hopelessness of the task."

"A fair comment," the other admitted, equably. "Even if one sets aside such irrelevancies as wars, empires and nations, we have not done well. We kept the telescope, the microscope and the principles of optics secret for 300 years, but they escaped us in the end. Steam we thought unlikely to make a vast social impact, for want of fuel, but we failed to anticipate the extent of the coal measures waiting to be excavated. The real tragedy, though, has been our failure to usurp the secrets of electricity. That genie was out of the bottle before we even had a chance to attempt its containment. No matter how many Faradays we might be able to draw into the fold, there will be many more–and the reanimators are already proliferating in their wake. This is our final challenge, Mr. Temple–our last throw of the dice. You may be able to understand our desperation."

"May I?" Temple counted. "You're talking to me face-to-face now, but you're hardly less a phantom than your 30 comrades. I don't know who you are, and don't expect to find out. I can't see the least reason to think that the secret of resurrecting the dead would be any safer in your hands than anyone else's, or that you have any moral claim to it whatsoever."

"It would be safer in our hands–especially if it could remain our monopoly for a while–because we would not use it to make slaves or soldiers. It would be safer in our hands because we would use it to preserve intellect and creativity, not brute force and greed. It would be safer in our hands because we would be deaf to the wailing of the multitude who want their *loved ones* restored but cannot see beyond the horizons of their own petty affections and lusts. It would be safer in our hands, Mr. Temple, because we are not radicals but conservationists, enthusiastic to maintain the order of the world irrespective of the ambitions and bloodthirst of empire-builders. Yes, we are a self-selected and self-appointed elite who believe that we have the right to determine the fates of our fellow men, irrespective of what they may think or believe–and we are proud of that fact, just as we are proud of the fact that our order began within the confines of monachism, not on a battlefield. Whether you will support our cause or not is up to you, Mr. Temple–but if you set yourself against us, you will be taking the side of violent and brutal men, of tyrants and terrorists, of the avaricious and the envious. You cannot begin to think about that, of course, until young Friedrich is safe once again in the bosom of the *vehmgerichte*, who are searching for him as we speak and will doubtless storm the convent without a second thought, with

259

guns blazing and swords red-tipped, if they contrive to locate us and think us too weak to resist. But when you *can* think of it, Mr. Temple, think about the kind of world that is nowadays in the making, and whether you believe the message that General Mortdieu asked Ned Knob to deliver on his behalf, forswearing any desire to make war upon the living."

Temple no longer had any retorts ready for delivery, and fell silent for a while. Eventually, he said: "Who are you, really?"

"I cannot tell you any more than I have already told you," the false Balsamo replied. "Should we ever meet again, in the outer world, you will recognize me, and will doubtless discover the name by which I am more generally known–but even then, Mr. Temple, you will know no more about who I *really* am than you know at this moment. I will have Friedrich Boehm brought into your cell, so that he might feel a little safer–but his best guarantee of safety is not your presence but his mother's temperance, Suzanne Thompson did no harm by appealing to you for help, but Sarah Boehm was unwise in the extreme to turn to her husband's former comrades for assistance. Whether they achieve anything or not, she is theirs now, and always will be–they will have her child far more securely and permanently in their grip than he is now in ours, and they will not make him the kind of man that you or I could admire."

"What do you want from me, Signor Balsamo?" Temple demanded.

"Nothing, at present," Balsamo replied, "since you have made it abundantly clear that you are unwilling to give anything. You know as well as I, though, that this will not be over when the last child is exchanged, no matter what we obtain in return. The *Empire of the Necromancers* is only just begun, and there will be a titanic struggle to determine the form of its hegemony. You are caught up in that struggle whether you like it or not, and you will have to take sides in situations far more complex than this one. You have met Mortdieu and you know Henri de Belcamp of old. It is for you to decide which of the players so far engaged offers the least of several evils. Personally, I still think that you are a natural ally rather than our enemy–but only you can decide. That is what I came to say to you. Goodbye, Mr. Temple–I am leaving the convent now, and it may be some time before we meet again."

After finishing this farewell speech, the false Balsamo rapped on the door, to signal the masked man outside to remove the bar. Then he went to Friedrich Boehm's cell, and brought the boy to Temple's, as he had promised.

It was not until the bar had fallen back into place, and the corridor was silent again, that Temple realized that he had not the slightest idea how to hold a conversation with a three-year-old boy–especially one whose first language was German.

"You must not be afraid," he hazarded, in limping German. "You must be strong."

The child drew himself up to his full height–which was unimpressive, even for a child of his age–and said: "I am a Boehm. I am not afraid."

Temple could imagine the other Friedrich–the recently-dead father–saying exactly the same thing, in exactly the same fashion, in frank defiance of his own lack of height and health.

"You are a Boehm," Temple agreed. "You and I shall befriend and protect one another, as good men should."

The little boy nodded his head, and Temple turned away from him, in order not to see his tears.

Chapter Seven
The Vehmgerichte*'s Rescue*

When Friedrich Boehm had gone to sleep, lying on the bed and wrapped in a blanket, Gregory Temple sat down on the floor of the cell with his back against the wall, facing the door. He became gradually drowsy, but did not go to sleep. He drew up his knees and folded his arms upon them in order to let his head slump forward, but he lifted his head again whenever his ears caught muffled sounds from the side or above–which they often did, as the convent's inhabitants went about their mysterious business.

Because his watch had been removed and he had been unable to observe the alternation of day and night Temple had no reliable means of knowing what time it was, but suspected that it must be the early hours of the morning when he heard the bar being removed from the outside of the door, in what seemed to him to be a stealthy fashion. The peephole had not been opened.

Temple came to his feet, ready to act. He was poised for action by the time the door swung inwards to reveal a man in the customary black habit–with the hood up–and death's-head mask. The only unusual thing about him was that he was holding a sabre in his right hand. Temple could not possibly recognize the man–but he started as he recognized the weapon as a German duelling-blade. The newcomer raised the upraised forefinger of his left hand to his lips; Temple nodded his head to signify that he understood.

The newcomer looked down at the dark-haired boy on the bed, and nodded his head slightly in apparent satisfaction. Then he knelt down, and pushed the mask on to the top of his head before putting out a gnarled hand to wake the child. Temple did not recognize the man, but he was unsurprised to see duelling-scars on his cheek and forehead.

When the boy opened his eyes, the knight of the *vehm* whispered to him in German, so rapidly that Temple could not catch the full significance of what was said. It included a reassurance, and an instruction to be very quiet.

The child seemed reassured to hear his native tongue. Although there must have been some among his captors who spoke it fluently, this was obviously a different sort of man, more closely akin to the servants who had looked after him in his infancy.

When the child had signified his consent, the rescuer brought him to his feet and wrapped the blanket more tightly around him. Then he signaled to Temple, indicating that he must pick the boy up. Temple nodded to signify that he understood, and assented to the request. Friedrich Boehm made no objection to being picked up, and seemed perfectly ready to play the game required of him.

The German readjusted his disguise. He had not brought a light of his own, but he picked up the candle from the night-stand to light his way back along the corridor. He moved through the bowels of the convent confidently, apparently having no doubt as to the route he must take. The way was tortuous, involving three flights of stone stairs and numerous turnings, but in the end they came to a small door that let them out into a small chapel. From there, they made their way into the nave of a larger church. There were other men waiting in the shadows of the church, all of them wearing death's-head masks–but they were obviously allied with Temple's companion, for they returned his silent salute–which must have included a private signal of some sort–and moved off into the chapel from which he had come. They were not dressed in the same fashion as Temple's earlier interrogators–they wore ordinary traveling-cloaks over secular costumes–but Temple supposed that the convent's residents must dress is a similar fashion when they went abroad, and that the death's-heads would protect them from instant recognition as invaders,

The rescuer and his two charges made their exit from the church through the vestry, and continued to move very carefully until they were clear of its surrounding buildings. The German blew out the candle then, although the moonlight and starlight were very hazy and it was difficult to see their way in the neat-total darkness. They went forward carefully, eventually reaching a clump of trees 200 paces further on, beyond a fallow meadow. There were at least a dozen horses tethered in the gloom within the copse. So far as Temple could tell, there was only one man guarding the horses, who uttered a whispered challenge in German, and was immediately satisfied by the password their guide returned.

"Is that Friedrich?" the sentry asked, suggesting to Temple that the agents of the *vehmergichte* had not been certain until now which child had been taken to the second exchange.

"It's Count Boehm, alive and well," the other replied, again pushing his mask up to the top of his head so that he might see a little better. Temple's German was not good enough to follow exactly what the man went on to say, but it was something along the lines of: "Herr Temple and I will take him to the meeting-point and guard him until dawn. We'll gather then to take the Pontoise Road as a company, whether we have the gold or not. Is that understood?"

The sentry nodded.

"Are you able to ride with the boy?" the German asked Temple, in slurred English.

"I can hold him securely enough," Temple replied, in the same language, "and keep him warm–but we'd best proceed slowly."

The other nodded, and they did indeed proceed very slowly across open country, for two miles or more, until they reached a wall of thorn-bushes. Their rescuer led Temple and Friedrich Boehm into a clearing within the bushes, to which the crag formed a rear wall, and where there was a small hut. There was smoke belching from the chimney, promising a good fire within.

"You will be safe here," the German said, still speaking English. "I will stand guard outside."

"You'd be warmer inside," Temple said–but a knight of the *vehm* was too proud to be intimidated by mere autumnal cold.

Temple carried the boy indoors. There was a candle already lit within, and a man sitting on a stool beside the hearth.

"I'm delighted to see you, Mr. Temple," John Devil said, in English. "I wanted to rescue you myself, of course, to seal our new alliance, but our friends would not hear of it. It's not so much that they don't trust me, but they have their own priorities. They would never have found you without my help, mind–I knew the country well enough to set them on the trail, although not as well as I imagined. Who would have imagined that it might be possible, in 1821, to find not one but two priories of the *Civitas Solis* so close to Pontoise? Is that my son you're carrying?"

"Temple answered the last question first. "It's Friedrich Boehm," he said. "Armand was taken to Miremont some hours ago. The second exchange should be complete by now, and your son should be safe at home."

John Devil frowned, perhaps in disappointment that he was not to meet his son, and perhaps partly in puzzlement, having expected a different order of exchange.

"I suppose that I would have been less surprised had you appeared in my cell yourself than I am to find you sitting out the action here," Temple said, setting his burden down with great care. "Would it not be better if our entire company were to set off immediately, without waiting for dawn?"

"It might," John Devil agreed, "but it's difficult and exceedingly uncomfortable traveling by night in weather like this, and it's less than an hour till dawn. I'm not in a position to give orders–my position is slightly delicate, as you'll readily understand–and my friends were determined to search for the gold while the convent was so lightly defended, even though that very fact suggested that it had been removed in the course of the general exodus."

"I'm afraid that I don't understand your position at all," Temple told him, as he persuaded Friedrich to lie down on the hearth, still wrapped in the blanket. "I have no idea what is going on. Your German is presumably far better than mine–can you explain to Friedrich that he is safe?"

John Devil knelt down to talk to the boy, and did so in such a soothing fashion that the child seemed completely reassured. When he stood up again, he turned to face Temple and said: "I'm sorry that I didn't join you in Dover as we arranged, Mr. Temple, but an opportunity turned up that seemed too good to miss. It led me into unexpected trouble, but I've always had a knack of turning trouble to my advantage. The situation remains delicate, as I say, but it seems that all three children are safe now–which was our primary objective. I assume that Jeanne will be able to produce the required ransom?"

"I believe so," Temple confirmed.

John Devil nodded, and sat down on his stool again, pointing Temple towards an identical one. "I'll tell you my story, in brief," the blond man said. "When Ned Knob brought me Suzanne's letter, I was in company with a few old friends–Tom Brown's friends, I fear–who immediately volunteered to help. I sent one to the river shore to inquire as to the disposition and sailing plans of any vessels that might be useful, and another to procure horses for a ride to Dover. When I returned, I discovered that there was a vessel moored not far from Southwark Bridge which intended to sail for Antwerp via Ostend before dawn. She had no engine, but the weather reports promised a favorable tide and a brisk northerly wind. It seemed likely to be the safer course, given the difficulties that might arise in riding to Dover on winter ground, so I hastened to beg a passage, along with two of my friends.

"The tide and the wind were exactly as anticipated, and the captain of the vessel assured me that I would have no trouble making my way from Ostend to Calais by sea or land–or, if it seemed preferable, going directly from there to Paris. Because my friends were so obviously English, I thought it best not to travel as Henri Moreau, and it happened that I had papers on me that I had used several years before, when I traveled regularly via Ostend and Antwerp on my way to and from the university where I studied in Germany. They were in the name of George Palmer–which is, of course, familiar to you, although I recklessly assumed that everyone else would have forgotten it. Not so–there were Germans in the crew who had exotic connections and long memories. George Palmer, it seems, was wanted for questioning in Germany–not by the authorities, but by one of the relics of the old *vehms*, which refused to die when Napoleon's minion was supposed to have killed them off."

"So the murder of Maurice O'Brien has not been entirely forgotten," Temple observed.

"That was hardly a crime, in the reckoning of the *vehms*," John Devil told him. "No matter how much favor he had accumulated, O'Brien had been a mercenary officer in Napoleon's army, and was not considered a man of honor. What had not been forgotten was the abduction of his daughter, Sarah O'Brien, who was a ward of the Emperor Francis I, and thus had a significantly different status. In itself, that might not have been afforded any great importance, but the efforts made by Count Boehm to trace her–in advance of his fateful meeting with you in London–had not only placed the members of his own society on the alert but had sent signals to every port from Le Havre to Copenhagen. The police and customs knew nothing of it, but George Palmer has been a hunted man since 1814. The fact that George Palmer had ceased to exist in 1813 confounded the search–but the years that had elapsed before his abrupt resurrection was not time enough for the name to be forgotten, and Count Boehm had never thought to call it off when he found the object of his desire.

"At any rate, I was ambushed and seized before the ship put in at Ostend, and compelled to complete the journey to Antwerp as a prisoner. My friends could do nothing, and were left behind. From Antwerp, I was taken overland to Brussels, and then to Liège–with all due haste, thank God. Liège is not a city where a *vehm* could normally be convened, but the word had already gone out from Central Westphalia bidding members of the society from Maastricht, Aachen and Bonn to make their way there with all possible speed for a special convention. That was no coincidence, of course–the reason for the command was a message received from the widowed Sarah Boehm, appealing for help in the recovery of her kidnapped son.

"The convoluted politics of the *vehmgerichte* are of little relevance to outsiders, but you will understand that a certain tension existed between the *vehm*– which had seen two of its strongest and bravest members assassinated in the persons of Friedrich Boehm's older brothers–and the Irish widow of the enfeebled heir to their fortune. There was no evident enmity, but relations had been a trifle cold. Her appeal for help was, in its way, a small godsend, promising that the relationship would be much warmer in future–and, more importantly, ensuring that young Friedrich would be committed to the society from his earliest youth, to be educated in its traditions and ambitions.

"As you will imagine, the assembly was not grateful to be interrupted by the delivery of a prisoner it had not time to try, but when I explained to them that I was not George Palmer at present, but the similarly dead Comte Henri de Belcamp, and thus intimately familiar with Miremont and its surroundings–I might have stretched the truth slightly in that regard–and also the father of one of the other kidnapped children, their attitude changed dramatically. I was immediately recruited to their cause.

"We had already wasted too much time to be able to reach Miremont ahead of you, so we did not arrive in time to discover what was happening on Little Switzerland, but we did contrive to pick up the trail of Ned Knob, who was attempting to follow the tracks of the man who had given the message to that poltroon Besnard. Ned had picked up the trail–and was in too much of a hurry to cover up his own. We were able to track him, and were close behind him when he walked into the trap that had been set for him. We followed his captors easily enough to an ancient convent in the middle of nowhere. At first, I thought it a mere shell serving as a temporary refuge for common bandits, but as we watched it I guessed–much to my astonishment–that we might actually be dealing with something far more exotic. Although there were no documents of any kind, I was amazed to discover evidence once we got inside that we really were dealing with an echo of the *Civitas Solis*."

"Of which I have never heard," Temple put in.

"That's not surprising, even for a secret policeman–Scotland Yard's records can hardly go back *that* far. The society has rarely had much success in its dealings in England since it recruited Roger Bacon, and the dissolution of the monasteries by Henry VIII was greatly to its disadvantage. Rumor has it that it was prevented from recruiting Leonard Digges thereafter, despite Mary's accession to the throne, and failed to recruit his colleague John Dee–although it punished him for it, and would not forgive him when he begged for reconsideration during his journey to the heart of the Empire. How they would have loved to snare Isaac Newton! I dare say they feel the same now about Faraday–but that's by the by. The significant point is that, although they used to consider themselves above the Papal Throne, they always operated more far comfortably in Catholic countries than Protestant ones–including France, despite what they call the Great Catastrophe."

"The man who called himself Giuseppe Balsamo mentioned that," Temple remembered.

"Balsamo? You meant Count Cagliostro?"

"No–that was merely the name he gave me. They seem to imagine themselves to be real alchemists, cleverly hiding themselves by masquerading as charlatans–but they might well be charlatans themselves."

"They might–but the alternative is the more exciting prospect, wouldn't you agree? Everything I knew about them until today is ancient hearsay, implying that they no longer exist–but if they *are* still active, even as bandits, that would be a wonder of sorts."

"*Civitas Solis* means *city of the sun*," Temple said. "Was that really the name of their society?"

"Societies of that sort always have several names," John Devil replied. "But yes–that is the one by which it is most commonly known to those who have heard of it. It was formed at much the same time as Augustine published his *Civitas Dei*, which argued that Christendom need not regret the fall of Rome too much, because the city of God was an idea contained in the hearts of men, not a mere place. The *Civitas Solis* aspired to be a city in the same sense: a city of enlightenment, located in the hearts and minds of scholar monks."

"And the Great Catastrophe?" Temple queried.

"Pride goeth before destruction, the Bible warns," John Devil observed. "The *Civitas* should have heeded that warning, no matter how much of the scriptures it had set aside. When the organization was at the very height of its power and wealth, its militant and commercial arm–almost the whole of its corporate body, in fact–was rudely and brutally excised by Philippe le Bel of France, who was in dire need of its money."

"*The Knights Templar?*" Temple said, incredulously. "You're saying that these clowns in death's-head masks are the relic of the Templars."

"No, I'm telling you that the Templars were an extension of the *Civitas Solis*, whose humbled brain survived the murder of its extended body for a while–longer than a while, it seems. They struggled afterwards, of course–such stored wealth as they contrived to save was gradually expended in order to secure the remnants of the order. They must have sunk to a very low level–almost as low, perhaps, as the relics of the *vehms*–but if they still have secrets to keep... did they interrogate you?"

"Yes," Temple replied, "but not brutally."

"But they believed you when you explained that you knew less that they had hoped?"

"Yes," Temple repeated. "They seemed particularly bitter about my inability to tell them where they might find you."

"Did they, indeed? Well, to resume my story, we thought at first that the children must be held in the convent to which they took Ned Knob. While my tempestuous allies were making plans to attack it, though, we saw a substantial number of men ride out, mostly leaving in ones and twos at intervals of several minutes. I had not confided my suspicions regarding the *Civitas Solis* to my companions, but they deduced immediately that the monks must be heading for a conventicle at some other abbey.

"When the exodus was complete it was a much simpler business to invade the building and release Ned Knob. There was little resistance, and no one was badly hurt. As I told you, I took the opportunity to look for evidence as to the true nature of the convent's tenants, and found enough to interest me. When Ned had told us what he could, we sent him back to Miremont to tell Sarah that we would do what we could to rescue the remaining children. He wanted to go with us, but my new friends were suspicious enough of me and did not want a second outsider in their midst.

"The convent where you were held seemed a much tougher nut to crack, and we had not even begun to conceive a sensible plan of campaign when a company rode out–keeping tightly together, this time–with a child in their midst. The boy was wrapped up too well to be identifiable, but what Ned had told me allowed me to deduce that the three children must now be in three different places–one in Miremont, one on the road to Miremont and one still in the convent.

"Our company was not large enough to split into two, and it seemed best to let the second exchange take place while we secured the child who remained in the convent, if that were possible. Again, the task became much easier in short order as the pattern of the first exodus was reversed; monks again began to leave in ones and twos, presumably dispersing before returning to the base we had already sacked.

"My inclination was to forsake the ransom payments, but my companions were differently minded. They wanted to seize the one already paid, and then make plans to ambush the men returning with the second. I suppose that I shall be given no alternative but to join them in the second project–but they will take due care to make sure that you and young Friedrich are not exposed to any risk. They will return you to Miremont with an escort of two or three riders. If I can, I shall rejoin you there in a matter of hours, and face the various accusations and resentments that are my just desserts. You have, I suppose, informed my widow that my death was more apparent than physical?"

"I could not lie to her, even by omission," Temple said.

"Of course not. I did not ask you to do so. You have always been an honest man."

"Unlike you, Mr. Brown," Temple pointed out.

"Unlike Tom Brown, and unlike Henri de Belcamp," John Devil agreed, readily enough. "But they are dead and gone now–one hanged, one shot. I have made a fresh start, not for the first time. I suppose that I should not have brought George Palmer back to life, even as a temporary flag of convenience–but it worked out for the best, I think... and it was, after all, Tom Brown, not George Palmer, who murdered Maurice O'Brien and Constance Bartolozzi."

"I can see why the members of the *Civitas Solis* are so interested in you," Temple observed. "That one mere body can contain so many different persons, alive and dead, is a remarkable natural phenomenon."

"So it is," John Devil, agreed. "I should not have been tempted to wear a Quaker hat in London, either–but the weather was so cold and the hat so warm! I wish I had it now. Does it seem to you to be getting darker outside rather than light?"

The hut's only window was shuttered, but the shutters were as ill-fitting as the door, and the texture of the darkness was evident through the cracks."

"The Moon has set and the mist is getting thicker," Temple judged. "The starlight is so feeble now that one would need to be a cat to make much of it. I think there may be hint of twilight in the east, though–dawn surely can't be more than a few minutes away."

"Let's hope that it illuminates more than freezing fog," John Devil said. "I suppose our alliance is almost at an end. That's a pity, in a way."

"Is it?" Temple queried, archly. Then, suddenly recalling the portrait hanging in the drawing-room at the Chateau de Belcamp, he said: "How did you know, in Newgate, about the locket I wore around my neck? Did Suzanne tell you?"

John Devil was sitting in such a fashion as to keep his facial expression shadowed from the candlelight, but the voice that answered seemed surprised. "Is that what you thought?" the bandit asked. "If I were you, I'd have had more faith in the loyalty of a daughter such as her, even though I had succeeded in blackmailing her for lesser favors. No, I saw it when I was James Davy, and took a closer look when I once found you asleep, after an exceedingly hard night's work. I was struck by the lady's resemblance to my mother, and the co-incidence of the initials. Indeed, I half-convinced myself that the lady must actually have been my mother, and took such great amusement in the thought that she might once have seduced you, while you were a married man... but I never had the chance to ask her, and I doubt that it was possible. It was a fine story, though, was it not? My hidden ace... almost, but not quite, good enough to complete the slam. I knew when I left you, though, that you wouldn't die, and wouldn't be driven permanently mad. It's strange, I know, but I couldn't entirely regret it. I had always admired you, Mr. Temple–I wanted to believe that you could endure the worst that John Devil could do to you, and survive to fight another day, even against me. Is that odd, do you think?"

"Insane," Temple judged.

"Perhaps, Mr. Temple, ours is a *folie à deux*," John Devil said. "We bring out the worst in one another... or the most bizarre, at least. You were wrong to think that Suzanne might be to blame, though, and I hope you'll beg her pardon for entertaining the suspicion."

"If it's James Davy I must blame," Temple said, "then it's James Davy I shall hunt down. Or is he dead too?"

"As a doornail, I fear. A pity, in a way–he'd have been well-placed to intercept the news when Lord Liverpool's agents figure out where Mortdieu took the *Outremort*. A ship and company of that sort can't escape the eagle eyes of the ruler of the seven seas for long, can she?"

"You'll never bring your reanimated Napoleon to heel," Temple opined. "Nor would you ever have been able to use him as you hoped had you actually succeeded in freeing him from St. Helena before he died."

"Perhaps not," John Devil agreed. "But he has grey men with him who might have far more in common with me than with him, if they only had a choice of tutors. Sawney Ross and poor re-embodied John are not his kind at all–nor is Germain Patou, in spite of his desertion at Greenhithe."

"What do you mean, exactly, by *re-embodied* John?" Temple wanted to know.

"Exactly what I say," was John Devil's infuriating reply. "As the *Civitas Solis* must have discovered, life can be hard for a sound brain in an irreparably damaged body–but as my Swiss predecessor found out, the vital principle contained in electricity can do more than renew life in pre-existent corpses. I was only at the beginning of my studies, you know–there was so much more to discover, so much more too attempt. Germain is brilliant, but he lacks my imagination. He and Mortdieu do not realize how much they need me...

"You were right about that hint of twilight, I think–but the Sun isn't making much impact on the mist as yet, and I don't hear any riders approaching, singing German drinking-songs as they come–as they would be, if they'd won a victory with their swords and seized a fortune in gold."

"It wasn't such a vast fortune," Temple said, almost absent-mindedly, as his eyes followed John Devil's to the cracks in the shutters. It was definitely brighter now, but there seemed to be a wall of mist surrounding the hut, which would reduce visibility to a matter of a few yards even though the Sun had unmistakably risen.

John Devil did not reply to Temple's remark. Instead, he went to the door and opened it. He looked out, and cursed. He called out in German, but received no reply. He drew his rapier.

"I'm sorry, Mr. Temple," John Devil said, softly. "It seems that the sequence of traps had one more layer than I anticipated."

Temple cursed himself for not having taken time to think about that possibility, even though he knew that it was Comte Henri de Belcamp, and not the not-so-vast ransom, who had been the true objective of the tangled plot.

First, Temple moved instinctively to stand astride the sleeping boy. Then unable to tolerate the thought of not being able to see what was happening, he picked him up and went to the door,

Black figures were appearing in the mist, on every side of the hut but the one backed by the wall of rock. It was not obvious, at first, that their hoods were the hoods of monastic habits rather than traveling cloaks, but their faces stood out more clearly in the grey mist than anything else: the faces of leering, fleshless skulls. There were at least eight of them, all on foot and all armed–some with swords, and some with pistols. The horse on which Temple had arrived was still tethered to a tree nearby, but there was no sign of the German sentry.

"They read the *vehm* more accurately than I did," John Devil murmured, mournfully. "Whether the brave knights were taken prisoner or whether they've simply sold us out, the result's the same–but we're not taken yet."

Chapter Eight
Friedrich Boehm's Return

"Put down your sword, Monsieur de Belcamp," a soft voice said, in French. "We mean you no harm." As in the council meeting, it was difficult to determined which of the masked men had spoken.

"Why, there do not seem to be more than a dozen of you," John Devil retorted, lightly. "Cyrano de Bergerac put a hundred to flight, so legend has it–and they were authentic bravos, while you are mere scholars in fancy dress. You might shoot me, of course–but what use would I be to you dead or mortally wounded? I, on the other hand, do not care in the least how many of you I hurt." While he spoke he placed himself *en garde*, taking up a protective position in front of Gregory Temple, which the detective did not like at all.

"Don't be a fool, man," he murmured. "Drop your weapon."

"I'm delighted that it will distress you to see me killed, Mr. Temple," John Devil said, in a voice far louder than a murmur, which must have been audible to everyone present. "Please don't worry too much about the fate of my soul,"

"There is no need for anyone to be hurt, Monsieur de Belcamp," said the soft voice. "None of your German friends has been killed, nor any of our people. We have no wish to harm you, and you have no reason to wish harm to us. Would it not be best to bring this matter to a peaceful conclusion?"

Temple was strongly reminded of the awkward situation that had developed aboard the *Outremort*, when little Ned Knob had made John Devil and Mortdieu see sense–but Ned Knob was not here now.

"That's not my way," John Devil said. "I was born reckless–sired by Satan, I wrote in my autobiography, although I'll allow that there was a certain satirical self-aggrandisement in that. I'll make you a bargain, though, if you wish it–I've always had a fondness for diabolical pacts."

"You're in no position to make terms, Monsieur," the voice told him.

"Am I not? Damn me, I'll make them anyway. Let Gregory Temple mount up and take the child safely back to his mother, and I'll not only drop my sword but swear to tell you everything I know about the means to reverse death. You'll get no more ransom money–but my friend was telling me just a moment ago that the ransom wasn't such a vast fortune anyway, so I deduce that you're at least as interested in me as you are in the gold. If I fight, you know, I'll be a very difficult opponent to put down, given that there are far less than a hundred of you. Which of you will take the lead, by the way?"

Temple knew that the other was playing a game, and putting on a show–but the men in masks did not seem so sure.

"Temple can go," the voice of the death's-head conceded, as if it were a matter of no importance whatsoever. "He may take the child. Now, please drop your sword."

"Wake the boy and mount up, Mr. Temple," John Devil said. "If you travel a few points north of east, orientating yourself by the dawn, you'll come to the Pontoise road eventually. Turn left. From Pontoise, the way to Miremont is signposted, if you don't know it. Go now, before I'm tempted to fight them anyway."

Temple knew that for an empty boast, but he thought that he understood why John Devil was putting on his show of reluctance and recklessness. Meekly, he did as he was told. "This does not make us better friends, Monsieur de Belcamp," he said, as he set the dazed child carefully in position before climbing into the saddle, bidding him to be silent with a warning hiss.

"Of course not," John Devil replied. "But you won't find it nearly so easy to hunt me down once I'm wearing a death's-head mask and have a thousand convents scattered half across the world in which to hide. Don't worry about who is trapping whom, Mr. Temple–just get Sarah's boy safely home to her, and tell her to be careful of the *vehmgerichte*, which is yet another company of fools uneasily ignorant of the redundancy of their cause."

Temple did not reply to that, but he moved his horse towards the gap between two thorn bushes that marked the exit from the clearing. The two masked men blocking the path moved aside to let him through, and no one else tried to stop him once he was on the open heath again.

He found the Pontoise Road easily enough, and had no difficulty then finding the route back to Miremont. No one came after him, and he soon allowed the horse to relax into a safe and steady pace.

"Nearly home," he said to his tiny companion, in English.

"*Danke*," the boy replied, as if to chide him for his lapse.

The mist lingered long into the morning, but the cloak in which Friedrich was swaddled kept the cold at bay. The boy seemed uncommonly patient and quiet; whether that was because he had been brought up in a disciplined fashion, or because he was in shock after all that had happened to him, or whether he simply had no confidence in his protector's German, Temple could not tell.

By the time they reached the gate of the château, Temple knew that the effects of the drug that had been used to render him unconscious had completely worn off. His limbs and face were numb with cold, and his aggravating exhaustion had returned in full force. He rang the bell, and waited for help to come.

At least a dozen people came rushing out. As soon as Pierre Louchet had opened the gate, Sarah Boehm rushed forward to collect her son. She showered Temple with effusive thanks as he got down from the horse, but he shrugged them off, telling her that the friends she had summoned from Germany had actually contrived the rescue, and advising her to take the boy home and get him warm without delay. Her carriage was reharnessed in a matter of minutes, and she set off in company with Robert Surrisy and her servants before Temple had had time to go inside the château, flanked by Suzanne and Richard Thompson.

"I'm all right," he assured them, "and I don't deserve any congratulations. I didn't free the boy; I merely brought him home."

He was ushered into one of the smaller reception-rooms, where a fire was blazing and an assortment of chairs had been arranged about the hearth. This must have been the room in which they had all been waiting, for there were more seats than people now. Ned Knob—who seemed to be avoiding Temple's eye—took it upon himself to effect the necessary rearrangement.

"Thank you, Mr. Temple," said Jeanne de Belcamp, when he had slumped into an armchair as close to the burning logs as he could, "for whatever part you played. My son was returned at midnight last night, exactly as specified in your letter."

"I doubt that you will see your money again, milady," he replied. "I don't know what happened when Sarah's pocket army of obsolete knights went in search of the first consignment of gold, but the kidnappers were well-prepared. Reinforcements must have arrived in force as soon as they discovered what had happened at the second convent–the one where Master Knob was being held, after walking into their trap. Either the knights were trapped and disarmed, or they made a bargain to sell us out. Fortunately, the kidnappers were more interested in securing Henri de Belcamp's peaceful co-operation than holding on to Friedrich–when he threatened them, they let us go."

"I was a fool to be taken so easily," Ned Knob put in. "But you must admit, Mr. Temple, that neither of us suspected the sheer numbers we were up against. I was thinking in terms of eight or ten adversaries skulking in a cottage or a barn, not a hundred false monks with more than one priory at their disposal." He was still not meeting Temple's eye, doubtless expecting a stinging rebuke for having passed Suzanne's letter to John Devil rather than delivering it himself.

All Temple said was: "They weren't false monks–not, at least, in the sense that they were merely pretending to be monks. If they and Monsieur de Belcamp are to be believed, their organization might date back further than the days of St Benedict and the cenobites of the Thebaid. There might well be documents stored in Whitehall that refer to them, but they're probably rotting in a vault with other produce of Tudor and Jacobean spies. They obviously don't consider themselves a spent force, though, in spite of their intense interest in resurrection."

"You have seen Monsieur de Belcamp?" Jeanne de Belcamp asked, keeping her voice quite level. It was a simple prompt; she knew that he had

"I parted from him a little while ago, milady," Temple told her. "He traded his freedom for Friedrich Boehm's–or, at least, made a great pantomime of doing so. My guess is that he was delighted to discover who the convent's proprietors were, and was very enthusiastic to join them. I dare say that he will do his utmost to use his supposed captors for his own ends, just as he tried to use the Brotherhood of the Deliverance. At this very moment, if I read him right, he thinks himself their potential master, and is planning how to deploy their resources in his own cause. He does not change.

"In all fairness, though, it might well have been your husband's ability to manage the *vehmgerichte* that got Friedrich safely out. I don't believe that the kidnappers ever intended to harm the boy, and they will presumably be well satisfied with the trade they made, but things could have gone badly awry had the agents of the *vehm* taken matters into their own reckless hands. If word of this gets around, milady–as it surely will, thanks to the involvement of the *vehm*'s self-styled knights–you will have to pay more attention to your son's protection. You need better fences and a larger staff. Pierre Louchet is a good and loyal man, but he cannot defend a château."

"Did Henri see his son?" was all the Comtesse said by way of reply. "Armand has no memory of seeing him, but..."

"No, milady," Temple said. "He could not get close to him. I do not think he will try again, at least for a while. I do not pretend to understand why he has not contacted you during these last three years, when there were abundant opportunities, but now that the boy is safe, I suspect that he will continue to consider you a widow—and himself, I suppose, a ghost."

There were no tears in Jeanne de Belcamp's eyes, although Suzanne's were moist.

"I know that you hate him, sir," Richard Thompson said, "but he is not entirely a bad man."

"He put the noose around your neck from which he eventually condescended to save you," Temple said, harshly. "With more than a little help from Ned Knob. You owe him nothing, Richard."

"But I owe him everything," the Comtesse de Belcamp said. "He really did save my life, and he really did love me, with all his heart. He still does—and that, however perverse it may seem, is why he believes that he must remain dead."

Suzanne got up from the settee where she was sitting with Richard. "I must go to my son," she said. "I'm sorry—I know that it's absurd, but I am too anxious when he is out of my sight even for a few minutes. Will you come and see us, father, before you go?"

"Go?" Richard echoed. "You're surely not intending to go, sir? Not today."

"You are very welcome to stay for as long as you want, Mr. Temple," the Comtesse said—although Temple could see that she understood well enough why he would not linger long.

Temple did not answer Richard, who only hesitated momentarily before following his wife.

"Will you leave us alone for a few moments, Ned?" Jeanne de Belcamp asked. Ned hopped down from his chair, bowed and left the room.

"Is he well?" the Comtesse asked, when the door had closed.

"Yes, milady," Temple said. "I never saw a dead man looking so well, and there was a real fire in his eye at the end. He's still very young, and his dreams have not abated in the least. If he no longer plans to conquer India, it's because he cannot think of anything less, now, than the conquest of death itself. He pretended to be somewhat dismissive of the society into whose custody he has delivered himself, but he is highly delighted with the notion of resuming his work with their collaboration. They will be a hundred times more useful to him than Germain Patou—and I suspect that he is more than capable of taking control of the organization that considers him its prisoner and its instrument."

"He will not be coming home for quite some time, then."

"He has no home, milady. He came here once because he wanted to make use of his father. He was astonished to find you here—and was thrown completely off balance by the discovery, as headstrong and purposive men often are by the unexpected. He might as easily have killed you as fall in love with you, but he's a man of very powerful passions, however perverse they may be."

"And now that your alliance is over, you'll resume the business of hunting him down."

274

"Until five days ago," Temple said, grimly, "I had had no business with him for three long years. I have a job to do, and a duty to perform, which have nothing to do with him–or had not. It will be very difficult indeed to persuade my blinkered superiors that the grey men are the seed of a revolution in human affairs far more powerful than the one envisaged by the poor fellows in St. Peter's Fields, who are merely asking for the right to vote for the government that rules their lives–but I shall have to try. What they will command me to do about it, I have no idea. I am not even certain in my own mind what I ought to suggest. They may well be interested in the society that he has joined, though, if not in him. Secret police are jealous folk by nature, intolerant of any rivalry."

"Who are they?" the comtesse asked, at last.

"Like the *vehmgerichte*, they appear to be the residue of a reality that ought to have dwindled away to mere legend–but there are a great many men in today's world who are trying to live out the legends of the past. The account their representative gave me and the one that your husband subsequently supplied are doubtless shot through with illusions and impostures, but they are men of flesh and blood, who do more than hold meetings in fancy dress. They have a mission now, and will pursue it with all the gladness of men who have been without a clear and achievable purpose for far too long. When I explain that in London... yes, milady, I dare say that I shall be set to hunt your husband again, if only as a first step in a much broader campaign."

"I'm glad of that," the Comtesse de Belcamp said. "I cannot expect you to violate the trust of your profession, of course–but I hope that I might learn something of your progress, and hence of his. You will maintain contact with your daughter now, I presume–unlike my husband, you will not continue, perversely, to play dead?"

"I have been a unforgiving fool," Temple admitted. "My own cardinal fault is stubbornness–but you're right. I shall maintain contact with my daughter, if only by letter, and it's not impossible that you might learn something of my progress, insofar as my duty will permit me to let it be known."

"Would you like to see my son?" she asked, out of the blue.

He only had to meet her eyes to understand. She did not expect to see her husband in the foreseeable future, but she hoped that Gregory Temple might– and she wanted Temple to be able to tell the late Comte de Belcamp that he had seen his son, the rightful Marquis de Belcamp.

"Yes, milady," Temple said. "But I should like to see my grandson first, and my daughter. There is an order of priority that ought to be observed–and enough warmth has now returned to my ancient bones to permit me to follow it."

He stood up, and she stood too. He bowed, but she was not content wth that and offered him her hand.

"I would like to be your friend, Mr. Temple," she said. "I hope that will be possible, given that my husband, your former enemy, is dead. I would like to think that you and I could start afresh, with nothing between us but the gratitude I owe you for coming so promptly to our assistance when you were called. Can we do that?"

Temple took the proffered hand, and kissed it. "Yes, milady," he said. "I will be your friend, and a friend to young Armand, if I can."

"And Sarah?" the Comtesse de Belcamp ventured to ask.

"That might be more difficult," Temple admitted, "especially now that she is inextricably tangled with the *vehm*. But I will certainly go to see her and Surrisy before I leave, and build what bridges I can."

"Good," the Comtesse said. "Now, I must follow your daughter's good example. I shall expect to see you in Armand's room when you are able to come."

On the way to Suzanne's apartment, Temple met Ned Knob, who was loitering in a corridor in the obvious expectation of such a meeting. The little man still seemed anxious.

"I did what seemed best, Mr. Temple," the little man said, defiantly.

"You did right," Temple conceded, grudgingly. "Just as you did at Greenhithe. I know better than to ask a loyal radical like yourself whether he would be interested in a position with Lord Liverpool's secret police, but will you at least condescend to travel back to England in my company?"

Ned seemed startled by that, and then suspicious–perhaps fearful that Temple only wanted to pump him for information about his radical acquaintances–but in the end he nodded. It was Temple who offered to shake hands.

Then he went in to meet his grandson, and to make amends for his desertion of his daughter. The fault was not mended in a minute, or even an hour, but he found the time eventually to meet Armand de Belcamp too, and memorize as many details of his existence as a paternal ghost might justly find interesting. By the time he went to the new château, night was falling again, so he had no alternative to postpone his journey plans until the next day.

Sarah O'Brien, as he had expected, was not much interested in counting him a friend, but she was still grateful for what he had done for her son. She had received a letter from the men she had begged for help, which assured her that Temple had, in fact, done nothing, and that it was they who had saved her the necessity of paying any ransom, but Friedrich had apparently told her a different story.

Surrisy was suspicious of Temple too, simply because the former lieutenant had spent so much of his precious youth in fighting the English, but Surrisy had always respected him, and was perfectly ready to renew that respect. It was, in fact, Surrisy who eventually took him aside and said: "What is your opinion of this magical means of restoring life to the dead, Mr. Temple? What kind of upheaval is it likely to cause in the affairs of men?"

"In my affairs, very little," Temple told him. "In yours, perhaps, a good deal more. In the lives of Friedrich, Armand and little Richard... no one can tell, as yet. Everything depends on matters not yet ascertained by trial and error. If a reliable means can be found to make all the grey men as mindful and competent as General Mortdieu, then the world will be changed out of all recognition within a generation. If, as John Devil supposes, the brains of dead men can be relocated in new and sturdier bodies, the change will be even greater. If, as Ned Knob once proposed, the grey people will eventually be able to produce children of their own who were never alive in the usual sense... but all of that remains to be discovered.

"When the contest to discover such things was a hole-in-the-corner affair involving lone men of dubious soundness of mind, it was bound to progress slowly–but that is no longer the case. Now there is a considerable organization involved, which is already party to uncommon knowledge, and has first-rate scientific minds among its ranks. It is not so very improbable that Michael Faraday, and every other student of electricity in England, will be working on the question within a year, and that the British Empire–like every other in Europe and the world–will be a Empire of Necromancers within a decade."

Surrisy had gone quite white. "I had not realized..." he stammered.

"Given the innate conservatism of the European aristocracies," Temple added, "and the authority of the Church, diehard opposition might slow that timetable by a factor of ten–but it can only be slowed, not stopped. We passed the point of no return some time ago. The world as you and I knew it is already ended. Even if the existing grey men were to be exterminated, and the means of reanimating more were prohibited by law, that would only drive the necromancers underground–where many of them have been well used to living for centuries. If the world is not to become a Gothic nightmare, it will have to discipline its dreams."

"I see," Surrisy said, and paused for a moment before adding: "My mother is not long dead..."

"Exactly," Temple agreed. "Mothers, fathers, brothers, sisters, sons and daughters are dying daily, very few of them unloved. Humankind has been the helpless victim of grief and tragedy since the dawn of consciousness and conscience. Now, the war has begun in earnest. You might try to make your government see that, as I shall try to do in England. It will not be easy."

"No," Surrisy conceded. "It will not."

The next day was the first of December, but the cold relented somewhat as clouds came in from the Atlantic, bringing a steady rain to harass the roads. It did not deter Gregory Temple and Ned Knob from waiting at Miremont crossroads for the *patache* to Paris.

"Since you have forgiven me for giving Suzanne's letter to Henri, and for being on friendly terms with your daughter while you were not," Ned Knob announced, portentously. "I shall forgive you for having me knocked over the head on the quay near London Bridge and arresting me in Jenny Paddock's. You will remain my enemy, of course, while you remain Lord Liverpool's lackey and spy, but you shall have my respect."

Temple shook his head wearily. "That is very civil of you, Mr. Knob," he said, in a voice that sounded very unlike his own, in tone and sentiment alike. "I, in my turn, shall hope that I am not forced by circumstance to have you arrested or hit over the head again."

"You might be forced to do something of the sort," Ned Knob conceded. "Some things never change, despite the fact that everything does. I suppose we ought to be grateful for that, or there would be no sense to life at all."

There was no denying it, so Temple contented himself with saying "True" as the *patache* rolled up–no more than ten minutes behind its stated time–to start them on the long journey home.

END OF PART TWO

Part Three of The Empire of the Necromancers, *"The Return of Frankenstein,"* *will appear in* Tales of the Shadowmen 4, *and subsequent episodes will hopefully continue to appear as long as the series may endure–unless, of course, I become incapacitated before Black Coat Press does. A roman feuilleton whose episodes appear annually is inevitably different from one whose episodes are published daily or weekly, as the episodes of all the great French romans feuilletons were, but its presentation as a series of more-or-less self-contained novellas will hopefully counter some of the problems associated with the long time lapse. One of the benefits of writing alternate history is that a series can be extrapolated, along with the history, indefinitely. All literary "endings" are, in any case–as Percy Shelley probably observed while Gregory Temple was deliberately not listening to him–mere aesthetic artefacts, so it will not matter in the least how long the series might eventually turn out to be.*

Brian Stableford

Sherlock Holmes
by Daylon (2005)

Credits

The Heart of the Moon

Starring:	Created by:
Doctor Omega	Arnould Galopin
Telzey Amberdon	James H. Schmitz
Captain Kronos	Brian Clemens
Hyeronimos Grost	Brian Clemens
Solomon Kane	Robert E. Howard
Maciste	Giovanni Pastrone
	& Gabriele d'Annunzio
Baron Iscariot	Paul Féval
Baroness Phryne	Paul Féval
Count Orlok	Henrik Galeen
	& F. W. Murnau

Introducing:	
Yvgeny	Matthew Baugh
Also Starring:	
Prince Vseslav	
And:	
Selene, the Vampire City	Paul Féval

Written by:

Matthew BAUGH is a 43-year-old ordained minister who lives and works in Sedona, Arizona, with his wife Mary and two cats. He is a longtime fan of pulp fiction, cliffhanger serials, old time radio, and is the proud owner of the silent *Judex* serial on DVD. He has written a number of articles on lesser known pop-culture characters like Dr. Syn, Jules de Grandin and Sailor Steve Costigan for the Wold-Newton Universe Internet website. His article on Zorro was published in *Myths for the Modern Age* (2005). He is a regular contributor to *Tales of the Shadowmen*.

Long Live Fantômas

Starring:	Created by:
Doctor Krampft	Marcel Allain
Enrico Gioja	Paul Féval
Saladin	Paul Féval
Clampin (a.k.a. Pistolet)	Paul Féval

Claudius Bombarnac	Jules Verne
Lord Edward Beltham	Marcel Allain
	& Pierre Souvestre
Paterson	Pierre-Alexis
	Ponson du Terrail
Father Rodin	Eugène Sue
Professor Moriarty	Sir Arthur Conan Doyle
Gurn	Marcel Allain
	& Pierre Souvestre
Lady Maud Beltham	Marcel Allain
	& Pierre Souvestre

Also Starring:
Kaiser Wilhelm
Heinrich Schliemann
Hyppolite Marinoni

Written by:

Alfredo CASTELLI was born in Milan in 1947. He started his career in comics in 1965, when he became an editor for *Kolosso* and drew *Scheletrino* for *Diabolik*. A year later, he founded the popular and influential fanzine *Comics Club 104*. He has become best known for writing comics, which he started doing in 1967. In 1978, he adapted *Allan Quatermain* in comics for the magazine *Supergulp*. Castelli's most famous creation is *Martin Mystère*, which started in 1982, drawn by Giancarlo Alessandrini. Since then, Castelli has also written issues of *Dylan Dog, Zagor, Mister No* and *Zona X*.

Next!

Starring:	**Created by:**
Barbarella	Jean-Claude Forest
James T. Kirk	Gene Roddenberry
Ying Ko (a.k.a. The Shadow)	Walter Gibson

Written by:

Bill CUNNINGHAM is a pulp screenwriter-producer specializing in the DVD market and a regular contributor to *Tales of the Shadowmen*. A recognized authority and speaker on low-budget filmmaking, his web-site, www.D2DVD.blogspot.com, offers screenwriters and filmmakers useful tips and insight into the DVD industry. He is currently producing the motion pictures *Stainless* and *The Gore Gore Gore-met* with legendary exploitation filmmaker Herschell Gordon Lewis.

Au Vent Mauvais...

Starring:
Madame Atomos
Gaspard Zemba III

Ozu
Also Starring:
Walter Cronkite
Arthur C. Clarke
Robert Heinlein
Neil Armstrong
Buzz Aldrin

Created by:
André Caroff
Jean-Marc Lofficier
based on Walter Gibson
François Darnaudet

Written by:
François DARNAUDET began his writing career with the critically-acclaimed thriller *Le Taxidermiste* (1985), before contributing numerous short stories to a variety of genre magazines and anthologies, including the prestigious *Territoire de l'Inquiétude* (1993). During that time, he also wrote two horror novels in 1989 and 1990. His works include the fantasy thriller *Le Fantôme d'Orsay* (1999) and its sequel, *Les Dieux de Cluny* (2003). He has also published two science fiction novels for the Rivière Blanche imprint: *La Lagune des Mensonges* (2003) and *Le Regard qui Tue* (2004; co-written with Pascal Metge). Darnaudet lives south of Perpignan on France's *côte vermeille*.

Return to the 20th Century

Starring:
The 20th Century

Professor Calculus
The Cat Women of the Moon
Also Starring:
Jungle Alli (a.k.a. Alice
Bradley Sheldon, a.k.a. James
Tiptree, Jr.)

Created by:
Albert Robida
with additional material by
Paul DiFilippo
Hergé
Roy Hamilton

Written by:
Paul DiFILIPPO's career began either in 1977, when his first story appeared in *Unearth* magazine; or in 1982, when he quit his job as a COBOL programmer to devote himself fulltime to writing; or in 1985, when his second and third stories appeared in *The Magazine of Fantasy & Science Fiction* and *The Twilight Zone*

Magazine; or in 1995, when his first book, *The Steampunk Trilogy*, debuted. Whichever date one chooses, 2006 will see the publication of his 25th book, *Top 10: Beyond the Farthest Precinct*, a milestone he is very proud of. He intends to retire now in stages over the next 40 years.

Les Lèvres Rouges

Starring:	**Created by:**
Ilona Harczy	Pierre Drouot, Jean Ferry, Manfred R. Köhler & Harry Kümel
Countess Elisabeth Bathory	Pierre Drouot, Jean Ferry, Manfred R. Köhler & Harry Kümel
Nestor Burma	Léo Malet
Doc Ardan	Guy d'Armen Lester Dent
Lt. Montferrand (a.k.a. Roger Noël)	Vladimir Volkoff
Jens Rolf	Anonymous
S.N.I.F.	Vladimir Volkoff
Florimond Faroux	Léo Malet
Le Chiffre	Ian Fleming
Plaster	Will Eisner
Cabiria	Federico Fellini, Ennio Flaiano & Tullio Pinelli
Manon Lescaut	Henri-Georges Clouzot & Jean Ferry based on Abbé Prévost
Zavatter	Léo Malet
The fish-men	H. P. Lovecraft
Audrey (a.k.a. The Vine)	Charles B. Griffith
Also Starring:	
Adélaïde Lupin (a.k.a. Monique d'Andresy)	Win Scott Eckert
And:	
The Silver Eye of Dagon	Roy Thomas based on Robert E. Howard & H.P. Lovecraft
Le *Cordon Jaune*	Ian Fleming
Radium-X	John Colton, Howard Higgin & Douglas Hodges

Written by:
Win Scott ECKERT holds a B.A. in Anthropology and a Juris Doctorate. In 1997, he posted the first site on the Internet devoted to expanding Philip José Farmer's concept of the Wold Newton Family. He is the editor of and contributor to *Myths for the Modern Age: Philip José Farmer's Wold Newton Universe* (2005) and a contributor to *Lance Star, Sky Ranger* (2006). His article "The Black Forest and the Wold Newton Universe" is included in *The Black Forest 2: Castle of Shadows* (2005), and he recently contributed the Foreword to the new edition of Farmer's seminal "fictional biography," *Tarzan Alive: A Definitive Biography of Lord Greystoke* (2006). He is a regular contributor to *Tales of the Shadowmen*.

Beware the Beasts

Starring:	Created by:
Doctor Omega	Arnould Galopin
Tiziraou	Arnould Galopin
Jinn	Pierre Boulle
Phyllis	Pierre Boulle
Q	Gene Roddenberry & D. C. Fontana

Written by:
G.L. GICK lives in Indiana and has been a pulp fan since he first picked up a Doc Savage paperback. His other interests include old-time radio, Golden and Silver Age comics, cryptozoology, classic animation, British SF TV and C.S. Lewis and G.K. Chesterton. He is, in other words, a nerd and damn proud of it. He is a regular contributor to *Tales of the Shadowmen*.

The Ape Gigans

Starring:	Created by:
Becky Sharp	William Makepeace Thackeray
Professor Lidenbrock	Jules Verne
Talisa the Mahar (a.k.a. Fatima Talisa)	Micah Harris based on Edgar Rice Burroughs
Lemuel Beesley	Micah Harris based on Michael Moorcock
Captain Obed Marsh	H. P. Lovecraft
Kong (a.k.a. The *Ape Gigans*)	Merian C. Cooper & Edgar Wallace and Jules Verne

Also Starring:
Benjamin Disraeli
And:
Kôr

Skull Island

Pellucidar

H. Rider Haggard
Merian C. Cooper
& Edgar Wallace
Edgar Rice Burroughs

Written by:
Micah HARRIS is the author (with artist Michael Gaydos) of the graphic novel *Heaven's War*, a historical fantasy pitting authors Charles Williams, C.S. Lewis and J.R.R. Tolkien against occultist Aleister Crowley. Micah teaches composition, literature and film at Pitt Community College in North Carolina. He is currently developing several comics and prose projects including *When the Stars Are Right: the Eldritch New Adventures of Becky Sharp*.

A Dance of Night and Death

Starring:
Irma Vep
Fantômas

Satanas

Created by:
Louis Feuillade
Marcel Allain
& Pierre Souvestre
Louis Feuillade

Written by:
Travis HILTZ started making up stories at a young age. Years later, he began writing them down. In high school, he discovered that some writers actually got paid and decided to give it a try. He has since gathered a a modest collection of rejection letters and had a one-act play produced. Travis lives in the wilds of New Hampshire with his very loving and tolerant wife, two above average children and a staggering amount of comic books and *Doctor Who* novels. This is his first published story.

The Lady in the Black Gloves

Starring:
Madame Fourneau

Irene Chupin/Tupin (a.k.a. Irina Putine)
Josephine Balsamo
Catarina Koluchy (a.k.a. Mrs. Moriarty)

Created by:
Narciso Ibañez-Serrador
& Juan Tébar
Narciso Ibañez-Serrador
& Juan Tébar
Maurice Leblanc
L. T. Meade
& Robert Eustace

The Black Coats	Paul Féval
Louis/Luis Fourneau (a.k.a. Maurice d'Andresy)	Narciso Ibañez-Serrador & Juan Tébar
Gaston Morrell (a.k.a. Blue-beard)	Pierre Gendron, Arnold Phillips & Werner H. Furst
Mabuse (a.k.a. Dr. Mau-beuge)	Norbert Jacques
Dr. Biron	Marcel Allain & Pierre Souvestre
Mary Holder	Sir Arthur Conan Doyle
Helen Lipsius	Arthur Machen
Inspector Lefevre	Pierre Gendron, Arnold Phillips & Werner H. Furst
Isadora Klein (a.k.a. Jacques Saillard)	Sir Arthur Conan Doyle E. W. Hornung
Also Starring:	
Maurice Joyant	
And:	
Van Klopen, *Tailleur pour Dames*	Emile Gaboriau

Written by:
Rick LAI is a computer programmer living in Bethpage, New York. During the 1980s and 1990s, he wrote articles utilizing Philip José Farmer's Wold Newton Universe concepts for pulp magazine fanzines such as *Nemesis Inc*, *Echoes*, *Golden Perils*, *Pulp Vault* and *Pulp Collector*. Rick has also created chronologies of such heroes as Doc Savage and the Shadow. He is a regular contributor to *Tales of the Shadowmen*.

The Murder of Randolph Carter

Starring:	**Created by:**
Hercule Poirot	Agatha Christie
Randolph Carter	H. P. Lovecraft
Inspector Owen	Thomas Owen
Charles Dexter Ward	H. P. Lovecraft
Lavinia Whateley	H. P. Lovecraft
David Marsh	H. P. Lovecraft
Malpertuis	Jean Ray
Also Starring:	
Jean Ray	

Hercule Poirot
by Fernando Calvi (2006)

Written by:

Jean-Marc & Randy LOFFICIER, the authors of the *Shadowmen* non-fiction series, have also collaborated on five screenplays, a dozen books and numerous comic books and translations, including *Arsène Lupin, Doc Ardan, Doctor Omega* and *The Phantom of the Opera*, all published by Black Coat Press. They have written a number of animation teleplays, including episodes of *Duck Tales* and *The Real Ghostbusters* and such popular comic book heroes as *Superman* and *Doctor Strange*. In 1999, in recognition of their distinguished career as comic book writers, editors and translators, they were presented with the Inkpot award for Outstanding Achievement in Comic Arts. Randy is a member of the Writers Guild of America, West and Mystery Writers of America.

A Day in the Life of Madame Atomos

Starring: **Created by:**
Madame Atomos   André Caroff
Madame Hydra   Jim Steranko
Fah Lo Suee   Sax Rohmer
Derek Flint   Hal Fimberg
Sumuru   Sax Rohmer
John Steed   Sydney Newman
Tara King   Brian Clemens
Alouh T'Ho   Jean de La Hire
Clarissa de Courtney-Scott   Peter O'Donnell
Greta Morgan   Leslie Charteris
Tania Orloff   Henri Vernes
The Black Lizard   Edogawa Rampo
Miss Ylang-Ylang   Henri Vernes
Catherine Cornelius   Michael Moorcock
Mephista   Maurice Limat
Mrs. Butterworth   Anthony Skene
Vic St. Val   G. Morris
Modesty Blaise   Peter O'Donnell
Willie Garvin   Peter O'Donnell

Also Starring:
Shoichi Yokoi

And:
The Depository Bank of   Dan Brown
Zurich
The Pink Panther   Blake Edwards
                                                 & Maurice Richlin

Written by:
Xavier MAUMÉJEAN won the renowned Gerardmer Award in 2000 for his psychological thriller *The Memoirs of the Elephant Man*. His other works include *Gotham* (2002), *The League of Heroes*, which won the 2003 Imaginaire Award of the City of Brussels and was translated by Black Coat Press (2005), *La Vénus Anatomique* (2004), which won the 2005 Rosny Award, and *Car je suis Légion* (2005). Xavier has a diploma in philosophy and the science of religions and works as a teacher in the North of France, where he resides, with his wife and his daughter, Zelda.

Bullets Over Bombay

Starring:	**Created by:**
Captain John Good, RN	H. Rider Haggard
Docteur Mystère	Paul d'Ivoi
Cigale	Paul d'Ivoi
Sandy Arbuthnot	John Buchan
Also Starring:	
The Lumière Brothers	

Written by:

David A. McINTEE has written many spin-off novels based on the BBC science fiction television series *Doctor Who*, as well as one each based on *Final Destination* and *Space: 1999*. He has also written non-fiction books on *Star Trek* and the *Aliens* and *Predator* movie franchises. He has written several audio plays and contributed to various magazines including *Dreamwatch*, *SFX*, *Star Trek Communicator* and *The Official Star Wars Fact Files*. He currently writes for the UK's Asian-entertainment magazine, *Neo*.

All's Fair...

Starring:	**Created by:**
Pigalle (a.k.a. P'Gell)	Will Eisner
James Bond	Ian Fleming
Maurice Champot (a.k.a. *La Grammaire*)	Pierre Dac & Francis Blanche
Frédéric-Jean Orth (a.k.a. *L'Ombre*)	Alain Page
Hubert Bonisseur de la Bath (a.k.a. OSS 117)	Jean Bruce
Commissaire Voisin	Alain Page
Simon Templar (a.k.a. The Saint)	Leslie Charteris
And:	
Picratt's	Georges Simenon
The Jewel of Gizeh	Will Eisner

Written by:

Brad MENGEL lives in Australia, with his wife, daughters and dog. Over the years, he has worked as a barman, teacher and librarian. Currently, he is engaged in a study of the "Aggressors," the often violent action adventure series of the 1970s, 1980s and 1990s, such as *The Executioner*, *The Destroyer* and *The Punisher*, which he plans to turn into an encyclopaedia and one day publish. He was a contributor to *Myths for the Modern Age: Philip Jose Farmer's Wold Newton Universe*.

The Affair of the Bassin Les Hivers

Starring:	Created by:
Lapointe	Georges Simenon
Zenith the Albino	Anthony Skene
Una Persson	Michael Moorcock
Vera Pym (a.k.a. Irma Vep)	Louis Feuillade
Sarah Gobseck	Honoré de Balzac
Vautrin	Honoré de Balzac
Introducing:	
LeBec	Michael Moorcock

Written by:
Michael **MOORCOCK** became editor of *Tarzan Adventures* in 1956, at the age of 16, and later moved on to edit *The Sexton Blake Library*. As editor of *New Worlds* from 1964 until 1971, he had a hand in the development of the New Wave. Moorcock's best-known creation is the Eternal Champion saga in which various heroes, such as Elric, Hawkmoon, Corum, etc. are multiple identities of the same champion across many dimensions called the Multiverse. Moorcock's other literary accomplishments also include the Jerry Cornelius (himself an avatar of the Eternal Champion) series and the Colonel Pyat tetralogy which began in 1981 with *Byzantium Endures*.

The Successful Failure

Starring:	Created by:
Isidore Beautrelet	Maurice Leblanc
Xavier Guichard	Georges Simenon
M. Poitevin	John Peel
James Bigglesworth	W. E. Johns
Also Starring:	
M. Voisin	

Written by:
John **PEEL** was born in Nottingham, England, and started writing stories at age 10. John moved to the U.S. in 1981 to marry his pen-pal. He, his wife ("Mrs. Peel") and their 13 dogs now live on Long Island, New York. John has written just over 100 books to date, mostly for young adults. He is the only author to have written novels based on both *Doctor Who* and *Star Trek*. His most popular work is *Diadem*, a fantasy series; he has written ten volumes to date.

The Butterfly Files

Starring:
William Mulder

Madame Atomos
The Lone Gunmen

Fu Manchu
Prof. Aldridge
Also Starring:
Shiro Ishii

Created by:
Chris Carter, David Duchovny
& Frank Spotnitz
André Caroff
Chris Carter, Vince Milligan,
John Shiban & Frank Spotnitz
Sax Rohmer
W. A. Harbinson

Written by:

Joseph ALTAIRAC is a French writer and essayist who has published numerous articles on science fiction and fantasy writers (including an award-winning study of H. G. Wells) and translated a collection of H. P. Lovecraft's letters. He is also the host of a popular genre radio show on *France-Culture*.

Jean-Luc RIVERA is the editor of the French *Gazette Fortéenne* devoted to Charle Fort and one of founding members of *L'Oeil du Sphinx*, a small press devoted to publishing books and magazines on science fiction, fantasy, the occult and the paranormal.

The Famous Ape

Starring:
Thomas Recorde (a.k.a. Zephir)
George Boleyn (a.k.a. Curious George)
Isabelle
Also Starring:
Olur
Poutifour
Babar (The Elephant King)
Hatchibombotar
Solovar
Mohor
Grodd
Huc

Created by:
Jean de Brunhoff

H. A. Rey & Margret Rey

Jean de Brunhoff

Jean de Brunhoff
Jean de Brunhoff
Jean de Brunhoff
Jean de Brunhoff
John Broome
Franco Oneta
John Broome
Jean de Brunhoff

Francis Arnaud Moreau (a.k.a. God)	H.G. Wells & Edgar Rice Burroughs
Red Peter	Franz Kafka
Flora	Jean de Brunhoff
Kaspa	C.T. Stoneham
Zembla	Franco Oneta
Ka-Zar	Bob Byrd
Nyoka	Edgar Rice Burroughs
Sheena	Will Eisner & S.M. Iger
Jann	Don Rico
Malb'yat	Edgar Rice Burroughs
Bonzo	Ted Berkman, Raphael Blau, Lou Breslow, Val Burton
Wolsey	Edgar Rice Burroughs
Aristobald	Edgar Rice Burroughs
Emily	John Collier
Chim-Chim	Tatsuo Yoshida & Tadashi Hirose
Magilla	William Hanna & Joseph Barbera
Bear	Glen A. Larson
Grape	William Hanna & Joseph Barbera
Old Lady	Jean de Brunhoff
Fandango	Jean de Brunhoff
Capoulosse	Jean de Brunhoff
Podular	Jean de Brunhoff
And:	
Animalism	George Orwell
Celesteville	Jean de Brunhoff
Karunda	Franco Oneta
The Ba Baoro'm	Hergé
The Bansutos	Edgar Rice Burroughs
Omwamwi Falls	Edgar Rice Burroughs
Gorilla City	John Broome
Anthar	Franco Oneta
Rataxesburg	Jean de Brunhoff

Written by:
Chris ROBERSON's novels include *Here, There & Everywhere, The Voyage of Night Shining White, Paragaea: A Planetary Romance,* and the forthcoming *Set the Seas on Fire, End of the Century, Iron Jaw & Hummingbird* and *The Dragon's Nine Sons.* His short stories have appeared in such magazines as *Asi-*

mov's Science Fiction, Postscripts and *Subterranean*, and in anthologies such as *Live Without a Net, The Many Faces of Van Helsing, FutureShocks* and *Forbidden Planets*. Along with his business partner and spouse Allison Baker, he is the publisher of MonkeyBrain Books, an independent publishing house specializing in genre fiction and nonfiction genre studies, and he is the editor of the *Adventure* anthology series. He has been a finalist for the World Fantasy Award three times–once each for writing, publishing and editing–twice a finalist for the John W. Campbell Award for Best New Writer, and twice for the Sidewise Award for Best Alternate History Short Form (winning in 2004 with his story "O One"). Chris and Allison live in Austin, Texas with their daughter Georgia.

Two Hunters

Starring:	Created by:
Nikolas Rokoff	Edgar Rice Burroughs
Judex (a.k.a. Vallières)	Arthur Bernède
	& Louis Feuillade
Favraux	Arthur Bernède
	& Louis Feuillade
Paul d'Arnot	Edgar Rice Burroughs
Lord Greystoke	Edgar Rice Burroughs
Jane Porter	Edgar Rice Burroughs

Written by:
Robert L. ROBINSON, Jr. was first introduced to the world of comic books, radio shows and movie serials as a child in the 1960s by his father, who had no idea the damage it would do to this fragile mind. Seeing *Planet of the Apes* on the big screen at age seven when it came out added film to the areas that fascinated him. Bob's Outer Edge Entertainment company is currently in preproduction on a remake of *Judex*, for which he wrote the screenplay When not escaping into worlds of fantasy and imagination, Bob coaches Soccer (eight years at it now with a record of 32-4-4) and basketball. He has a patient wife in Ann and their four kids, Abby, Rob, Matt and Kara (named after the lass from Krypton). *Two Hunters* is his first short story.

The Child-Stealers

Starring:	Created by:
Gregory Temple	Paul Féval
John Devil (a.k.a. Henri de Belcamp, etc.)	Paul Féval
Robert Walton (one of the literary gentlemen)	Mary Shelley

Giuseppe Balsamo	Alexandre Dumas
Pierre Louchet	Paul Féval
Jeanne Herbet, Comtesse de Belcamp	Paul Féval
Suzanne Thompson	Paul Féval
Richard Thompson	Paul Féval
"Don Juan" Besnard	Paul Féval
Sarah O'Brien, Countess Boehm	Paul Féval
Richard Surrisy	Paul Féval
Ned Knob	Paul Féval
Also Starring:	
Percy Bysshe Shelley (the other literary gentleman)	

Written by:

Brian M. STABLEFORD has been a professional writer since 1965. He has published more than 50 novels and 200 short stories, as well as several non-fiction books, thousands of articles for periodicals and reference books and a number of anthologies. He is also a part-time Lecturer in Creative Writing at King Alfred's College Winchester. Brian's novels include *The Empire of Fear* (1988), *Young Blood* (1992), *The Wayward Muse* (2005) and his future history series comprising *Inherit the Earth* (1998), *Architects of Emortality* (1999), *The Fountains of Youth* (2000), *The Cassandra Complex* (2001), *Dark Ararat* (2002) and *The Omega Expedition* (2002). His non-fiction includes *Scientific Romance in Britain* (1985), *Teach Yourself Writing Fantasy and Science Fiction* (1997), *Yesterday's Bestsellers* (1998) and *Glorious Perversity: The Decline and Fall of Literary Decadence* (1998). Brian's translations for Black Coat Press include Paul Féval's *John Devil, Knightshade, Revenants, Vampire City, The Vampire Countess, The Wandering Jew's Daughter, The Black Coats: 'Salem Street* and *The Black Coats: The Invisible Weapon.*

TALES OF THE SHADOWMEN

Volume 1: The Modern Babylon (2005)

Volume 2: Gentlemen of the Night (2006)

WATCH OUT FOR
VOLUME 4: LORDS OF TERROR
TO BE RELEASED EARLY 2008

Printed in the United Kingdom
by Lightning Source UK Ltd.
116812UKS00001B/216